by award-winning author

Becky /HEALANI/ Banks

Published by:

Maui, Hawaiʻi | Portland, Oregon
haiku-press.com

Cover design by James T. Egan of Bookfly Design.

beckybanksbooks.com

ISBN: 978-0-9882614-7-1 (e-book)

ISBN: 978-0-9882614-8-8 (paperback)

For Maui.

AUTHOR'S NOTE_

Regarding the technical jargon in this book, I'd like to note that I've been heavy-handed with the fiction. Some of what I've written is real and achievable, and some is "total sci-fi," as my husband, computer engineer, high-performance computing expert, and haxor-lite, has informed me. The knowledgeable will know which is which, and the rest? Enjoy the story.

ʻŌLELO HAWAIʻI

In the rear of the novel, you will find a glossary of Hawaiian language used in the book. I drew on the work of the well-respected duo Mary Kawena Pukui and Samuel H. Elbert (*Hawaiian Dictionary*, University of Hawaiʻi Press, 1986), as well as terms I learned in school and grew up hearing in our home. Our family on the islands spans generations, and the Hawaiian that was spoken by our friends and family is colloquial and sometimes grammatically different from what is in textbooks. I give my humble thanks to my family, Hawaiian language educators, and the generations that came before me; any grammatical errors within this book are all my own.

The last name of our main character, Hoyt Kahoʻokalakupua is derived from the word *ho'okalakupua*, which is a dynamic word with supernatural and magical meanings, including "extraordinary fisherman." Because Hoyt's family are fishers and their family 'aumakua is manō, my humble intention was to create a fictional last name that honored those connections—and that helped to create a fictional atmosphere that my Hawai'i community can enjoy.

Midway through the final edit of this novel, tragedy struck my home island of Maui. I've written and rewritten this section several times over the last few weeks since the wildfire. At first, I let out my grief. Then, knowing my family would be reading this, I dialed it back to just the facts of the event. And now, months later, I'm still struggling with the right words. Today, my message is to my friends and family: As we go through this, me ke aloha pumehana. I give you my strength and my aloha and am holding you tight in my arms. Together, as a community, hand in hand, we are getting through this. We will get through this.

For ways to help or get help, please visit any one of these sites:

- beckybanksbooks.com/Maui
- haiku-press.com/Maui
- Maui County's mauinuistrong.info

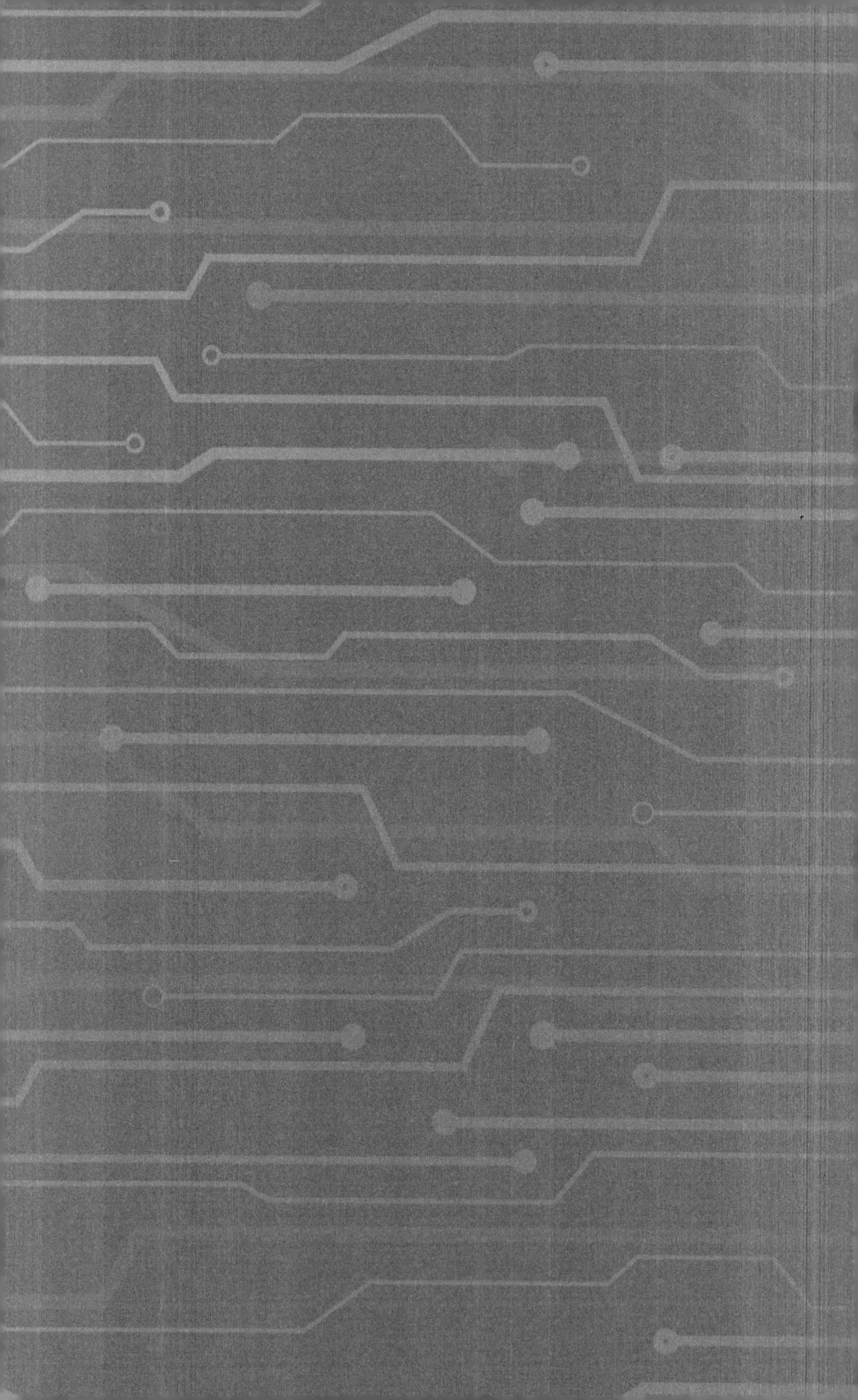

PROLOGUE_

One year ago.

Standing in the abandoned scrapyard warehouse, Vega blew out a breath. It had been a long time since she'd been in her hometown. It was both a relief to be closer to her little sister and also a bitter pill to be back in the place that had caused so much pain.

"Fists up, kid." Vega remembered her foster father, Junior, coaching her in the boxing gym in a repurposed warehouse not much different from this one and not far from where she currently stood on the southeast side of the city. She'd been light on her feet with him.

Ms. Maggie, Junior's wife, a kind woman with a short bob of gray hair, had taken to Vega and Scout, bringing them treats when she'd stop by the gym to give Junior his dinners when he stayed for evening sessions. Vega liked to watch the bodies in the ring, fists up, feet shuffling. She liked the idea of getting in the ring. There were rules to follow, and they were strictly enforced. Junior had invited her in more than once, and Ms. Maggie had encouraged her too, her gaze lightly touching the bruises on a young Vega's arms before handing her a crisp package of a Franz hand pie, but trust was still a hard thing for Vega to do, even back then. Vega took the treats she brought but shook her head; she wasn't going in. Plus, she usually had her kid sister in tow, and a boxing gym didn't sound like the place for Scout, even though it was exactly what had saved them, one desperate day.

That day, the day Vega and Junior had gone from circling each other to being family, hadn't been great, and at twelve, Vega had already lived a string of days that weren't great. Her identification numbers, with associated personal information—the golden ticket of ID theft, originally taken and sold by her dick stepdad—had manifested two knee-breakers outside her middle school, looking for the actual human attached to the digital disaster named Melanie Alexander, the birth name she once identified with. The digital Melanie Alexander had hustled the wrong drug dealer, and the knee-breakers were keen on getting that money back. Even if the dimwits thought it could be a scrappy twelve-year-old girl.

She was thankful, on that parched September day, that Scout, formerly known as Harmony, was still at after-school care. Her scuffed Converses slapped the asphalt as she ran through the parking lots and alleyways, unthinkingly moving toward Junior's gym, the men just behind her. Sweat made her arms sticky as she sailed down the last alley, only to find she was being flushed out. A dark-blue sedan halted at the end of the alley, its tires chirping on the sidewalk. Her exit was blocked.

Torn shorts, a boy's tank, and long legs were all she had to work with, but it was enough. She tossed bins of garbage, recycling, and towers of cardboard behind her. Glass shattered. Fermenting food waste spewed into the narrow space. Shouts erupted from behind her as the two on her tail hit her chaos.

Ahead, the car doors opened. Vega saw the greased hair and flashing gold watch of the catcher as he got out.

She was lanky. Thin. *Easy to grab* was likely their thought. But Vega knew even then that lanky meant light, and light was fast. She had one shot to not get grabbed. She was back to sprinting as she aimed for the hood of the car. Then leaped.

Knees up, her ass hit the hood, and she slid. Middle fingers up, she sailed past the windshield, giving the driver a piece of her mind before she careened off the other side.

"Goddammit!" the driver yelled at her as she ran across the then-empty street.

Down the block, Junior, the man she'd only known in motion behind the ropes, was standing on the sidewalk talking with a client in front of the gym's open garage doors. If he hadn't been outside in that moment, if his eyes hadn't been kind that day, she would have run in another direction. He was a tall and imposing man with a salt-and-pepper buzz cut and built as if he were made to move mountains. His warm brown gaze matched the color of his skin, and when that gaze lighted on hers, he smiled. Then he looked behind her, and his smile vanished.

He waved her into the garage, understanding enough of the situation without having to be told what he was witnessing. "Come. Get inside."

Then he reached through the open warehouse door and picked up a bat.

After that, Vega and her little cub of a sister knew why people like them would go to Junior's gym. If they weren't at school or with Cindy and Peace, Vega's best friends and the only two who knew what Vega and Scout's home was really like, they were at the gym, high on practice jabs and chocolate chip cookies. It was at the gym that she overheard Maggie talking to Junior about adding Vega and Scout to their home. They had raised up what they thought would be their last bunch of foster kids and were now in their early retirement years. But when her gaze traveled over Junior's shoulder and landed on Vega, who was running through the ropes with Scout, Vega had the first inclination that Maggie would do it again for two girls she and Junior had come to care about.

"We can't," Vega heard Junior remind his wife gently. "Her stepfather still has custody."

That was the first time Vega had a clear idea of what a future without her stepfather, Lloyd, would look like, and the idea nestled like a golden seed in her abdomen and sprouted hope. Over the next month, it grew with a vigor that had Vega breathless with the possibilities when she thought about it too long.

Curled into Scout's bed, tucked into her little sister's pink sheets and fluffy unicorn comforter, Vega watched the glow of her never-sleeping computer over her sleeping sister's shoulder. Lloyd had quietly taught Vega how to use SFTP to hack into websites, and eventually, a shady friend taught him the dark art of rooting the box. That full control of another system meant opening the digital back door and gleaning what was there. Even young Vega knew they were doing something wrong, but Lloyd had told her they had to, that she and Scout were expensive. Only that too had been a lie, like everything else Vega had witnessed in her young life. Except now, she had a plan, fueled by hope acting as the accelerant. A plan to send Lloyd to prison that she perfected with the help of Cindy and Peace, who had enough desire to pull Vega and Scout out of their world and into Cindy and Peace's and the naiveté to pursue such a complicated and dangerous plan with gusto. A plan to clear the way for Junior and Maggie to step in. A plan that saw Vega, Cindy, and Peace in the school and county libraries every chance they had, perfecting it within an inch of the law.

All Vega had to do was capture information about Lloyd's activities, the names of the people he was working with, the things they were doing—digitally washing money, defrauding the unsuspecting, writing checks that held new names that came with fresh identities like her's, Melanie Alexander's—and report it to the authorities. She figured they just had to survive another week while she worked.

It would turn out that they didn't have seven days to spare. They didn't even have a night.

Of all the information she was hiding that week, it was the oldest piece of info, the piece she was protecting and was not part of the plan, Vega mused now, walking the inside perimeter of the warehouse, her warehouse, that had nearly ended them. She and Scout had arrived home that night the way they always did, creeping in to avoid running into Lloyd. Through the dried grass and weeds of the backyard to their bedroom window they went. Vega slid the glass to the side, but before she could lift Scout in, her stomach dropped. The bedroom was in disarray; Scout's unicorn lamp lay on the floor, no longer prancing to new heights. Every drawer was open, its contents spewed, and the manila envelope of Scout's papers containing her personal information that had been taped to the underside of Vega's desk was on her tossed bed. Torn open and now empty.

Vega helped Scout into the room and followed her in. Anger of a thousand bees swarmed through her veins. The envelope had contained the last virgin item of the Scout and Vega duo. It had been the pristine identity of Harmony Alexander tucked safely away from the monster who would take it from them, be it Lloyd or, even young Vega had guessed, the people he owed. If her stepfather had been up against a wall with what Lloyd called "clients," he'd take from his dead wife's kids yet again.

Carefully opening the door, Vega looked down the hall, with Scout holding on to her back pocket. She, it seemed, even for so young a person, could feel the tension that was erupting out of her sister.

The short hall down to the open kitchen and living area was clear and quiet save for the sound of keystrokes coming from the kitchen table.

Vega's heart raced, and pulling out her small phone, she clicked in messages to Peace and Cindy. And another to Junior and Maggie, asking if she could come by later. She didn't want to spend another night in that house.

Vega undid Scout's hands from her pockets, and crouching, she whispered, "Stay here, bug. I'll be right back." She put her finger to her lips. Then, considering something, she added, "And remember, if I tell you to run, you go back out the window to the neighbor and tell them, what?"

Scout's soft voice squeaked out the answer: "Help. Nine. One. One."

Vega kissed her cheek and smiled, trying to keep the worry off her face. "That's right. Nine-one-one. And you keep on telling until they do it. Now, wait here."

Scout let out a soft whimper, not wanting to be left alone, but did as she was asked and stayed in the doorway.

Vega moved down the hall until she could see Lloyd at the kitchen table. He was in the same thing he wore every day, a worn black graphic tee with jeans. His strawberry-blond hair was thinning at the top. He was squinting at his laptop screen when Vega's pocket buzzed.

Cindy had finished softball practice, got her friend's message, and convinced her mom to drive by Vega's place. Another followed: Peace was coming by on bike.

Vega kept her body language casual—aggression had gotten her punched before—and came into the kitchen. Lloyd, deep in his "work," didn't look up when she said, "Hey."

He grunted in response.

"What's up, Lloyd."

"Father, to you" was his automatic answer.

Vega looked down at the scarred and stained wood top of their kitchen table and felt the last of her good mortal soul leave her body and dark venom fill its place. She'd been right. On the table was Scout's identification. The number she would need to enter school, higher education, drive, get a job that paid more than the minimum wage and have a 401K. Her path out of that world that Lloyd had trapped them in was being digitally sold to pay off a debt he owed. Scout's tiny digital life was about to become saturated with dark and thirsty hands that would use her information and then discard it like an orange rind after the sweet flesh had all been consumed. All before she knew how to spell *fraud* or say *misdemeanor*.

"What the fuck are you doing?"

He gave her an angry glance. "Getting us clear. That's what."

"The fuck you are!" Vega knew no one was getting clear of anything if Scout had to pay the price. Vega snatched the papers off the table.

She was suddenly being slammed against the kitchen counter, Lloyd's hand at her throat, squeezing.

"You don't talk to your *father* that way. Now, give it back."

The papers were scrunched in her hand. Blood pooled in her

head under the squeeze of his hand, but she kept the papers out of reach. Then she kneed "father" in the nuts.

His hand slipped off her throat, and she screamed.

"RUN, SCOUT, RUN!"

"You fucking cunt."

She didn't get in another hit.

He had her on the ground with a single strike of his fist.

The room spun as she remembered too late Junior's counsel to keep her hands up.

Papers clenched in her fist, as if they were the actual body of her sister she kept from him, she put up her arms as he hit her again. He was on his knees straddling her when the nightmare got worse.

Scout hadn't run. She came to Vega's "rescue" and jumped on Lloyd's back, pounding it with her small fists. Lloyd tossed her off and into the table. Her head hit the table leg, and after she lay stunned, her screams filled the room.

Vega tried to get up. Scout's screams were like tethers to her body, and after each hit Vega took, she made for her sister. Lloyd was too focused on Vega to notice the front door opening and Scout's screams ceasing.

Everything was happening fast: Vega watching Peace rush in, Cindy on her heels, ignoring her mother's cries, and grab Scout; Cindy's mother calling the police. Cindy had her bat from practice and entered the kitchen swinging. She connected with Lloyd's temple with a crack, sending him backward off Vega. But not before Cindy, her mother, and Peace, who held Scout in her arms with a hand over her eyes, witnessed Lloyd's fist hit Vega's face one last time, smashing her septum and loosening her front teeth.

Junior told her later that if Lloyd hadn't gone to prison, he would have sent him to hell in a pine box. Vega grimaced now at the memory and scuffed her black thick-soled boot in the dust on the concrete floor of her warehouse.

Beauty flows precariously, but it had flowed for at least a moment then. Lloyd lost custody of his charges. Junior and Maggie were already in the foster care system as well-qualified guardians and picked up the girls from the care of child protective services in the emergency room the night Lloyd was arrested. Lloyd argued later in court that his daughters, Melanie and Harmony Alexander, were his and that prison wasn't for the likes of a single father with girls to protect. Only the records the court was given showed him having two charges, from his last wife, named Vega and Scout Flux. With his poor representation in the face of provable serious allegations, and on top of that his seeming to be a fool of a man who didn't know the names of the children, he was removed as their guardian and awarded twenty-five years in prison on multiple charges of fraud and child endangerment.

Vega smiled now in the dark of her new warehouse. Being in her home city was bittersweet and tinged with the dark unknown, but she, Cindy, and Peace were older now. The project they started at twelve had blossomed, and it was only fitting that she be back where it all started. Vega's road to get there had been rough, but she was ready now. Ready to be closer to the women she loved. Ready to settle down, stop betting big, and put her past to bed.

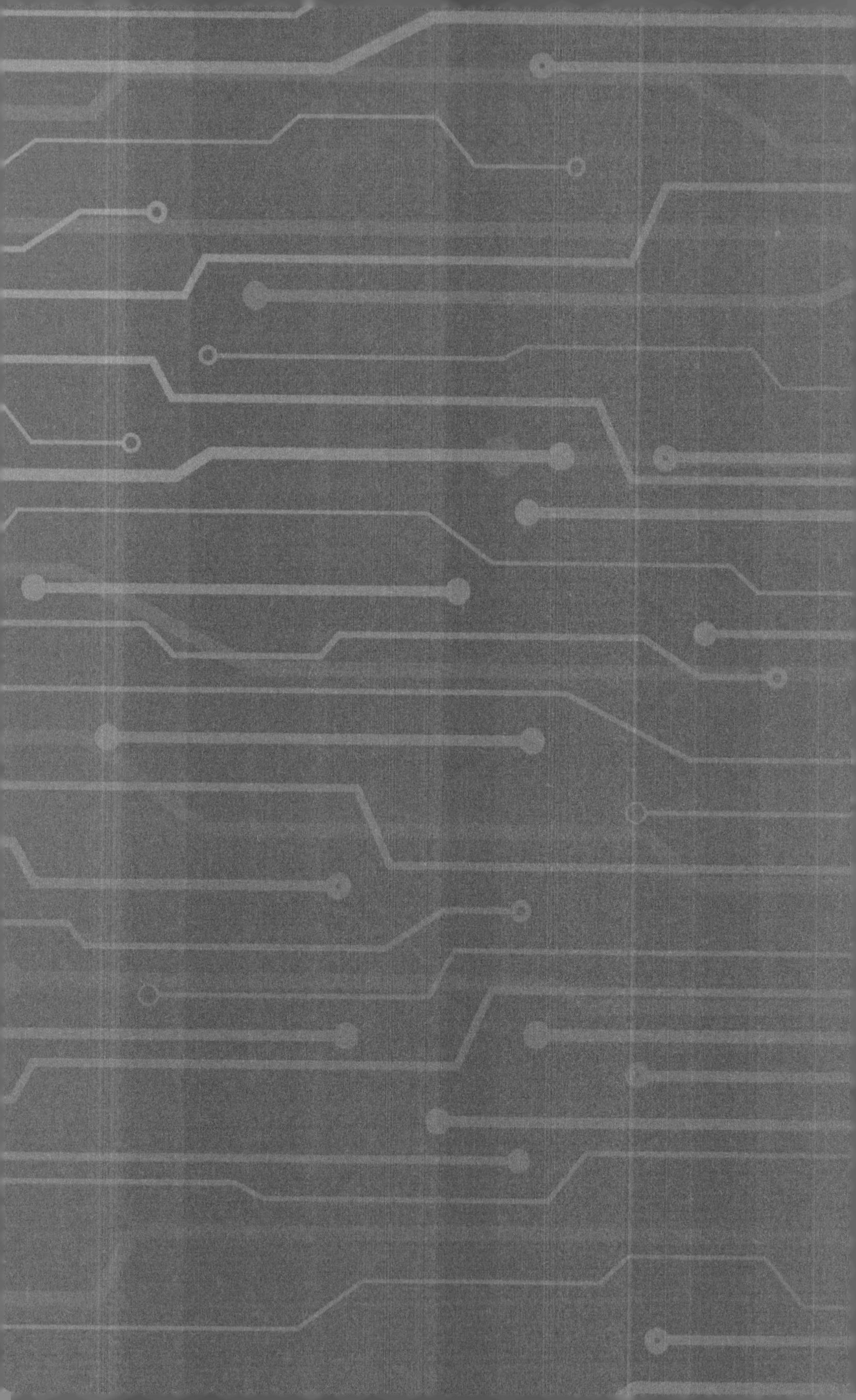

WHAT DO YOU DESIRE?_

Rain struck the kitchen window of the sprawling home nestled deep in the forest of the West Hills, the pot on the stove mimicking the plunk of rain as the popcorn kernels hit its sides.

"You're kidding, right?" Lei asked her older brother as they sat at the long wood-topped kitchen island.

"Not kidding," Hoyt replied. He had hoped it could be a nice, peaceful night in, but his younger sister was out to prove a point as they tossed back handfuls of popcorn their father was making in batches at the stove.

"Ho'o," she pressed, using the nickname he had gotten his first year playing college football over fifteen years ago. "This time last year you were loving single life and being on that *Forbes* tech billionaires list, and that local one—what's it called?"

He didn't want to answer, but unanswered questions gave him heartburn. "*Rose City*—"

"Yes! *Rose City Review*'s top ten bachelors list. Now, you're all grump-tastic, saying, 'It's time for me to settle down,' and, 'Marriage is serious.' What you and Londyn have is none of that—"

"It is." He hoped his curtness would get his sister to drop it. But she was too much like him—and not just in their shared black hair, hers long and always in a top knot, brown skin, and weird eyes that didn't know if they were brown or hazel and usually ended up looking a disarming gold—to let him off the hook. He may have even known she was right about the woman he had asked to marry him a month ago.

Londyn was the third in a string of bad time-investments and from an elite marriage broker who had promised him results. Instead, she'd said he was difficult and particularly discerning. But the thought of spending the rest of his life with someone should mean he could ask for the best. He shouldn't have to settle for mediocrity. Then again, he wasn't sure exactly what he was looking for. Just that he'd know her when he saw her. Thinking of Londyn now, however, made his stomach ache, as if he'd had ahi poke that had been left out for a few days.

"Admit it, Londyn isn't your type. Even Amy could see it in your face the other day, and if she can see it over a video call, that's not good. The marriage broker was wrong. Again. She pushed Londyn on you because her daddy is a shipping magnate who paid tons of money for the match. And she was the perfect angel when you two were under contract. Now? She's a party girl, booze and Ecstasy at the clubs. She's like a younger version of you—"

"I never did Ecstasy."

"Right, like, that is my point. Let's face it—she's a different person. You and the matchmaker got hustled." When he said nothing, she repeated, "Admit it."

"Not doing that." He reached for the fresh bowl their father had just set down, wondering if HR would allow him to fire Lei as his director of engineering at Hoyt Securities. It was *his* company after all.

"Fine, then, I will. Londyn 2.0 isn't the one. Let me tell your marriage broker what you really need. You totally have a soft spot for antiheroes. And Londyn is so far from being an antihero she's an actual hero. Hero of social media selfies to make young girls feel inadequate."

Their father chimed in from the stove. "Lei, that was unkind."

Curtis was a tall, soft-spoken man whose hair had gone gray at the temples. His tan skin was the deep color of his plain morning coffee, evidence that he spent his days fishing, and now that he and his wife, Ginny, were both retired, golfing. Ginny would say she would never retire, as she continued to manage the Kahoʻokalakupua Estate and Trust. Curtis pressed his youngest child, "Londyn is going to be family. She's ʻohana—treat her with more respect."

"Fine."

"Come, Hoyt, bring her around more. So we can stop this nonsense, ya?" He pointedly glanced at Lei to tell her to quit her Londyn bashing.

Hoyt mumbled, "Yeah, sure." Thinking the opposite was what he was going to do.

"Or," Lei said, tossing her father's advice to the side, "you can forget this matchmaker business and bring someone you actually like. Someone like the antiheroes from your comics you worshipped when we were kids."

Their father tsked from the stove.

"I'm too old for comics, Lei. And Londyn and I are fine." He heard the lie in his voice, his monotone as dry as his unbuttered popcorn.

Their father shook the large stainless-steel pot as the oily pings of the kernels struck the sides.

"I can hear that Marvel show, *Jennifer Jones—*"

"*Jessica—*"

"On your phone while you poop."

"I don't do that here."

"Why does it take you an hour in there? Are you hiding?"

He threw his arm out at her. "And you wonder why? What's with the interrogation?"

The pot on the stove gained steam once more until the covered pot sounded like it contained firecrackers. The mini explosions mimicked the rapidity of the thoughts in Hoyt's brain.

Lei shrugged. "Tomorrow you go to Festivál for Zane's thing at the club, and I'm just saying, maybe you should let loose. Find someone new and have a good time. I'm giving you permission to let her go.

Why you proposed, I dunno. Are you desperate? You got a three-for-one: the first two sucked, but if you marry the third, the match cost is free?"

"That's insulting and makes no sense." He was definitely firing his sister.

"Lei," came from their father, "mai hana kuli."

"Sorry, Dad, I know. I'll be quiet. It's just that, Hoyt, you just don't seem happy, and you're here all the time, and I'm guessing it's because you don't like being at your place. And I wanna help."

"Lei..." Curtis pressed. "Leave him be."

"Yeah, leave me alone," he grumbled, standing.

"I'm just saying that a month is long enough. No more marriage broker. You should be honest about what you really want, not what you think you need. Having a wife should be more like what Amy and I have, a partnership, not whatever it is that you told the marriage broker. You have two eyes, and you need to trust your gut. And take down that wall you have around your heart. I swear you built Titan's Wall then made a second one around your emotions."

"I'll meet you in the movie room." Standing, Hoyt ended the conversation with finality. As he left, he caught a glimpse of his father giving Lei a stern look.

Hoyt didn't need the haranguing from his sister about his choice of fiancée—he was doing enough of that all by himself. Had he noticed he rarely went home these days? Yeah. Had he noticed that Londyn was happy in her wing of the penthouse and gave him only an air kiss if their paths did cross? Yeah. Had he noticed that she didn't want to talk with him since moving in? Had he noticed that since the ring hit her finger, they had zero intimacy?

He could use a hug.

And he definitely didn't want one from Londyn. He was convinced Londyn didn't want one from him either. She'd already made it clear that the things that defined him she wanted removed. The talisman around his neck she wanted put in a drawer, and the ink on his body she wanted covered, and then one morning, she didn't want him all together.

It didn't take a rocket scientist to see his marriage choice was a bad one. Their relationship, despite what he'd thought when he put a ring on her finger, was barely social, much less civil. Somehow Londyn had skated through the matchmaking with promise, and the marriage broker's notes matched Hoyt's own: Londyn was engaging and interesting. She had him convinced that she was a sure bet. It turned out he was her sure bet. He needed to make the call to end it and start another round of dating, and he would. The only problem was that he was tired. This was his third serious attempt at finding a life companion, and it felt like doomsday. And if he made the call, ended things, and started over, the engagement announcement the broker had already sent and the social media posts that congratulated him would make everyone think they had permission to ask questions. Questions he could give a shit about, but they were exhausting. He had an international, high-level-security company to run. And this was the pilikia he'd hired a marriage broker to avoid. Now he had to find another broker. Or say fuck it to the whole thing. The only silver lining was that while he figured out what to do, he would enjoy the quiet. Date requests from others had all but vanished now that he was thought to have a fiancée, and that, he thought, was close to priceless.

Lei followed her brother only a few minutes later. The movie room was on the house's lowest level, where it tucked into the hillside. The décor mimicked the underground atmosphere with walls and furnishings in deep earth tones that absorbed light. The plush, velvety couches made a large *U*-shape that blended into the shadows and invited a person to snuggle into the pillows and luxurious throws. Hoyt was already stretched out on the far leg of the *U*, making his side of the couch seem small under his six-foot-plus frame.

Lei plopped down next to him, wedging between them a large bowl of popcorn now sprinkled with dark flakes of furikake seaweed and toasted amber nuggets of mochi crunch to make it island style.

"Look," she said, taking off right where he'd physically left, "I want you to be happy, and I think you need to find your Jessica Jones or Selina Kyle or—"

"Those were fantasies of an adolescent, Lei. I'm running a multi-billion-dollar company with thousands of people dependent on me." He fed her the excuse he told himself: "I need someone who has her own life, so when I'm not around, she's not heartbroken. I need someone who won't be corrupted by all the money either. It's a lot."

"And you think that matchmaker was right—Londyn is the one?"

"It's a marriage broker, and sure. Londyn comes from money, Lei—"

"But she spends it like she's never had a dollar in her whole life."

"Lei..."

"Look, I'm just saying, I want to see you happy or at least pursuing more of that proclaimed bachelor life you wanted until a year ago until you woke up and decided forty was coming up on you fast and you wanted a bride on your arm before then."

"Lei, fuck off."

"Fine," she said. "You guys settle on a wedding date yet?"

"What movie are we watching?"

"Dunno, something Dad will like."

"Superhero then." He picked up the remote and got things started.

"Londyn would have a date locked down— Oh."

"What do you think of this one?"

Lei looked at the screen where the hero stood in a solid stance, ten rings on his arm, then to her brother. "Ho'o...I'm sorry. You *are* thinking of breaking up with her?"

"It's a new idea. I don't want to talk about it."

"I know how much you hate quitting things." For a minute, his sister sounded thoughtful before she snapped back to her original purpose: "But think of it as another game that didn't go well: learn from it and move on—"

He pointed the remote at her. "Lei...just because Amy, your perfect wife, is stationed overseas so you have extra time to dive into other people's shit doesn't mean I want you in mine."

Lei grabbed the remote from him and switched streaming services. “Here, let’s watch your girlfriend, vigilante and all-around—”

“Alcoholic.”

“Badass.”

“Fine,” he said giving in. He tossed a blanket over his legs and tucked his hands under his crossed arms. His personal life was shit, but he could dream.

It was ridiculous to crave a fantasy superhero type, but he definitely wanted a woman with powerful confidence who wouldn’t shy away from him. He wanted someone to look at him and see *him*. Not his career stats or titles: MVP and legendary tight end for the Seattle Seahawks. Nor his second-career stats as tech-security billionaire.

His dad caught up with them then, coming into the room with a tray of fruit punch for himself and Lei and a glass of ice water for Hoyt.

He passed them out before settling in his movie-watching seat. “Oh, good, this show. That’s the one we were just talking about. Let’s do it.”

Lei grinned at Hoyt and got it started.

Their father added, pointing at the raven-haired woman on the screen, “It’s a good thing she doesn’t exist, or Hoyt would follow her everywhere she went.”

“Not true,” Hoyt mumbled. But he couldn’t hide the smile that broke out inside. It was completely true. He wouldn’t mind getting obsessed with someone as strong as him, someone who didn’t want to ride his money train and didn’t feed him false narratives she thought he wanted to hear. And yeah, she had to have that save-the-underdog thing going.

He sighed at his own reality, watching the stomping combat boots and snarling red lips of the actor who played the dark vigilante on screen. He was going to be alone for the rest of his fucking life.

LET'S PARTY_

"VEGA, VEGA, VEG-ASS!!!" A SECOND BEFORE THE CHANTING STARTED, the door to Vega Flux's apartment had burst open, shocking her fingers up off her keyboard. Into her low-lit space swept her childhood friends Cindy and Peace like models showcasing the latest in glittering nightclub attire. They were still shouting her name as they kicked her door shut.

"Ugh!" Vega feigned disgust, rolling back in her chair and taking in her beautiful friends. "What are you guys wearing? Are those tube tops supposed to be dresses? And no! I don't want whatever you're up to," she hollered, although she already knew why her gazelles were there.

Vega smothered her grin as they lit up her dark industrial apartment that was as classy as a second-story defunct-scrapyard office space could get. Once a maze of cubicles, it was now one cavernous room. Brick walls and single-paned windows were nods to its Prohibition-era construction, when the view to the river was decent. Now she had to look around the concrete footings of the I-84/I-5 interchange.

"Aw! Come on, Vega!" Peace Scott trained her cornflower-blue eyes on Vega. Her fine blond hair was pulled into a braid that danced down her back. She turned toward Cindy, who was already elbow deep in Vega's snack pantry. The cabinet had once held parts that made bombs during the WWII. Now it just held sugar bombs.

Cindy tossed back a mini chocolate chip cookie before saying, "Come on, you have to come to this one! It's literally two blocks away." Giacintha Merino-Perez went by Cindy off the clock and liked rum, chocolate, and chocolate-drenched rum parties. And handcuffs. On and off the clock. On the clock, she was Special Agent Merino-Perez. A job both Peace, who was a corporate attorney, and Vega, a haxor, found useful in their passion project, Project Valkyrie.

Cindy dropped the cookie bag on the counter and bent to see in Vega's antiquated fridge, exposing the lower curve of her bum as she dug through like a big sister inspecting how her little sis lived. "You know, one day these leftovers will kill you." Vega heard the clang of the kitchen trash lid pop open and objects dumped into it.

"I'm busy!" Vega said before sliding even lower behind her wall of monitors. She popped back up for a moment to holler at Cindy, who had more takeout boxes in hand at the garbage bin. "And those weren't that old!"

As Cindy looked over her shoulder at Vega, her bossy black curls slid out of the way of her glare. "You're busy? With what? We closed all the Project Valkyrie cases for this week. Or are you breaking the rules and fucking someone up?"

Vega slid low again. Being good for a year sucked, and it made her want to shout at happy people. "For the record, no, I'm not breaking the rules. And, two, I *could* be busy with something else!"

Peace sauntered over, her unfastened breasts lightly bouncing under the thin fuchsia fabric of her dress. She and Cindy were glittering spotlights among Vega's dark and brooding things, from the dark stain of the linseed-oiled old timber floors to the black desk and the dimmed semicircle of monitors that made up Vega's command center.

Peace's voice was soft and soothing. "Are you, though? Busy?"

"Yeah. I totally am."

Peace scrunched her nose and watched Vega pick at the corner of her thumbnail. She squeezed her shoulders up in a shrug as if she really wanted to believe Vega, but it was a stretch even for her, and she had the tenderest heart of them all.

"Peace," Vega said, "I'm pretty sure I just saw your vag. Don't shrug while you're wearing that sparkle-bandana."

"It's a dress."

"Exactly. And I don't wear tube tops that pretend to be dresses."

Peace's countenance warmed as she knew that arguing was just stage one of getting Vega ready to party.

"Yeah, you only wear knee-high combat boots, a hoodie in scathing black, and pants that look like they've been through razor wire, twice."

Vega poked at her skin peeking out from between the frayed threads at her knees. "Yup." She winked at Peace. "And that means I'm not going wherever you are going."

"You might change your mind..."

"We're meeting some guys—"

Vega's scoff interrupted Peace. "Oh, some *guys*? Then even harder pass."

"You haven't heard who they are. Their portfolios and physiques are to be admired, Vee. Be open-minded."

"They're next-level hot," Cindy decoded.

"And one in particular has a profile that we think you especially will appreciate. Appreciate so much you'll leave your computers behind."

"No one's worth leaving my command center for. And a woman needs a man—"

"Like a fish needs a bicycle, we know. But this one's different."

"Yes, Cin and I are in agreement—this is someone you could actually get distracted with," Peace encouraged.

Vega felt her lip curl at her friend's implication that someone in a group of "hot" guys was anywhere near what she considered distraction-worthy. In Vega's experience, stereotypically hot men were a couple bricks short of a full load. It wasn't their fault—she assumed that happened when people cooed at your face your whole life—but she didn't need someone in her life who never had to apply themselves.

"For being my best friends, you sure—"

Cindy held up a hand. "Your *only* friends, but yes, do go on."

"That's even worse—my only friends have no idea what motivates me. Hot guys are fun for a nanosecond; then they open their mouths, and dumb shit falls out. Do you remember the last time you said I had to meet a hot guy?"

They collectively groaned. "That was once, Vee." Cindy held up a finger. "One time."

"All it takes is once."

"This is different."

"Different? I'm not flying wingman, then?"

"Technically..." Peace started.

"And if he asks me if all bitches are feminists?"

"I believe we remember vividly, Vee. That *one* time."

"And the lawsuit that I had to help you dodge," Peace added.

Cindy dogpiled: "And the relocation we all helped with."

"There was that." She beamed her charming I-couldn't-have-done-it-without-you smile. "I appreciated the help. I know you were worried that he would expose our operations, but he had no idea it was me..." Her grin changed into a grimace. "Until I asked what he thought of feminists now, and told him who I was, and what I could do to him. That was a false move, I see that now. But seriously, before that was fun." Her grin was back.

"You're an adrenaline junkie," Cindy chastised. "And need to start going to Gamblers Anonymous meetings again."

"Sure, I'll get around to it. One day. Look," Vega said, back to Mr. One Time, "he gave me a come-on I couldn't refuse. 'One night I'd never forget.' And he was right—I've never forgotten it."

"And neither has he," Peace said.

Cindy was as unimpressed by the memory as she had been by her friend's actions in the moment and now folded her arms under her ample bosom. "So, instead of excusing yourself, you took a bet you shouldn't have with money that wasn't yours and slipped a bot in his phone...all before getting banned for life from the casino for counting cards."

"When you put it like that..." Vega stretched out on her black rolling chair that looked as if it could double as a Formula 1 driver's seat. "Remember, I was just giving him what he wanted—he got to fuck me earlier that night, and in return, I got to fuck him. A win-win, and let's be real—he got to witness one of my finer products after I lost his life savings at blackjack. He got a good little Bunny bot that was just having some fun until we saw who Hot Guy really was when the chips were down: a suddenly broke bro who—surprise, surprise—downloaded free porn like it was water in a wasteland and fat-shamed women online."

Cindy and Peace let out a collective sigh. That had been the moment they knew they'd lost the fight to get Vega's bot off his phone. When his actions put him squarely into the Project Valkyrie zone of noncompliance. Their silence at the time had been their unspoken agreement that it was OK to remove Vega's limitations and let her do what she did best. Up until that point, she'd just been having fun, like a cat with a mouse, but then the mouse turned out to be a feminist-phobic prick with a god complex.

"That was fun. Or at least it was until he got freaked out and got the cops involved."

"Making you have to move yet again." Cindy raised her brows to drive home her point.

"Which—silver lining—brought me home to Scout." She thought of her little sister then added with a sad face at her frowning friends. "Just out of curiosity, why do you keep asking me to these things? *No one* is 100 percent aboveboard."

"Because you work too hard, and you need to have time to focus on yourself and let go. It keeps the darkness away."

"You spiral when you work too hard, and that makes you reckless."

They knew why Vega punished herself to achieve the things she did for other women online. If she could protect one, she would. Only, right behind that one, was another, and behind her was just one more. Every one was important, and every one she identified with. And because of that, she'd gladly lose herself in trying to protect them all.

"One night," Cindy reiterated. She glanced at Peace. "This one is different."

Peace, glee coloring her tone, launched into the details. "It's a launch party. I was invited by the CEO, and he's got a friend..." Incredibly, from inside her tiny dress, Peace pulled out a playing card–sized invite and handed it to Vega.

Vega analyzed the body-warmed cardstock and its gold-embossed text. "Printed invites. I hate them already." She picked up one of the six phones sitting on her desk and using the camera pulled the invite data into her main terminal's search bar. The party sponsor's website came up on her monitor, and then there were the executives.

Cindy and Peace, giddy with something they both seemed to think was exciting, vibrated, waiting for her to see it too. Vega looked at the group of twelve men and women standing like dopes in front of the fresh-faced façade of a place called Big Friends Bigger Hearts in downtown and did not think, *Hell yes! Let's party!* The one labeled Zane Winters, CEO of Big Friends Bigger Hearts looked like an actual athlete. "What is he, like, a pro football player or something? Why is his jaw so wide? Why is he so hot?"

Peace was humble. "His heart is a magnificent thing to behold. I really like him. And yes, he's retired from the NFL for a few years now, and he is friends with—"

"Are. You. *Fucking.* Kidding me?!" Vega had been giving Peace a mental high-five on her new guy friend while using her facial recognition overlay to review the names and data dumps for every other person in the photo. "Your date, Peace, is friends with the man known as Ho'o Kaho'okalakupua?" Hoyt "Ho'o" Kaho'okalakupua. Tech billionaire. Founder of Hoyt Security. And egotistical maniac.

Peace clapped, her expression simultaneously hopeful and optimistic. Wringing her hands as if squeezing her excess excitement out of them, she said, "He's a major investor and close friend of Zane's from their football days. They, the two of them, go all the way back to college."

Vega breathed out and looked back to the screen. Hoyt was built like he could step back onto the field at a moment's notice. The sharp cut of his open-collared white shirt beneath a gray linen suit jacket, the kind that financiers preferred, would have left an average white tech nerd looking simultaneously wan and sickly and trying too hard, but the broad-chested, 253-pound former All-American tight end from Maui, so said the stats that were still rolling by on her monitor, still looked like a champ. Tan, proud, and smart as fuck, Hoyt had earned a reputation for creating an unhackable security system, which he kept unhackable with the double team of tech brainiacs he employed. One team to break it in-house, another to fix it.

Their constant stress testing had proved out its name: Titan's Wall.

The tech security community knew that Titan's Wall cost a mint to even attempt a breach. As in, enough money to buy an army of bots, a team of university experts, and somewhere to store the million-dollar cash prize that that egotistical maniac put on any person who could hack it. Hence why that amber-eyed towering giant had a billion dollars of net worth. Add that to his reputation as a powerhouse on the NFL field, and he was handshaking every pharma and energy bro from here to Brussels.

"Fuck," Vega whispered, taking in his gaze that said he was amused, even though his mouth wasn't smiling. He seemed genuinely happy in the photo, but she'd bet her tech that when it was game on, that gaze went sharp and calculating. She shouldn't bet; she was trying not to do that anymore.

Cindy brought her back to the apartment. "So, will you come?"

Vega had the itch to have a go at it. Titan's never came up as a wall she had to scale—her clients weren't that high up. The prospect of going up against him... Vega knew it would be delicious. In person? It could be mind-bending. So many technology bros graduated with a BS, sometimes figuratively too, in business finance. They may, *may*, know the ins and outs of revenue and sustained growth on a spreadsheet, but they left the in-the-trenches engineering to their top dogs. They knew fuck-all about the minutia of their own tech. Or the ones who had been young-pup developers too often got sloppy as the years passed. Sure, this football god looked like he was better at the fifty-yard dash than C++, but his work was supposedly legit. That he kept his code as tight as Peace's dress by still having a steady hand in the game. Vega wanted to find out more about those rumors and those hands. Did he keep his skills as a developer as tight as he obviously did his body?

"I tell you what," Vega said to her friends, "if I can't hack into just one of his personal devices, I'll go. If I can, he's just another pretty face." Vega knew Titan's Wall would have all business phones locked down tight. But the odds that his personal cell did? His first cell? Hell yes. Second? Maybe, but new phones required updates to Titan's Wall to be compatible with the new firmware, and she was sure by phone five, he had said fuck it trying to make his kit compatible. Titan's Wall was geared for corporate data centers, and he had better things to do.

"No, wait, Vee, that sounds like a bet." Cindy called her out.

"Think of it more like a litmus test."

She started three of her homemade programs to find his devices: Hunter, Seek n Find, and Sing. Hunter was as it was titled, a hunting application that combed through social media and communications from the IP address of Hoyt Securities. Seek n Find was the program she used to get stats on the board of directors, and Sing was the app baby Vega was most proud of. Another stellar program that used the cell phone tower data of every smart device in use to triangulate where someone in particular was located using voice recognition. She'd track him using voice prints taken off his voicemail and YouTube TED Talks.

From next to her, Peace asked, "Is any of what you're doing legal, Vee?"

"Legal in what sense?" Vega asked absently as her heart rate kicked up at the potential of engaging a man like Hoyt Kaho'okalakupua. For the first time in a year she began to feel genuine excitement glow deep inside.

Cindy looked worried at the green code flying up on the three programing windows Vega had open. "Instead of walking up to him digitally, come with us and talk to him in person. Let's keep it light, Vee. Don't go deep."

Vega swatted at Cindy's hands as they tried to grab her arm, a bit of a trick in her overlarge hoodie. "Nope, if he's a dunce, I don't wanna go. It's too much work to get pissed off over nothing."

"But what if you have fun anyway? You'll have a good conversation with someone, some dancing, with us at least, and maybe even some anonymous make-out session—then back to work tomorrow all refreshed."

"I just want to know if he's gone soft— Got him," she said, and both women leaned in.

"Where? There's only all that coding stuff."

"He's at Festivál already, which, let's face it, I probably didn't need Hunter and Seek n Find for that. Now, let's watch what happens when you get to be a billionaire: you lose focus on the little things." From within that glow that had begun, Vega hoped she was wrong.

Cindy, voice low in agent mode and full of confidence, said, "How about I hit your closet and get you something to wear."

Vega didn't hear her as she plowed through the three app's results. She found his personal device and its firewall, like any good tech, but this one wasn't strictly Titan's Wall. It was, and it wasn't. It was dynamic, not just an impenetrable surface like classic Titan's Wall, but rather, fail to guess the riddles three, the application's programming interface protection key triggered a defense she'd never seen before. It went on the offensive, collecting user data.

"Shit," Vega muttered as she started a slew of her own defenses, allowing her to stay at his wall anonymously. Then under the barrage of thousands of bot-bees, she fired up a basic hack of coming at the firewall in an attempt to force his device to route her to a denial-of-service error path. Then she hoped the engineers were lazy and didn't lock the error path door, leaving her uninhibited access to his device. Only, it wasn't some random device; this was Hoyt of Hoyt Security, and her defense programs were logging data hitting *her* firewall. They were holding; he'd have no idea who attempted the breach as long as she could hold him off long enough for her secondary systems to boot. She swallowed a tickle of apprehension at the out-of-the-gate aggression. Then smiled. "He's good."

Cindy was back in front of her, something glittering in her hands. "Excellent. Time to get dressed."

TAKEN TO TASK_

Hoyt took up half of the corner booth. Even there on the lower floor, away from the main party upstairs, the place was as it always was: packed with the energy and opportunity of a promised good time.

Only it was the land of opportunity for everyone but him. When he saw Londyn next, he'd break things off with her, and he'd do so with the marriage broker too. He might not know what he wanted, making him "particularly discerning," as the broker had said, but he did know he didn't have the energy to put himself out there any longer. His sister's random quip about having Titan's Wall around his emotions was probably true. And he had no idea how to take it down or even if he should.

That night, however, wasn't about him. It was his buddy Zane Winter's first venture, and the future of Big Friends Bigger Hearts was something Hoyt also personally believed in and would dump every cent of his personal capital into if Zane needed it. This was the only reason he was physically there at the club their mutual friend Nate Vellanova owned. He loved Nate like a brother, but their tastes were opposites. The club was as successful as it was because Nate had a pulse on what humanity found stimulating. Hoyt preferred to not have hundreds of bodies colliding against him; he'd rather leave that for game day.

Just when he thought it was time to say his goodbyes and leave, his watch vibrated, alerting him that there had been an attempted breach of one or more of his personal devices.

Curious, Hoyt took out his phone and checked the status of the intrusion detection. He corrected himself, the *ongoing* attempt. The beta software installed on his personal devices was doing as he wanted, going on the offensive, the legality of which was still being debated by Congress and the FCC. He had no taste for breaking the law but knew that his legal team was ecstatic to be attempting to create legal precedent. He just wanted internet trolls to stop feeling like they were invincible, and for now, his personal devices could do just that.

The denial-of-service hack attempt seemed to be coming from five hundred thousand different IP addresses, all attempting to connect to his device at once. His system was holding. What were they attempting? To have his firewall crash with just a half-million bots? If he were a junior coder with half a brain cell, he'd know that wouldn't work to access *his* devices. Who was this group?

He checked the logs on the IP address trace and watched as his beta software Titan 2.0 attempted a capture but instead was being sent on a wild goose chase all over the world.

Outside in the cool damp of the night air, Vega marched with Cindy and Peace over water-filled dips and breaks in the sidewalk to Festivál. She felt it then—opportunity and exhilaration smoked her nerve endings, setting her skin alight. She felt that thrill of potential electrify her bones; it was party time; it was chaos-creation time. Peace squealed as a passing car splashed water up onto the sidewalk. Vega didn't notice her boots get wet nor that her fishnet stockings had muddy droplets on them now, like dark crystals. Her eyes were on the horizon, toward which they strode in their glittering dresses, to the thump and thunder of Festivál.

The line to enter Festivál was, as it always was, down the block. Vega let the towering soles of her black boots take her past the line as if she were the owner of all the world's shit and this line, like any other, was only for those who followed the rules. *Oh yes, this night, just this night, she'd break the rules. Just a little.*

Peace, satisfied with the back of the line, stopped and hollered at the other two that the end was back where she was. Cindy doubled back and grabbed Peace's arm with a laugh, dragging her after Vega, who was headed for the warehouse's neon lights and double-door entrance. Sticking to her back, they stumbled in after her as she pushed past the line manager and those waiting behind the velvet rope at the door. Inside she blew a kiss to the bouncer on his stool; happy to see them, he waved back and pointed to where the VIP party was upstairs. He'd gotten Vega's message.

A team of women at the door were incensed and hollered for them to "get to the back of the fucking line." Peace hid her face as Cindy laughed at the chaos that Vega had already conjured. Vega heard the cussing from the doorway and turned, blowing the girls behind the rope a kiss too, against her middle finger.

"Once I break his phone," Vega shouted over the thump of the club, "I'm out."

Cindy rolled her eyes. "And remember, keep it light, have some fun!"

"Come, he's over here!" Peace grabbed Cindy and made for the crowd and the man she'd come for.

Vega paused to watch her friends dive into the crush of bodies, skin to skin moving with the grind of the DJ's playlist. It'd been a year since she'd been out, and the bodies, the music, the flashing lights were intoxicating. She'd told Cindy that she'd break him and leave, but Cindy had read her right. She was there to play.

Nervous, excited energy rushed through her body. Hoyt's system was the perfect playground for a specific scientific test she was quietly collaborating on. She hadn't told the girls since it was just a pet project with a university professor who hadn't given her specific permission for that night, nor had it worked properly in the last hundred attempts. But that night—she had a feeling—it would work. It had to. Everything was too perfectly aligned for it not to.

The neon rainbow of the strobe lights bounced off sequins, glitter, and black-light nails. Cindy's dark curls disappeared into the shadows while only the very top of Peace's blond hair was visible, reflecting the changing colors. Vega watched as Peace zeroed in on a man in a sport suit moving as if he needed a week of hot yoga to loosen up his body for Festivál's dance floor.

Vega turned. Her target was not there. She had to find him, and quickly. Her little bots could create only so much chaos until the master of Titan's Wall caught up with them, closing the window she had to work her magic in and ultimately revealing to him who she was. Billionaires tended to be the protective and vindictive sort. The kind that made perfect targets...for the foolish. Vega felt herself smile for the first time in a long time—that was her kind of odds.

She moved through the club and up the frosted-glass stairs, the boom and cascade of the music rattling through her skeleton and down into her boots. In the VIP section, Vega took in the few investors sipping water or dirty martinis, but none of them were six feet four and built like SEAL Team 6. Combined.

It was as she was coming back down the stairs, through the clear glass treads, that she glimpsed him. There, below her, separate from the rest, his arm wide over the back of the curved booth cushion as if an invisible date was nuzzled in next to him, was Titan's master. She wanted him to look up right then, to meet her gaze, so he'd know she found him. He was looking at her, but from a totally different angle, through his device. Her handiwork was currently being analyzed in his wide hand.

This knowledge sent another thrill down her spine. He was not a couch performer; he was very much still in the game, and the thing her bots were coming up against was what she had assumed—it was some of his own personal handiwork. The average chief technology officer didn't track breach attempts on his own phone.

She whispered down to him, "No time like the present, my friend." Her voice drowned in the music.

. . .

HOYT LOOKED UP, FEELING EYES ON HIM. THE CROWD PULSED JUST beyond his table; bodies crowded the stairs as a set of laces-and-leather punk-style black platform boots worked their way down. An odd feeling struck him like déjà vu, a pleasant feeling of recognition, that somehow this moment was important or had happened before in another life. He shook off the feeling and let his attention go back down to his phone. He was looking at the progress his system was making against the invasion when that feeling of eyes on him made him look up once more. The boots had worked their way along the edge of the club and were now stopped as their owner, hip cocked one way, head cocked the other way, watched him from her dark corner. He saw the chunky cuts of black hair sweep around her shoulders and touch her jaw, a rockstar's style. Or that of a scraggly cat eyeing him from atop a fence.

Having gained his gaze, she moved out of the dark and into the dim light surrounding his table. He amended his earlier thought; *she is no scraggly cat.* As the sequined curves of the woman stepped into the low light of his booth, he felt his insides swoop. Maybe coming to the club had been a good idea after all.

Her eyes were dark, smoky in black, and her dress, one handshake away from being a napkin, sparked and glittered over her tight, lean body. She approached with the kind of familiarity that he was once accustomed to. Only the fans from his time in the NFL had been one of two kinds. Fans of his stats and fans wanting to fuck. With this woman, he had the odd sensation that she was coming *for him.*

Her lips twisted wryly as she bumped his table with her hip before sliding her hand over the black marble. She looked like a porcelain statue, bored and ready for a nap. Only her heavy-lidded gaze was like lightning aiming for him. He felt his skin go warm and his shirt too tight. She looked as if she was ready to play, play at what, he had no idea, but her eyes beckoned, both playfully and dangerously, to him.

Her lips, a dark red that reminded him of blood on jerseys, parted. "Are we having fun yet?"

He wasn't sure he'd heard her right over the club music. "Are we what?"

"Having fun," and in the next second, she plucked his phone from his hand and spun it across the table.

"Hey" was all he managed before she caught it and slid into the other side of his booth. In what felt like a practiced move, she opened a small clutch at her waist and pulled out her own old-school cell and a connection cord. Alarm bells went off in his mind.

She connected the phones and popped the screen up on hers before using her thumbs on the keypad and starting what looked like a physical attempt to crack open his device. The screen of his phone went black as his own special protections went into place.

He was definitely *not* prepared for what just sat down at his booth.

"What the fuck are you doing?" he asked as he stood. He wanted her to see his height and think twice about what she was attempting. It wouldn't be the first time someone felt confident to flex on him when he was sitting.

Instead of startling, she put her boot to the booth seat and pushed herself farther in, taking the phones with her. When she answered him, her voice was sultry, almost indistinguishable under the music. "Why," she said, "I'm playing with you. What else would I be doing in a thundering club on a Saturday when I could be at home with snacks? But to be honest, this is starting to feel a lot like that." She winked in a way he didn't know how to interpret.

The woman was some kind of agent connected with the ongoing attack. Her bot team weren't so much trying to break in as they were being a distraction. He wasn't sure what kind of beautiful psycho she was, but he did know that he didn't want to underestimate what a direct port into his phone could do. He didn't want his proprietary beta program breached by a hottie at a night club. There was a lot there he couldn't defend to his engineering and legal team.

"Nope," he said and reached for his phone.

INVADERS_

Hoyt's reach for his phone only made the woman slide farther away, forcing him to get back into the booth. With every move he made to get closer, she used the wide-topped table as a center point, moving around it like hands on a clock. Every time she paused, she leaned on the table like it was a bar, her cleavage rounded up where it rested on her forearm, reminding him of the length of time it had been since he'd had a hug, let alone more. Despite her allure, he wished then that Nate hadn't bolted the tables to the floor. He had the urge to flip it out from between them. Her fingers were like the wind over her mini keyboard.

"Enough." He stood again, and when she tucked back into the booth, he followed and reached to grab her, any part of her, but she put her boot to his chest.

Braced against the back of the booth to keep him firmly back, she said, "I'll be just a moment more, darling. I know you desperately want your phone, and I'll get it back to you, in just a second. I am so close to winning this bet, you see, and setting precedent. Meanwhile, let's chat. This tech is"—she took a deep, appreciative breath as if sampling his defenses was like tasting a fine wine—"nuanced, layered, and complex, with a defense wall that's...dynamic. Who wrote it?"

Looking down at the thick sole of her boot on his pale-blue dress shirt, he was surprised. He should have been pissed, and he'd get there, no doubt, but she was unconventional, and he had to admit there was a part of him that was liking the flex that she was bringing. Nothing so dangerously beautiful had taken him on like this before. He was disturbed to find that he liked that she was impressed with his beta tech, and it made him curious to see how far she'd get.

"*I* did," he answered her.

"Ah, yes, I thought so. You've still got it, my friend."

"You know who I am," he stated the obvious. "Who are you?"

"Just a friend who's taking your trick ride for a spin."

"And if I say no?"

Her eyes left the screen for just a moment to light on his, making him feel as if she were looking past everything that was superficial about him and like his phone was putting a direct tether into him. "Are you? Saying no?"

He should definitely say no. He should absolutely say it. *Say no,* he thought.

When he was silent another beat, she smiled. "That's what I thought."

His phone now on her chest, she'd gotten the phone to reboot without Titan 2.0. His mind tripped over itself. No matter if it had been a direct port or a wireless request to connect his system; on that device, it should have stayed locked down. The woman was breaching encryptions that should take an experienced team of hackers months, even years, to break. And by then his key would have digitally changed over a thousand times.

She was doing something that shouldn't be possible, no matter how much time someone had. She was doing something he'd never seen before.

"Who do you work for?" He should not look down at her long fishnet-covered leg and into the spread *V* of her thighs as her other leg, hooked over the booth seat, ticked that foot in time to the beat of the music. Nor should he take a longer glance at that strip of dark lace that rested at the apex of her thighs like a present for his eyes only.

"No one," she answered. "You're just an experiment, a friendly bet, like I said. Or did you think that this woman in a minidress and tats was joking, Hoyt of Hoyt Security?" She looked up, giving him a lip lift that was a threat and a grin rolled into one.

He noticed her tats then, tiny, on her fingers and forearms. They looked to be mathematical symbols; he could see the infinity symbol and a triangle that he interpreted to be the Greek symbol delta, for change. Then he spied one under her arm, behind the generous curve of her breast; the part of the black-and-gray design that he could see was of the rear of a car, a time-traveling Delorian. He memorized each as clues to who she was.

Just as he took his eyes off her arm, she had his phone rebooted. His stomach churned. He put his hand gently on the leather and laces of her ankle and easily lifted her foot off his chest. She stayed focused on the phone, but he felt her watching him in her periphery.

He pulled her in. "Do you want a job? Are you trying to break my software? If you're taking the Titan's Wall challenge seriously, then you'll know it has rules, and my personal devices are off the table." She was dragged a few inches before her other boot was against his chest. It landed with a gentle thump, stopping her movement. It was an odd game they were playing. It was as if they both knew that he had the physical capability to yank her out of that booth and get his phone back at any time and that it was a risk she was willing to take. Fuck the consequences.

He took her other boot off his chest, and with both ankles in his hands, he pulled her gently but purposefully across the seat to him. He tucked her ankles behind him, trapping her legs between him and the back of the booth.

"Nope." She twisted, her dress riding up, as she reached overhead, taking both cells with her. He saw she'd gotten down to the administrator screen. The lower crescents of her fishnet-covered buttocks popped out from under the glittering hem of her dress as she tried to wriggle away. The administrator screen was a kind of atomic bomb they both were racing toward. Him against, her for it.

Hand across the backs of her thighs, he pinned her. His pinkie may have brushed against the warm curve of her butt, and he registered that the lace beneath the fishnets formed a thong. He pressed down just hard enough and reached over her body for his phone. She wriggled harder to keep his phone out of reach. While he was focused and intent on retrieving his phone, his love-starved body welcomed her uninhibited push back against him; the curves of her that pressed against his abdomen felt like foreplay, and his heart responded with a jolt of joy. With his body against her back, he bent his head and told her against the shell of her ear, "'A'ole, I don't think so."

He shot his hand out and grabbed the cord, and with a flick of his wrist, he freed his phone.

She slumped under him, the game over.

She turned over then, and he was close enough to see the lightning in the storm clouds of her irises before they lightened in a sunburst. "Damn," she whispered.

He tried to keep his gaze casual as he reached over her and plucked his device off the cushion. Like a cat, she stretched out under him as if they were lovers in bed and not strangers in a club, before cushioning her head on her arms, and said, "So close."

He should raise his voice at her for taking advantage. He should get her name. He should not unscrew the dim light bulb of that already darkened booth and adjust her into a better position up onto his lap.

Reading his thoughts as if they were closed-captioned, she grinned, her lips twisting devilishly, and she slowly pulled one leg then the other out from behind him before sitting up and adjusting her dress back down. Her eyes scoured his form, studying him as she wound up the cord attached to her own device and returned it to her pouch.

"Who are you?" he asked, gaining brain space in the physical space between them. "Tell me who you are." He hoped she couldn't hear the pleading in his voice.

"It's been fun" was her only answer before she popped open the back of her cell and removed the battery, then cracked the SIM card. He didn't give a shit about her phone; he only cared about who *she* was. One more clue: she had the paranoid feel of someone who had hacked hackers before. No one else bricked their devices like that.

Her long look was both warm and keen. "You win. Good game. But we both know that I was one second away from popping open your phone like a digital library and having Hoyt Security all to myself."

"What is it that you want with Hoyt Securities?"

The woman shrugged. "Not today, big man."

"You need to tell me who you are and who you work for, *now*." He didn't want to let her leave. As she pushed to leave the booth, he thought about physically grabbing her.

"I wouldn't, big guy," she said, properly reading his expression. "And I wonder, why so demanding now? You had ages to get me to stop, but you wanted to know, didn't you? You were curious, weren't you? How far would I get? And now you know. So, say thank you, and I'll say you're welcome and, now, goodbye."

Vega eyed the man named Hoyt Kaho'okalakupua. He was clearly incensed but still hadn't started screaming or yelling for bodyguards or calling her a crazy bitch. All of which she expected from a tech billionaire at a club. It made her want to stay a while beneath his bracing arm, his warm, hard body pinning her in the booth. It made her want to ask him questions, like, how far could she push him to get him to react? What emotion would it be? Would it be more of what he had now, a fire in his eyes that said he'd track her down? Just that thought alone made her shiver with excitement.

But *now* was the proper time to leave. She had to get home, check the test logs to her project, clean up her digital trail, and pray to the tech gods he wasn't as vengeful as his own security defenses made him out to be.

He slid out of the booth too, and her pulse kicked up at all six-plus feet of him. "Let me walk you to your car."

Vega took in his towering form. He filled out his suit nicely, and it was broad-shouldered with hard edges, tailor-made. She wanted to know if he could pick her up. She knew his offer was more about him wanting a license plate, more time under the security camera for a facial recognition, anything to start digging into her. Something she both wanted and was afraid to have happen.

With one last smile, she said, "I'm good. Bye," and not for the first time, since her year of restraint started, she did the opposite of what she really wanted to do, which was to stay and chat, to dive into the minutia of his system and dig into his mind. He was the first man she'd met whose aggressive intellect matched his aggressive gym skills. And his face, purposeful jaw, neck as wide as her thigh, and black brows and lashes that were like brushstrokes on his tan skin were definitely going to be on her mind when she let her asshole boyfriend, Jax, get hip deep with her again.

She took a deep breath to keep from diving back into the booth. She had to walk away. Not straddle his lap there in the club and pop a couple of his shirt buttons and taste his skin. Or let him pin her to the booth cushion once more—only that time she'd invite his hands up her dress.

He stepped closer to her, and with a thrill up her spine, she spun to leave, and plowed headfirst into Peace and Cindy.

"Umph," Cindy grunted.

"Where are you going?" Peace asked then looked over Vega's shoulder. "Oh, that's him." Then to Vega: "You didn't."

Vega's stern look silently told her loose lips sink ships. "I might have. I have to go now." She felt the reality and complication of friends and a man like Hoyt. They'd have to lie through their teeth to their dates about their relationship with Vega. She cursed; things were getting complicated fast.

Cindy looked to the towering Hoyt as his friends joined them, also looking to Hoyt, who was wearing a pleasant smile, a boot print on his shirt, and a threat in his eyes. *You can run, but you cannot hide from me.*

Peace's date, Zane, a leaner male still well over six feet tall with the jawbone a carpenter's square would be proud of, put something together.

To Peace, he said, "This is your friend who's into computers, right?" He looked to Vega then to Hoyt as if it were Christmas and the present that had been given was a good one. Glee coloring his tone as it had Peace's earlier that evening in Vega's apartment, he said, "Damn, did she do it? She hacked you?"

Hoyt's gaze sizzled onto Vega's. "No. And she's lucky I'm polite."

Vega couldn't resist stepping back into the fray. "Polite? My, my, my. You sound like you want to tangle again, Titan. How about this time you can use those hands more judiciously. You can hold me while I take you, and what's yours."

Cindy grabbed the back of her arm in warning. "Cool it down," she said under her breath then, "You go; we've got this."

But Vega loved the Titan's murderous gaze and desperately wanted that next round despite the alarm bells going off all around her. "I had your kit in my hot little hands, and I would have broken it if you didn't physically interfere."

Cindy tightened up on her arm. "Time to go, *Joan*." Joan of Arc as her code name had been her idea.

Vega said to Hoyt, "I take that as suitable evidence that I breached your phone's defenses adequately, and now," she said to her friends, "I've earned that wager, er, litmus test, and get to go home. With another notch in my belt."

With one last look over her shoulder at Hoyt, who was giving her a stare that said they were far from over, she smiled. She'd had fun, but now she had to run like hell.

"You won't hear from me again, no hard feelings. See you later, big guy." And blew him a three-fingered kiss.

TRACKING_

Hoyt resisted the urge to follow her. Watching her leave, and her friends hurrying after her, he asked Zane, "Who'd you say that was?"

"Peace's friend Joan. Last name Arc, I think..."

"Yeah, not her real name," Hoyt said. "Where does Peace know her from?" He looked down at his phone, opening its operating logs. Everything looked fine. It had registered a connection but nothing more. "Who the fuck is she?" he asked aloud to his phone, more pointed this time.

"Dunno. Peace said they came late because they had to convince her to come. Apparently, she took one look at you and decided it was worth her time. They said she couldn't crack you, so I think there was some sort of wager made... I don't know any more than that— Peace was worried she'd said too much. When I asked where she worked, she totally clammed up. You don't know her?"

"Did she mess you up?" Nate, who'd joined them, chimed in.

"No. She didn't get in, but it was too close. She's...really talented."

Nate and Zane exchanged glances.

Zane added, "*Talented*, huh?" He laughed and touched a finger to his friend's chest. "Is that her boot print on you, man?"

"Maybe." His eyes trained on the door, he repeated to himself, "Who is she?"

Zane gently punched Hoyt's shoulder to knock him out of his trance. "She did break your shit, didn't she?"

"Close isn't *in*."

They knew that phrase from their days on the field. Close wasn't in when it was the fourth down at the one-yard line.

"Hoyt, lemme get you some comps. You shouldn't have to deal with something like that at my place."

"No."

Nate smirked and slouched in his expensive suit that made him look as if he had Hoyt's net worth, wiped his fingers over his mouth, needing a cigarette, and added, "So, you're into that kind of shit. Kinky booth shit with random girls. Dump Londyn, I'll have you hooked up by week's end."

"Tempting."

Hoyt didn't want that night to be the last play of the game. He wanted another round with the woman named Joan Arc, a round where he could take a closer look at what she'd done. Because the only thing that made sense was that she'd used tech that was theoretical. Though its name evoked images of branching timelines in a science-fiction world, quantum computing offered the only way he could fathom that she'd been able to knock down his multiple 512 kilobyte security encryption layers in such short order.

"Time to go?"

"Yeah," Hoyt said, finally meeting Zane's gaze. He wanted to get to his terminal and start up his own systems to find her. Titan 2.0 should have made some kind of headway with the IP trace, but his last readout showed them in Nova Scotia. And if they didn't catch a bot, she was in the wind.

Zane handed him his phone. "Hold this—gotta take a leak before we go."

Hoyt took the phone and waited a polite second as his bro slipped back into the rear of the club.

Nate's eyebrows pinched together, a silent question of why Zane didn't just keep his phone in his pocket.

Hoyt answered as he flicked through the contacts, copying Peace's number before locking it and pocketing it.

VEGA LAY IN THE SEMIDARKNESS, HER WAREHOUSE WINDOWS DRAPED with sheets against the day's warming light.

She was still obsessing about that six-foot-four man who let her take a joy ride with his kit. He'd been fuming at the end, but not "call security" fuming. She mused he was pissed that it had been so one-way. It made her want to do something foolish, like ping his phone and ask if he liked it as much as she did, and was he up for another round?

She threw her legs out of bed, and the rest of her reluctantly followed. In just her socks and underwear, her hair mussed, half up and the rest trickling down her back, she shuffled across the room and slumped into her command chair. She looked at her phones, including the one from last night, the one with the broken SIM. She wanted to know if he was on the hunt or if he'd just brushed her off. Was he thinking of her too?

She shook her head as if saying no to her moronic train of thought. It was on a dangerous and foolish path.

But was it?

She'd swept her trail clean, but now, she wanted to drop a crumb.

Vega tsked at herself and let it go. She shouldn't wander down that path without a chaperone.

As quickly as she'd sat, she was up again, getting dressed—this day needed to begin—and then once again back at her computer. Vega went through her routine of checking online message boards and setting up project lists for her, Cindy's, and Peace's Project Valkyrie work.

Their first case, as not even teenagers, was helping Vega escape her stepdad with her little sister, Scout. Thanks to addiction, bad luck, bad timing, and one mom dying on them, Vega and Scout, who were half-siblings from the same mom, ended up in the care of Mom's final husband, Lloyd, who was stepdad to them both. Lloyd had a low-paying job with a high penchant for bitching about how everyone else had it so easy, so when the creditors and debt collectors started calling the moment, it seemed, their mother left the earthly plain for heaven above, he began to look for ways to make quick cash. That was when their lives took a sharp detour.

Scout was lucky, all things considered, and survived what Lloyd put them through relatively unscathed. Being too young to remember things clearly was sometimes a blessing. Not so much Vega. The time-traveling flux_capacitor, Vega's handle, was born a demon. The demon who said "fuck no" to abusers in every form. The fat-shaming troll, the sandwich "artist" who got handsy with his coworker who didn't want any of it, and those further down the despicable turd bucket scale. It was dark work, no matter how "light" the offense, but with each project, they—Vega, along with Cindy, Peace, and maybe someday, not now, but someday, Scout, who was in undergrad prepping for law school in Portland—liberated a woman or someone else oppressed. Each time, they gouged a line into the brick wall of the warehouse as a reminder of the solid presence each of them held in the world. The short side of the rectangular warehouse was full. Tick marks now started on the long rear wall. Hundreds of thousands of women were safe.

By early afternoon Vega had gathered enough info to start another round of Valkyrie projects, once Peace and Cindy reviewed them. She stood and stretched, and seeing what might be one of the last nice fall days through her windows, she pinged her sister up at the university, grabbed her hoodie, and called an Uber with her hacked app.

In the car, Vega slipped on her sunglasses, lowered the window, and let the sun and cool fall air wash over her face as her hair danced in the wind. Her mind was blissfully blank.

Her phone vibrated.

She looked.

It was a message from a number that made excitement sizzle across her skin. Her mind was definitely no longer quiet.

Hi.

She double-checked as her insides flip-flopped. It was a number being directly connected to her device, not through her routing systems, from Hoyt Securities. She took a deep breath, trying to still herself. She had no idea who was on the other end. It could be a talented engineer he tossed her breach to, but her instincts said it wasn't. She replied.

New phone, who dis?

There was silence, and Vega wanted to take back her joke and confirm it was her and confess she knew who he was and beg him to not quit texting, but she stilled her fingers. The Uber stopped, and as she hopped out, tossing behind her cash the driver hollered he couldn't accept, her phone vibrated again.

She read the message as the sun hit the side of her face as she walked through the quad to where she knew Scout liked to study.

Taking a class? Intro to Hacking?

Vega knew she shouldn't take the bait. But now that he'd proved that he had the tenacity and haxor skills to find her—he didn't need, or want, any crumbs she dropped—she gave in.

Teaching. Wanna join?

Sessions start at a billion dollars but are one-on-one. I've got an opening right now.

That's a little pricey coming from a woman with no portfolio to show me. How do I know if I'm getting my money's worth?

Vega paused on a bench. She was there for Scout, but she'd have to handle the Titan first.

Did you try a Google search for "woman at club taking me to task"?

Came back with right around zero. Who are you meeting?

Why? Are you jealous?

Maybe I'm meeting my lover for a tryst in the quad. Wanna watch?

No. Are you a student there?

Goodness, you're forward.

Feels like you're trying to get more information on me...

I think it might be my life's work now.

Vega laughed, startling two birds out of their perch above her.

God, that's sexy.

That's a threat. It's not meant to be sexy.

Too late, it was sexy, you can't take it back.

And yes, I was fantasizing about you as well.

We should grab a coffee sometime. Naked.

Let's.

Clothed.

I have a few things to ask you.

Like...?

Vega waited and then, standing, typed:

Bye for now, Titan.

His response this time was immediate:

Js wiat

She wrote as she walked once more to find Scout:

?

It was some time again before he responded, and Vega began to wonder if she should brick her phone.

I'm trying to run a multibillion-dollar company
at the moment—just wait.

Why are you working, sir—it's Sunday.

Some things can't wait.

Like trying to find a psycho from a club?

I doubt she's psycho. I believe she's cunning
and relies on powerful people
underestimating her.

Vega looked at his words a good long while. If she hadn't met him, she'd take his tone as flirtatious. Since she had met him, and had a sense how he spoke, she figured he was just stating a fact. But decided to take it as flirting anyway.

Are you trying to get me naked?

It's working. Where are you? I want to show
you my navel ring.

I ask the questions. Who are you?

Who are any of us but pawns in a rich man's
game?

One hint. For this rich man's game.

Now Vega stayed silent.

Just one.

No, I want you desperate, Mr. Kaho'okalakupua.

Why?

So that you know how I felt after meeting you. It's a sin to be so handsome AND smart. Where's your fatal flaw?

Not sure I'm the person to be asking that.

Good point—let me call your mom? Do you have one, or were you born fully formed right from the earth?

That's personal.

Just how I like it.

Vega waited for his response. She checked her watch, giving herself at least two more minutes before she would pop the battery out.

A question appeared:

What's your fatal flaw?

How much time do you have?

All day.

Vega sighed. She didn't, and yet she wanted more.

Do you feel it too?

Feel what?

Vega mentally kicked herself and started scanning for her sister. His texts were starting to take on a distracted flare she didn't like.

Her heart skipped a beat when, across the quad, still in the well-fitting pants and shirt from the night before—only now his collar was open and his suit coat was gone—he took in the courtyard, searching for someone.

Vega let out a scared giggle and popped open the back of her phone. *Yeah,* she told herself, *he could feel it.*

His gaze dropped to check his phone that looked small in his wide palm. He looked up and made eye contact with Vega across the courtyard.

She slipped her shades back on and with her heart hammering, stepped into a well-timed crowd of girls passing by. Weaving through their bodies, she used them as cover before tucking down the steps into the basement entrance of the nearest building.

Hoyt lost her signal after his last text, and as though the Universe knew that an old-fashioned meet-cute needed to step in, the next time he looked up, between the shadows and bright fall sunlight, his eyes found her. A hundred yards across the packed quad her dark gaze met his as she was already tucking pieces of her phone into her pockets.

She'd slipped on fluorescent-pink heart-shaped sunglasses he'd bet anything weren't hers, even though he barely knew her. As if on cue, a batch of sorority girls entered the courtyard, and she was gone. He'd been too far away and didn't want to mow anyone down just to get to her, but a few minutes later, on the ride to his cousin's law office, he cursed himself. He should have sprinted to her.

HELLO, VEGA_

The next day broke bright through Vega's eyelids. Through one slit eye, her phone told her it was noon. She should roll over for another hour of sleep, but something felt off. She lifted her tired face off her pillow. Seated at the center of her *U*-shaped command center was a large man tossing and catching her stress ball as if he lived there too.

Adrenaline blew into her system. She kicked off her blankets and stood, her head swimming. It was too early for this shit. As Hoyt Kahoʻokalakupua's gold eyes scoured her from foot to crown, she was glad that she'd worn her pj shorts *and* hoodie to bed. As she caught her breath, she watched his mouth grow into a winner's smile. He was looking impeccable in another suit, this one in indigo, as if he were taking a power lunch in her studio.

"Hello, how are you, *Vega Flux*, whose list of outstanding warrants is as long as my arm?"

Vega's guts bottomed out. "I'm well, thanks for asking. Ah, now, get out?" Her mind skittered. *How long has he been at my terminal?* She had seriously underestimated his desire to find her.

Hoyt looked at her with curiosity. "Is there an 'or' at the end of that question?"

"Yeah, like 'Or stay and make me breakfast and fuck my brains out'? I dunno, what do you want?"

His eyebrows rose slightly. While he attempted to respond further, Vega plopped back down on her bed, trying to pretend she was just enjoying a surprise visit from a friend. She crossed her legs, and leaning forward, she slipped her hands into her hoodie pouch. Cell in hand, she began a blind boot of her nuclear reset program. She didn't have much fire power in her cell, but the magnet outside—which would be suicide for her stuff but would nuke his phone too—did.

"Toss me your phone."

"Nope," she said and, found out, brought her phone into the open. Now with the speed of both thumbs and her eyes, she opened the homemade app and typed commands like mad.

He leaped out of her chair.

"Shit," Vega said.

With a hand on the tabletop, he came over it. Vega cursed the elasticity of his tailor-made suit as he cleared it easily. She dove under another long table at the end of her command center, knocking boxes of supplies and tumbleweeds of cords. Phone still in her hands, she scurried to the kitchen and put the dented island counter between them. Her naked knees felt the scuff of the floor as she got the program started, creating a whine in the room.

"What the..." he said as, with one push from his hand, he moved the long table out of his way, refusing to follow her under it. "What's that sound?" His gold eyes had gone to hard gemstones. The sweep of high cheekbones gave his face a natural look of mischievous joy, but now he looked menacing.

"Just a little wipeout. Can't have Mr. Security getting his hands on all this."

He put his hand out to her as if she were a skittish kitty. "Stop, I just wanna talk."

The whining intensified as the low rumble of a diesel engine kicked on.

"Seriously, I just—"

Vega's fingers flew, but when the crane lifting the magnetic ring, a leftover from the scrapyard that once had been out back, hit the side of the building, she could see that Hoyt realized how deep the shit he'd waded into was. The bookshelf of parts against the rear wall shook with the strike.

He flinched. "What the..." he said again, looking out the metal-rimmed panes at the magnet and then back at her. "Don't turn that on."

"Sorry, I have rules. I don't know what you're really here for, but whatever it is, you won't have the evidence to prove it."

"Turn that on, and you'll kill us," he growled.

"Nope, just my data," *and my navel ring*, she thought. That was going to hurt like hell when it got ripped out.

Before she could confirm the go command, he was sprinting. His speed as an NFL tight end caught her off guard. She managed, "Oh, shit..." before she flinched. His shoulder clipped hers. Her phone flew, and she ricocheted off the cabinets before sprawling to the floor. He grabbed her phone where it had clattered onto the countertop and shut down the program, undoing everything she had set in motion.

She heard the diesel motor go silent, and she groaned, sprawled out on the floor. Blinking, she tried to get the wood-timbered ceiling to right itself. "Fuck...I think you broke me."

He cursed before tossing her phone back onto the counter. "What you were about to just pull would have killed us both. A knife out of your cutlery drawer could have sliced you up on its way across the room."

"You assume"—she groaned—"that I have silverware."

He looked down at her. "You don't live here?"

"Yeah, I do, but it doesn't mean I have to have silverware." Vega's face pinched in pain as she pushed herself away from him. She was sure she popped a rib.

He squatted. "Did I really hurt you?" She could see the strain of the material at his knees and had the odd thought that every time they met, his suit got at least a little fucked up. He added, sounding surprised, "You seem invincible."

She smiled wanly. "Well, I think you found the limits of my physical endurance."

He cursed. "Sorry. If you're hurt, let me get an ambulance."

He pulled his phone out, and Vega reached over, wincing against the pull of her rib, and stilled his hand. "Don't. You know I can't go to a hospital. If I go to the hospital, I get picked up for all those outstanding warrants."

"Still, if I hurt you, I should help, or can I take you somewhere? Can you stand?"

"Again, no. And yes, I can stand. If this is some plot to get me incarcerated, you should know that I'll use all that time inside to break you. So, you'd also better plan on being my bail bondsman,"

His eyes' mischievous joy returned. "That's more like the response I was expecting," Then he sobered. "I'm sorry..."

"I'm fine. Really, big guy. Just be a doll and hand me my phone."

"No. You're scary. Like I said, your list of warrants is downright frightening. And I don't trust you with that magnet."

"Yeah, well, welcome to the dark side. Those warrants are thanks to bogus dillwads who didn't like being flexed on after they pulled shit on women that required me to teach them a lesson. I try not to do that anymore. In real life." Vega tried to get up and found herself back on her back, panting.

Hoyt laid a heavy hand gently on her stomach. "Please don't move." He added, "Stay still. I'll call in a personal favor. I know a doctor who owes me one."

"Nope, no favors needed here." Sharply inhaling through her gritted teeth, Vega rolled, and his warm, wide hand slid off her, and made it to sitting. "I think I'm just rattled. Some dude is in my apartment, first thing in the morning—"

"It's well after noon."

"And he's trying to scare me then tackles me." She leaned back against the cabinets and gave him a wan grin. "I think you knocked a couple marbles right out of my head. I'm dumber now. Thanks a lot."

"Ms. Flux..."

She barely heard him. She needed him out of her apartment and to scrub it clean before going after his phone. Then move to another shitty location. Possibly in a nonextradition country. Cindy and Peace would understand. Her sister, maybe not.

"No, look," and she staggered to standing; the pain was definitely coming from a rib. "Get out. You don't get to play doctor while threatening me with whatever you're here to threaten me with."

He looked baffled. "I want to hire you, Ms. Flux." A lock of his hair, dark brown, the color of haunted forests in her childhood picture books, had fallen loose, and he pushed it back into place as he stood. Even his haircut was fast, she noticed. Closely cut on the sides, visible razor lines, a creative touch, like racing stripes on a racecar, with a long top that had been styled as a sweep-back.

She made her way to the corner where her chest freezer was and popped it open, pushed aside film, and pulled out an ice pack she used on her head on hot summer days. Putting it to her back, she said, "What now?"

"I want to hire you. I've not seen anyone with the kind of firepower you have. I thought a hacker group was trying to make an example out of me, but it turns out it was just one person. And she lives in my city? Yeah, I'm going to make sure we're friends. Surprise, I'm not a moron." It sounded like a phrase he had used more than once.

Vega felt the truce he offered. "Burly dude breaking stereotypes. I like it, but the shit I do, we can't be friends. I don't trust billionaires. When my work gets on you, and it will, you'll bury things. Meaning, me. So how about we say pass?"

"Ms. Flux, we can help each other here—"

She held up a hand. "I should say, it's a pass unless you just want to break some furniture together, you know, once my back is better. I've never been called Ms. Flux. I like it. We can start there then work our way to—"

"I have a fiancée," he said, and that line too sounded like a reflex. He continued without pause, "No one has seen the software you tore through last night. And it was tight, or at least I assumed it was until you blew through it."

"What are you saying? You want me to break your shit?"

Both of them feeling the ease seep into the space between them, Hoyt casually leaned against her counter, tucking his hands under his arms, enjoying the negotiation. "Yes."

Vega felt her insides squirm pleasantly. This egotistical maniac was humble enough to show up at her place and ask for *her* help? But once the joy he had for her left, and it quickly did in Vega's experience—people liked her energy until they didn't—the Titan would grow tired of "dealing with" her and her expectations and nuke their deal.

"Like I said, the world I live in is shadows and cash. Your income bracket alone means you're dodging taxes without fear of penalty and making more in a year than the GDP of a third of the world's countries, so let's not pretend we're on level footing."

"I'd say let's make an iron-clad contract to put you at ease, but you've already said you don't live in the real world. What can I do to have you believe that I'm serious?"

"You gotta walk away."

He nodded, a solemn move that made Vega want to apologize, but caught herself before that feeling settled in. What was it with this man? It was as if he was cut from a cloth that said there was more in this life than money, and really believed it. It made her want to be touched by him, softly and tenderly. But she was also broken, so she fantasized about his power being put against her. Rough could be just as fun.

"Fine." He underscored his nod with that word, not looking fine with it at all.

"One question before you go. What'd you take, and how'd you find me? Damn, that was two."

"I took nothing, and how do you think I found you?"

Vega scrunched her face in disgust then opened her snack cabinet and took out a warm diet soda, and after a crack and a hiss, she took a long drag off it, wishing it had whiskey in it. "You fucked Cindy, didn't you?"

That earned her a dry look.

"No?"

"Peace has a very talkative intern working at her office."

Fuck. Vega was her own kind of Titan's Wall that surrounded Scout and protected her from the realities of their childhood. Which was why Scout told a tall NFL god everything he wanted to know about her big sis, whom she loves like a real mommy.

She lifted her brow as if that was news that her baby sister worked there, but probably overplayed her hand. "Peace has loads of kids doing shit for free there, and yet she freaks out at me when I don't pay for stuff." She shrugged as if her heart wasn't hammering. "Go figure."

"Scout looks up to you, but it's obvious she has no idea who you are, or what you do."

She took a loud slurp of her soda. "Huh, interesting. What is it that I do?"

"You are the dark knight of women's causes online. When all hope is lost, people come find you. You give them hope again in the form of law-breaking chaos."

She tore open a bag of cheese puffs and tossed one into her mouth. It felt really good to have him say that. It sucked he wasn't there to have sex; that would be a new kink for her. Have this towering man say nice things to her while she rode high on his thick erection… That must be what Peace kept telling her love felt like.

"All men deserve it."

He smiled at her, recognizing the trap she was luring him into. He pushed off the counter and looked down as he rebuttoned his impeccable sport coat. "Work for me."

"No. Well, maybe, if you say more things about me that sound nice." She gave him a grin along with the challenge. Only he looked as if he might not accept her challenge, as if he knew it was a slippery slope with her and he was holding back.

"At the club. You were able to make quick work of my security layers. I've had a long time to think about it." He massaged his face as if he'd been up all night. The dark stubble of his five o'clock shadow bristled in the quiet. "That means you have theoretical tech."

Vega struggled to keep her face impassive. She needed him to leave, not broach another subject she wanted, *really wanted*, to talk with him about. The chair, two steps behind him, had her thinking they should sit and chat about her pet project that miraculously worked the night at the club. As in, push him into the chair and straddle his lap—that kind of chat. Her fantasy list was taking on a singular focus. Talk, straddle, and watch this Titan come loose. No sexual partner had ever seen this part of her world. Much less talked about security in the technologically advanced space of breaking 512 KB encryption.

She swallowed down the urge. "Goodbye, mountain man. And erase your search history of me when you get home. Or give me your phone, and I'll do it for you."

He gave her last line a dry look. "Ms. Flux. You're better than good, and I need you. Work for me."

Knees still watery from being bodychecked by him, or it was the way his resonant voice said, *I need you*. She walked him to the door. "I'd love to, busy schedule, etc. Bye now."

Turning back at the open door, he said, "The offer will be permanently standing for you, Vega Flux. Or do you prefer, flux_capacitor?"

"Sounds like a *Back to the Future* reference—how old are you? Forget I asked. Goodbye, beautiful human, lose my number, erase your search history, bye *now*." Vega slammed the door after him then pulled her phone and watched through the security camera as he reluctantly left her door and worked his way down the stairs and out the warehouse door. She watched his expensive SUV exit her parking lot before she ran a diagnostic on all her equipment.

Her heart pounding and palms beginning to sweat, she let herself think. He'd been to see Scout. And knew her shadow world names. With his beauty no longer in front of her, distracting her, she let that realization bottom out her guts. The founder of the security agency that created Titan's Wall knew her in both worlds. And knew the one person who meant more to her than anything.

She screamed, "Fuck!" until she was hoarse and, pulling out boxes, started the move.

HIT PLAY_

Sitting at her computer, half-filled boxes surrounding her, Vega rotated the USB key between her fingers. Her mind ran a similar rat's wheel, going around and around. In her hand was a tiny surprise. The kind of tiny surprise that had powerful ripple effects. Like a match before it's lit. And she mused that maybe, just maybe, she didn't have to move.

Vega didn't get to be where she was in the underworld by having an ego the size of the Milky Way. She learned to be quiet, unassuming, and to write smart, camouflaged code that didn't cause a fuss, until she needed it to. Still, even she was surprised by the data capture.

At that moment, one of her original pieces of tech, a little program called Bunny, had hatched and was being a good little dude. He was collecting colorful nuggets of information in a very powerful man's cell. She'd made that Sunday her own personal Easter.

She hadn't been sure that she'd gotten that administrative access in that final moment of wrestling with Hoyt at the club. Plus, her quantum computer, which was based on tech she had but also on tech she...borrowed, and most of the time, the borrowed servers weren't fully functioning. But she'd gambled, and after a hundred attempts to test the university-based system, that night, she'd been right, the deck was stacked in her favor, and it had worked.

Even with the systems aligned, she was sure Bunny had been discovered and nuked. But he hadn't. Quietly, Bunny was doing his job, and changing the personal game she had with herself in the process. He sent nothing unless the Titan's phone itself did. Little packets of data were being gathered and sent off his device with each text message, email, and phone call. Like lint off a shirt. Now, she twirled the data between her finger and thumb like a fidget spinner. What, oh, what to do with the sceptor of a powerful man?

Her outdoor sensors alerted Vega to visitors. Checking the cameras, she saw that her gazelles were back.

In under five minutes Cindy and Peace were in her studio and at the snack pantry. The music was on high. They reeked of rum and men's cologne.

Cindy eventually turned down the music, and Vega told them the whole story. Resting a hip on the partially clear workbench, she popped a Cheeto into her mouth. "Freaky he got by your systems. Double freaky the hot tech god himself stops by, you freak out and almost kill you both, and he just walks away?"

Peace was busy texting.

"Peace, you can't be texting your boy any of this."

"Yeah, but he has a friend who's a sports chiropractor, and he can help pop your back into place or at least tell you if there's serious damage. With all the work you do at your computer, your back can't be effed."

"Yeah, sure, I'm fine, Peace—" Vega's phone system alerted her that one of her numbers had an incoming call. She routed it to the cell on her desk. It rang, and her little sister's face was smiling. "Hey there, sweet thing."

"Hey, sis..."

Vega heard it in her voice. "What's up, sweets?"

"Put me on video. I miss your face."

"You called to tell me you missed my face? I just saw you on campus yesterday, bug." *After losing Hoyt in the quad,* she thought.

"Yeah, I wanna see your face, so when I tell you I met a guy today, I see how you react."

"Ugh, Scout, don't meet guys. Please try and find a nice woman to settle down with."

Scout giggled and responded as she always did. "I'm letting love find me in whatever form they take."

"Yeah, yeah, OK," but Vega knew what man came to see her, and probably right at the butt crack of dawn at 8:00 a.m. "And for the record, I already heard about you talking to a dude this morning."

"You did? Jeez, he works fast. So, he asked you?"

"We talked about a lot of stuff, Scout. I'm more interested in what that interaction between you two was like. He just popped by to say hi and...?"

Vega looked to her girls, and Peace looked guilty. Vega would talk to her later about how her sister came to be a topic with either her boy toy dude, Zane, or his best bud, Hoyt. She knew part of it was that they'd been insulated for so long that it was wearing them all down.

A year had passed since she was relocated by Cindy from her last city, Reno, back to Portland. It was to be a new start for all of them. After decades of living under the radar, they were all tired. Peace had jumped from city to city with Vega, and their insulated bubble meant they did everything together. It was time for more, and Vega knew half of it was squarely in her court. Peace, emotionally, couldn't keep moving. And Cindy couldn't keep Vega off her superiors' radar if she didn't keep her head down. In the last year, they had taken a gamble on Vega. Hoping they could live in their hometown, stretch out and settle down. Just breathe, make friends, and at least for Peace and Cindy, make connections that went beyond one night. The normalcy that Peace craved was understandable and infectious. But it also warranted a reminder that Vega wasn't in a place to share personal information with a square-jawed stranger from a club.

Scout prattled on, not knowing her security had been threatened. "No, he was here at work for some other reason and recognized my last name."

Vega rolled her eyes; sure, he recognized her last name. His lying game was average.

"He said he has a job for you but that he couldn't find you. I tried texting you, but your phone is all glitchy again. Look, remember what I said, you have to update that job references profile I set up for you on the LinkPeeps site. So people like him can find you. I tried to find it to pass it along, and the page was gone. I think if you're not active, they take it down...so stay active on it, Vega, sheesh."

"Uh-huh, sure, those pages don't really work for me, though, sweets." Vega rolled up to her computer, and waking her command center, she went to work taking down the page that Scout had started again.

"Yeah, but, Vee, it might help you get bigger clients. Like this guy. He seems to really want to hire you. I think he sees what I do."

"He sees me like a big sis?" she said with a Cheeto crunch and licked her fingers to avoid spreading the nuclear-orange dust onto her keyboard.

"No, you know what I mean!" Scout said with a laugh. Her big sis was just so funny. Vega wished she could live the web designer life that Scout thought she did.

"I just think, he seems nice and has a company to get you a stable job. You can get a real place."

"Scout, it's my job to look after you, not you look after me." She sighed and fed her a lie that would get Scout to drop it. "Listen, he's an ex, and he wanted my address to come say hi."

"Oh...really?" It sounded like Scout knew this was bull. She was getting more argumentative the deeper into her pre-law degree she got. "He isn't really an ex, is he?"

Vega mumbled, "Could be."

"Look, I'm sorry, he's just so..."

So fucking hot it's hard to refuse anything he asks. Even if it's to sit in his temperature-controlled offices and work for him, just to catch a glimpse of his towering physique every day.

"...convincing, and kind. He also knew, like, half the office."

Vega finished the page takedown and walked away from the

watchful eyes of Cindy and Peace to the grimy windows looking out over the back where the magnet still hung in the air. "He did?"

"Yeah, apparently, we did some work with Hoyt Securities in the past. He's a beloved ex-client." So, she knew who he was.

"Why's he an ex-client?" God, she couldn't stop asking questions.

"His business needs changed, and he needed in-house counsel."

Vega nodded as if her sister could see her. "Right, makes sense."

"Call him, Vee. More than one coworker overheard his request, and they gave me the impression that he doesn't ask for things, ever."

"Ever?"

"Prides himself on being self-sufficient, apparently, so him asking about you and having me reach out to you made some jaws drop. You're a big deal to him. And now at the office."

Vega swallowed down the panic at all the attention but then let the hum of pleasure at him looking for her vibrate at the back of her neck as if his voice was there now, making a low rumble.

"Oh, huh."

"Anyways...I have to talk to you about the university—" Scout segued hard.

At the mention of school, Vega panicked. "Shit, did I miss a payment?" She turned back toward her command center. "I thought they were taking payments by the semester; did they change it up? I can pay it tomorrow."

"Oh, no. I just...there's another course that I'd like to add to this semester that involves an overseas internship...?"

"I'm ready—how much is it?" Vega put on a cheery voice.

"It's like... Oh man, I shouldn't ask; you live so broke. It's selfishly the other reason I mentioned this job offer. Maybe with it, you can help me get some loans? I really want to go. Sorry, is that too much?"

"It's no trouble. I'll take a few extra jobs; some of these websites I build can pay good money, or I'll do a bunch of little ones. It's fine, Scout. Seriously, you're my little sis, and what you do, I live vicariously through, remember? That's why I moved back," she said, feeding her the line, which was at least partially true. She didn't need any more of a life than she already had, but she was glad to be near Scout again. "So, talk to me about it."

When Vega finally hung up, the pain in her back was worse. She went to the washroom in the back corner, where she also developed film, and from the cinder-block shelf there, she took a couple of pain pills. Back in the kitchen, she washed them down with a gulp of Jack Daniels.

Hissing in the after-burn, Vega met Cindy's eyes. "That bad, huh? Do you have to bury a body?" her friend asked.

"Worse."

Peace had taken up residence on Vega's bed, massaging her feet, her heels finally off. She scrunched her face. "Is she all right?"

"She needs 'just a couple grand'..."

"Oh, that's not bad. I saw your stack of cash under the bed."

"Times ten, it turns out."

The gazelles grimaced. "How are you going to make that kind of cash by...when?"

"This week."

"She can't get a loan that fast," Cindy said.

"I know, not to mention, how the fuck do I get her a passport without raising suspicions?"

Peace leaped off the bed and joined them in the kitchen looking hopeful. "Looks like you'll have to take Hoyt up on his offer of employment. That way you'll have a legit source of income, she won't need a loan, and maybe she won't ask where you've been hiding her passport all this time."

"Nope." Vega was still chewing on the side of her nail. Not only did she love her freedom, but attempting to hump the founder in his office wasn't acceptable, she was sure. But she had another idea. Last night at the club and Bunny's hard work had all made her think that Titan's Wall was a mountain she *could* scale. "There's a pot of gold for the person who can crack Titan's Wall. It grows each year. Right now, it's at one point five."

Air squeezed out of Peace, making her voice pitch up an octave. "You saw his skill finding you after the club. Going after Hoyt

Security's Titan's Wall will make trouble for us, Vega. Just take the straight-and-narrow path—we can't hide from a man like him. Vee, please. Just accept his job offer; he's a good guy. And we have rules about good guys."

"You're right, Peace."

Cindy's head whipped to Vega. "What'd you just say?"

Peace was giddy. "You'll do it?"

Cindy interrupted. "You *just* said that you were going to take an online bet to break his wall."

Vega held up a finger. "No, very clear, no, this is not a bet. I'm done with that. Mostly."

"This feels like a precursor to one of your betting spirals, Vee." Cindy put her cop gaze to Peace. "Catnip, and now look at her."

"Hoyt isn't catnip, Cindy. I still stand by my decision: the club was a good idea, and it'll be fine."

Vega felt as if the gazelles were having a conversation above her pay grade.

"Look, it's not a bet. That pot of gold? It's his, Hoyt's."

When they both stared blankly, she elaborated. "He has a standing challenge: break Titan's Wall. He just keeps increasing the pot until someone does. And the jury is out on the club. Pretty sure I shouldn't have gone. But that's on me. I'll get us out of this."

Cindy looked incredulous. "Wait. It's his money? Cut the shit. No way, who does that?"

"Serious tech security companies, hon. And also, a very confident man. And to answer your next question, no one has done it. It, being a full penetrating breach through the firewall and into the internal systems. People have attempted it, and failed. It was lightly breached five years ago—a bunch of doctoral students at Carnegie Mellon breached the firewall's initial defense, but that's all. They didn't get in and, say, roam around and glean user data." Another thought flicked into Vega's mind: Hoyt had still awarded them the money. *Close enough; take this and use it to learn more.* Who does *that*? Before she could get too sappy feeling, Vega said, "So, yeah, Titan's Wall stands impenetrable."

Cindy shook her head. "And if you can't breach it?"

Vega shrugged and pulled a packet of Red Vines down and put one in her mouth. It flopped as she talked. "I have a shot." She didn't want to tell the girls that the night at the club she'd torpedoed through his API key with the very lucky help of Juggernaut, a quantum computer. So lucky, in fact, that had it not worked, there was no way Titan's Wall would be scalable for a haxor like her. The information she gleaned that night was the equivalent of snatching a golden key out of the air while riding a broom. A one-time ride on a persnickety, prone-to-failure system that even at her level of gambling acumen couldn't justify using again outside of the scientific boundaries it was created in and for.

"By the time Scout needs the money?"

Vega smiled. "You don't like those odds?"

"No," they answered.

"Fine, I have some *key* information. It's the only reason I think I can even attempt this."

"OK," Cindy said analyzing her as if she were in an interrogation room, "can you just do the little bit that the contest thing requires? Will you be able to *just* breach?"

Peace echoed, "Yeah, and not, say, breach and fuck up? Because if it's the latter, I...I don't know if I can move again."

Vega's gut churned. She knew Peace was ready for a calmer life, but it was hard to hear it said aloud. "I know, hon. I promised I wouldn't fuck this up. I know what it means to be back here. I won't fuck him up either. I doubt I get much past the initial defense, like the Carnagie Mellon kids, before Titan's Wall goes on defense and I have to shut things down."

If Carnagie kids got awarded, would he take pity on Vega getting somewhere, even partway, for her sister's education? The memory of his face, hard gemstone eyes when she'd gotten to the last reboot screen at the club, came to her. He'd been fucking impressed. More than that, he'd wanted to play with her. "I don't think so," he'd protested. While that whisper had sounded in the moment warm and sensual, diving straight into her brain and unlocking her body to him as she'd felt him slyly brush her buttocks, and the memory made her shiver and want to take her clothes off, there had been something more in his gaze, a sadness that the game was now over. She recognized that look now that she'd seen it again, today, in her apartment, when she told him that he had to walk away. He'd wanted more.

Vega thought that maybe he missed the competitive adrenaline rush of game day. That this new game she was planning would be another kind of game day, and she had a feeling he would want to be in for all four quarters.

"Just breach-lite. And no fuckup," she reiterated. "Even though that's the best kind of fun."

COME TO ME_

HOYT WAS ON THE PHONE LOOKING OUT THE WINDOW AT THE GRAY skyline; the mountain in the near distance was snow-capped, a puff-ball on the hood shape. The memory of Vega sparked on his every other synapse, making him go quietly insane. She was a lit fuse that he had to walk away from, but he couldn't entirely. He'd been catching up on her through the handle she used, flux_capacitor. The general assumption, from the forums to the message boards that he'd dug deep to find, was that she was a seriously badass *dude*. They had no idea the wrecking ball behind that handle was a woman, and he understood part of why she kept it that way. Equality in tech was a far cry from being equal. He knew by just looking at his engineering room. Then there was the Wild West of the online gaming world where he'd seen firsthand how his sister was treated in teams versus how he was. Though any human with a working brain cell who spent any time researching the digital fingerprint of flux_capacitor would, as he did now, recognize the Delorian GIF and references tagged to each of the online incidences that went above and beyond for the benefit of individual women and sometimes others who were oppressed either by society or circumstances.

He mused, her list of warrants would be a whole lot smaller, too, if they weren't grievances from men who thought they could call her crazy to make her go away. As in, Hoyt was sure the guy who reported that she put his hand in a panini press first put that hand of his on her or someone she knew when they didn't want him to. But that was her in real life, when she had raven hair and flashing onyx eyes. Online message boards, forums, and social media feeds tipped their hat at flux_capacitor and her tire-smoking Delorian GIF for taking down leaked personal information, reworking entire stock portfolios, and wreaking general havoc on those whom she deemed deserving of it.

He wanted to hire her still. Now more than ever. Asking him to give her space was going to make him obsessive. He already thought about her constantly, wanting to one-up her hacker skills, to see her tech, and...to repeat the wrestling in the booth at Festivál. Only this time he'd savor it. The moment she broke out quantum tech on him, he wanted to watch it in slow motion, catch a piece of how she did it.

Then there was that other thing he wanted. The thing he tried not to think about.

But maybe he should?

Technically he had a fiancée, but it wasn't that. There were things in life that were stable, and there were things that were too hot to touch. Vega Flux? She was molten lava. The kind that Kilauea blew into the skies under Pele's orders. Pursuing anything further than her quantum tech was like playing in a lava flow and hoping not to get burned.

But he liked a good match as much as the next person, and Vega was a first-class hacker who was equal, or better, than him. Playing with her would improve his skill. She woke something deep inside that made him want to take his coat off, loosen his tie, and uncuff his shirtsleeves. In a purely gamesmanship way. *That is all,* he argued with himself.

She woke his competitive spirit, *that's all.*

Suddenly the dial tone was loud in his ear. He blinked the mountain back into focus. He wasn't sure how long he'd been holding the phone to his ear after his investigator hung up. She was doing her own searches into Vega Flux.

He turned, putting the receiver back into the cradle on his expansive teak desk. It, like the rest of the office, and the whole executive floor, was all wood and glass with a view to the river and mountains beyond. The room also held a meeting table and plush chairs clustered for informal gatherings. Floating shelving were stacked with books and football memorabilia his cousin, an interior designer, said made him look more...something. He couldn't remember. His office in the engineering department didn't have any of this There, he was productive; here held his public persona.

Escalating voices reached him through his open office door. From where he stood, he had a partial view down the hall to the executive reception area where an argument was happening.

Moving around his desk to the doorway, he felt his insides dip with excitement. Hector was keeping a beautiful black-haired menace from moving down the hall.

His mind was suddenly alert. It was game day. He mentally took his coat off, loosened his tie, and undid his cuffs. She really had wanted some space. But knowing Vega, as he was beginning to strangely feel he did, this wouldn't be any normal visit.

Hoyt leaned against the doorframe watching the show. She was fire and smoke with lightning in her eyes.

THE YOUNG ASSISTANT WAS STANDING IN VEGA'S WAY. HER LUCK would have it that at the moment she stepped off the elevator, he was up blocking the hallway on an errand. He had turned to her immediately, surprised that the elevator held her and not someone, Vega was assuming, with ten-thousand-dollar shoes and a smile to match. She definitely wasn't on the appointment books for that afternoon.

"Who are you?" His tone was clear. He meant, who was someone like her to the well-manicured interiors of the Hoyt Securities executive floor.

Vega twirled her homemade key card on her finger. "Buy me dinner, and I'll tell you."

His brown eyes behind designer dark-rimmed glasses took her in quickly. "How'd you get up here?"

Vega held up her card for inspection. "All-access pass, my friend. Now, if you'll please excuse moi..." She sidestepped him only to have him block her. Vega liked his tenacity, but she was on a mission. "Beep-beep. I have a football god to destroy."

His glossy, pert mouth fell open. "Oh hell no. Get your snatched ass back into the elevator—"

Vega paused at that, instantly falling in love with Hoyt's door demon. "Ohh, hello. Thanks—I do squats." She demonstrated, winking as she popped back up.

He wasn't impressed. "Git. Shoo." He pointed to the open elevator behind her.

Vega cocked her hip and tilted her head at him.

"Hector, is it?" She knew door demons were the ones who caused the most interference, so of course she'd looked into the Titan's. Low-paid but the closest to the royal jewels, they'd bite off their own hand to keep that proximity to power. "You know, that hot young thing your ex is clubbing with isn't actually a college freshman..."

Hector's pout transformed into a gasp. "How do you know that?" Then caught himself: "I don't care; go away."

"I know because I'm not your average alley cat, H. Can I call you H?"

"No."

"Yeah, well"—her voice went secretive and low—"I'm the kind of alley cat who can delete pretty boy's number out of your ex's phone. You know, fuck with him. Just a little. Or I can transfer his entire savings into yours. Up to you. Use me." She put her black nails to her chest and smiled conspiratorially.

"No! All to go assault Mr. Ho'o? No way, what do you take me for?"

Vega lived with Hector in a relationship the size of a microsecond. If she kept the conversation about things he wanted to know about, he'd keep listening. And if he was listening, he wasn't calling security.

"Whoa, I meant destroy in a different way than you're thinking. More like...no, yeah, OK, maybe you have a point there," Vega said. She flipped through her mental file on him. "How about..." she said, pulling out her phone and pulling up the screen she'd been obsessing about all summer. Something made her think he'd love it too. She showed him. "An unopened, discontinued tube of MAC Lipglass in Fuck Me Like a Pony red."

Hector winced. For a second, she worried she'd guessed wrong. Instead, he said, "It doesn't exist. That's a unicorn."

"And I have the keys to the stable. Lemme be your courier and gift you this."

He swallowed and looked at the naughty red tube as he whispered, "What do you really want with him?"

Vega smiled and gave him truth. "To fuck him gently until he screams my name for mercy."

Hector jumped to the wrong conclusion, as she'd intended. "Well, why didn't you say so? You don't have to do this if you have *that* kind of business with Mr. Ho'o." He glanced over his shoulder, and Vega saw him then, leaning like a massive Douglas fir against his doorframe at the end of the hall. Hands firmly tucked under his arms and a sly expression as if he had been watching from the moment she got off the elevator.

His smile seemed to confirm the narrative that Hector had jumped to, and Hector said with some shame at realizing his perfect boss might not be so perfect, "No, please, no. Just go."

Vega pushed the order through anyway. "You're a good human, Hector. Where on earth did he find you?"

Hector answered automatically, his features looking vacant and overwhelmed, "He's my mom's cousin."

Vega's brows arched. "Interesting..." She moved past him, giving him an air kiss. "Stay sweet, my friend. Your order arrives in an hour. Don't ever call me a hustler—a deal is a deal." And her boots carried her down the hall to the towering giant at the end of it.

"Were you mean to Hector?" Hoyt said once she was in earshot of his low rumble.

Vega feigned disgust.

He was even more glorious up close in his deep Mediterranean blue collared shirt. His gaze was as dark but a tightness at his mouth's corners told her he was hopped up on just as much adrenaline to see her as she was him. And he was struggling to hold it back.

"How dare you. He just might be the sweetest thing on planet earth. I gave him a treat for being so sweet. Lemme know if he needs anything more from me—I want him to love me."

This made Hoyt grin, straight, glorious, bone-white teeth making Vega think of frothing surf and ocean spray. "You're a menace, Ms. Flux."

"Only smart men see that."

He closed his eyes as if grateful. "Thank you for stroking my ego."

His voice purred over the word *stroking*, and Vega felt something move through her knees again, making her right give out just a little, like a trick switch lived there now and it was attached to the broad-shouldered man in front of her.

"Are you going to invite me in, or do I have to do all the things I promised Hector I was here to do to you out here in the hallway?"

"And what exactly did you tell Hector you were here to do?"

"I told him I was here to fuck you gently until you screamed my name for mercy."

His eyes closed again; then a low laugh started deep in his chest before bursting out.

Vega liked it. All of it. The bottomless pit that cratered out in her abdomen when she was within arm's reach of him and when he slithered into her mind. She hadn't thought of contacting Jax since meeting Hoyt. But that was the devil talking: wanting things that were off limits. She didn't fuck around on nice guys or with nice guys. Jax was an asshole, so he didn't matter. But Hoyt was engaged, and she was sure this game they had going was just that. A game. Anytime she thought it was more, that was probably just her one last molecule of hope screaming from the black core of her soul.

He put two fingers in his mouth and whistled down the hall like a rancher in a pasture. Vega winced at the piercing sound. Heads popped out of offices, and Hector, fumbling with his headset, peered around the corner. Hoyt pointed one finger down at the top of Vega's head, and she looked up at it as he hollered, "She's not a prostitute, and I'm not fucking her."

Hector nodded, his eyes wide at what Vega assumed was unprecedented behavior from the company's founder.

With a sweep of his arm into his office, Hoyt said, "E komo mai."

"Thanks. I'm assuming that was 'welcome in' and not 'take your pants off.'"

He shut the door behind him with a smile. "It was."

SWEETEN THE POT_

"Wow." Vega took in his office like a tourist in Greece; the gorgeously appointed room with a view that no one else in the city had made her feel like they were on sacred ground at the top of Mt. Olympus. Trophies took up one wall, and on another, an impressive display of books. Some she was sure a designer put there to make photo ops look classy. Though Hoyt would look classy anywhere.

"This is some office." She flopped into a large leather chair with the best angle on the view, letting her legs dangle off the side.

She watched him as he relocked a narrow drawer in his desk, a file in one hand, then went over to the meeting table and let it fall with a slap. She really wanted to read what was in that file. Why did it have to be locked up? Was it for his eyes only, and now for hers too? Was it a BDSM contract? If so, yes, please.

He sat on the edge of the table and slipped his hands into his pant pockets as if he were simply an ordinary man waiting for an ordinary woman to walk over to him.

The silence expanded between them.

"What's that?" she said, giving in.

"Come look."

"No." She slouched deeper into his comfortable guest chair.

Maybe he'd pick her up, she thought for the second time since meeting him.

"What'd you come here for, then?"

"Is that an employment application?"

"Technically, no."

She swore and swung her boots to the floor and made her way to the table. Standing next to him, she found herself looking into the sparks of stars within the brown and amber of his eyes and tried not to lean into his warmth. Or kiss his wide mouth or the soft freckles that were invisible on his cheeks unless a person was as close as she was.

"What is this?" she managed to say.

His glance up from her mouth to her eyes felt like it took a decade. "Scared?" he asked, his voice low, matching hers.

"Fucking frightened. Now that you asked. Lawsuit?"

His expression was gleeful.

She let her shoulder lean against his. He *was* warm, and built strong. He didn't flinch away but rather stayed put, like a solid wall. Making her feel as if he welcomed her touch.

"Open it."

She shivered. "No."

He pressed his shoulder back against hers, giving her a gentle nudge, urging her on. "Do it."

"Fuck," she said and flipped it open.

There in the black file folder were five pages of legalese. She read through them swiftly to get the gist. A contract that Hoyt Securities would employ an anonymous contractor to accomplish tasks on an as-needed basis; they would work as long as all terms were agreeable, and said contractor could leave the agreement at any time. The only catch was that the nondisclosure and noncompete and confidentiality terms were tighter than those for an NSA asset.

"Name my price?"

"Yes."

"And I can work for no one else but you for"—she checked the paperwork—"forever. This is employment in golden handcuffs. Is that legal?"

"I want you," he said, looking down with a frown as if hearing what he'd said out loud, and while it was true, it was not what he meant. He cleared his throat and tried again. "I want you to work for me. No one else. Pick another profession when you're done with me."

"You mean, done with Hoyt Securities?"

He studied her face. "One and the same."

She liked the warmth of his body, the whisper of his voice over her shoulder as he talked to her about getting into a binding contract and him pretending it wasn't some kind of kinky foreplay. She didn't agree that Hoyt Securities the firm was one and the same with Hoyt the human. It felt like the business was a cover for what he really wanted, and that contract was clear as day. It said, *Mine.* All she had to do was sign on the dotted line, and she'd be his. And vice versa, because the paperwork made it clear that Hoyt was the only point of contact. She'd never been so turned on in such a sexually benign situation. If she signed it, she could tick each of her fantasies about him off her list by week's end.

She had to bring in some ice water. "This seems pointedly personal. What does your fiancée think of this contract?"

"Londyn?"

"Is that her name?" He was close enough that she could lean just so across his shoulder and touch her lips to his. Would he resist if she tried to push him into the conference room chair at his knee?

He smiled in a way that said he knew she was a fibber; she knew who Londyn was. "She doesn't care about the business side of my life."

Vega sat on the table next to him, eliminating the temptation to taste his mouth. They both looked out into the cool, open room. "I meant contracts as personally binding to you as this one is, but why doesn't she care to hear about your business deals, or you don't think she has the head for it?"

From over his shoulder at her: "Are you getting pissy?"

"Trying to."

"You think I don't value women?"

Vega believed he did. She was getting pissy because there was something about his fiancée that rankled her. It had taken her a long, burning-hot shower that morning to realize it, during which she had been fantasizing that Hoyt was in that cramped cast-iron tub with her. His hands had been on her hips, and after fantasy-he made her scream his name, something moved into her chest that was laced with venom. As she toweled off, she realized what it was: she was jealous. This unique god of a man belonged to someone else, and right then she wanted what Londyn had. Not that dumbass name, but everything else. She wanted to slip into bed with him at night, she wanted to watch him eat his breakfast, she wanted to crawl into his world and very carefully see if she could set him on fire.

"Is she in tech?"

"You tell me."

Vega had done a superficial dive on Londyn and knew she was one of two things to Hoyt, and now Vega tried the one she was the most hopeful for.

"She's a cover. You wear her so that no one troubles you for a relationship because most likely they just want a relationship with your money and power. Does she even like you, or is she just using you in return?"

"Let's get off Londyn."

"You first."

"You going to sign the contract, or do I have to wait some more?" Vega heard something in his voice, the tone and tilt of it, that said he had an accent he was keeping hidden.

"Now who's pissy?" she said.

"Me." Vega liked the first sign of heat in his eyes.

She should course correct, get things back onto what she was really there for, but that was what chaos was good for: sousing out trouble before it had the potential to ruin something good.

"Yup, you don't like talking about Londyn." She hoped that was because she was a cover. And not, say, the second in a deeply personal relationship that he shared with no one else.

"To you? No, I don't. What we have is business—"

"Nope, no business nothing. We have no relationship, except that of one special night at the club, in which we both left wanting more." She had the itch to pretend she was his fiancée and spread her palms over his pectorals to see if she could feel the heat of him through his crisp cotton shirt. Instead, having to deny herself, she over-corrected with a touch too much temper. "I didn't come here to sign these forms and be your pet. I came here for more. To be polite in telling you that I'm going to take a crack at Titan's Wall. Get your cash ready. No checks or IOUs."

He scrubbed his face and went to the bank of windows and slid his hands safely into his pockets.

Vega huffed out a laugh and leaned back against the high-shine table, crossing her ankles before giving her feet a swing. "*There* you are. The real, distant you. Stop being nice to me, Hoyt. You love to wear a scowl, and I love to watch you wear it."

"You're familiar with the rules? No breaking the rules, Ms. Flux, or you won't get paid." The hint of his hidden accent was fading.

She liked that he didn't talk her out of it or tell her she couldn't. He looked like a man who was preparing in his mind for the onslaught that was coming.

"Everyone knows the rules. I'll be gentle, just a quick in and out."

He looked darkly over his shoulder. "If you take data, I'll come for you."

Her insides quivered with something that felt like a thrill wrapped in joy. She hadn't planned on taking, but now, she wasn't sure.

"Like a billionaire would."

"Like I would. You act like the world is more powerful than you, but you also have power Vega," he said, losing the Ms.; they were on the playing field now. "And your threats are legitimate. I see the woman who views the world as her playground. There's no wall, firewall, or 'no' that you can't surpass. I've been lucky to have gone unnoticed by you until now. I'm not asking you to be gentle—I'm just saying, even if you don't see it yourself, I see the ingenuity that you can unleash on our systems. I believe we're ready; thanks for the heads-up. That was...kind of you."

Vega was used to fighting, going toe to toe, but this, his combat-with-praise, she didn't know what to do with. She also didn't like the way his jaw worked, as if she was about to hurt him, as if he couldn't trust her. That was her brand, but she wasn't sure, for the first time, that she liked it.

She cleared her throat and tried to wear a business cloak too. "I'll help you expose where the wall is weakest. *If* I'm able to get through."

He nodded. "I appreciate it. I said we're ready for you, but that quantum shit you have, I don't think we're ready for that. All of that is theory—where'd you learn it?"

"Quantum what?"

He faced her then. "If you breach us with quantum computing technology, you have to create a patch for the hole you make. Or teach me how you did it—if I can't figure it out."

She stood and wiped her hands on her black jeans. She was both scared and impressed he'd figured out how she'd pushed past the protections on his phone.

"No," she responded to his request to teach him. She'd done what she came for. This was the time when, Cindy and Peace kept instructing her, she walked away. Just like at the club, lingering led to talking, and with Hoyt, she wanted nothing more than to talk and touch. What stood before her was a nice guy, albeit a hot egomaniac with a fiancée, but if she lingered, she'd pursue that fantasy to pop a couple of his shirt buttons and tell him everything she knew about that futuristic tech that was more than just theory for her and her university professor, Dr. Branch. A mentor who had not been impressed by her joy ride in the system, dubbed Juggernaut, when she stopped by for an impromptu visit after her campus visit to meet Scout.

She had to keep things aboveboard.

"Goodbye, Hoyt."

"Wait." The desperate pitch of his baritone pulled her back to him. "Why go a' the wall now? Is this for the notoriety or for the money? Wha's your drive?"

Now his accent was clear, and Vega felt as if that meant something. Was his guard down? Desperation?

"I want both. And now seemed better than never."

He shook his head as if he was seeing something in her face and he was calling her bullshit. "Money? I can help you with tha'—how much you need?"

"Why, are you going to peel off a cool twenty grand for me right now?"

"I could. If that's what you want."

"One point five, my friend—"

"In cash?"

"In a bank account will do."

"What will that get you? Will that be what you really want, Vega?"

"Why do you care? Are you scared about what I'm going to do? I've already promised I'll be gentle."

He looked as if he were wrestling with whether to say something. Then: "What made you want to do what you do? Defend women and the oppressed online?"

Vega wasn't ready for that level of getting personal with the founder of Hoyt Securities. She watched him instead of answering, the way his gaze was light brown now like chocolate-coated honeycomb. The way it stayed on hers as if it were a genuine question he truly wanted an answer to. If she wasn't mistaken, he was wanting personal information as if they were friends.

She didn't like that he'd been guarded with her earlier, and it was that, she supposed, that made her say, "The first girl I saved was my little sis."

"Scout?"

Vega wasn't sure why it felt good to tell him, but it did.

"Yes."

He took a step closer. "Can I ask who you saved her from?"

"Our stepdad."

He nodded, taking into his hands the dark morsels of her soul. "From our limited interaction, Scout seems proud of her big sister."

Vega watched him a beat longer. What she shouldn't be doing was sharing secrets.

She took a step back toward the door.

"Too far?" he asked, and the genuine concern was back on his face.

"Too far."

He nodded. "Work for me instead of trying to break Titan's Wall. Show me what you can do."

"I have."

"This time I want to watch."

Candy unwrapped inside her at his words. His ability to speak in double meaning, at least to her mind, was delicious. As if he had spoken in code for so long that his ones and zeros had gotten skewed into a reality.

Vega looked down at her boots as they took swaggering steps toward him, and just before her belt touched the front of his pants, she looked up. "I'll let you watch me anytime, anywhere, Hoyt. Tell Londyn that you want to take a six-month hiatus to break some furniture with me, and then let's play."

His gemstone eyes registered her overt sexual come-on, and something like glee flitted across his irises before he smothered it.

"Let's sweeten the pot of this competition, then."

Vega groaned. "That sounds like a bet. I've been advised to not do bets... I'm trying real hard to not be the adrenaline junkie I once was."

He digested that then said, "I see. This is where your brash honesty comes from, some twelve-step program?"

She let him think that. "It's important to be honest with folks."

"Honest that you're going to fuck someone up being the main one?"

"If that's the situation, sure. But that's not you. Is it? You have an entire staff of engineers and developers at your disposal. I mean, let's face it, big guy, you'll be fine. Your net worth has more zeros than I've had boyfriends."

The glitter was back. "But is it more zeros than you've had fuck buddies?"

"You know..." She considered it. "No. It's not more zeros." She baited him just to watch his glitter turn into fire: "Again, set aside Londyn for a beat, and I could add you to that long list."

He was unimpressed, and Vega missed the chance of an inferno. "Gosh, what an offer."

"Is that a no?"

His accent was hidden once more. "For this task you've set to, breaking through Titan's Wall, since you're so confident, if you fail, you should have to lose something to me."

"Again, Billions, you have nothing to lose in any situation other than a nasty nosedive off the stock market. No."

"Let's make it personal, then."

Vega could feel that lure of upping the stakes. "I'm listening."

"You fail. By which I mean, you can't breach us in the next week, and you work for me." He looked over at the contract.

She looked at the contract too. She heard Cindy remind her that bets were slippery. Bets led to losing your head and getting emotional, but this one... Losing her employment freedom to a man she wanted to get trapped in an elevator with, naked, had strong allure.

Only, and realistically, Hoyt's contract wouldn't hold her. Which he'd find out the moment he showed it to his legal team. She had that effect with things based on legitimacy in court. But his bet had the weighted construct of danger that she liked. If she lost, he'd pursue her to fulfill his contract and she had a moment of clarity that it was that, right there, that had her putting her hand out.

"Fine."

His surprise was written on his face, and tentatively, he put his massive paw into hers and shook. The warmth of his dry palm flowed into her, and she gave him equal pressure back as that glitter turned to smoke in his gaze. It made pleasure dip though her.

His words rumbled over her skin: “Pōmaikaʻi, good luck. May the best player win.”

WANTING_

Hoyt was in the kitchen of his South Waterfront penthouse mixing his fitness powders into his small bullet-shaped blender carafe. The evening was fading faster these days, with the slant of the November gloam promising winter soon. The fireplace in the sunken living room and the lights throughout the front rooms were now programed to turn on low the moment he stepped into the penthouse.

He neither saw the purpling sky nor heard the whir of the blender. Vega was running like a favorite song on repeat in his mind. Who did that? Who came into an executive's office and told them that they were about to be breached? Vega wasn't one to pussyfoot around, sure, but she was the kind to just send a text with a list of threatening emojis—she'd as much said so, telling him she usually didn't reach out to her targets. He technically wasn't a target, so she'd treated him differently. And it was that difference he wanted explained.

Her casual dominating vigor was like jumper cables to his heart. When he'd offered to make it personal, it had electrified her, and he wasn't immune to watching her dark eyes go from curious to sparking with intrigue. And then he had a handshake promise that she would work for him after her attempted breach.

In one heart-stopping moment during that handshake, she had taken his palm and laid it on her left breast, over her heart, as she whispered, "Cross my heart and swear to die I'll work for you... But you won't win."

He was still trying to get feeling back into that hand. Now, he paused the blending to take a deep breath and brace himself against the counter as if he'd done sprints on the playing field. She robbed the blood out of his head, this headstrong woman who'd stepped directly out of the pages of his fantasies and into his real life. She provoked an obsession that very likely was going to kill him if he couldn't soothe it.

The penthouse elevator chimed, and Hoyt shuttered his thoughts as his AI said, "Welcome home, Londyn."

Londyn's blond hair with stylish brown roots was pulled back into a tight twist, and her lips were as they always were, larger than life. Her white cashmere coat rested on her shoulders as her enormous leather bag hung on her forearm. She smiled as if he were a camera and she were taking a selfie. "You're home."

He nodded, trying not to hear the twinge of disappointment in her voice. "Do you have a second, Londyn? I'd like to talk with you."

She waited a beat before heading down the marble hall. As her heels clapped for attention, she called back to him, her voice a kind of sing-song pitch used for children, "Sure! I'll drop my things and be right back!" He heard the click of her door to her wing of the penthouse.

Leaning back against the counter, he shook his mixture by hand in its tumbler. She wasn't coming back out. He'd been with her for long enough to know when she was telling him what he wanted to hear and not what was the truth. It still rankled, how wrong he'd been to rush into putting a ring on her finger.

Things had started out perfectly. He knew now that she'd been coached to parrot the things the dating coach suggested, and instead of keeping that persona, Londyn dumped it the moment the ring slipped onto her finger and her bags were unpacked. It felt like the longest mistake he'd tried to figure out how to delicately fix. Though he knew it was only his second-most delicate. And it was the first one he'd need to fix alone.

His parents, who now spent half their time in the sprawling family home tucked into the forest in the West Hills and the other half back home in Peahi, were always a grounding force in his life. His mother, an educator, had recognized his gift for code and engineering when he was young. He had helped his aunties change their screen settings when he was in kindergarten and then turbo-charged their operating systems when he was in middle school. He had been the family anomaly, a little too smart, a little too aggressive, and always questioning the order of things. Instead of shunning him, his family welcomed his differences and collectively helped to raise him. They showed him outlets for his energy and desire to take things apart. His father and uncles woke him before sunrise to take him fishing and work out his excess energy; his mom and aunties pushed him to put the small appliances he demolished back together.

His parents had always understood that people who worked with computers were the next generation of forward thinkers and wanted their son, and then their daughter, when she showed similar inherent talents and interests, to be on that front line. It would lift him up, and he in turn could lift up his community and show the world that white wasn't the only color tech smarts came in.

But they didn't have the money to send him to a premier mainland college that could be his launch pad into the Silicon Valley circles where he could be among peers. Fortunately, he had something just as good as money. The fall of freshman year, after a growth spurt over the summer, the high school JV coach asked him to try out for football. Football ended up being his ticket to a mainland college that in turn allowed him to earn a degree in computer science.

After graduation, football continued to open doors for him, and he signed on with his first NFL team. At first, he got swept up in the money and screaming fans. He lost his way. In school, he'd been focused on creating the beta version of Titan's Wall, studying, and training. As a pro, the atmosphere allowed him to have a singular focus, and he soon forgot Titan's Wall. He chased one high after another, first, wins on the field, then, alcohol and any woman who was willing off the field. The more the merrier. His debauchery was fueled by parties and fans quoting his stats and wanting to be him.

The alcohol started to hit him harder, inflaming his body and preventing him from healing quickly, until he was blowing out a knee one week and a shoulder the next. Team docs tried to talk to him about his diet, lifestyle, and mental health, but he just wanted the shots to his joints that put him back into play. Until they weren't enough, and he added pills to the drinking.

Then his mother showed up and let herself into his apartment.

He had been too out of control back then to give a shit that she'd flown over three thousand miles to be there. He knew now that he had been teetering on the last rung that led to the darkness of rock bottom. His contract had been under serious scrutiny, and though his agent was trying to get him to rally, he'd given away his last fuck.

In a hail Mary pass to save his career, his agent had called his mother for help.

He remembered that morning he walked into his kitchen to find her there, her winter jacket still on. His head and mouth were filled with cotton, and he was so angry. But she reminded him that he wasn't alone and that the man he was trying to be with the drugs and the girls was like a coat that didn't fit. She pushed a pouch toward him across the counter.

Even now, Hoyt kept that memory close. When his firm's revenue stream and its appearance of success said it was fine for him to ease up, to let loose, to not be as diligent, he didn't. It was a slippery slope back into hollow wins and wondering if he'd ever be good enough up there in that mammoth professional arena of the mainland. He remembered his mother's words that day. She had opened the pouch, letting the silver-dollar-sized shark's tooth shake out with a clatter. "Don't forget who you are, and where you come from, Ho'o. Let your 'aumakua remind you." She pressed the triangle into his palm so hard his skin bloomed around the jagged edges that had once torn flesh from cartilage. For him, his ʻaumakua, manō, was a protector.

He still remembered the day she'd first come to him. He had been a teenager spearfishing when a tiger shark had grabbed his dive bag, ripped his catch out, and left a tooth behind. That too became a memory that delivered an emotional punch every time he touched the tooth, which always hung around his neck. *Don't keep all that you catch; leave some for her, like an offering, so she doesn't take your dive bag,* his father counseled. With her in his life, and in the water, he could go deeper, explore new areas, and as long as he kept her as a guide, he'd have her strength, cunning, and counsel.

Now, he reached into his shirt, and of course there on its fine black cord was his tiger shark's, his manō's, tooth. And there in his apartment up in the Oregon skies, he still smelled the ʻehu kai of the shore break, felt his dive mask tight on his face, tasted salty ocean water. He looked at it and then down the hall where Londyn had gone.

He'd failed in that first half of his NFL contract with the Seahawks and put his future and the hopes of his family in jeopardy. After his mother's visit, he mentally went back to where he came from. He'd been raised in harmony with the land, the ʻāina, and he now remembered that delicate and sacred bond that was worth honoring. Sports commentators reported his comeback as a miracle, but he knew it was hard work and clean fuel. His body was like the land; it performed at its peak when it was unpolluted.

The first time Hoyt and Londyn made love, he sensed a hesitation from her. Eventually, she flicked the tooth dangling from his neck and said it unnerved her. As did his heritage tats over his thigh and manō across his back. The story of Maui pulling the islands from the sea with his magical fish hook she tolerated but didn't want to understand why Maui was important to him. He had taken off the necklace, thinking that he wanted her to feel comfortable with him. Once the feeling of shame for intimidating her passed, he realized that it wasn't his perceptions that needed to course correct. So, he put the necklace back on and tried to educate her about the world he came from. Londyn hadn't appreciated his perspective.

Now, he was back in that spot of needing manō's counsel. He could feel the inked teeth, the miniature triangles that represented his 'aumakua on his thigh and back, pull his skin tight as if talking to him through his skin. Though, he supposed, manō had been speaking to him all along, and he was only now quiet enough to listen.

He wanted someone to respect him for all that he was. It was that that he wanted the marriage broker to find for him. If that was even possible.

Looking to the tooth resting on his fingertips, his mind went to Vega's choppy black locks. She had a shark's force of nature. Someone like her was who he would have the marriage broker try to find for him. And in a week's time, to quell his professional needs, Vega would be working for him.

That tightness across his chest and down to his groin came back with just his thoughts about her working for him—she'd be within his reach *daily*. He rolled his shoulders as if to ease the grip that his shirt—that *she*—had on him. She fed that insatiable hunger that gnawed at his belly and that put him on the field every morning and at the top of his securities game. When she wasn't in front of him, he wanted to seek her out, circle around her until she reached out and touched him.

Vega, he had a strong feeling, wouldn't flinch at his inked body or ask him to take his 'aumakua amulet off. And not for the first time he wanted get her somewhere dark and quiet and put that theory to the test.

STALKING_

Across the street from the downtown US National Bank building, Vega got to work. The cold wind that came in off the river shot through her hoodie as if she were wearing a tank top. Goose bumps broke out as she held her 1972 Minolta camera up to her eye, getting a tight bead on the architecture from the roof of the neighboring building. The slippery click of the physical shutter was satisfying. The week was slowly moving into what would certainly be an action-packed weekend. Her bots were busy assessing Titan's Wall and telling her if the secret information she had tucked in her back pocket, thanks to Bunny's data, would be needed. She first wanted to just flex on the wall and see how far she could go with low-key skills. If it held, then it was time to legitimately power up the glitchy Juggernaut housed at the university and have a quantifiable run at it.

Until then, Vega was reaching out to recurring clients—clients who paid to have odd niche projects accomplished: a particular piece of code created, the odd investigator she passed work to who then needed help in return—to see if they needed assistance as she had an "unscheduled" opening. Cornices, as she called him, had put in a request immediately. Which was why she was up on that rooftop on a forty-degree windy day taking pictures of exterior architecture. He was a weird one, but he paid well for gritty architecture shots.

As she took pictures, she monitored a third project. The thing that was strictly for her, a social sciences experiment come to life. She had been watching Londyn all morning through the tracker Bunny. It had taken a few days before her and Hoyt's phones overlapped, but when they did, Vega was in.

Vega wanted to follow her, watch her, mimic her. Study this woman who held such a coveted spot by Hoyt's side. What did this woman do? How many boards of directors did she sit on? How did she get to be a tech genius's preferred human? What'd she say to him? How'd she do it? How'd she take her coffee? What did she see in Hoyt—the same things Vega saw or a side to him that was even more extra-special? She wanted to see it too. Vega looked at her own arm, letting the black-and-silver camera rest around her neck—would her arm look good with a bulky black leather and gold purse, which she'd just seen Londyn posing in a photo with?

The rest of the morning she electronically traveled the places Londyn went: Brunch that went untouched except for a bite of honeydew and a sip of mimosa. Cheek kisses and selfies. Londyn's acquaintances from her messaging traffic were mostly in New York and LA, one in Seattle who sounded like a relative and was wholly ignored. Another was in Portland and was filed in her contacts under *P2*. Londyn had spent that morning laughing with and arranging to meet and go over some event with this contact.

Vega wanted to plan events. Would there be cake and champagne? Cheese and charcuterie boards? Vega was making a mental list of what to buy with the rest of the million and a half from breaking Titan's Wall. So far, it included coats she'd wear only on her shoulders, a large leather bag with gold detailing, and a personal chauffeur. And none of it felt real. But what did she know? She'd never had a billion dollars, much less the opportunity to sleep with a man who did.

That afternoon, at the coffee shop, Londyn stood in line texting. Vega was physically there too but watching through the window, hood pulled up, leaning against a light pole. Through the café's front glass, Vega watched Londyn check her watch. A diamond-encrusted gold hunk that looked like it could singlehandedly buy Vega's warehouse, with change left over. Vega looked down at her own wrist. Had Hoyt bought that for her? Not a single message had come or gone between Hoyt and Londyn. Not even *I'm going to be late*, or, *Put down the goddamn toilet seat, asshole.*

Just as Vega was realizing that, Londyn sent him one:

> I have reservations tonight at Woodland Sushi.

Vega's stomach swirled. She wanted to see them together. She'd know, then, if she was just a cover for him or if this was true love. Would she feed him, touch him under the table? Fuck him in the bathroom?

God, I have to stop.

Londyn got her coffee; her coffee app told Vega it was a caramel macchiato, extra shot of espresso, skim milk, sugar-free syrup, and whipped cream topping. She took two sips and threw the rest away, then got into the back of her chauffeured black SUV. Vega, in her Uber, followed, wondering what swanky place the meeting with P2 was taking place in.

Hoyt's return text came in.

> Can't tonight. Don't forget the gala Saturday. You haven't said if you're attending. They need to know if you'll be there. And we need to talk.

Vega wondered why the man Londyn was marrying had no idea if she'd be going to some fancy party with him. And why she had no time to talk. Was she too busy? Vega wanted to know her business interests. So far Vega's online research showed Londyn as not sitting on a single board save for the one at her father's shipping empire. The real picture was taking shape, and Vega let it.

The car stopped, and Vega tossed cash and exited the car before the driver could shout at her that he couldn't accept cash. The building was the Ritz. Vega took in the glittering lights of the downtown and bustling cars honking their frustration in the heavy traffic.

Ducking into the hotel, she oriented quickly and guessed her way to the lounge where palms and marble dominated and delicate piano music tinkled like crystal rain. The maître d' asked if she needed a table for one or two.

Vega enjoyed the fact that in Portland, Vega might have looked like a goth ruffian, but she could expect the same service as anyone else. Well, maybe that was less about Portland being weird and more about it being in a nation like the US, where cash was still queen. She pulled out a folded fifty and tapped her palm with it.

"Pretty woman, blond, screams money, she come this way?"

The maître d' shook his head.

"That's too bad."

"But I did see her go upstairs."

Vega winked. "You're the best. Is there a meeting hall up there or an event today?"

He shook his head. "Just rooms, ma'am."

"Huh, well, thanks," she said and shook his hand.

"You're welcome," he said and slipped her fifty into his pocket. "Anytime."

Vega left the building and made her way to the roof of a neighboring one, the building with the best view of the side of the Ritz Londyn's phone was on.

As Vega hunkered down, eyeing the penthouse rooms, Londyn's phone received another text. It was Hoyt wanting an answer for Saturday. Then another saying that maybe he could make that night's reservation, pressing again that they needed to talk. It felt like he was trying to make some kind of effort with her.

She responded:

> Don't be rude. I was just letting you know as a courtesy.

> And I'm not asking you to come with me. As for Saturday, I don't appreciate the pressure to decide.
>
> I have things to take care of right now.

Vega didn't like the feel of it, at all. Looking down at the camera at her chest, she had a real good idea on the kind of meeting Londyn was having in the penthouse suite of the Ritz.

Hoyt didn't respond. And she didn't expect him to. Londyn had acted as if his inquiry had been the inquisition.

Vega felt the sour direction the day was taking and mentally returned all the items she had bought with the billionaire's fiancée in mind. There was no boss lesson to be learned there, no woman to be jealous or envious of, to seek her good approval and learn from her, to mimic her. No, Londyn was like a pup who had everything but couldn't resist rolling in garbage for a good time.

LATE THAT NIGHT, HER APARTMENT WASHROOM NOW A RED-LIT ROOM, Vega developed her film. The architecture pieces were well-composed, "urban" shots that her client would love. Once that roll, as well as the other Vega had snapped that day, was developed, she came out to find Cindy and Peace ransacking the snack pantry.

"We missed you tonight," Peace said, moving as if she were still drunk and dancing.

"After last week, I'm never going out again. You two are dangerous."

"Aw! You say the sweetest things!" As Vega started pinning up the freshly developed film to dry, Cindy crunched on salt-dusted chips. "Oh my god, not that cornices guy again?"

"He's the best. Pays on time, and his work is almost like nature photography. Like going on a building safari. Love him."

"Yeah, but why you? Why not just take them himself?"

"He likes stuff up close and with vintage flair, and I ask no questions. Plus, it's part of his kink—he needs the pictures to show up like ransomed bordello shots."

"Whaaat. No one is into that. What is his angle?"

"I told you, his wife's an architect, and some of the buildings are ones she's designed and others are ones that she loves. He jizzes on them and leaves them around for her to find. Remember?"

Peace coughed up a mouthful of chips. "What?"

Cindy grimaced. "Ugh. Was I drunk? I would have remembered that."

"Hey, man, it's his kink, and his wife's; no one's getting hurt, and they're having a blast. Good for them. Not everyone is so lucky."

Vega knew the next set in her hand was going to be like a small bomb in the room.

"Still, seriously, that's..." Cindy's gaze had gone to the photo Vega had just pinned then the next and the next.

"Who. Is. That?" Her mouth gaped as her jaw went slack. "Is she taking it in with her... Oh my lord, these are—"

"Porn."

Peace came over to inspect what was obviously bodies in various states of coitus.

"Oh my. Did you have permission for these—"

Cindy interrupted, "The curtains are wide open. She doesn't need permission for these."

"I see." Peace was sobering up watching the photos dry on the line. "Is that...I know that blond. Vega, what is, oh, that's not—"

"Hoyt," Cindy finished.

"No, it sure isn't," Vega said.

"How many did you take?"

"I thought I could take enough shots to make a flip book, but I ran out of film. It'll be a fun coffee table book."

Peace squealed, "I know him!"

"Yup," Vega said, "he owns five sushi restaurants across the city."

"That's Phillip Patel. He's banging Hoyt's fiancée? What the hell!"

When Vega pinned up the last photograph, she turned to them. They were back down at the beginning of the clothesline that ran the length of the east-facing windows. They were taking them in, moving slowly past each one as if at the opening of a fine gallery that served cheap snacks.

She let them digest the gravity of the revelation. How had her life taken this latest sharp turn? It started with a party at a club, and suddenly her year of quiet solitude had ended, and loudly.

Vega that afternoon hadn't expected to watch Londyn fuck another man, but she did—watched as she rode her own personal erotic pleasures all afternoon. Though, now, Vega's emotions caught up to her, and the low boil of hate she had for Londyn was hard to deny.

From Hoyt's text messages, Vega had a vague notion of what that serious-feeling talk was likely about. If Hoyt was half as smart as Vega thought he was, Hoyt was either going to talk with her about her status as his cover or break it off all together. Only it didn't help the swamp of emotions that welled up within her. Vega had rules. No nice guys. And this was why. Nice guys were so rare it wasn't fair to hurt the ones who did exist. Not when there was a whole population of assholes to fuck over.

"Vega..." Peace asked tentatively. "What are you thinking?"

She shrugged, feigning nonchalance. "Nothing. I don't owe him anything. We're not friends."

Cindy objected, "If we didn't know you from little-kid times, we'd take that to the bank and cash it. But you get stars in your eyes when you talk about him. He knocked you flat and broke into your apartment, and you didn't torch his life. You went to him the next day to tell him you were throwing your hat into the ring for that challenge. He's shaking up your ideals on what all men are like. And to top it off, I would have thought you'd be contacting your fuckboy Jax by now to blow off steam, but you're not. Why?"

"I haven't been in the mood—"

"Why?"

"Because."

"Why, Vega?" Cindy was in cop mode.

Vega blew out a breath, feeling the pressure of the situation build in her chest. "I don't get her," Vega said, flicking the drying photo where, palms to Patel's well-groomed dark chest, Londyn's pale hands stood out as she rode him. "She has a human being like Hoyt by her side, and yet she's out fucking some dude who's nice to look at, but, I mean, he's a trust fund kid who's had daddy's money his whole life—I checked. Hoyt is a self-made man, sharp as fuck, with a body... Let's just leave it there, enough said: his *body*."

Peace and Cindy groaned in understanding. "His body," they said as an amen.

Vega's hand fisted and released. "It's one thing to use a man if everyone is getting something, and maybe they are. Maybe she's a cover for him, but I doubt it. So that means she's using him and lying, and that's fucked up. I wanted to be her this morning, to figure out how she got there, by his side, keeping up with him, making him smile, and now, I know they don't have that, and I want to wash her off of me and out of my brain where I made space for her. And maybe, too, to push her off a bridge." She held up two fingers in a small gesture. "A little bridge."

"And then?" Cindy asked.

"There's no 'and then.'"

"You're sure?"

Vega grinned. "Kinda."

SET IT OFF_

Londyn had great dresses. And lingerie and diamonds on watches, cuffs of platinum, earrings in a rainbow of gemstones, hair pieces that looked themselves like jewelry. Her closet was the size of an average studio apartment. Vega pressed her heels into the thick white carpet, her right one falling particularly hard, and dragged her fingers along the glass-topped surface of the center island of drawers, leaving behind oily smudges atop the kaleidoscope of colors. Everything from her updo to her boots was reflected in the myriad of mirrors.

Hoyt's security system was linked to the building's elevators, which required a key card. Get by the guard in the lobby, and the lower fifteen floors were available to the average rider, but the penthouse required a key card. Using the data she gleaned from Bunny, Vega had inserted her key card attached to her device and punched the button for the penthouse.

The doors had swung open, and the AI had welcomed Londyn home.

By GPS, Vega had Londyn's steps in the penthouse logged, and followed that path to the rear of the penthouse. It was also the only overlap she had with Hoyt's tracker, there in the hallway. It was how

Vega had come to see that they lived in separate parts of the penthouse. Focused on Londyn, she had made her way down the main hall before catching Hoyt's scent from the first room, and the smells of salt spray and crisp linens had stopped her short. There in the hall she'd wrestled with staying on task and the yearning in her belly to open Hoyt's door. She wasn't there for him. And yet...

With one slow step back then another, she was at his closed door. He was also gone at the gala, and she wanted to go in, take her clothes off, and slip between his sheets. She slid her hand down the smooth surface of the heavy wood door. She wanted to be his Goldilocks, sampling everything of his and surprising him in his bed.

Her hand went to the lever-style door handle, and before her mind could argue, her body acted; the latch popped, and the toe of her boot smacked the door into a yawn.

"Oops."

As Hoyt's arm had swung wide at his office days before, the door welcomed her to his bedroom, giving her an uninhibited view of the well-appointed space: thick carpet, dark wood, sturdy bed frame, deep jewel tone of his sheets. The sheets in midnight plum looked like flax linen, the craftsmanship perfected over the centuries such that they would slide like warm milk over the skin. She glided to a closed door—the closet.

The lights flickered on in the deep closet that held neat parallel rows of suit coats above and pants below. A mirror at the end showed her in all black, eyes wide, touching his shirts, her fingers floating over the sleeves. Then it watched as she unzipped her hoodie, pulled a maroon suit coat off the hanger and slipped it on. It hung on her, her fingertips reaching the cuff only when she held her arms aloft.

Then, there was his smell. The suitcoats were all freshly laundered, and Vega had to lift the collar and press it to her nose to catch his scent. It was muted but there, and Vega filled her nostrils with ocean spray, linen, and the touch of musk that said his skin had laid against the silken inseam and left a bit of him behind. She lifted pants off and held them up, the waist coming all the way to her breasts, then found a shirt, a plain black tee she hadn't seen him wear nor was ever likely to. Putting everything back, she stripped naked and slipped on his tee, and with excitement, the thrill of the shadows electrocuting her nerve endings, she slipped between the sheets in his well-made bed.

Vega groaned and made a snow angel in the buttery softness of his French linen sheets, "So good," she whispered to herself. He was there, in the bed, on his pillow, the fir and sandalwood of his soap and more ocean spray and heavy musk. She buried her face in his pillow and pulled him deep into her lungs.

She was *fucked*.

Lying still on her back, arms out, Vega took in the soft amber glow of the room, admiring the deep closet and the beams that made the room seem as if she were in a luxurious mountain home with deep architectural roots.

This, Vega thought, was as close as she'd ever get to the man. And if she didn't get her little butt out of his bed, a restraining order was gonna make that distance legal. She put her own clothes back on over his shirt—damn the consequences—and once everything was tidy again, went to the door.

"Focus," she whispered and after taking one last long look at the room, broke eye contact with it as if it were her lover. Then, because she wasn't Vega if the stakes weren't high, she had left the door open as a kind of question for Hoyt later and gone to the end of the hall where the entire western wing had been decorated for Londyn. Pictures lined the halls, mostly sexy black-and-whites of her in purring, breast-thrusting poses. Off the bedroom through the luxurious white-marbled bath and into the closet, Vega felt like she'd walked into a social influencer's orgasm.

She dug in, investigating the silk sheets, the jewelry boxes, and the clothes on silk hangers. She uncovered only one sex toy, and it was still in its clear plastic packaging.

Vega twisted the box containing the violent-pink dildo back and forth. "Londyn, this is your problem. You gotta use this babe and not fuck real dicks until you've cleared your pussy of her promises and contracts." Vega tossed it back where she'd found it before moving to the trash bins. They were pristine, as if they were emptied and polished as soon as the occupant used them. Vega had the urge to wad up a tissue and throw it away to conjure the cleaner, so she could interview the person responsible for the glistening bins, porcelains, and baseboards.

Vega ran her fingers between cushions and along the back of Londyn's nightstand and found what the vacuum did not. There were the messy remnants of condom wrappers, shoved there in a hurry then forgotten. Vega sanitized her hands and continued working the white and mirrored furniture around the room, and at the heavily lit vanity between the floor-to-ceiling windows that held a view of the river, Vega hit a locked drawer. She jiggled then smacked it with the side of her fist, but it didn't move. Digging through her hair that she'd braided, twisted, and piled up on top of her head for the gala, Vega pulled out a couple pins; with another jiggle and a twist, the simple lock gave.

Yanking the drawer open, Vega sighed. A tablet with a tripod clip was in the drawer. Vega swiped at the screen—and it opened.

"Oh, Londyn, no, girl. Haven't you learned anything from Hoyt?"

Londyn's lack of security was not the most disappointing thing about the tablet. On it was a small library of videos Vega hoped were just content for her influencer reels but lost hope at the sight of the first one. They were of Londyn and the sushi magnate fucking the daylights out of each other in every room in the penthouse.

Vega's lip curled in disgust as Londyn sloppily caught, or more often didn't, cum with her mouth, back, or belly. Even with a cleaning staff, below the black light, Hoyt's penthouse would be a Jackson Pollock painting. It was as if it was purposeful desecration.

Being a glutton for punishment, Vega watched one then another and let the burn in her stomach catch fire. Their kink wasn't just making a mess—it was a catch-me-in-the-act kink. Hoyt was an unknowing third in Londyn and her boy toy's sexual escapades. And that hit like a fist to Vega's sternum.

Now, watching Londyn and Phillip pretend to be scared that Hoyt was coming home, little dramatic glances at doors and scaring each other with moaning exclamations of "Oh no, he's here!" before making a mess on the rug, Vega set to work protecting Hoyt. Cindy wouldn't approve—Hoyt was neither a woman nor in a desperate situation begging for her help—but Vega's guts were on fire.

She set the tablet down, got her phone out, and grabbed a five-second clip to go with the photos, before lifting her boot. She slid the heel open for her travel-sized nuclear option. From it she pulled a small but powerful rare earth magnet the size of her palm. She set it on top of Londyn's device and swiped. With slow and purposeful strokes, the magnet slid back and forth across the tablet as if painting line by line the macabre black that her device would now forever display. Then she flipped it over and did it again, and again, for five minutes straight until the device forgot everything it knew including the command to use the battery to power on.

Vega tucked the magnet away and slipped Londyn's bricked tablet back into the drawer and resisted the urge to leave a note: *Dear Londyn, this is the fucking you get for the fucking you got.*

After relocking the drawer, she moved back into the closet, stripping as she went, a little tune on her lips.

"London bridges falling down..."

Vega pulled down seemingly the only black gown Londyn owned and popped on the lights to the makeup station to prepare for war. She hated swapping Hoyt's T-shirt for anything of Londyn's, but she had a gala to crash.

CLEAN HOUSE_

The car ride to the gala had been a disaster.

Hoyt had held the door open for Londyn, gently loaded her into the back of the chauffeured SUV, then half way to the event told Londyn it was over. He had expected some emotion but not the level she'd delivered at.

"Londyn, after tonight, I think it best you move your things out of the penthouse."

As his words settled between them, Londyn's eyes darted up from her screen. He saw in them anger just before the tyrannical screaming began. He'd been avoiding it, and now, maybe he understood why. It was yet another example of how he failed at the thing others seemed so good at. Reading people and their subversive plans and expectations was a skill he lacked. Honesty, in whatever form, was data he could understand.

When she caught her breath, he impatiently asked, "Are you done?"

She wasn't. Nelson, his driver, had been with him long enough to read instructions in Hoyt's eyes, and he circled the block as Londyn continued. Hoyt wished he could signal Nelson to let him out immediately, but he knew he had to finish this.

"How could you, Hoyt!"

"This cannot be a surprise for you."

Her eyebrows shot up. "Not a surprise?! This is a complete surprise! Are you fucking someone else?" She was back to screaming.

"No."

She was shouting now about what her family would think. Hoyt had already given quite a lot of thought to what her family would think. Her father was a shipping magnate, and one of Hoyt's largest customers. Young and Co. had Titan's Wall installed across every facility around the globe. That couldn't keep Hoyt from breaking it off with his daughter, but if Hoyt wanted to keep Young's business, he'd have to be careful not to reduce himself to Londyn's petty antics —no matter how much her behavior over their last few weeks together made him want to dive into his baser self.

"No? No? No!?" Her blue contact lenses were not filled with tears, he noticed, but her neck showed her frustration in red blotches. He liked it—it seemed real. Finally.

"No."

Since the conversation didn't seem to be going anywhere, Hoyt signaled Nelson, and the man immediately pulled them to the curb with a chirp of the tires. Hoyt braced himself at the sudden braking and didn't blame him. He didn't want to continue to hear her shrieks either.

Outside the car, she took in the distance to the event then glared back at him, clearly displeased they were parked so far from the entrance. "Wait till my father hears about this."

"Hears that I don't love you, you don't love me, or I'm breaking off this sham?" He adjusted his cuffs before meeting her gaze.

Her eyes had narrowed to slits as if her emotions were too heavy to hold. "He was the one who wanted me to try as hard as I did to 'land you,'" she said, and he thought her fingers might snap off as hard as she air-quoted. "And I did." She took a deep breath, and her voice quieted on the next line. "My parents wanted this to succeed despite your *disadvantages*." Her eyes darted to parts of his body as if they were checking off a list of things that made him less-than to her,

"You're new money, so you wouldn't understand." Hoyt wondered what made her admit that, and if she was saying it to him or more to herself. Before he could ask her what the fuck she meant by that, her volume notched up again, and she spat, "He's your largest client and will bury you because of this."

Suddenly, Hoyt really didn't care if Young and Co. was one of his largest clients. He'd pay his annual salary to be anywhere but where he was standing right then. "Let me be clear: in no world were we ever compatible. We're done."

"He'll bury you," she reiterated.

Hoyt took a deep, stabilizing breath in before saying to her, "Londyn, what you've failed to realize in our short dating history is a lesson you would have learned had you actually been interested in me: you can't bury a man you can't touch."

Hoyt had been threatened before. When he was younger and didn't know his own value, it would spark rage in him, but now he was clearheaded enough to see the woman before him was no opponent. Just an immature soul trying to move forward in life in the only way she knew how. Maybe he was learning how to read people after all.

An odd thought distracted Hoyt; Vega was an opponent. A unique one who had blown into his life like a hurricane, and when she tangled with him, all he could do was hold on. But when her winds died down, he was on the bow of his ship looking for her, just to do it all again. He'd let Vega bury him. Because every second would be a glimpse into the unknown, and he wanted to face that power she wielded, and flex back. That was a game he'd play for every second the clock was running.

"We're over, Londyn. I'll give you a week to find another place and six months of cash to get you to your next..." He wasn't sure what to say there. "To your next man" was probably accurate but felt wrong to say aloud, and "gig" would mean she was interested in working. "Thing," he ended lamely.

"You'll give me a year—it's what you promised me."

He held his hand out, a vision of acquiescence. She placed her hand in his, and he surprised her by slipping the ten-carat ring off her finger and handing it to her. He'd never promised her a year, but he wanted this severed, no more screaming. "This is worth a year of support from me."

She called him a sour name. Took the ring and picked up the front of her dress and turned down the sidewalk toward the gala. He was a little surprised she didn't just get back in the car.

Was it over? It was over. He felt relieved and lighter. But also, as if there was something he was missing.

He pushed thoughts of Londyn away. He had a role to play tonight: best friend to Zane and premier sponsor of this first black-tie benefit for Big Buddies Bigger Hearts. The gala was at the exclusive Waterford Building downtown. They'd celebrated the nonprofit's launch at Nate's Festivál, and tonight they'd raise money to pay for operations over the next five years. Hoyt's firm had footed the bill for the hall and the catering. Hoyt would introduce Zane during the scripted portion and then shake hands, encouraging guests to dine, wine, and open their pocketbooks for the silent auction.

Those conversations were always the same no matter the topic—the other person was always pretending Hoyt didn't have a net worth of three point two billion dollars and that they weren't there to take some of it off his hands. For toothbrushes that ran on solar, for a supercomputer that could map alien genomes—"We'll be landing on Mars soon"—or for a sleek shower trimmer for a woman's bikini line. That person had produced a sketch on their phone, which showed a streamlined pearl-colored device with a skin-soft cylindrical silicone handle that had settings for rhythmic vibrations.

That one had been shared at an event just the night before, and as soon as he truly understood the sketch, he had thought of Vega. He'd love to get her decisive and illuminating answer on how she'd use such a device. Then her come-on, which he'd push away as if his whole body weren't screaming *yes* to perform erotic acts with a hacker he'd just met. He'd barely excused himself from the pitch in time to save some dignity.

Now, up the marble steps and standing at the expansive doors to

Zane's gala, Hoyt paused, steeling himself. While he enjoyed fake conversations as much as a squirrel liked being in a pen full of dogs, at least tonight was worth it to be there for his friend.

And there was that friend now. "You ready, buddy?" Zane said and slung his arm over his shoulders before the two stepped into the Gatsby-esque fever dream. The domed space was all thrown-open iron-framed glass doors and windows as the foyer soared up into a glass atrium, each level filled with lush planters. The second-floor ballroom opened to a rooftop garden. Somewhere a fountain burbled. The sighs of violins. Laughter and chatter. Gowns in ruby, ocean, and ebony rustled and glittered. The men wore tuxedos that reminded Hoyt of a Bond movie. His own suit was hand-tailored, like all of his clothes, and fit conservatively through his shoulders. He'd have to be careful to not rip a seam.

Zane flicked his lapel. "This shit's tight. I think my granny had a headscarf made out of this. Paisley and silk? Damn. Leave it to you to pull that off."

Nate joined them, looking put out in a form-fitting tux Hoyt knew was one of thirty the bar owner had. "When is this thing over? Eva took the baby to her pop's place tonight, and I need to get back to make sure she's...OK." he finished, and they all knew "making sure Eva was OK" involved having his pants off.

Zane laughed. "You just got here."

"Yeah, and when the guard dogs Mr. Genius here has surrounding the place asked for my invite—which I didn't bring—I almost went home."

Hoyt raised his brows at his grumpy friend. "I would have thought this would be your scene."

"Fuck yeah. But not when the baby is at Grandpa's house."

Zane was curious. "So, how did you get in?"

"Some goth girl told him to check his list again, and I was on there."

"You were always on the list, Nate."

"I wasn't."

"Did you RSVP?"

"Should I have?"

Zane gave Nate's arm a soft tap with his fist and shook his head with a smile. "I appreciate you giving up alone time with Eva to be here."

Event coordinators buzzed around them, checking tablets and talking into comms.

Zane took in the room. "Man, there's so many people here."

Hoyt said, "Yeah, initial numbers are good. You'll have enough funding to cover the next five years, eight, if you're conservative."

Zane's eyes went glossy with emotion. "Eight years?"

"That's right."

Zane turned and held up his hand, and Hoyt put his into it before Zane yanked him in for a hug. He smacked Hoyt's back and choked out, "You're a good friend, man."

Hoyt gave him a firm squeeze before letting go. "It's worth it. You're worth it."

Nate nodded in agreement. "Worth it. Hoyt paid for my plate, but it was worth it."

Zane laughed and gave his shoulder a squeeze. "The thought, right? It's the thought that counts."

Nate wiped his fingers over his grin as if halfway to his mouth he realized he didn't have a cigarette in his hand.

They were quiet, taking in the moment. Zane and Hoyt had been together since college and played football with and against each other in the pros before retiring, and Hoyt's added success was icing. For Hoyt, and then for Zane, and eventually for Nate when he was released from prison and needed an ally in the small Portland investment community. His high-end Euro import garage needed customers, and Hoyt had acquaintances who had expensive Euro cars and who needed a mechanic. When Nate wanted to diversify his assets, he pitched Hoyt on Festivál. When Hoyt invested and promoted the ventures of his friends, who were both outstanding humans, no matter past mistakes, it created the community he wanted and was raised with. What was good for one was good for all.

Nate broke the silence. "Your girl from the club coming?"

"Who?" Hoyt's hands suddenly felt awkward, and he busied them by pushing back a lock of hair.

"Right," Nate said. "Try not to look like you've been electrocuted."

"She's not my girl."

Zane added, "I've been talking to Peace. She's nice."

Nate looked between the two. "Nice? You guys gotta get more expansive with your vocabulary. It's no wonder you're so old and still single."

Hoyt's watch buzzed as he heard Zane laugh and quip back at Nate. He checked the message. His assistant had gotten Hoyt's note that Londyn was no longer afforded privileges and was making the changes he requested.

Something Zane said made Nate snap his fingers. "I thought that goth chick—the one who told your door guard to look again for me on the list—looked familiar. She reminded me of your girl from the club, Hoʻo."

Hoyt's insides lurched. He'd been speeding along with this evening, and suddenly he hit the brakes and looked around the room. Was she there among all the bare shoulders, laughing red lips, and glittering eyes? Servers passed through the room, their polished silver trays laden with small appetizers and tall flutes of champagne.

"You all right, buddy?" he heard Zane ask.

"Yeah, why?"

"Because I think you got whiplash looking around the room. You excited to see her or scared?"

Nate added, "Fuck, man, your face looks like your body is having engine trouble. You wanna sit down?"

Hoyt sneered.

"Yeah, that look. Pretty. Keep wearing that look, no one will talk to you."

"I'll keep that under advisement."

"Oh, ho, ho." Nate adjusted his tie with exaggerated movements. "Under advisement," he parroted Hoyt, to his annoyance. "She's under your skin. You tell Londyn goodbye yet?"

"Did in the car here."

Their faces fell. "Aw, shit." Zane put a firm hand on his shoulder. "I'm really sorry, man." He squeezed.

Nate tucked his hands in his pockets, looking like he wished he had something nicer to say than "How'd she take it?"

"Like shit. Nelson had to circle the block, repeatedly, till she stopped her shouting."

"Fuck."

"Yeah. But it's done. I think."

"What do you mean?"

"She asked for a year of support. I gave it to her—I let her keep the ring—but there's still more to do, the apartment, keys, cards, fuck, I don't care. It's done."

Something caught Nate's eye across the room, and he squinted. He asked absently, "So, now you're a free agent, right?"

The emcee announced to the room that they'd be getting started shortly.

"I'm not going to get into another relationship anytime soon, so let's say I'm not a free agent. I'm contracted to myself for the foreseeable future."

Nate grunted an affirmative while Zane gave him another shoulder pat before an event assistant pulled him aside to discuss something.

Nate continued, his eyes tracking, "So, you wouldn't care if that chick from the club, Joan Arc somebody, was here?"

Hoyt's gaze darted out to the sea of well-dressed people.

"Where?"

Nate gave him a knowing smile. "I thought you said you weren't a free agent?"

"I'm not. She and I... She has business... I have... It's business with her. She wasn't invited to this. Where'd you see her?"

"I saw her duck into the side hall."

Hoyt felt his whole body alight. Apprehension, excitement, and a deep-seated yearning to see her in something fit for a black-tie gala.

He was making for the hall Nate had pointed to when he was stopped by another event coordinator.

"Sir? It's time."

LET ME DREAM FOR ONE NIGHT_

Earlier.

Vega had her phone out and was talking in hushed tones to the sous chef on his smoke break. Hoyt's security for the event was tighter than the Virgin Mary's holy tunnel on her wedding night. She wanted to find him and tell him that to his face. And see what he was wearing. What did a man who wore suits meant for Italian models on an average Tuesday look like at a gala? How'd he turn up the volume on perfection? She'd never stood so straight for so long pretending she was worth in excess of a hundred million dollars and deserved to be there. Hoyt's systems had caught her faked credentials and flagged her, and just inside the door she'd been escorted out. Now the sous chef was taking too long to accept her bribe to get in through the service entrance while event guards Jacked and Stacked were headed down the alley to them.

"I mean," the sous chef said, wiping his mouth with his hands, "it looks legit..."

Over her shoulder, Jacked, bald and thicker than Hoyt, spoke into his wrist. Stacked was coming from the other way, lankier, but he looked like he wouldn't mind punching a faux-fancy lady for getting by him, a second time.

"Enjoy your smoke, and it'll be here in fifteen, bud," Vega said, shaking the order screen.

He looked up, surprised, his brown eyes soft but wary as if she and her hustle were definitely not a good thing for his day. "I really need this job, though, lady. You look like you should be in there, so if you're not on the list, there must be a good reason. If I let you in, and whatever you do gets back to me, I'm fired. And this gig has healthcare."

Fuck.

"You're right. But here's the thing." Vega glanced at her impending doom patrol about to descend on them. "Josh is dodging my calls. He knows he owes me alimony, but he's out with his new young thing." She spoke like an auctioneer at the podium. "And he thinks he can walk away from me and our baby. You understand, don't you? I raised her all by myself—the least Jake could do is pay his fair share."

He blinked. "I thought you said his name was Josh."

"Fuck. Sorry, bud." She took another look at Jacked and Stacked who read her right and started running. She shoved past the sous chef and into the kitchen.

Steam and barked demands filled the room. She hustled through the maze of prep chefs and stainless steel into a concrete brick hallway and followed the sounds of the party.

"Get back here!" came from behind her, and Vega darted into the first stairwell. She slowed her pace at the top so she was breathing normally as she stepped out of the service door and into the open hall that led into the ballroom through archways that reminded Vega of a Greek coliseum.

She tucked into the crowd and started looking for Londyn in earnest. Everyone looked like they enjoyed Chopin and dark den gambling. The kind who actually wore diamonds when they played tennis and calculated your worth before they shook your hand. Vega loved it. They were there to brush up against the wealthiest man in the city and bought a $20,000 plate of food just to dine in his presence. And she'd had the pleasure of being alone in his presence more than once.

With that joy in her mind, Vega snatched a champagne flute and continued searching the sea of faces: black, beige, dark brown, and white, Hoyt knew how to draw them all. None of these folks were taking a selfie on a stick with the ring light set to soft amber. In fact... Vega dipped out of the way of being caught by one of the hired professional photographers.

Moving in the opposite direction of the flash, Vega caught "Pull your head out of your ass, George." Vega stopped and took another sip of champagne.

"Your idea is good, and I didn't buy us plates at this event for you to sit and search your soul for an ounce of your father's moxy. You have it—now go tell him your idea."

Vega glanced at the speaker, an elderly woman heavily weighted with marble-sized pearls, in a black-sequined dress, and wearing Chanel No. 5 thick enough for it to be an insecticide. She'd envisioned a middle-aged woman encouraging her young son, but instead the son was in his sixties.

Vega raised her brows as George, with soft shoulders in a brown suit that looked to be from *Mad Men* days, worked his way through the crowd before stopping a server for a quick chat and a snack off their silver tray.

Vega couldn't resist and fell into a slow step with George as the server left. George was meandering through the posh crowd toward the front of the expansive ballroom.

"What's your idea?"

George flinched. "What's that?" Owlish eyes stared back at Vega before taking her in from boot to messy updo.

His green eyes reminded Vega of sea glass and philosophy majors as they sat behind wire-rimmed specs.

"Your idea." She threw a thumb behind her. "I heard your mom. I'm close with Mr. Kaho'okalakupua." In every fantasy of hers lately, she was close with him. Real close. And she liked to fake it till she made it. "I'll tell you if he'll like it or not."

"I, ah..." he stammered.

She gave him a smile to put him at ease. "Your idea."

"Yes, well. Who are you?"

Vega put her hand out. "I'm Ms. Arc. Mr. Kaho'okalakupua's agent for change in cybersecurity." Not quite a lie.

"Oh, well." He seemed to relax. "That's nice of you. I have an idea that I think will change the world."

Vega was excited. Changing the world was a big idea, and everyone had a different take on what that change looked like. She was a student of the internet and expected a popcorn-worthy speech.

"I think that Mr. Kaho'okalakupua should pay for every child who graduates high school in the metro to go to a four-year college of their choice."

Vega blinked. She was expecting something more like someone should feed the chipmunks in the park so they grow fat and docile, enabling parkgoers to dress them up like dolls.

"I'm the son of the late Dex Clements, forestry baron of Philomath, and our family set up college scholarships for every graduate. We've since run out of money to continue the fund, and it's had a devastating impact on the town. It's these opportunities that are life-changing chances for families. How do you change society? You reach individuals and give them the opportunities a man like Mr. Kaho'okalakupua can afford to give. Bring higher education to the metro then to every corner of our state and watch us flourish fiscally and intellectually."

Vega swallowed. It was beautiful and simple. Long-term vision for enacting sustainable change. "Yeah."

"Yeah? You think he'd like it?"

She blinked. "I think you should try your damnedest to talk with him."

His face illuminated with what she assumed was a rare appearance of hope. "Will you tell him my idea?" He pulled a card from his chest pocket.

"Oh, I—" Vega looked to the dais at the front of the room as a woman took the microphone and announced they'd start shortly. Nearby were three brickhouses of men Vega knew all too well. Zane and Nate were in respectable James Bond–style black-and-white tuxedos while Hoyt's designer suit was deep maroon with a silk stripe giving it a luster that was tempered by a soft black shirt and tie. Anyone else in that would look color blind. Against his tan skin, he looked expensive, down to his hand-crafted Italian suede shoes. Stylists would hate the brown-and-black combo. But again, on him, it looked purposeful, on point, a style that couldn't be mimicked. All on a body that said power. Vega drank him in. She had the urge to go to him.

His eyes were as gemstone dark and shiny as the buttons on his coat. Even from across the room she could see something intense had happened recently to him. Had he found her bots? She had the itch to pull out her phone and text him. But no, it looked deeper than that. It etched his cheekbones and jaw with hard lines. She took a step toward him before she caught the eye of his friend Nate.

His gaze was trying to place her again. He'd given her that same searching look when he thanked her when she'd slid his name onto the bouncer's list. She had the feeling that in just a moment more she would become the topic of discussion between the men. And she wasn't there for Hoyt, despite her boots wanting to run directly to him so she could ask him if he thought that everyone should have access to higher education. She had to keep on task. He needed protecting.

"Good chat." She gave George's shoulder a pat and was headed toward the back of the gala when she spotted Jacked and Stacked scanning the crowd. "Shit."

From behind her, she heard George say, "So you'll do it, you'll tell Mr. Kaho'okalakupua about my idea?"

Back to him, panic in her eyes: "Sure, yeah, buddy." Jacked and Stacked looked serious now, like grab-and-toss serious, and she'd hate to fuck up her makeup. Londyn had expensive shit, and she didn't want to smudge it just yet.

She blew a kiss to George and headed for a side door.

"Thanks!" he called to her.

The hallway's gold-and-garnet carpet made Vega think of palaces. As did the royal-looking fucks hissing at each other at the other end.

Vega grinned at her luck. “Well, well, well, look who it is.”

Londyn, hand to Phillip’s chest, was saying something, begging him for something. A something that Phillip wasn’t excited about. Her shiny manicure was a stunning contrast against his bold turquoise dress shirt. An orange sari-patterned tie brought it together with Londyn’s dress.

Londyn’s chin snapped over her shoulder at Vega’s comment, her straight blond locks swinging out. Vega expected her unnaturally blue eyes to hiss and her mouth to be filled with blood as her fangs retreated.

“Who are you?” she asked instead.

Vega stepped into their alcove with them. A window above them, at the second-floor height, framed the purples and blues of the setting sun on the deepening clouds.

“Just someone who’d like some answers.” Vega pulled the photos out from where they had been held by her wide belt. Did Londyn recognize the dress and belt?

“What’s this?” Londyn looked to the black envelope then to her, accusation in her gaze. “Papers? He’s fucking serving me papers? What the fuck for? Breaking up with me wasn’t enough—he wants to fuck me over now?”

This gave Vega pause. “What?”

Londyn slapped the envelope out of her hand, sending it to the floor where the photos erupted out of the envelope, reminding all three of them how flexible Londyn was with Phillip on a king-sized bed at the Ritz.

She heard Phillip’s voice that sounded like he was speaking through his nasal passages while holding a golden spoon to his lips. “What the…”

“Fuck is this?” Londyn finished. All eyes were on the floor. “What the fuck is this?” she asked again, louder. Her voice then lifted to decibels that impressed Vega. “What the fuck is this!?”

Phillip uttered, his dark brown skin going gray as blood drained out of his face, “Blackmail.”

Vega tsked. “Look, I had this whole explanation before you were to open the envelope. Londyn, stop screaming; you're really ruining this—"

"Who the fuck are you?!"

"See?" Vega said to the two sets of eyes on her now. "This is what happens when you do things out of order—now you're just creating chaos. When all I'm trying to tell you is—"

Phillip's voice whined, "It is blackmail! I'm screwed!"

Londyn whirled around at him. "You're screwed? I have nowhere to go, and now he's attacking me!"

"Guys? Look, this isn't blackmail. I'm trying to tell you—"

"You work for him, don't you?" Londyn screamed at Vega. "You showed him these, and that's why he's broken things off." She balled her hands into fists. "You fucking—"

"Oh, for fuck's sake," Vega cut in. It was as if she were trying to give two cats a bath. "These images are a warning—"

"I can't believe he'd do this!"

Vega had traveled the halls of hell and knew it was paved with screamers. She knew if you could tune out the vocal scratch, you could stay on task.

Vega looked down to the images that Phillip was hastily shoving back into the envelope. "Not as kinky now, is it?"

Londyn hissed, "I'm going to sue you."

Vega angled her head. "Cool. You want to sue me? Sounds good. What's my name?" In the pause, Vega said, "'Get the fuck out of Hoyt's life' was what I was going to say, but it sounds like he's taken care of that already. But you"—Vega looked to Phillip—"sucks that you see the fallacy of what you've done only now when it's too late, and rules are rules. You've hurt and shamed a man who has no idea that you've done it. And we're going to keep it that way. But starting today, I'm going to need to you buckle up."

"Buckle up?" Phillip asked.

"I'm going to take you on a ride that, frankly, is gonna suck for you. It's a punishment for touching her." Then to Londyn: "It should be you I bury, but we women get the shit end of the stick too often, and your misguided grasp for love shouldn't be punished. But I won't let you spin tales. Move on. Or I will make you."

Londyn opened her mouth to respond, when her eyes darted over Vega's one shoulder then her other, and Vega knew then that Jacked and Stacked had found her.

To Londyn, Jacked asked, "My apologies, ma'am, but is this woman with you?"

Vega thought she could hear Londyn fill her lungs with screaming energy before she shrieked, "She's trying to blackmail us!"

Meaty hands grabbed Vega's upper arms, and Vega knew that the dress, her makeup, the rest of the night was about to be toast. She nodded at Londyn as they yanked her down the hall. "Bye, babe. Don't forget"—to Phillip—"the fucking you're about to get is for the fucking you got."

Stacked shook her a bit. "Watch your mouth. You kiss your daddy with that mouth?"

"My daddy?" she said down at the hand before looking up into his growly face. "I would, but my momma died and left me in a strange man's house to be raised like a feral cat. Yeah, I suppose I'd kiss him with this mouth. Right after I bit his face off."

His lip curled back. They dragged her down the hall, and Vega tried to pull her arms out of their twin grips as her boots fought to catch purchase on the rug. With one look back at the ballroom, she wished she had more time. Between the arched columns, her eyes searched for Hoyt. He wasn't on stage or in one of the clustered groups, as she'd expected. Instead, he was moving through the crowd toward her. His face set in a kind of determination that said someone was gonna pay.

Vega smiled over her shoulder at him. She must be a vision of sexy in her slinky black gown being towed out of the party like a grifter.

Up to the men who had her: "Boys. It's been fun, but heads-up. Your boss is in-bound on your six."

Stacked gave her a shake for her impertinence. "Shut up."

From behind them came Hoyt's voice. "Do that again, and I'll personally see to it you never work again."

Jacked and Stacked stopped abruptly and turned. "Sir?"

"Release her." Hoyt punctuated it with a growled "Now."

"Sir. Yes, sir."

They dropped Vega without ceremony, and Vega shook out her arms, getting the feeling back into them and down to her fingertips. She said to the guards, simultaneous pats on the shoulders, "No hard feelings. Have a good night."

To them, Hoyt's voice held an edge of danger. "Get back to work."

They gave him a "Sir," before moving down the hall, chancing glances back as if they thought they'd see Vega somehow sinking 253 pounds of man all on her own. Which, of course, she had been dreaming of.

Vega couldn't resist. "My hero."

His gaze went to hers, and she could see the dark shadows were deeper up close. That night was a strain on him.

"What are you doing here?" he asked, and Vega watched his hand move—to touch her, cradle her arm, or rest on her hip? She didn't know which because he tucked it into his pants pocket before he did.

"Taking care of some business. You?"

He stepped in closer, so Vega had to stand up straight to look him in the eye. "What business could be had here at a gala for you, Vega?"

Her eyes roamed over his mouth before answering his amber eyes. "Protection."

That oddly seemed to satisfy him. "Did you complete your mission?"

"Yes."

"Now what?"

"As you were witness to, I was just leaving."

"Were you?"

"I was. There are some aggressive guards here for some reason."

He gave her a whisper of a smile; the glint in his eye was returning. "Thanks for letting Nate in."

"No problem. Although he wasn't happy I helped him out."

He took in her face as if he were an appreciator of fine art. "He's not."

She let out a soft huff of a laugh. "You have weird friends."

"So, is this goodbye?"

Vega took in the buttons on his tux coat and counted them with her fingertip, five in total and made of obsidian.

"Vega."

Back up to his eyes. "Yes?"

"Join me? Stay." His eyes were growing lighter by the second.

"Are you sure you know what you're doing by asking me to stay?"

"I believe you're the only person here who has the ability to make this night interesting."

She matched his whisper, touching his silky lapel. "Are you about to fuck shit up, sir? Because no one who asks me to stand next to them has highbrow ideas."

"I believe I've earned the right to, tonight, fuck shit up, only, very politely." He held his hand out.

She put hers into his before he tucked it like a gentleman into the crook of his elbow. "Why, then, yes, sir, I'll join you. But no photos. Please."

His grin washed over her like ocean spray. "By the way, you clean up real nice, Ms. Flux."

She looked down at herself, how the belt shaped her into an hourglass, and flicked invisible lint off the gossamer black gown that billowed like a cloud around her when she walked. "Joke's on you," she said as she tucked her silver nails in tight. "I might look the part, but I can't dance the waltz, and I've already promised a guy you'd pay for every kid in the city to go to college."

He laughed, loud and ringing, causing more than one set of eyes to land on them. Fuck yeah, she thought, he was her kind of man. He might not officially be hers, but for that night, she'd own the hell out of him.

CRASH 'N' BURN_

HAVING VEGA FLUX ON HIS ARM FELT LIKE HAVING THE POWER AND HEAT of Pele, the goddess of volcanic fire, at his side. It was dangerous to have her there—especially if she was there for some protection thing—but having her close, he could, for just a night, keep an eye on her, talk to her, see if she'd tell him anything more about that quantum technology she pretended to not have. He texted his assistant to add another plate next to him for Joan Arc, and it would be the first time he had looked forward to a gala dinner.

On the dance floor, Hoyt thanked his years of dance training, done first for coordination on the football field and then to impress at events. With Vega pressed up against his body and the music moving into a rare tango beat in the heavily waltz-weighted playlist, he put his hand against her back and pressed her body against his. He bent his head, putting his mouth to her ear. She smelled like waffle cones and lemonade. "Follow my lead, and you'll be fine."

"And if—"

His grip tightened up, and he pushed them across the floor. The strings set a quick beat to ensure pulses stayed high. Her hand firmed up at his shoulder as his legs pressed between hers in an intimate walk that could easily be leading her to bed.

"Oh," he heard her utter, as the music's staccato beats punctuated their steps. He hadn't ever loved dancing as much as he did right then. Vega was trying to look over her shoulder to see where they were going, to anticipate their movements, when he reminded her against her ear, "Let me move you."

"I'm trying to."

"Look at me."

She did, but without ease.

"Do you trust me?"

She closed her eyes then, and he felt something give. She pressed her chest against his before whispering against his jaw, her breath warming his skin, "I trust no one."

"Not with your life. With this, trust me, just with this. That I won't plow you into another couple."

Her head rested on his lapel, and he hoped she couldn't feel the pound of his heart against her cheek. The pound that said he was in trouble. He'd lied to himself that she was just business. The physical demands of the tango required his hands to be active on her body, to push with his pelvis and chest against hers. His hands on her back and hip pressed her even closer; he released, twirling her out as if he were done with her, only to hate the cold emptiness he'd sent her to, and he yanked her back.

Finally, she fell into step with him, her body languid and fluid. "This dance is erotic. I can't figure out if I should—"

He pushed her out before pulling her back in again, feeling the strain on his tux's shoulders.

"Be embarrassed at all the people watching us have sex with our clothes on, or if it's really just dancing we're doing."

"It's just dancing," he murmured without conviction. He felt it too, that hypnotic pace they were setting with their bodies that reminded him of the intimacy of full-bodied skin-to-skin contact.

The song came to an end too soon, and as he pulled Vega against him, a flash went off. Vega had turned her head, and he could see then what he'd done, put Vega in a spotlight by inviting her to dance with the evening's host. He put up his hand and smiled at the photographer as he tucked Vega behind his shoulder as the rest of the dancers caught their breath and laughed at the high-spirited dance.

Her fingers laced between his as if she was just as loathe to stop touching him as he was her.

To the photographer, he said, "Could you grab a photo of Zane for me as we head into dining hall?" He redirected the photographer, and with his hand still intwined with hers, he guided Vega outside through wide gilded glass doors.

Out into the cool night air and the well-manicured garden that held paths and alcoves within the shrubbery he walked with Vega. A water fountain, modeled after the statue *Portlandia*, burbled and splashed, filling the air with aquatic white noise.

"Sorry about that." He added, "Maybe dinner might be too high profile."

"It's all right, Titan. This was worth staying for as long as I did. I should go, though."

Thinking about her leaving made him feel as if something precious was being taken from him. He asked her a question to prolong their time together. "Was that your first time ballroom dancing?"

Her lips, as red as the stripes on the Hawaiian flag, broke into a grin. "How'd you guess?"

"The panic."

"Yeah, I haven't done anything so highbrow...ever. Or so erotic. How is that legal without a license?"

He just smiled as they walked past the splashing fountain; Vega knocked a small pebble down the path with the toe of her boot. Then she pointed at the gate on the far end of the garden. "I'll take my leave. Goodnight, Billions."

"Wait a second..." His wrist vibrated, and he mumbled, "My assistant."

"Your assistant?" she asked, walking backward down the path.

His finger swiped up and read the cryptic message Hector had sent him. Something about Londyn apparently suing over photos. "Londyn photos?" he mumbled.

Vega paused, and her gaze went by him, looking back into the gala. He watched her swallow before asking, "What's that about photos?"

She looked as if she knew the answer. "Vega..."

"Strange you should hear about that from Hector. What'd he say?"

"Londyn is looking to sue the person who gave some photos to her, and Hector is making sure I know about it."

Vega's lip lifted in disgust. "So she's really going to try then, huh?"

Hoyt felt his guts bottom out. "It was you. What did you do?"

Vega turned her smoky gaze, blurred at the edges with iridescent silver, back to him. "In a moment of curiosity, I followed her, trying to find out what kind of woman earned the right to stand next to you. That's what I've done my whole life. I see something I want; I study it to find out how to do or become it."

In her tone, in her eyes, he understood her meaning. Her intent stole his breath and twisted his guts with a desire so strong it bent his mind as his imagination scrabbled to make Vega's words about becoming the woman by his side a reality. He squashed the dangerous urge to push her into an alcove and press his body against hers. She was volcanic. Too hot to touch, he reminded himself.

Swallowing hard, he kept it professional. "You wanted to learn how to become her? Explain how that is helping you breach Titan's Wall."

She looked around. "Is that what we're doing right now? And no, it's not. Man, those crab cakes were good," she said, eyeing the gala once more.

"You followed her. You took pictures?"

"Yeah, look," she said, avoiding his gaze, "it's done with, I'll have a little chat with Londyn and it, and I will be out of your hair."

"What pictures," he pressed, feeling like he was coming up against a hard defensive line. Vega was making him go slowly insane.

"I told you not to dig. This competition is about flexing your skill on Titan's Wall. Digging into my life any further will disqualify you."

She held up a hand. "I get that. I get that I'm not normal. I don't do things by the book, but I wanted to see who you deemed to be good enough to spend forever at your side. Who you spent time on to find a ring, get it sized for just her finger and slip it on, a smile on your face. Who you begged to have marry you."

"You've said that once before, and I'll remind you, that's not at all how that happened."

This made her eyes spark with curiosity as she agreed with him. "It's not, is it."

"What are the photographs Hector is talking about?"

She responded with a question of her own. "Why Londyn? Why her, out of all the eligible partners available to you? Why that particular one?"

"She was... She had been..." He nearly answered her. It was that way with her. No one else had ever tried to crawl into his mind like she did. *Get your shit tighter,* he admonished himself. He pinched his eyes. He felt like he knew her and could trust her, but could he really? There was a good chance he was seeing something that wasn't there between them, and he took a careful step back, knowing she doled out punishment to the unworthy. "Now, what is it really about Londyn that you're after? Whatever you've done to her to get to me, undo it."

Vega looked surprised before taking a breath as if to stabilize herself. "She's fine. Maybe a little too fine. She's got a lot more balls than I initially gave her credit for. I'll go now and sort things out with her."

She turned to go, and he hesitated to grab her.

"Vega." He heard the tone in his voice. He was losing his carefully maintained composure.

She turned back to him, and her hands fisted then released before she asked, "Do you believe in the saying that secrets make us sicker?"

He wasn't sure secrets and Londyn were something he wanted to get into with Vega, but it was like a train wreck he couldn't look away from. "Sure. Come clean."

She blew out a breath. "I like you. I don't like most men because, in my experience, most men aren't nice."

He was getting impatient. "I'm not nice."

"Egotistical? Maybe. But compared to me? You're a sweetheart."

"Spit it out."

"I've been monitoring your devices since the day you visited me. I spread out to Londyn's phone, and two days ago, I trailed her. Like I said, I wanted to learn about her but realized you two lead separate lives. Then, now, *right now*, I can't help but think, are you like that with all the women you're with? You get them then can't keep them? You said putting a ring on her finger didn't happen the way I described. How did it happen? Hector get the ring and give it to her? You couldn't be bothered?"

He stopped listening after she said that she'd been monitoring his devices since the day he first visited her. He felt the shadow of her metaphoric hand slip into his pocket and touch his phone. *How?* He'd checked his phone. More than once. *Fuck.*

"You have a bot in my phone… How far did you get? Did you already breach the wall?"

"I just asked you about Londyn, and your question is about your firewall?"

He felt her temper flint. About right since that was where he was at too.

"Did any of the women you've been with ever matter to you? Or are they just an item on your to-do list? Get milk. Get eggs. Get laid."

He snapped back, feeling the control of Hoyt Securities slip out of his hands and into hers. "Answer me about tha' bot. An' get the fuck off my personal life. I can't be any clearer—it's none of your business."

Vega nodded, shaking a lock of dark hair loose. "You're right—it isn't." She pulled something out of the back of her belt. Her phone.

"What are you doing?"

She angrily looked for something on it. "I gotta ask. Because I didn't think you were like them. I didn't think you were like the rest. But maybe you are. Maybe this year of being good has killed my instincts." Back at him: "Did Londyn ever matter to you? Or did you wear her like an expensive timepiece to show off your wealth? Did all your money and power make you lose touch with your humanity, and because there's so many of us, you just took what you wanted from Londyn, giving her nothing of yourself in return? You can get another when you're done with her, and she had your money, so she should be happy too, shouldn't she? Guess what, girls need hugs too, fuckface."

Her words made his flinting temper catch fire. "Wha' the fuck you take me for?" His hand went to her arm holding her cell and gently wrapped his fingers around it before gripping tight. Vega's gaze darted to his hand, and she let him steer her farther into the alcove and push her up against the green shadow of the conifer hedge.

"Careful, Billions," she growled.

His breath was catching in his chest as his head swam with colliding emotions. He wanted to fight, fuck, and scream all at once.

"I am. Always." He whispered, "I'm going to let that comment slide 'bout how I treat women, because I owe you nothing. Do you understand me? *Nothing.*"

"But?"

He hated that she didn't react to him like others did. Instead of being intimidated, she looked him in the eye and asked for more. It felt like she was under his skin, poking around to reveal something he hadn't ever told a soul.

It felt ripped out of him: "Londyn...broke what we had when she devalued the things tha' make me who I am. It was she who said she couldn't love a brute like me."

Her chin flinched as if she'd been hit.

He continued, "What's in your phone? Proof of the breach?"

"Brute? Bullshit. Of course she can." Then demanded from him: "What do you mean by that? Why would she say that?"

"Those words were from her own mouth; now, what kind of blackmail are you about to hit me with?"

IT'S NOT BLACKMAIL_

LONDYN HAD TOLD HIM THAT SHE COULDN'T LOVE A MAN LIKE HIM? Vega put her palm at the center of her forehead and rubbed. What was she doing? It had been clear from the penthouse alone, Londyn could only love herself. But now Londyn was pushing things, exposing Hoyt to shame and embarrassment.

Those photos on her phone, which were insurance, would be like a nail through his chest. She should just put her phone away and leave. She should find Londyn and finish things.

Hoyt wanted her phone, however, and his hand gripped tight around her wrist and turned it. "Shit, Hoyt, no. Stop. It's not blackmail." Her guts bottomed out as she pointed her phone down. But he was strong enough to lift her arm so he could see it.

Vega dropped her phone, and it hit the ground, and for the first time in the history of phones, it didn't crack, its screen, crystal clear, spewing its toxic contents. "Shit, no—"

Curses whined out of her as Hoyt's hand fell off her. She dropped to her knees covering the phone. Her finger closed the window, but open in another program was the five-second recording she'd taken from Londyn's device. Moans cried out from her dinky cell's speakers. The video was pressure she hadn't needed to put on Londyn earlier when she confronted her and Patel. Pressure that now was a bomb in Vega's face. "Close your eyes," she said to Hoyt. "Fuck. I'm dumb. Cover your ears."

She fumbled with her phone, her hands having gone numb with her own shame coursing through her body. She got it stopped and looked up. Hoyt hadn't closed his eyes. Instead, they were like obsidian stones as they took in the phone and Vega on her knees. Coarse pebbles scuffed her knees and panic at what she'd just done paralyzed her.

"Hoyt, I'm sorry."

"Are you?" His voice had gone as stony as his gaze. "This feels like a kind of punishment you'd dole out. Tell me, what have I done to deserve this?"

Vega's heart went cold as she felt her lungs go tight. She was drowning in her own guilt and shame. "Goddammit, this isn't punishment. I'm—"

"Then this *is* blackmail?"

Vega stayed on her knees. It felt appropriate to beg from there. "It's not blackmail. I didn't go looking for this... I've already confronted her—"

"Where are the photos?"

"Londyn has them."

"You expect me to believe that you breached security tonight, after tailing a woman I was seeing, just to play some misguided protector of me?" His gaze cut to hers, and his eyes were the dark orbs of a shark. "I'm not someone you fuck with, and right now it feels like you're fucking with me. So, Ms. Flux, before I torch your life, tell me how much those photos and that snippet are worth to you."

Vega felt the heat of his threat pull her up off the ground. He was a man who could indeed torch her life. One call, and she'd be in prison. What little trust that she'd given him shattered. As she stood, she moved angles, putting the alcove's opening at her back. She opened her phone and sent him a copy of Londyn's sexcapades before having him watch as she deleted the photos and video off her phone.

His lip lifted in disgust as his wrist chimed with an incoming file download.

"What I won't do is repeat myself, so listen closely." She pulled the dark cloak of the world she lived in around her shoulders and lied with the vehemence of a dream crushed. "Twenty thousand in small bills. Nothing larger than a five. I want it to be as tedious for you as you've been for me."

"I have that in my nightstand."

"Of course you do—"

"This is for being a man or being a billionaire? Or being smarter than you?"

His ego surfaced, and Vega felt her body go hot as a fire. "That's some shit talk from a man who's got my bot worming through his code making doors in your wall." She took a step back. "That twenty thousand is a down payment, because as we speak, my bots are sitting in your system waiting for my command to ignite." Bunny wasn't a worm nor an ignition switch, but Hoyt didn't know that.

This made him lose the last of his control, and he took a step toward her. "You *have* breached the wall. I told you just breach, don't fuck up."

She lifted her chin, hearing in those words an echo of what Cindy and Peace had also told her. She knew he was flexing on her only in his own defense. And despite this, her own emotional reaction to him swamped her. He didn't need the chaos she'd just brought him, but she couldn't stop it. It was old hat, and sometimes that hat fit so easy.

"I've been in for *days*," she said, taking another step. "Tell the authorities who I am and where I live, and I'll break Hoyt Securities in pieces so small your current life will seem like a far-off dream."

"Stop," he demanded. "What do you mean, days?"

"Breached, days ago. Should I start a fire so you can find me?"

His lip lifted in disgust. "I call bullshit."

She could feel her skin go blotchy with anger and hurt. "Just because you don't see me doesn't mean I'm not there. That's what you men forget: it's always quiet before the storm, and this girl wants to start a hurricane. So, how about I send you a screenshot of a few client files or, let's say, your emails that come through tonight? Or turn the power off for a week?"

"You do that, and you won't like what you've started."

She took another step back then another before shaking her head and uttering, "What's the point? I already hate what I've done."

Vega left him there. His smoke-and-whiskey gaze burned her skin as she walked away toward the far gate of the gardens. She made her way through the darkened conifers, not seeing the boxy hedges or overflowing pots of winter flowers. She wanted only to be out of there and running. To save what she had of her life before he could find her online warren and torch her. She'd have to start again in another city. Cindy and Peace would be furious. She had bet big and lost everything.

MURDER MY FEELINGS_

Vega, her emotions charred, stalked into the two-bedroom bungalow a mile from her warehouse in Southeast Portland still in her black gown and soaking wet from the rainstorm she'd walked in. The flat-screen TV on the far wall played monotone music while showing a woman taking a cock the size of an anaconda down her throat. The house was as filthy as the last time she'd been there to see Jax, who was now on the couch with more women than should reasonably be on one asshole.

Vega slammed the door, causing empty red cups to fall off the table in the adjacent kitchen. She dripped onto the carpet as Jax, half-naked, looked up from between a pair of unusually pert breasts. "What the fuck?"

Vega, hating herself and the hurt she'd seen in Hoyt, held her hands out at her sides. "You want a go or not?"

The pill-dealing frat bro, who Vega noticed was attempting to grow a short patchy beard on his overly bronzed face, looked at the three women on him. "Join us!"

Vega wanted to murder him. "I don't do groups." She peeled two hundred dollars in twenties from the stack of cash she should have used for her Uber rides that night tucked in the back of her belt and held the bills up to the women. “Stay or take two hundred and go.”

All three looked to each other before making a collective decision that two hundred dollars was better than Jax.

“No, no! Don’t go!” Jax grabbed for the women as they slipped off him, his pants around his knees; his dick, red and wet, flopped around dizzyingly.

They grabbed their things, pulled on shirts and skirts, and gave Vega a once-over before snatching the bills from her hand.

“Aw! Come on, Joan!” he said, using the only name he knew for Vega. “You would have had a blast! We were all juiced and ready to go!” Jax tucked his softening penis into his athletic shorts.

She snapped her fingers. “Up” was all she could manage. She’d come there for one thing and one thing only: she had to murder her feelings, and Jax was the knife that could gut her.

She’d been so careful for so long. Men always came then left. Always. But this one, this one was different, and she had to rid her body of his beauty; it was toxic to her system. She was afraid she would always want more from him, and after tonight, she knew he’d never give it. The most devastating part of all was that she’d lost the prestige of being in his presence, and the only thing she wanted now was to gnaw her own hand off to stay there. But she was stronger than that. She was her own kind of titan, and because the one person she could consistently rely upon was herself, she’d get what she wanted. And what she wanted was a man on his knees. And with the lights out, Jax would do.

“Whoa,” he said with a nervous laugh as she pushed him down the hall to his bedroom. The sixties orange-and-mustard short shag carpet was stiff under her boots. Pushing him onto his bed, she watched as he eagerly shoved his athletic shorts down again. “Fuck, you’re hot when you’re like this.”

She wanted that 253-pound All-American football tight end from Maui, even though she hated him. The things he said hurt. *Ms. Flux, before I torch your life...* She could feel the crack of their camaraderie snap in half as he accused her of being nothing more than a blackmailer and not smart enough to gain access to his systems. That she was just a hustler there to punish him for being a man. It still burned. Even though it was she who had been rough with him. But it wasn't her place to wait for him to calm down then try once more to explain. She had rules. And Vega had already begged from her knees once. She'd not do it again.

"Where's your rope?"

His hands stilled. "My what?"

Vega was pulling out drawers and letting them fall to the floor. Lube and condoms fell to the floor. She found the bondage rope on the upper shelf of his broken bookcase and rewinding the wad of it, looked at him sprawled on the half-made bed.

"Feet and hands" was all she could manage to say without her voice breaking. Men like Hoyt didn't connect with women like her. How, she asked herself, had she expected the interaction that night to have gone? That he would have danced all night, put her next to him at dinner, then slipped a ring on her finger? Did any of that scenario exist in the reality that was Vega's life? It didn't. The only relationship she had had with a man for more than a night was the one who was about to be tied down. And he knew nothing about her.

Looking like a jack-o-lantern at the sight of the rope in her hands, Jax sprawled his buff upper arms to the headboard and his legs that missed leg day on the regular to the footboard. "Remember, *Barney Rubble* is my safe word. I want pancakes served in bed for being a good boy. And two hundred dollars, same as you gave the ladies." He waggled his eyebrows at her.

Vega swallowed. She had condoms and Plan B in her belt, if she lost her goddamned mind. Evidence of how far her expectations had fallen that night.

"Deal."

As she tied Jax's wrists to the bedposts, she could feel Hoyt's disgust on the back of her neck. He'd ask her what the fuck she was doing. He'd tell her to be that warrior she was for every other woman online, to fight for what she wanted, to prove him wrong.

Her hands started to shake. Jax looked down over his sculpted and waxed pectorals to where Vega was squatting with his second ankle. The smell of his cologne was giving her a headache. A bead of sweat dripped down from her hairline, and she wiped it away with a shoulder shrug.

"You OK, man?"

"Fuck you," she said, stood, and hit the lights.

"Aw, yeah, baby, fuck me raw." She heard him test the restraints, making the metal frame creak.

Vega's insides roiled. She picked up a sock off the bed and rammed it into his mouth. "Shut up."

He squealed in delight.

She felt a hot tear of her own failures work its way down her cheek. Vega looked to the bed and the eager wriggling outline of Jax and took her belt off. "Fuck it."

DEFENSE_

"Why'd she dump you, Hoyt?" his mom asked after giving him a hug and his cheek a quick kiss.

His dad was finishing chopping what she needed for the midnight chow fun that would feed twenty.

And his cousins, two of his three brothers, and Lei were also in the house, though, mercifully, only Lei was at the kitchen island.

Londyn's things were gone from the penthouse since the night of the gala, but now Hoyt didn't want to be at the penthouse either, so after work, where he'd maniacally checked and rechecked systems, Hoyt had come to the family home. It being the middle of the night, he hadn't expected anyone to be awake, let alone cooking a feast. But he should have known—his troubles had a ripple effect in his 'ohana.

"She didn't dump me, Ma," he said, scrubbing his face. He should just go to a hotel.

Lei countered, pointed at her phone, "Yeah, but that's not what she's saying. Well, she's been weirdly quiet. So, not what her friends are saying that she said."

He squinted at his sister, hoping she could feel the darts in his gaze. "How do you even know what her friends are saying?"

"As soon as she announced she was dating you, they friended me."

His mother turned from the stove, pointing a spoon at Hoyt. "This is the third one. What she do? Yawn when you tried to talk tech with her? How dare she!" she said sarcastically.

Hoyt thought he'd reply with a dose of Vega-style honesty. He didn't like to upset his parents, but his insides were on fire, and he couldn't quite put his finger on the exact ignition point. "She was stepping out on me with the Woodland Sushi restaurant guy."

The room went silent, and he realized in the silence that the TV in the adjacent living room had been muted too. Everyone wanted to hear better. "The one downtown?"

Hoyt gritted his teeth. "Or the one in Southeast or... All the same guy."

Lei's jaw was slack. "How do you know this?" She looked down as her phone vibrated, then back, her gaze chastising. "I texted Sam earlier when we found out, lawyer cousin Sam, not Lesley's husband Sam. He says he was there at the gala, but you were too busy with a girl in black to talk with him? So, you stepping out too?"

He glared at her. She was the most like him, questioning, loud, headstrong. Quick to assumptions. "What do you think?"

"I think you're not telling us everything."

So, gripping his hair as if that could relieve the pressure in his head, he told them everything. About Vega, everyone. The only thing he left out was that, if he was being honest with himself, he'd played a part by not rousting Londyn sooner.

His mother stood in front of the stove, spoon frozen mid-stir.

Hoyt looked to the stove. "Should I stir that?"

His mother shook off the shock as Lei exclaimed, "Londyn, that bitch! I'm going to smack her off her heels! Who's this Vega? How do I get ahold of her and thank her?"

"Vega Flux is a ghost."

His sister blinked, "What'd you say? Flux? Not like the notorious hacker flux_capacitor, though, ya?"

Hoyt nodded. "One and the same." He was done keeping her a secret.

Lei swallowed and put her phone down, then picked it up. Then stood. Sat back down. "Oh, Hoyt." Her tone called him a moron.

"Spit it out."

"I know her. And you know who she is to me," she said pointedly, but he didn't and was glad when she continued, "My roommate in college, remember?"

"Yeah," he lied.

"She got drunk at a college party, and a guy took naked pics of her and posted them online. Her parents' life, her life, everything got toasted by this guy. He did this to, like, thirty other girls too. My roommate lost her scholarships. Then she stopped eating... They sued him, but their court date kept getting pushed out... Hoyt...this was the shit—"

"Language," their father said from the end of the island where he was tasked with folding wontons.

"Sorry, Dad. Hoyt, this is the pilikia you were talking about defending against even back then, trolls on the internet. It's like the Wild West; law enforcement doesn't have the resources to track down every offender.

"When she stopped eating, I knew I had to do something. You were too busy with football." He grimaced, but she waved her hand. That wasn't the point. "And my computer science advisor...she pointed me to this flux_capacitor. It took about a week to find the right message board for her, but she... Man, I can't believe this. You, like, *know* her." Lei just looked wide-eyed at him.

He was impatient to know what Vega had done. "What happened?"

His parents were also. "Yeah, Lei, what happened?"

"Oh, um, just, everything. She took down the pictures, of course —but, like, all traces of them. Then..." Lei leaned back in her bar-height chair. "Since there were still so many girls he'd done this to... She, um, I don't condone this, but she, um..."

Hoyt had a good idea of what she did. "Destroyed his life." He had

had a taste of what that would be like and didn't want to have a full meal of it.

Lei nodded. "Last I checked, he's still in every database of wanted criminals, registries for pedophiles and convicted felons... His life has effectively been blown up. There's no social media presence either." She sighed as if it were hard to have a hero with a dark side. "My old roommate is teaching up in Seattle, married, two kids, living her best life. I don't think she'd have that if flux_capacitor hadn't stepped in. And the other women this guy targeted, my roommate found two of them—they didn't know what had happened; they attributed it to God hearing their prayers."

Hoyt put his thumb into the corner of his eye socket to see if that would relieve some pressure there. "Sounds like her."

Lei looked at him like they were kids again and he was a cool big brother. "My hero knows my brother." She pronounced it *bruddah*. She reached over and smacked his shoulder. "What the hell are you doing here?! Go! Go find her, grovel, beg, anything to get her back. Maybe put some moves on her if she's into 'roided-out dudes who used to wear spandex."

He looked at her sharply. "'Roided out? Thanks, kika. You're an asshole."

"Hoyt," his father said in warning as his mother said to Lei, "Stop picking on your brother."

"Look," Lei said to Hoyt, "my bucket list would like to add her as a sister-in-law. So, if she's willing to do what she did for you? There's a chance she might want to sleep with you." Fingers laced under her chin, she begged, "Do it. Marry her. I need this, Ho'oooooo!" she crooned.

His dad stood, seemingly under the impression that Lei's begging would move him to see Vega that night, and food was the obvious gift to bring. "I'll get to-go containers."

"'A'ole, Dad. Lei, I'm not going to pursue a relationship with her."

"You just murdered the little kid in you that spanked off to all those superheroes in your comic books, Ho'o."

He ground his teeth. "You're fired."

"Keiki..." their father warned his children.

"Why not pursue her, huh?" Lei pressed.

"Because she's blackmailing me."

The silence returned to the room.

"With what? Why? What'd you do?"

"She was going to destroy my company. And she can."

"Why?"

"She just made vague threats."

"Tell me *exactly* what she said."

Hoyt sighed and didn't see what the point was but did and gave thorough details to piss her off, but the opposite happened. His mother and his sister now watched him with wonder as if his ignorance was shocking.

"What?"

Lei was incredulous. "You're a lōlō, Hoyt."

His temper caught at the red button his sister knew was there. "I'm not a moron!"

"She said it wasn't blackmail, Ho'o!"

He shouted back, "You don't understand—"

"What can't we understand!"

His mother pointed her spoon at them both. "Kulikuli, you two." Then she pointed the spoon at Hoyt and swept it out the door. "Go see her. Apologize. I didn't raise you to be like that."

"I'm not going anywhere tonight. I have to think. She can single-handedly take down Hoyt Securities."

"Has she?" his mother asked.

"That's not the point. She wanted twenty thousand..." Hoyt remembered then how her eyes had gone from begging while she'd been on her knees to flinting when he'd threatened her in return. Only, maybe what he'd registered as a threat hadn't been one; maybe he'd more been reacting to the jolt of finding out that Hoyt Securities was not impenetrable. That still shocked his system.

His father sat back down as if unsure he should get the to-go items as his son worked through his thoughts.

His mom said, reading his body language, "So, Lei is right—she a protector, then? The other night at the gala, she went there to protect you, Ho'o?"

Hoyt's face was back in his hands. He should just go to a hotel, except it'd probably be even more tormenting, alone with only his own thoughts spinning. "No, this is punishment for something I didn't see."

Lei was back on her phone. "Sam followed up with some video... He took it to show his fiancée as a possible wedding location and said he caught this." His mom came around the corner of the island, spoon still in hand, and watched over Lei's shoulder as the video caught Vega having cornered Londyn and Phillip. Phillip had photos in his hand. Hoyt knew what those were. Phillip and Londyn were incensed. He couldn't hear what was being said before his guards arrived and hauled her off.

"That the Vega girl?" his mother asked.

All he could do was nod, realizing she had indeed been there on Project Valkyrie business. Protecting him from what Londyn had been doing with a sushi magnate and what could become fodder for newspapers and shame for his family. He murmured, "My personal nightmare and...Valkyrie."

His mother's eyes shot to him. "Not Valkyrie. You know who this is..." She let that statement balloon into the room. She pointed out the obvious that his emotions had clouded: "Manō has grown legs."

"She is not manō."

His mother's eyes went wide at his retort, and Lei slid back in her bar seat to be out from between the two of them.

His mother pointed the spoon at the screen still in Lei's hand. "She protected you from a woman who wanted you for nothing more than the money you gave her." The spoon was pointed at him next. "Where is it? Show me."

He looked up at the ceiling as if it were a portal off earth. "Ma."

"Show me."

"Ma."

He knew as soon as she saw it, her point would be proven, and he didn't like thinking of Vega as his 'aumakua, his manō, but he undid the top button of his dress shirt, his work tie was long gone, and reached in, pulling out the tooth.

Lei said, "Maybe she's not manō, but manō is guiding her."

Hoyt took a deep breath and waded into his childhood and its spiritual depths. Could a piece of his home have crossed the Pacific and touched a woman here? "Maybe, but she wanted money for the pictures," he said weakly.

"Did she ask for money first, or did you make that fat assumption, brother of mine who thinks nothing in life is free?"

"It's not."

His mother tsked, went back to the stove and dropped the last ingredient, chopped green onions, on the chow fun, and said again, "I never taught you that."

He pushed up from his seat, ready for his bed upstairs and the long night that awaited him thinking about how everything had gotten so fucked up and what a pissed-off hacker with quantum tech could do to his carefully maintained ecosystem at Hoyt Securities.

"Ho'o." His sister caught his attention. "If she's flux_capacitor, the things she's done to level the playing field for women, and especially for women in the gaming industry and in tech, I'm sorry, but I just don't see her going after Londyn one moment then blackmailing you the next."

"Manō..." he heard their mother say at the stove.

Lei shrugged. "Manō or not, it's cool someone of her caliber wanted to be close to you. Maybe you could be her friend back? Ask her about the twenty grand. I bet it's not what you think."

SPIRALING_

The night after the gala, Vega was back in her dark lair at the illuminated *U*-shaped command center, the light from her monitors the only ones in the room. She'd washed Jax's place off her body. Twice. And Bunny had found a printer with old software he'd gotten to know in the mailroom at Hoyt Towers. The printer was connected to the data infrastructure of the building, and using it, Vega accessed the server room and downloaded her crew of apps.

She'd promised Hoyt a good game, and now it was on. She'd set up a virtual computer on an innocuous data server, and from there she would tunnel into his base-level binary code of the security software until it couldn't recognize where she began and it ended. It'd take time—this was like manual labor for her programs—and she had to let them run. Unlike breaking 512 KB encryption layers with the Juggernaut, this was caveman work. She picked up her stress ball and squeezed it. Then she stood and went to her snack pantry. Jax hadn't helped, and now she was worse off. She could feel a spiral coming on. A spiral that would end in a penthouse across town.

She wondered what that man in his tall tower was doing. If he was pulling the strings needed to indeed torch Vega's life. She should be running, but something was keeping her from doing it. That thing was his reputation. It was the paperwork locked in his desk. Vega remembered back to when she had first started to hear about him; his reputation then was of a good guy. This Clark Kent type who had created code at a *state* university that was causing a stir. Then it eventually became the protection standard in the industry. He was walking, talking protection, and it was that which made her want to stay, to hope that, despite her being his antithesis incarnate, deep down he might notice they were very much the same.

Vega had spent the day continuing to knock all the dominoes out of Londyn's hand before she could lay them down again. Vega wouldn't go after her fully, not like her boy toy, who was already hating life after the health inspector called. And again, when the OLCC pulled his liquor licenses at all five of his restaurants. It would be a banner year of suckage for Phillip after aggressively reaching too far off his mountaintop. He got to his peak in business, and instead of settling in and enjoying the view, he had tried to touch the sun. Like fucking a billionaire's fiancée without consequence. Vega "helped" Phillip reprioritize his life. That kind of business strain was what had been missing, just a little life-affirming shake-up for him. Vega smiled with zero mirth. Her shame and anger would find its outlet.

For Londyn, Vega would use silk gloves to wipe away her social media sob stories. She'd make her ass pick up a phone and call someone to tell them. There would be no sad selfies or fluffy feels from emotionally distant people giving her false support. She'd have to sit in her own shit for what was likely the first time for her. It was tempting for Vega to post her cheating images to her social media sites, but Vega had rules. Sisters didn't tear down sisters. But hold them accountable? Yes.

Despite it being protection work, it wasn't what she really wanted.

She felt the itch to catch a ride across the river.

She texted her girls: *Where are you?*

Her perimeter alarms alerted her to a breach just before she heard a crash against the warehouse doors downstairs then laughter in the stairwell before her door burst open.

"Shit!" Cindy hollered. "It's dark! I thought you had auto lights!"

Vega felt their chaos pull her up from her nosedive toward talking to Hoyt, begging him to listen, that she wasn't blackmailing him. His forgiveness felt like it could save her world from crashing down. But also likely was that he was gunning for her. And that felt like a bullet to her heart.

"I did, but I put them out for tonight. I didn't know you were coming."

"But we got your text!" Peace said and with her lower lip sticking out grasped Vega's hoodie at her collarbone and shook. "You look sad. What happened?" Peace smelled like lemons and vodka.

"I thought you guys were Netflixing and chilling?"

"We were, but then Zane invited us out. Today was opening day for the administrators of Big Friends Bigger Hearts. Next week the facility fully opens for business, and who knows when we'll see each other again. Cindy was an absolute peach and said yes to delaying our Netflix and chill."

Cindy explained, "He's got reservations at places I thought I'd never see the inside of with my federal paycheck—I'm not gonna say no. I'll happily be a third wheel and pump people for information all night. Did you know that one of the other investors is friends with our state senator? Like, drinks-and-holiday-parties friends. These are good people to know."

Peace, flush from hours with Zane and a cocktail bar, pointed out, "But Hoyt wasn't there. Zane said he's not returning their texts."

At the mention of Hoyt's name, Vega's stomach pinched.

Cindy said, "Before here, we were waiting for a table at Munchies next door to Festivál. But it was an hour wait, so we ambushed you here. Plus, dream boat over there," she said toward Peace, who made her way to the rear were the toilet was, "had to pee. What happened, Vee? You showed them to him, didn't you? That's why he's not out."

From inside the bathroom, Peace yelled, "He's sad and crying over Londyn, isn't he?"

Vega wanted to hope that he was crying. She knew it wasn't over Londyn. She hoped he was pressing pause on nuking Vega's life because a part of him was scared shitless that she might indeed take down Hoyt Towers if he did. But then that didn't feel right. She'd already made him feel pain. She wanted to tell her girls to drive her to him so she could feed him ice cream while straddling his lap, begging him with each bite to forgive her.

Instead, she told them about the gala.

When she was finished, Cindy said, "Ugh."

The toilet flushed, and Peace emerged drying her hands and cried out in a kind of bittersweet angst, "But dancing with him... Oh my god, Vega, that must have killed you when he accused you of blackmail. After everything we've been through, that hurts." Peace's blue eyes welled with pain for Vega.

Vega wiped a crumb off her workstation. "Yeah, it did," she mumbled. She had wanted to dance more with him. If simply dancing with him felt that good, she couldn't imagine what being naked would be like. "I fucked up at the end there. He's a nice guy."

Cindy nodded but reminded her, "You shouldn't have gone; he didn't need protection. He's a solid man who can fix his own problems."

Only Vega didn't see it that way. She had seen a problem that needed fixing for a person she'd started to care about. She'd acted. Damn the consequences.

"This is why we have—"

"Rules," Vega finished.

"Exactly. So that we don't end up having to move you again," Cindy said then asked, "Any movement on his end? I assume you're monitoring him?"

"I am. He's spending the majority of his time at a home in the West Hills. Everything else seems normal."

"What do you want to do? You're already half packed from when he paid you a surprise visit two weeks ago."

"I know. No...I think it's fine. He's likely going to just move on. Hopefully, I'm too much trouble for him to actually invest any time in."

"Aw," Peace said, seeing below Vega's tough exterior, "you're not too much trouble."

"If I have to move, I'm doing it alone, Peace."

Peace looked at the ground. "OK," she whispered, "This time I'll let you..."

Vega added, "From now on, if I fuck up, it's just me that pays the price."

Cindy shook her head. "This is just a blip. I don't see Hoyt gunning for you, Vee. Not after that contract he set up for you. That was a set of soft and fuzzy handcuffs. He doesn't have that sociopathic billionaire thing that says he'll waste energy just to prove he's better than you. Now, obsessive about you? Yeah, I could see that. Who makes a contract that tight anyway?"

Beautiful egotistical maniacs, Vega thought, *that's who*.

And she knew the girls saw the clear reality of what was happening. Vega wanted Hoyt to want her back. But for her part, she had no idea how to make that happen. At the gala she learned that it wasn't with her brand of chaos that she could do it. That who she was, chaos in the darkness, was in effect a kind of repellent for good men. A person could fall in love and not know it until the rejection point. And that was new for her. Her feelings had gotten involved without her permission, and now her chest ached.

Peace, with a hiccup, tore open a bag of chips and shoved three into her mouth with a crunch. Around the salty pieces, she said, "I'm on Londyn's account right now. Do you think she's pursing her lips out that far on purpose? Is that sexually stimulating in some way?" Peace, still looking at her phone, pursed her lips, trying to perfect Londyn's pout. "Cindy's mom used to tell us when we crossed our eyes that if we kept doing it our eyes would stick like that."

Vega looked up. "Babe, what account are you looking at?"

"I'm saying!" Peace shouted as if it was her volume that was the problem. "She puts her lips out farther than her heart and gets stuck in performance mode instead of seeking fulfillment through self-love and building up those around her."

Vega was up and in the kitchen looking over Peace's shoulder. "No, what social media site is this? How many accounts does she fucking have," she whispered, not feeling like that was the point, but it was all her brain could manage right then.

Cindy murmured from Peace's other side, "What the..."

Peace said, enunciating slowly as if they were too drunk to understand her, "Londyn is looking for external validation via—"

"I know, hon," she said absently.

Vega didn't hear much else; she was back at her command center and scouring the alternate social media page Londyn was using. Then torpedoing it.

"Ew. She's making accusations that Hoyt had her followed and is now blackmailing her. Then she says, 'I should have known when a billionaire baller made me into a prized possession that he only wanted me for one thing whether I liked it or not.' What does she mean by that? It makes it seem like Hoyt was forcing her to have sex with him. And doesn't 'ballers' refer to basketball?"

Two sets of shining eyes stared at Vega as if waiting for her opinion.

Vega after a few keystrokes asked, "What?"

"Take it down."

Vega grinned. "What post?"

"And what does she mean by that?"

Vega knew, Londyn was making him out to be some kind of uncultured barbarian—his words, *Londyn...broke things when she said she couldn't love a brute like me.* There was a backstory there that she wanted to dig into. What was it that turned off a pampered shipping magnate's daughter?

"Who knows what Londyn is alluding to. And I'd rather not give it credence."

She watched as Peace refreshed the site, and seeing the account gone, Peace said, "Good. Because that was mean, and I'm sure she'll wake up tomorrow with a clear head and will be glad that account doesn't exist just so she could post mean things about him."

Cindy and Vega gave Peace adoring but sad smiles. "Sure, babe, let's live in that world."

Cindy raided the snack pantry before dragging a chair over and putting her heels up. "So, what's the next move?"

Vega watched Cindy try to catch the end of a long red straw of licorice as she replied, "Next move about what?"

"Hoyt."

"Monitor him. Properly break his system, like he wants me to." She gestured to her monitor where the programs were still running. "Then collect my million and a half. I'm sure he has that lying around, right? Get Scout the money she needs for the rest of her schooling, then get her a passport, then go dark for a while. I might need to move. We'll see how things shake out; fingers crossed we can stay on this path and not have to run from billionaire boy."

"Don't call him that."

"What?"

"Don't call him billionaire boy, like he doesn't matter to you."

Vega looked down at her hands and picked at the corner of her thumbnail. "He doesn't."

Peace had found queso dip and with a sloppy bite said, "You do care. No lying."

"Ugh!" Vega plowed her hands into her hair. "Why did I ask you guys over?"

"Because spiraling is worse."

Vega took a deep breath and stood, flipping a switch to small fairy lights that trimmed the room in atmospheric glow. "I know, I know, I just... Everything got intense, and it's over now, and I wish I'd never met him."

"But then you wouldn't know that you're good, if not better than this really hot billionaire tech genius and that you too could have a life like that."

"Thanks, Cin. But I can never have a life like that even if I didn't torch any potential tonight."

Around another bite of cheese dip, Peace said, "We've already laid out the path, Vee, for you to go clean. That's what we tested this last year. And you did good. We're," she said, gesturing between Cindy and herself, "taking care of everything we can aboveboard, and what we can't, you get. It's working. And Scout should have been told at eighteen who she really is—"

"This isn't about Scout," Vega said then defended her decision: "She's Scout. And being Scout is all she knows, and that is enough for her. She's happy. Moot point. Why are we talking about Scout?"

Ignoring her question, Peace pressed, "If she knew, then you wouldn't have to do illegal stuff for her identity and you could get on with living your own life. Unless you don't want to because you're scared."

"Fuck you," Vega whispered.

Peace blew her an air kiss. "Love you too, hottie babe with a lotta leg."

"It's not so simple. And what if I'm scared? You guys know how precarious this is. She doesn't need the baggage of her original, and stolen, name. We've been too lucky with that crazy day you guys had to grab her and run; she either blocked it or was too young to remember that day. Either way, she should live in bliss as Scout Flux. She has to focus on school, not on who Harmony Alexander is. She's happy. I'm not going to wreck that."

They gave her twin arm folds with stares that said they understood but it had to be done in order for Vega to fully live a life outside of the shadows.

"I"—Vega needed them to understand—"I plan to tell her when she graduates. Jesus, why are we talking about this?"

"You said that at sixteen, then eighteen, and now at graduation? From undergrad or the bar?"

Vega shrugged. "I want her to be a lawyer so that when I tell her, she can understand the muscle of the law and not emotionally what could have been. Lloyd made decisions that I'm afraid she'll rationalize now as just our stepdad trying to do what was best so no one got shot. It's hard to explain the nuance of people tracking you down with a gun because they think you're the Melanie Alexander who swindled them out of thousands of dollars. But you're not because your fucked stepdad sold your name and personal info so that someone else could use it to defraud people."

"That's a great place to start. Tell her that. She'll get it."

"And if she doesn't? He's one visit away at the state pen, and we all know what he can do with a sympathetic listener. Fuck, he sent birthday cards to Maggie every year for a while there, little reminders he could still get to us. That fuck."

"I know, but Vee, I think you're giving Scout too little and him too much credit in that scenario."

"Yeah, but whose paranoia has kept us alive and out of prison this long?"

Peace and Cindy answered, "Ours."

Cindy continued, "And, Vee, we know. You don't have to defend your childhood to us. We know. We helped get you guys out of there. We know."

Vega blew out a breath. She didn't want Scout having anything to do with that man. He could talk a mouse out of its cheese, and even in prison he likely still owed awful people more than he had.

"I don't want her in all this new independent glory she has now at college going down to prison and talking with him. To her, he's dead. That's why we were in foster, and that's why I got custody of her when I hit eighteen, so Maggie didn't have to answer questions and raise her by herself after Junior died."

"Breathe, Vega. It doesn't have to be today. But the passport is risky for you to get and for Scout to use. She should at least know the risks before she enrolls in this program and travels. Or, yeah, she might not forgive you."

Vega cursed. "Yeah, well. Just this last one. She's not ready for the truth. Soon, though."

Cindy rolled her chair over to Vega and put a hand on her arm. "Babe, I don't think this kind of stuff a person is ever ready for."

Peace came around the other side and wrapped her in a hug. "We'll do it together. Like we always planned."

Vega could only nod. There was a good chance that once she told Scout, she would want Vega out of her life. Vega needed that million-dollar prize money to find a new place to continue their Project Valkyrie work. Her place up in Seattle needed airing out. She probably would move there and keep her distance for a while. Somewhere she could give Scout space and somewhere from which she couldn't easily walk into Hoyt's office.

From the crook of her neck, in the folds of her hoodie and hair, she heard Peace say, "Hoyt could help here, you know."

"And how is that, exactly? The man is a domineering force for good and all that is in sync with the law. He's already admitted my warrant list scares him. Add my old Social Security number to the mix, and he'd have a heart attack. He won't want anything to do with this kind of baggage, especially after the gala. So, please, we're not adding him to the share list. I can't withstand being rejected twice by him, and you're drunk. These are all drunk ideas."

"But he's so hot, and he really likes you."

Vega's insides squirmed with anticipatory pleasure laced with angst. She didn't tell a soul, but her deepest, darkest thoughts told her she wasn't worthy of a man like him. She was the devil, and he was heaven's brightest angel.

Peace was still talking, "Zane says it's hard to talk to him now. Zane's worried that Hoyt is obsessing over work again. They lost him for a couple years while he started his business. Apparently, he can be a bit of a workaholic. But we all know that, really, it's our Vega." Peace leaned back and observed Vega like she was her sweet child, all through a vodka-fueled haze.

"Time for bed, Peace," Vega said, then to Cindy, "Netflix and chill?"

"Let's do it."

They pulled Peace toward Vega's enormous bed in the far corner where thick layers of faux fur blankets and fleece competed with plump, pale-gray flannel pillows.

Something began to buzz, and all three looked around for it before Peace pulled her phone out of her bra. "Our table is ready!"

CAN'T FORGET YOU_

The next morning dawned early and bright. Hoyt didn't believe in polluting his body with caffeine or alcohol—those days were over—but that morning he needed one of those aromatic chai latte things that his staff got in the executive lounge. Lei found him there struggling to get the machine to work.

"Jeez, you look like shit. Are your clothes mismatched?" she asked and plopped down the printouts she had in her hand and took his mug from him. "Here, I'll do that."

"Thanks," he said and leaned against the opposite counter. He'd slept through his 5:00 a.m. alarm and skipped his morning workout. In the reflections in the room, he could see dark crescents under his eyes and shadows in his cheeks, showing the world that he hadn't gotten to sleep until just before sun came up, for the third night in a row.

Lei was poking buttons on the colossal brass-and-black machine. "Masala chai is what you wanted?"

"Yeah."

More poking. "Mom says she can hear you tossing and turning and pacing in your room."

Now he felt even worse. He couldn't go home to the penthouse even if he wanted to because, in a fit, he'd told his cousin Cody, who'd been itching to renovate the place, that now was the time. Seemed good in the moment, to literally rip Londyn out of there...

When he said nothing, Lei added, "You talk with her yet?"

"Who, Mom?"

Lei shot him a dark look over her shoulder that reminded him of their mom. "No, the reason you're not sleeping."

"Yeah, no. She's not someone you casually text or email."

"You should."

"Why?"

"I found her breach."

That woke him up. "What? When?"

"Data logs show it was two nights ago. That tiny bot she put into your phone the night of the club had been dormant, from what I can tell, but there's a matching one in the servers. I'm still trying to debug the code, but I think I have a simple fix for it. I just need to know if we should restore an older version of our systems to before the night at the club or even before that? You didn't meet her before that night, right?"

"No, just the club..." Where she'd used her wits, and her body, to alter the course of every one of his thoughts from that point on.

His sister leaned against the counter as the machine hissed behind her. Her long black hair was twisted up in a bun held by a koa stick. "What are you thinking Ho'o? I can hear that mouse on a wheel in there."

"Leave it open."

"What? You lōlō??"

"Leave it open. Let her think that we haven't detected her yet."

"Why? I mean, I'm a huge fan of hers, but, Ho'o, we both know that she has the potential to be dangerous, and I don't know how pissed she is at you."

"She won't do anything to compromise data." He hoped the night of the gala had been a bluff on her part; now that they'd found her in his servers, he was hopeful again. "And I want an opportunity to end-run into her systems."

His idea was off brand for him, and his sister knew why and mischievously grinned. "You still all huhū with her about her hacking your phone in under five minutes?"

"She has some kind of quantum computing capabilities; I think she's keeping quiet about having learned how to do that. I would too. Especially on the black market in the wrong hands, it can be dangerous."

"And in yours?"

"I could protect people from it."

The machine began to foam behind her. "You mean, destroy it?"

"No, learn how it works then defend against it."

"So, give you a huge leg up in the marketplace where you already dominate?"

"I only dominate, Lei, if I continue to be aggressive."

"Ho'o..."

"What?"

She tsked as the machine behind her beeped, signaling that it was done. She handed him the large ceramic Hoyt Securities mug with froth teetering on top as warm cinnamon, cardamom, and star anise filled the air. "You can pretend in your head that you don't care about the scary, pretty malihini girl who sets your guts on fire, but not with me. Vega is scary, but she's the kind of awesome that dovetails nicely with it, and I think you've never met your match outside of your days playing pro. And here she comes, and you can't get a read on her, and it freaks you out, but it's also a little bit exhilarating? Not to mention ticks every box on your list of fantasies."

"I don't have fantasies."

"Fine, weaknesses."

It was times like this that Hoyt mentally revisited allowing his relatives to work for him. "No, dangerous is a risk, and we pride ourselves on being risk adverse."

"So, is that why we're leaving her bots alone to freewheel around in our systems?" she asked gently. "'Cause we're risk adverse? Or is it that you wanna watch her? Watch the work she does and use quantum computing as the excuse to eventually break the silence you've got going on?"

"How do you know we've been silent? Maybe she's been in contact with me and I didn't respond?" He knew he was being childish with his baby sister, but he couldn't help it. Somehow his emotions had been caught, and try as he might, he couldn't unhook them from where they were snagged: on a woman who wore tight black jeans that looked like they were one swift tear from showing him all of her. And he couldn't figure out if he still had a chance to rip them off her or if it was dust in his hands now.

Lei interrupted his thoughts. "That little bot she wrote? I followed it back to your phone, and there are no scandalous texts from her or you to an unknown number in days. I also see why you're scared of her; she came in hot." Lei raised her brows as if to challenge her brother to tell her Vega didn't.

He put his mug down and scrubbed his face again, this time to try and clear his mind. "Fuuuuuuck."

He heard Lei laugh; she knew she'd hit the nail on the head.

"She messed with my mind. She doesn't respect boundaries and is a goddamn menace."

"And?"

"She's the smartest person I know in and out of tech, she's got street smarts, foundational mechanics and mathematics understood like they were the back of her hand, and, and..."

"And?"

From behind his hands, his voice was muffled.

Lei leaned forward. "One more time—I couldn't hear you."

He dropped his hands in defeat. "She's fucking hot."

Lei laughed, the sound chiming around the small office kitchen. "That's more like it. You're such a sucker for the underdog and anti-hero stories, and she's all that tied up with a black bow."

Hoyt grinned at his sister who was picking up the papers she'd brought with her. "Patel had to close all five restaurants until further notice."

She looked at him knowingly and shook her head. "She's doling out her brand of justice. I'm just surprised your ex hasn't posted about all the horrible things that have happened to her. It's unlike Londyn not to take a picture of her morning shit, filter on vintage, let alone not spew about her grievances."

He gave her a look. "What'd you say about justice?"

Lei was quiet a moment, processing what he'd said. "Oh. Vega?"

"No doubt."

"You need to go apologize to Vega for saying you thought she was blackmailing you. Even as mad as you said she was, she's defending you even now. You owe her twenty grand and an apology."

He picked up his mug. "I'll think about it."

He was at the door when his sister said, "You know..."

He took a sip of his piping-hot beverage. "What?"

"Nothing."

He glared at his little sister.

"What?"

"It's just..."

"I'm going to revoke your executive floor privileges."

She smiled at him as if he were cute. "I derive evil joy from watching you get flustered. Nothing ever ruffles you, but talk about Vega, and you're like a golden retriever with a tennis ball: you can't focus on anything but her. That, and if you were really risk adverse, you'd talk with her about the quantum tech, not spy on her. *Talk* with her, Hoyt, not text or email or call. Talk, in person."

"That requires being face-to-face."

"Don't be scared."

He grinned before departing. "Too late."

THAT NIGHT IN HIS ROOM, WHEN HE REALIZED HE WAS PACING, HE SENT A silent apology to his mother and fell back onto his bed. He checked his phone for the millionth time that hour and resisted the urge to open his laptop. They had tracked Vega's bots to a computer in the mail room at midnight before he decided to go home. Now, hands resting on his abdomen, he studied the cedar beams in the ceiling.

The place had been designed and built in the sixties for a wealthy businessman and his family whose numbers had been as big as Hoyt's family. Despite its peaceful placement and spacious layout, there was no way he'd get any sleep that night.

The last words Vega had spoken to him, *I already hate what I've done*, ran through his mind.

Now that he had had days to process that skirmish, he saw his own panic. He'd been blindsided that Vega had been there for him and Project Valkyrie. They didn't protect wealthy men in positions of power. She targeted them. That had led to him fumbling the conversation and blowing up the relationship. She was the one person who could break his wall and his life in an afternoon, and he'd flipped his shit on her. But calmer now, he realized what she was trying to tell him, that she was there to punish Phillip Patel and Londyn for what they were doing to him. Her continued efforts against Londyn's insidious social media narrative was proof positive that he was being protected, not destroyed. Her words threatening him had been her own defense, words she'd used only to hit back.

He groaned. They'd tangled, and both had gotten hurt.

I already hate what I've done. What did that mean?

He wondered if he should be hating what he'd done too, telling Lei to stand down. The heat Vega could bring against him, his company, his clients—she could easily glean information from their normally hyper-secure servers and sell it to the highest bidder. And he was putting it all at risk to end-run into her systems for a glimpse at her quantum computing technology. Lei was right—it was a risky game of chicken.

He needed to treat Vega just like anyone else. But she wasn't just like anyone else. He should have Lei and her team roll back the systems to punt Vega's bot out. But he couldn't do it.

I already hate what I've done.

If she truly did, then there was hope. Hope that he hadn't grossly miscalculated her.

Another hour passed before Hoyt gave in. He needed answers.

Dressed in casual pants and a hoodie, he slipped on sneakers and headed down the stairs. He ducked into the hallway, where his father was, surprisingly, waiting for him.

His father was tying the plaid terrycloth robe he'd won in an amateur golfing tournament before nodding toward the kitchen. "Come."

Following the tall older man with soft footfalls, Hoyt kept his voice low out of respect for the late hour. "Dad...you should be in bed. Sorry if I woke you."

He waved off his son's apology and went to the fridge and pulled out glass containers of leftovers from another midnight cooking episode and began reheating them.

"Makua kāne...I'm not hungry."

He nodded. "But *she* might be."

Hoyt felt the weight of what his father saw in him. "Right," he murmured. Vega was always hungry. He sat on the barstool at the edge of the kitchen island and scrubbed the exhaustion from his face.

After the click of the gas stove then the sizzle of cold noodles hitting a hot pan, his father said to him, "You need to make peace with her, ya?"

"Yeah." Hoyt was too tired to answer any way but honestly.

"It's her presence in your mind that made you wake up or kept you from sleeping?"

"'Ae." Hoyt felt the calm of his father's understanding demeanor —one that knew where that night was taking his son physically and emotionally and was willing to help him through it.

"And when she's happy with you, you feel like what?"

Hoyt thought of the few times Vega had flexed on him with a smile or acerbic sexual fantasies, and he answered, "Feels like a Super Bowl win."

His father's lips tilted up at the corners before he put the reheated items into fresh glass containers. "Good friends are like that. And it takes trust to make it last." He opened a thermal carry-all bag and placed the hot containers into it.

"Yeah, well, I'm not sure if I can trust her. I'm not sure she wants it. Me. My trust, I mean."

"Maybe not, but do you trust yourself?"

"Of course."

"And what does your gut tell you: Stay away or get closer?" His father already knew the answer to that as he zipped up the bag with hot food for her.

"Closer."

"Maikaʻi. Now, go make sure she understands that's how you feel." He came around the island with the bag and handed it to his son. Then hugged him. "Whether she can trust you back or not doesn't take anything from you. You give and leave it. If she wants it, she'll take it. But you lose nothing by being honest, with her and yourself."

"I'm not sure about that. I can't help but feel..."

His father helped him out. "Scared?"

"Yeah, but not because I can't do it. Because, because...what if I misread every interaction with her and she's not who I thought she was? That in all that darkness there isn't a woman who has an iron-clad sense of right and wrong when it comes to helping people?"

"Is that what you truly feel, or is that what your fear is contorting your mind to believe?"

Hoyt grumbled, "Fear."

"Fear of what?"

"Not getting what I want."

"What is it that you want?"

Hoyt swallowed down all the images that came to his mind—all of them were Vega, all her various smiles and her hand to his chest like it belonged there.

His father said, "I see. Come, let's get you going. You have fear to overcome." He patted Hoyt's back before resting his hand on his shoulder and walking with him to the foyer.

"Dad, mahalo."

He waved it off. "This one is different," he said as they stepped into the damp night. "You've never lost sleep over a wahine before. A game? A delayed product launch? All the time."

"She's an enigma, and I think she's one of the few people I've respected off the field. Besides you guys, of course. She's teaching me things I didn't know about myself."

His dad quietly nodded as if he knew a secret his son had yet to learn and was happy to see him having that experience of discovery.

"What?"

"It's not something I can explain, but your fear... You fear the pain of possible rejection from her?"

"Sure."

"And the thought of her accepting you feels like you're falling, drowning, achieving the unachievable while invincible?"

Hoyt was shrewd. "I'm not in love, Dad."

Curtis gave his son a soft smile of understanding. In the dim orange light of the landscaping lights, he patted the hood of Hoyt's SUV before saying, "Drive safe—keep it under the speed limit."

FORGIVE ME_

Vega stretched in her command center chair. It was almost time for bed; the sun would be up in another couple hours, and her plan for Hoyt Towers was nearly complete. As she stood, her external vicinity alarm popped up on her screen and made her phone buzz, alerting her that she had a visitor. Checking the camera, she saw Hoyt's SUV in the parking area. She froze. Then she picked up her phone to dial Cindy when the least secure of her phones on her desktop chirped.

This you?

Her stomach twisted as pleasure at having Hoyt so close and pain at not knowing why he was there mixed. She was reminded of his own set of haxor skills at being able to tap into one of her open cells to send a message. She picked up the phone and started to text back and, biting her bottom lip, as if that could keep her hands quiet, set it down. Being open to Hoyt was a precarious position to be in. She wanted it, him, but she also didn't want to go to prison.

I'm sorry.

It felt genuine. Or drunk. But knowing Hoyt, it was more likely genuine. He was up in the middle of the night and at her place because of a genuine need to apologize.

That got her thumbs working, but she would try to be careful.

Why?

Truth?

And nothing but the truth.

Then added:

Please?

You scare me. I was shocked by the video, and I made assumptions based on bad data. And breaching my phone made me panic. I think you might be able to relate?

She didn't want to answer. He'd firmly put her in the power seat and set her own fears aside. It made her sloppy. It made her want to take the steps two at a time until she was in his passenger seat. But that was his superpower against her, so she continued to tread carefully.

Still there?

She left the rest of his confession aside and replied:

Yeah, I can relate.

Will you let me in?

She watched the one human who made her knees feel like water get out of his vehicle as his thumbs moved over his screen. He stopped at his passenger door and took a bag out.

I have something for you.

What's in the bag?

She sent at the same time.

She watched a smile bloom over his face as he read her text.

Watching me?

Monitoring an incoming potential threat.

His smile fell. She resisted the urge to put it back on his face. That was chaos. What she was trying for was truth.

He looked like he'd just slipped from bed, casual pants and a hoodie. Or like he'd just finished saving the city like it was no big deal and came home to find he'd gotten locked out with a grocery bag on his arm.

I have your 20K. And food.

Drop the food.

Keep that fucking 20k.

Vega's stomach rumbled, reminding her that she'd not eaten more than M&Ms and a Coke that day.

Fine. But I wanna talk.

We're currently talking.

Face-to-face. This feels fake.

Vega rolled back in her chair, devoting her entire attention to her phone.

Locks didn't stop you before.

That magnet scares me.

Vega knew she should play it cool and send him on, but watching him and listening to him, she took a chance and unlocked the warehouse door. It was a slippery slope, what she was doing, letting him in. But her molecule of hope was back and furiously converting every cell in her body over to its cause.

She heard Hoyt close the exterior door and throw the deadbolt again, then make his way through the warehouse and up the stairs. Her heart had settled into a steady thundering rhythm.

He opened the door with a tentative peek then wider before stepping in.

Seeing her in the dim space there behind her command center he said, "Hi," before closing the door and leaning against it.

She nodded to the bag. "What's really in there?"

"Food."

"Sounds like a trap made just for me. Are you wired?"

He gave a wan, tired smile. "I hadn't thought of that. No, I just have food. The only catch is that we have to talk while you eat."

"No. Drop the bag and leave."

He watched her for clues to how she really felt and went with "Do you really want me to leave?"

"I just want to know why you're up in the middle of the night and at my doorstep and all you want to do is talk. That's a lot for 'just a chat,'" she said with air quotes, "that could happen in daylight hours."

He looked down at his shoes, almost sheepishly, Vega thought. "I couldn't sleep. I need answers."

"We all need answers. What questions could a billionaire have at my doorstep?"

"Do you like chow fun, wontons, and musubi?"

Vega's stomach growled loudly. *Traitor.* "Depends, where'd you pick up takeout at this hour?"

“My mākua, parents’, kitchen.”

Vega felt something new wash over her. “Your parents,” she murmured, incredulous, “made me food?”

“My mom’s been cooking. They’re fresh and really good leftovers.” But quickly added, “My dad reheated them for you under the strict orders that you’re to eat them while hot.” He gestured to the kitchen. “May I?”

He didn’t wait for her to answer but instead set the thermal bag down on her kitchen island. “Do you have a light switch in here somewhere?”

She was keeping her answers short, so she didn’t blurt something ridiculous like *Please, please, forgive me and take me back as your friend and possible hump buddy for now and forever, amen.*

“You told your dad you were coming to see me?” His father reheating food that was intended for her deepened the urge to go to him.

Parents making food for their kids was catnip, a daydream that included happy adults and easy laughter. A daydream that had never manifested for her, and now it seemed that was what he was raised on. Another piece to his grounded-demeanor puzzle fit into place.

“He figured it out.”

“How...”

“Let’s just say they ask a lot of questions. And who I tangoed with then took into the gardens at Zane’s benefit gala has been a focal point.”

“What did you say?”

“A friend.”

“A friend?” Then she added, “What’s changed? Why are you really here? You were clear at the gala that you were going torch my life.”

He sighed. “I’ve had some time to think. Come eat.”

She pressed him. She had to know that singular detail, the one piece of trouble she hadn’t been able to suss out. “Tell me.”

“I’ll tell you while we eat.” It was as if the food was as important as the words they were sharing and not eating was in part denying the conversation.

He found the switch, and a warm glow illuminated the kitchen from the bare bulb high up in the vaulted ceiling. He pushed back his hoodie, and there in the soft light was a man who looked like he hadn't slept in days. A five o'clock shadow grazed his cheeks, making his whiskey eyes look haunted. She wanted to know what would haunt a man like him.

She eyed the steaming glass containers and felt the smells pull her in. Spicy noodles with sesame seeds and green onions dotting the top filled the room with its savory allure. Crunchy pockets of what smelled like pork wontons and another with spam musubi, rice bricks wrapped in seaweed.

HE HEARD HER STOMACH GROWL AGAIN ACROSS THE WIDE SPACE. SHE sat like a hungry sorcerer on her throne, but she was also reserved, and that made him feel uncomfortable. Vega reserved meant she'd cuffed herself and would either ignore him or murder him in his sleep, he didn't know which, and he hated it. He wanted to see her back in her element, not guarded and wary.

Food laid out, he folded his arms over his chest and said, getting to the heart of the matter, "I reacted badly when I saw Londyn getting plowed by that sushi magnate guy, Phillip. I shouldn't have treated you like a blackmailer, but I couldn't think straight with all that right in my face."

"I can understand that. But I've already apologized—on my knees—for what you saw. Which wasn't even for you. I don't make it a habit to apologize, but with you I've done it more than once now."

"We're both doing things we've never done before. But I have to ask, and you'll probably light me up for it, but I have to know: You crashed an exclusive gala to do what?"

"To get Londyn to knock it off and move on. But as it turns out, that wasn't necessary."

"Yeah, I did that all by myself."

"I just saw a problem and needed to fix it."

"You make it sound like you do that for every problem you see. Is that true or is there something different here? Why me?"

"Why not you?"

"I'm not your standard protection client. Don't be coy."

He heard her curse in the dark. "Look, you. You're..." she started and stopped while she poked at the side of her thumbnail, making her look guarded and apologetic. "Different. I saw what she was doing and couldn't help myself."

"I get that. I forget all that I am, all that I'm trying to achieve, the moment I'm with you. And I'm constantly having to check myself because you're a dangerous person to slip up with. Your respect I highly value. And I've let you get close. At the gala I felt my guard go down; then hearing you had infiltrated Hoyt Securities made me feel as if you'd used my downed guard to take a potshot at me."

She made a soft sound of understanding in the back of her throat, "I can see how you would, though it wasn't my intention. Things... with me, things can get off the rails pretty quickly."

He gave her a soft smile, "I've noticed."

She rubbed her hands on her thighs. "If we're being honest, you're someone I also want to have respect me, and to have you light me up, tell me I wasn't smart enough...I might have lost it then. That video was insurance with Londyn. It's ugly business, what I do for protection work, and you, being the person I was supposed to be protecting, should never have seen that."

Her admission that she'd been seeking his good opinion as well settled him. That thing between them was real. Hope returned. Maybe, just maybe, he hadn't nuked their relationship. Whatever, exactly, it was.

She continued, "When you said that night that she couldn't love a man like you. Why did she say that to you?"

"I'll tell you someday. Not right now."

He thought he could see her jaw working as if she'd rather act but was, maybe for the first time, not pressing for an answer.

He asked her a question in return, "Did you really want to be her? At the gala you said that."

"I wanted to figure out who she was and how she got to be where she was at."

"By my side." God, he couldn't stop. What would he do if she said yes? Then asked to take Londyn's place?

"That wasn't a lie, you're an anomaly that I can't figure out. At the club when we first met, you didn't call me a crazy bitch or have security escort me out. I went to you and told you I'd breach your systems, and you calmly took my challenge. Who the fuck does those things? I wanted to know, was it because of the woman at your side? It wasn't. It's your family. I see that now. But fuck me if I wasn't curious about who would be worthy enough to walk in step with you in this life. I still want to be her—I mean that I want to have that kind of power in this life."

Right there, he thought. Right *fucking* there, that potent honesty settled into his bones. He felt his heart flutter, skipping a beat, at her words.

"I think," he said, treading carefully, "that you know the kind of power you already wield in this life, Vega Flux. It's not a power that Londyn will ever hold, not because she can't but because she doesn't want to."

"What are you saying?" Her voice was so quiet he stopped breathing to hear her better.

He rearranged the hot dishes in front of him. "I'm saying..." he started, wanting to be honest but then opting for safe, "I don't need protecting."

She gave him a wry grin. "That's not what those photos said to me."

"I just hadn't gotten around to fixing my mistake."

"I still need—sorry—*I would like* to know why you put a ring on her finger. I see you and think you're incredibly decisive. You must have had a reason to put a ring on that particular finger. It must be a reason I couldn't see."

"I did. And as it turned out, my reason was solid, but it was also a mistake. She was the result of me delegating a task that I didn't think I knew how to do."

“What task?” she pressed.

“I spent the last eight years building Hoyt Securities around the single promise and platform that Titan’s Wall was impenetrable. I stayed up late nights and weekends to ensure I could deliver on that promise that began when I was in college. About a year ago I wanted more. Something felt missing. Maybe it’s because forty is on the horizon for me, I don’t know, but it seemed right to look for a partner for my life. But I’ve earned a reputation. Super Bowl MVP and tech billionaire. There were lots of dates who thought they knew me before I even sat down.”

He looked at Vega there in the dark behind her monitors that had gone to sleep, making her part of the large apartment darker. “I think you understand that those are things I accomplished, they’re not who I am.”

“Shit you do versus *being* the shit.”

He softly smiled. “Something like that. I hired a marriage broker who lined up a series of potentials. Londyn was the last one. She was charming and nice and took the advice of the woman running the service until she accepted my proposal and moved in. After that, it was as if she’d passed some kind of test and could go back to being who she was. I’m not sure. Seemed liked that. That person and I didn’t get along. Londyn became, or is, shallow and mean-spirited. She said things to me that allowed me to focus on my work and not on building our relationship.”

“She ‘said things,’” Vega asked, “like she couldn’t love a man like you?”

“*Brute like me*, and yes. She pointed out things that she wanted me to change. Things I can’t change.”

He expected her to dive after it and wasn’t disappointed.

“I’ve met brutes before. You’re much too classy to be a brute.”

“My tats, size, and how I speak have been reason enough for people to question my intelligence.”

“I take it that was before you had nine digits in your bank balance?”

“Even now. And in some cases, especially now. Earning my

billions with my skin color isn't the same as being born with it. And while certain elitists could overlook my skin color if I had been born with a silver spoon in my mouth, they don't because I wasn't."

"That's fucked."

"It is."

"I'm sorry humans are assholes."

"Let the assholes apologize. You? You've already done plenty of apologizing, and I want to apologize in return. I didn't hear you at the gala; I heard you'd breached our systems and felt like a fool for thinking you were there for...me."

Hoyt had never been so baldly vulnerable before with anyone for the purpose of rescuing a relationship. It hurt and scared him, especially when the person whom he was doing it with was for all intents and purposes a demonic goddess.

When she stayed silent, he pulled the envelope of cash out of his hoodie and, walking over to her desk, put it on her keyboard.

"What I owe you."

Her dark eyes under a curtain of black bangs hissed at him. Her words did too. "I don't want it. I never wanted it."

"Just one point five mil?"

Her chin came up. "Fuck yeah. That, I *earned*." Her eyes were back to sparking lightning bolts. "That I earned for being *smarter than you*."

He winced, recognizing his jab at her from the gala. "You need this for Scout's thing. I heard about it tonight. I'm staying at my parents' house for the time being, and my cousins who work with her mentioned her looking forward to the semester abroad and her sister spotting her the cash for it. That and Peace brought it up with Zane."

"Your parents' home is there, up in the West Hills?"

He couldn't help but feel a soft smile at that admission. "You *are* watching me."

"That's what I do with threats, Hoyt. I monitor them."

He pressed her. "You know I'm not a threat."

"You aren't? I've never let anyone get as close as you have. I should have packed days ago. Why not? 'Cause I'm fucking crazy enough to believe that maybe you won't make good on your promise at the gala. But it doesn't mean I won't monitor you, track you, and watch your phone to make sure I'm safe."

He felt the same, "And?"

"And what?"

"And what have you decided? Am I a threat? Because if you're monitoring my phone, you know that you were caught on video lighting up Londyn and Patel, and my family is having a grand time making memes out of it and sending them to me. The favorite being a meme of you in a superhero cape."

He heard the soft huff of her laugh before she looked up. "Bunny is monitoring threats on your phone, not memes."

"Bunny?"

"My seemingly innocuous little data-monitoring bot."

"I see."

Her reserve left, and she blurted, "Are you going to torch my life? If so, shoot me now. You can't give me food then light me up. Or you can, but it's not fair."

He groaned. "How do we make this better? How do I?"

"Stop being nice. Go away and be a dickhead again, so I can stop thinking about how I hurt you."

"Can't."

"Ugh, why?"

"I'm hungry," he said as an answer. "Will you come eat, please?"

He watched how his nice words made her squirm, so he gave her more. "Be patient with me? I've never had a friend who scares me."

With that, she smiled hesitantly. "Did you just call me a friend? After everything, you still want to have a part of this?" she said, gesturing to herself. "Why?"

"You're talented. My every other thought is about you, and I think maybe, just maybe, I can sleep again if we're friends. Or at least, if we're friendly."

She looked down at her keyboard, her hair falling forward, but he caught a smile on her face before she smothered it. She poked at the envelope on her keyboard. "Twenty grand is in here?"

"Yes, just not in small bills. Twenties mostly."

She picked up the envelope and weighed it with one hand. "I'll take the twenty grand...as earnest money for the big cash payout."

"No, let's call it friend money. You need it for Scout, and the breach will be in addition to this. Don't try and cheapen yourself with me." He tried for humor and was glad to see a full-wattage smile.

"Piss me off again, and I'll expect double," she played back.

He could feel his insides swoop with her return to her position in their relationship. "Deal."

She stood. "Or, really, I'll just give the twenty grand back because I, too, probably, somehow, fucked up."

He watched her come around her command center. She was in her tight, ripped pants, a hoodie that hid the curves beneath but not her long legs that were anchored with her boots that took her to his chin.

He followed and resisted the urge to pull her into a hug. He was happy that their battle was over.

At the island that was now a steaming buffet of food, he said, "You just caught me by surprise, Vega, and I doubt I'll threaten to torch your life again."

She went to the sink and produced a dingy fork. "I've been waiting days for the torching to begin, and tonight I thought you might be making good on your promise."

He hated that she'd been waiting for him to attack her, though he'd been doing the same. "I wouldn't do that to you. Ever."

"Aw, come on, don't say that. I kinda like pissed-off Hoyt, now that we're friends again. Just next time I see it, I hope it's aimed at someone else." She moved to the opposite side of her kitchen island and took aim at the large dish of spicy noodles.

He looked at her fork from the sink and winced. "Wait, is that your only fork? Is it clean?"

"Yup and probably," she said, and when she reached for the noodles, he grabbed her wrist. Her gaze darted to his grip, and he was reminded of the gala and wanting to push her into a dark alcove. That thing between them was back and just as strong if not stronger than before with the feelings of relief swimming through his system. It was just her wrist caught in his grip, but the heat moving between them felt like his hand was sliding down the front of her pants.

He pulled from the bag a clean set of chopsticks for her.

She cleared her throat as if her emotions had gotten clogged there too. Her voice scratching, she said, "Aw, you believed me when I told you I didn't have silverware."

"Vega, I remember everything you say."

FORGIVEN_

Vega had slid back into his orbit faster than she wanted but slow enough to feel that she'd done enough due diligence to forgive him all his trespasses. She was afraid the thing they had going would make her forgive him anything.

"What'd you do with the video?" she asked and slurped noodles and shoved crunchy, salty wontons into her mouth and suppressed the need to groan in pleasure as Hoyt looked for something in the bags.

"Nuked."

"Figured," she said around the food in her mouth.

"And Bunny? You find him in your stack?"

He slung her a sideways look. "Not yet. I will."

After a long pause during which Hoyt stole surreptitious glances at her, warming her cheek with his gaze, she asked, "So, are you really sorry, or are you just afraid of the door Bunny popped open and let me deposit my bots into? And you're really here to beg for mercy."

"Let's see: really sorry, explained myself, begged for mercy... Checklist is almost complete."

Vega grinned. "Good, because if it's for sex, you should know I paid my asshole boyfriend Jax a visit the night I left you at that posh party. I probably need a rabies shot."

"About your bots, and, no, I'm not here for sex. And why would I care what you do with your boyfriend?" Then added, surprised to learn she had a relationship: "And does he know you?"

"You mean, does he know me as flux_capacitor?"

"Yeah." His eyes were on hers now and were coming to a slow burn. It made her skin itch to be against his. Was he angry?

"Why? Does that bother you if he does? Is it the risk or that he knows me better than you?"

"The risk is too high. Does Jax know who you are? Does he appreciate who you are, all of you?"

She watched him as she slurped up another noodle. His mom was an amazing cook, and now she knew that this man with a hard jaw and peekaboo clavicles also had a dad who was kind and looked out for others— She mentally cursed the big bet in front of her. He made her want to go mad and throw away everything to have him.

And yet, she couldn't place his sudden anger; the only way it made sense was if... "Are you jealous of Jax?" she blurted out.

His hands went to the opposite sides of the countertop as if to either brace himself or rip it clean off. He looked as if she had hit a tender spot with him. She felt heat move across her skin like a sensual chili sweat.

"And if I am?"

Vega swallowed as her insides free-fell, and her hand with the chopsticks lost its crispy passenger mid-flight, and it plopped back down into the dish.

She murmured, "I didn't expect you to answer that honestly. What exactly does Jax make you jealous about?"

"Did you let him..." He stopped then started again. "Why did you go to... I didn't realize you were with someone; I should have asked. I just assumed..."

"That I was unfuckable?"

"Unfuckable," he murmured, and he sounded incredulous. Louder, he said, "That you couldn't afford a real relationship."

She gave him that and stabbed at her wonton again. "He thinks my name is Joan, has no idea where I live, and is a fuck buddy. If we're being honest. He's the longest fuck buddy I've had, so I call him an asshole boyfriend. I didn't mean to elevate his status. True boyfriends *are* a risk I can't afford." She gave him a pointed glance that he took as her misinterpreting him.

"I'm not asking to be your boyfriend; I've just exited a relationship."

Vega rolled with it. "Don't I know it. Did she post a selfie midway through?"

"Screamed the whole way to the gala."

Vega remembered her volume when she was on the other end of it. "Oh man, I'm familiar. She did not take the photos I showed her with grace and humility. Though, to be fair, no one does."

"I can imagine," he said then pulled her back to his earlier point. "I'm just assessing the risk there, of you with Jax."

Her head started to tilt the way it did when she analyzed something that didn't make sense. "Is that why your eyes are burning with rage in hearing about Jax and me?"

WANT_

Vega wasn't sure what was being injected into her veins, but it probably wasn't just whiskey anymore. His burning gaze was making her blood sizzle.

"Who is he?"

"He's a stoner who doesn't ask questions"—she kept her voice cool and calm like someone who could keep things together—"and is always down for whatever I march into his house demanding. Even if it's tying him to his bed and letting me straddle him while I cry."

It was Hoyt's turn to freeze with his chopsticks halfway to his lips.

"I didn't fuck him." She poked her noodles around and murmured, "Your fault."

"My fault?" he whispered back as if these were secrets that might be overheard.

"You're fucking amazing," she said, moving her open palm up and down as though to indicate him, all of him. "I mean, even after threatening me at the gala, I'm back on board. I mean, look at you. Standing here, having not slept, it looks like, sorry, but despite that, the cut of your cheekbones, the simple but pointed stature of a man who's familiar with *all* the gym equipment and maybe even long, hard runs?"

"I'm familiar, yeah."

"You wear that sweatshirt like it was crafted just for your body, *and* you have the technical capabilities to keep up with me? Let's face it, I'm not sure I'll ever want to fuck anyone else as bad as I do you. But even if you'd let me, I toasted whatever we had going. The girls tell me it's trust. I'm bad with it—it's too much like glass, and I'm constantly breaking it to get what I need. And sometimes my best just isn't good enough. And you seem like a guy who needs trust to fuck."

Vega watched him swallow hard before she heard something that sounded like "Yeah" escape from him.

"What?"

He looked away then back again as if he'd needed to edit his words out from under her steady gaze. "You're already forgiven." His whiskey eyes were warm and guarded as he walked with her in honesty. "I miss you. I want that thing back too. I can't...I don't know what it is. It's more than trust. You challenge me, and I've missed that. And I've only known you for a short time, and I already know I don't like quiet from you."

"Me too. Truce?"

"Truce. Except the bots. I'll find them all."

She took in his dominating stature making her open-plan kitchen, which could easily accommodate four people working in it, look like it was just a one-person galley on a small fishing vessel.

He pressed her. "Come by the office tomorrow. Let's talk about your bots. I've designed some low-rent scripts to hunt them."

She casually smiled, letting the gnawing heat that he'd awakened in her slide away. "If you need a prescription, talk to your doctor."

"Haha. We found only two. I figure, by morning, we'll have the hole you created."

"Who's on the hunt? Just you or your whole team?"

"My head engineer took point. She wants to meet you. Come by tomorrow," he repeated, packing up the containers before looking around her kitchen. I'll leave these for you? Do you have a refrigerator?"

She scoffed. "Do I have a refrigerator? Duh."

"Sorry, this fifties stainless-steel thing works as your fridge, right?"

"Just like new. They really don't make them like that anymore. Just let me change out those glass containers for mine. Those are so nice; your mom will miss them, then hate me."

"Nah, just keep them."

She looked around her warehouse before looking back at him. "I promise I can afford food storage containers." And cereal bowls. And a mixer she'd bought on a domestic whim the day she moved in. "I don't want to upset your mom." Her stomach twisted at the thought of the woman who called Hoyt son giving Vega the evil eye.

"They don't expect them back. Unless you want to wash and return them in person?"

Her head whipped around to look at him. "What?" she asked and hoped it didn't sound like a scream. "You'd let me meet your family?"

He looked at her with softness. "Vega, of course." Then as if he realized what he'd said, walked it back. "But, really, just keep these. They don't need them back."

She was lifting blankets off a heavy wooden ladder against the far wall and trying not to think that Hoyt Kahoʻokalakupua had invited her to his family home in the West Hills. He had gone mad. Or she was in a fever dream.

She tried for casual even though her mind was shattering. "Oh yeah, well, I'm still not keeping them."

"Fine. Where are your containers?"

"In the upper cabinet."

He looked around at the kitchen opening cabinet doors that revealed cables and black boxes of tech and other small parts. Incredulous, he asked, "Where?"

She pointed at the deep cabinet above the snack pantry.

Hoyt reached up and opened the cabinet as Vega said, "Show-off." Bringing the ladder over, she placed it against the pantry front.

The ladder had been in the warehouse since the day she moved in, and she was sure it had always been there, to reach the access hatch that led to the roof. The wood was sturdy, but heavy use and the uneven wood planks of the floor meant it was fun to climb. As in, one-step-away-from-being-a-shipwreck fun.

He eyed her skeptically. “What are you attempting? That looks like an OSHA violation.”

“Ha. Unlike you, I’m unable to reach up there with my two feet on the ground, so I use this device. It’s called a ladder.”

It wobbled, and the rungs groaned as she started up it, and his eyes squinted at her in concern as he grabbed the edge of it. “Vega, I can get them down.”

“Yeah, but I’m a self-sufficient woman, and my man is in need. I can call you that, right, my man?”

“Friend. We’re officially friends.”

“Man-friend. That seems inadequate.” At the top, she looked down at him, “How about best friends?”

“I’ve only known you for a short while and have so many unanswered questions. Best friends know everything about the other. Does Peace know all of you?”

“That sounds like entrapment.”

“How long has she known you?”

“What’s with all the questions about Peace?”

“She’s dating an actual best friend of mine, Zane—”

“Fuck.” Vega winced, feeling something like jealousy pull at her. “They’re officially dating now? He’s told you that?” That was new territory for any of the Project Valkyrie gazelles, yet it made sense that dreamy-eyed Peace would be the first to fall in love. And love meant relationships, which meant risk, which meant she’d likely be leaving their project in the not-too-distant future.

He studied her, trying to puzzle out the problem. “Is that not accurate?”

Vega shook off her thoughts. “No, that’s great.” She was happy for Peace, she was. She also wanted that too. She wanted a man at her thigh just as Peace had done with Zane. But she was not and never would be as normal and good as Peace was. She would have to settle for playing cat-and-mouse in this man’s systems. She’d take it; she would. Then murder someone over the pain she’d feel when he eventually found a woman who was more like the marriage-broker version of Londyn. That woman would give him sweet-tender kindness and normal love in equal return for his. And he'd stop playing cat-and-mouse with Vega because future Londyn would have him too busy setting up white picket fences and playing for eternal keeps.

With a wounded heart, she rammed the teetering stack of colorful plastic mixing bowls she'd gotten on that domestic whim and extra boxes of snacks to the side to get to the storage containers at the rear of the upper cabinet. The bowls tilted, and Vega tried to catch them with her elbow.

"Shit." The bowls toppled out, and Vega strung curses together as she attempted to catch them all one-handed. The bowls crashed down. Hoyt reached for some, but as Vega leaned over, the ladder careened.

BREAK ME_

"Whoa," Vega said as Hoyt cursed and grabbed her, simultaneously putting his foot on the bottom rung and slamming the ladder back into place as bowls bounced off the floor.

Vega felt her insides swoop. The back of her thigh was warm with the heat of Hoyt's forearm—because his hand was holding her left buttock, pressing her forcefully into the ladder. Five Hoyt fingertips dug into her rear as if he was gripping a football and was in a mad sprint to the end zone. She felt his breath, uneven as if his body was preparing for that sprint. His gaze traveled from her hip up over her waist, past her shoulder to her eyes. His gaze asked her if she was all right, but maybe also if he should stay like that for a while longer?

His grip softened, but he kept his hand on her ass, and Vega felt it then. That thing between them, and right behind his questioning gaze, she saw the golden fire she had been trying to provoke for weeks. The inner python who finally let her see what he really desired, and it wasn't soft, normal, or kind. He wanted to swallow her whole.

His voice choked out, "Are you all right?"

Slowly, watching his pupils dilate, she shook her head. She was not all right. All right was snack in hand, taking down internet trolls.

This was— Did he want to pull her off the ladder or move his face in closer? She wanted to watch.

"You're not?" His breath was warm through the tear in her pants closest to his mouth. He touched the tip of his nose to the rip's opening and breathed her into his lungs. She felt the beginning of a passionate fire that was going to set her world ablaze.

Vega's hand brushed over his cheek before her fingers threaded up into his hair. His groan was part misery, part exultation. Her fingers gripped a handful of his rich dark-chocolate hair, making his gaze snap to hers. A full shudder went through her body as his eyes spoke to her, telling her that he'd not be soft, he'd not be kind, and that she was likely the only opponent he could ask all of that from. He wanted her just as she was.

"Vega..." Her name rolled off his tongue like a beg. He was begging her to listen, and listen closely. "I didn't come here for this, but I've wanted it... I want *you*. Bad. I can't promise I can be restrained or gentle. I can set you down and leave if it's not what you want..."

"Or?"

"Or I can do all the things I've fantasized about since you gave me a taste in the club when we first met. Tell me what you want from me."

His grip on her buttock tightened, and panting for the sweet outlet and the baited promise of more, she pressed her knee farther open. At her side he took one last drugged pull off her thigh skin and made room for her knee to go by before settling it onto his shoulder.

"Want it" choked across her vocal cords. His dark gaze was like twin pools that were a promise to end her agony, but first she had to drown. "I want you. Unrestrained and not gentle. I can take you as you are, Hoyt. I'm strong enough."

She watched as he took her invitation and put his mouth to the crotch of her jeans.

Vega moaned at the intimate placement of his mouth and the sweet heat of his breath that made her feel ignited as it pushed through the cloth, making her head swim. It was a tease for what was to come, the warmup for the workout that his desires were going to put her through.

His hand crawled up from her buttock and gripped the waistband of her jeans before pulling. Vega had been so mesmerized by him, the dark of his gaze, his mouth so intimately placed, that she belatedly focused, understanding that for her to get what she wanted, she had to take her pants off.

Her hand left his hair then, going to the button fly of her jeans. Her fingers slipped, and she gripped harder. She couldn't get her fly open fast enough, and fear of losing the moment and the chance that went with it made her beg, "Please, Hoyt. Don't stop, don't go. Wait for me."

Another exhale at her crotch, as if patience and time were both things he had in abundance. "I'm not leaving. This...you like this... just know I've been hungry for days, and now that you're giving me an opportunity to have what I want, I won't leave until I've been fed."

Her black hair cascaded over her shoulders as she shivered at her luck; his words were a beautiful torment. "Good. You're fucking amazing. I wanna be the one to feed you." Then more decisively: "I'm going to feed you."

Hoyt heard the change in her tone and gripped her waistband more firmly and tugged. "Now. I want you *now*." He dragged his teeth over the seam of her crotch in a gentle bite.

"Fuck yeah." With an impatient tug, Vega ripped the buttons open and wriggled her pants down. Jeans down over one knee, she put her bare knee to his shoulder and watched, watched his hungry eyes devour the sight of her.

He gentled his forehead to the naked front of her pelvis where she was shaved in a tight strip. His breath warmed her outer lips that were suddenly rushing with blood at the proximity of his lips. He touched his nose to the top of her strip where she was parted and murmured across her labia, "Beautiful, scary woman."

He stayed there, as his hand traveled down to the top of her boot and undid the laces before yanking it off then her pant leg down. He wanted more room.

Vega shook the pant leg off while her voice squeezed out in an anticipatory whine as the cool air of her apartment skimmed across her naked rear down to her toes, enhancing the ocean sensation in her veins.

With another kiss to her closely shaved outer lips, he whispered, "Patience."

"I'm not good with that." She swallowed against a dry throat, as if all her moisture was rushing to where his mouth was in preparation. "You should know this about me: I'm usually harder, harder, faster, faster."

He smiled against her as he looked up, connecting her with his act through their gaze. He cradled her naked thigh and rear before pressing his nose farther in to touch her clit. "Why does that not surprise me?"

He set to parting her outer labia into a *V* with a gentle and purposeful touch. Then, just as carefully, deliberately, he tasted her clitoris with the tip of his tongue.

Vega let out the pressure of her pleasure. "Oh god, yes, Hoyt, *please*."

He responded with his own groan, an anticipatory sound that he was about to be fulfilling a fantasy.

"'Ae," he murmured against her clit before kissing it, "anything you wish, Vega. Anything," then gave it a long, luxurious lick before touching the tip of his tongue to her as if tasting the last drop of wine in the glass. He then covered her pearl nub with his mouth, putting his lips to work, massaging the hypersensitive skin there.

Demanding she do his bidding and come for him, his silent lips asked her pleasure center to wake, to talk to him, to ride his mouth and tongue. To let him draw blood to her under the gentle vibration of his jaw and suckles of his lips. To make the woman above him call his name as she orgasmed into his mouth, repeatedly, until she screamed for mercy.

Vega's mind went blank. Without her having to show him her favorite spots, he read her body's wants as if he'd had an ear to it for decades.

Hoyt's mouth released her and was replaced quickly with the backs of his fingers brushing down over her outer lips, waking the sensitive skin further. He stroked her outer folds, making Vega's insides ripple like a gentle wave crashing over the rocks on a beach, the energy pushing and pulsing with every one of his strokes and caresses. Her inner lips parted, sighing open and welcoming his fingertips to bathe in the wet warmth there. Then, slippery with her physical desire, she tilted her hips, pushing against his touch, knowing he was preparing to dive into her. And also begging him to take her with a firmer hand.

He answered.

Hoyt pressed his middle finger up inside of Vega, just to a single knuckle before pulling back out again, and it felt like a tease for Vega.

"Please," she gasped out again. "Hoyt, this, you're killing me."

"Patience, I just got here," he said into her folds. "You've been in my mind for days, teasing *me* with this dream, and I will not be rushed."

He pulled his finger out before gently pressing it back in, teasing the leap into the deep end.

Vega's knee went wider, wanting more, as she bit the corner of her lip to keep from screaming aloud in tormented pleasure. Hand gripping a fistful of his hair, she rode the powerful feelings that stormed and swirled inside of her. Never had she been so mentally and physically dominated and aroused; she stood on the edge of total oblivion. She just needed a firm hit from his wide fist and eloquent mouth and she would leave her body in total and complete orgasm.

Vega's voice moaned out of her in a gradual crescendo as she rode his fingers and mouth, holding on to him with one hand and the other on the ladder rung. Her hips tensed, locking in at a tight, instinctual rocking rhythm as her body spooled out pleasure waves from where his mouth and hand connected with her.

She needed more, just a touch, one iota more so that she could die right then and there.

"More," she choked, "don't stop, more, please, Hoyt, please."

He took her command and pressed a second finger up into her

and with a gentle curve mimicked a short but hard, wide cock sweeping in against her erotic trigger.

"Harder, Hoyt."

He nuzzled her clit before looking up, his eyes drugged, his thick erection in his loose-fitting pants making an impressive tent. "Harder? How hard?" And he demonstrated, fingers in deep until the flat fronts of his knuckles gently smacked against her opening as his mouth kissed her hood.

"Harder."

He did as she begged, and as she threw her head back, her body went electric with the pound of his fist against her vaginal opening as a second bigger wave of pleasure roared through her veins.

"Hoyt," she screamed, her voice echoing back at her from the cavernous space. And as his mouth sucked, his nose rubbed the cluster of nerves above her clitoris hood where every one of her orgasms lived in quiet harmony with their sisters. Until he undid them. He found their secret door and opened it wide, welcoming them into his mouth. They raced out with glee into her veins, setting her body cracking open and alight in release. Vega shook and cried out.

Her abdomen clenched, and Vega gripped the lip of the open cabinet just before her knee turned to water. Her standing leg gave, and feeling her weight, Hoyt's grip firmed up. With a heft of her body up onto his shoulder, he kicked the ladder away with the diligence of a man who was rudely interrupted and slammed her back into the pantry door.

The ladder crashed, mimicking her almost fully delivered orgasm. Hoyt pushed her thighs up onto his broad shoulders.

"Not done yet," he managed before putting his mouth back onto her.

With a groan that Vega felt through her legs at his own unrequited lusts, he slipped his fingers back inside of her.

Dizzy with the power, the devotion, and the diligence of him, she arched her hips, giving herself once again to him. She gripped the upper cabinet with one hand and his head with her other as she pressed her bare foot into his back, desperate for one more hit of his drug as his tongue worked in unison with the pound of his fingers. She came again, and he didn't stop until her body convulsed, releasing every pent-up orgasm she'd ever held back. She screamed for mercy as the electricity that raced through her turned into an aggressive tickle and she squeezed his cheeks with her thighs.

She laughed. "Stop, stop, stop!"

He slowed, nuzzling her softly before giving her oversensitive clit one last lick and a parting kiss. "Are you sure?"

"Yeah." Panting, she said, "I'm pretty sure some neighbor just called 9-1-1 to report a murder."

He grinned.

She bathed in his drugged gaze, "You murdered me, fucking ruined me, Hoyt."

"Oh yeah?" Then he did something that she would hold in her brain's basket of dirty images forever and ever.

He slowly, luxuriously, slid his wet fingers out of her tender vagina and while holding her gaze like a taut wire, slipped those fingers over his lips and into his mouth until they were knuckle deep before sucking them clean. His eyes closed in pleasure, and his voice hummed in his chest, reverberating through her thighs, as he murmured, "Mine."

She needed to seal that promise and bent over to kiss it and keep it. He let her down before pinning her again to the cabinet with his body and, resting her buttocks on his knee, put his lips to hers. For the first time.

Against his wet lips, she kissed him hard, murmuring, "Fuck yeah, I'm yours."

ON YOUR KNEES_

TUCKING HER INTO BED HAD BEEN THE HARDEST AND SWEETEST THING he'd ever done. He'd marked her in a primal and animalistic way that had, in retrospect, startled even himself. Hoyt hadn't realized the depths of his own emotions when it came to Vega. She opened something in him that demanded more. And each time he asked, he was given it. That night had been more than just a misjudgment, when he assumed he could just be friends with her. He could never give up having more from Vega now that he had it. And he'd only put his mouth on her. If he slipped into her, he knew it would alter his life permanently. He'd want rings, a shared home, and family dinners all with her by his side. And he had no idea if Vega Flux, online vigilante and beautiful menace, would want any of that too.

Now, back at his empty penthouse, he stood among the mid-renovation chaos staring across the river at Vega's warehouse. The way she had begged him had caught him off guard, sending crushing emotion through his chest. He was sure she begged for nothing in her life. But now, twice she had of him.

Up on that ladder she'd let him lay her bare, and made his cock go hard. She had wanted to return the favor, and any other time, he would be game, or do as she did, beg for it in return, but he wanted that night to be about prioritizing her. Which meant tucking her into bed and kissing her soft, warm lips that smiled under his.

It surprised him. And made him hope.

She was sweet, kind, and vulnerable. He'd never been with a woman who made him feel like he could do no wrong, that every thought of her filled him with excitement and desire.

He now needed daily doses of her, and her returned affection was something he was going to be obsessive about. He'd been obsessive about his work, and in retrospect, he knew why—he was filling his heart with something that he cared about. Now that hole felt finally full, overflowing even. She was a woman who in private was soft, but to the rest of the world, she went fists first. He wasn't sure why that felt powerful and empowering, but it did.

But all that wasn't the full reason he stood looking out over the river to the dark rectangle that was her building. What held him now was what happened the moment before he'd left her. He'd kissed her asleep, dodging her grabs for his still throbbing erection, and she'd drowsily said, "I think I love you, Hoyt Kaho'okalakupua."

He'd brushed wild black hair off her sleeping face and felt his chest cave in under the weight of it. He'd felt it then, that thing that his father had said to him. He felt like he was falling, drowning, achieving the unachievable while being invincible. It made him do irrational things like say in response to her sleepy whisper, "I think I love you too."

Unlike the night before, this night he'd sleep. He'd sleep deep right after that cold shower. His whole body was screaming to press his erection deep into her, to never leave her side and follow her through life, taking any morsel of attention she threw his way.

He'd put his hand to his still throbbing erection in the shower and relieve the pressure on his hardened cock. Braced against the tile, he would let the cold deluge mimic a waterfall against his back while his fist pretended to be the soft folds of Vega, and he'd remember the earth and salt of her intimate taste and the clamping feel of her orgasm on his fingers as he pumped. Only he'd be daydreaming that her thighs were spread wide, the dark shadow of her tight strip of hair parted. He'd press his hips to hers and slip himself in. He'd release that desire that clung to him, letting himself later sleep like the dead. Then, tomorrow, he'd figure out what it meant to love a haunted, vicious, full-hearted woman like Vega Flux.

THE NEXT MORNING HAD HIM UP EARLY AND IN THE OFFICE WITH THE kind of celebratory glee that followed him for weeks after the Super Bowl win. Vega was coming in that day; he'd already pinged her phone and now waited for his night owl to wake up and arrive sometime around noon. That was the thing about Vega—fucking her was only part of the joy of her; she knew how to play outside the bedroom too. And he wanted all of it.

In the elevator up to the executive suites, he thought of the schedule. First to the engineering department where Lei was ready to show her the work they'd done. Next would be to have Vega explain how she got in, then figure out where to send the million-plus to a woman who didn't have a Social Security number.

Stepping off the elevator, Hoyt pulled up short as Hector whisper-shouted from behind his desk, "She's here. I don't know how she got in, but she's here."

At first, Hoyt thought of Vega, but he knew it couldn't be her. There could be only one other person making Hector hiss like that. His mood plummeted. He'd been foolish to think that Londyn wouldn't attempt to get more from him about Vega. He'd already told Hector to tell Londyn to go pound sand.

With a frown, he said to Hector, "I'll take care of it."

"Should I call security?"

"Yes."

He pulled off his cross-body bag with one hand and at the end of the hall threw open the door to his office. His wide wing-backed chair was facing the view. "Get out," he growled.

"Aww," came from the chair, and it made his scalp tingle with a thrill before cascading down his spine. Vega turned the chair around. "You sound grumpy—did I surprise you?"

Cheerfully, he turned and hollered down the hall, "Hector, cancel security."

His head popped around the corner, his headset cradled again in his hands. "Are you sure?"

With a laugh: "Oh yeah, I'm sure I've got this." To Vega, who now had her booted feet up on his desk: "You're up incredibly early."

Laughter danced in her smoky dark eyes. "So are you, you maniac."

He shut the door and dropped his bag and came to her. One hand on each armrest, he leaned over her, his silk tie falling onto her folded hands. She gathered up the end of his tie and pulled tight, locking him in close.

"Aloha kakahiaka. Good morning," he said. He knew he hadn't stopped grinning.

"Good morning," she cooed back at him, and he put his lips to hers, softly telling her hello and that he liked the familiarity they now shared.

Her cool hand went to the side of his face and cradled his jaw as she kissed him back before pressing her fingertip into the small indent she'd noticed on his chin. She fell back into his leather chair and sighed.

"I got the workout of my life last night and as such woke at the butt crack of dawn, five minutes ago, and raced over. I feel like a kid in the candy store. Or rather, Hector's candy store where he needs bribes every time I see him. Worry not, he's coming around."

"He called security on you."

She clicked her tongue. "Shucks, I thought we were getting somewhere."

Hoyt reached one hand behind him and, giving her a brief kiss, pressed something from his back pocket into her hand. "Yours."

She took the key card, and Hoyt watched warmth flush her cheeks and eyes. "This is dangerous. Are you sure you know what you're getting into? Maybe we should just stick to fucking and games."

He tilted her chin up and kissed her again. "You can already get in. Now you have the same access as I do. Use it wisely. As for what I'm getting into, I don't settle for less than 100 percent. I'll have fucking, games, and you, all of you. Even the darkest parts. Even the lightest parts."

She whispered, sobering. "You say that now. But I'll be ready for you when you kick me out. It'll hurt, but I get it."

He held his hands out and pulled her up, "Have you ever been with someone like me?"

"A cunning man who eats me out like a fine buffet? Nope, can't say I have."

"That was fun. I have a new fondness for ladders."

"You should buy some."

"Five hundred in all shapes and sizes are being unloaded in my apartment as we speak."

Vega laughed deep in her throat. "Can't. Fucking. Wait."

He gave her another kiss before going serious. "Vega."

She touched his chest, sensing the change. "Ugh, serious already."

"Don't go back to Jax."

She winced. "Gross."

"I'm not a moron. At some point I'm going to piss you off, and, hurt, you're going to do something to quiet the pain. Run, bungee jump, rock climb, something, anything, other than go to him."

She looked at her hand on his chest and turned it over; he slid his into it. She gripped tight, "This feels like you're asking me to see you exclusively for sex and sex-related things."

"I'm asking you to see me exclusively. Period."

Her gaze went up to his, and he felt the sudden precipice under his feet, the make-or-break moment with Vega.

"What if I say no?"

His heart suddenly was a jackhammer in his chest, but he knew what the right answer was and gave it to her. "That's OK to say no."

Her eyes narrowed. "I can feel the beat of your heart. I'm gonna call you a liar."

He closed his eyes to break the spell she had him under. "It has to be fine—you're an independent human with free will."

"It wouldn't crush you?"

His eyes opened then, and as her head tilted, taking in his gaze, she smiled. "That's more like it. Don't hide behind politeness with me. I want truth, I want it hard-won and to burn across my skin. Tell me the truth: What if I say no?"

He turned it on her. "What if I started seeing Londyn again?"

She was quick to reply. "I'd murder you and burn down the city."

"Any other woman?"

"Murder."

"Then you have my answer too."

She clicked her tongue, and it sounded like a ticking bomb. "Then say it, Hoyt. If I don't hear the truth from your lips, I will make poor decisions based on assumed or bad data."

He smiled quietly. "I don't want you to have bad data. I also don't want to get hurt if I misjudge things, but since you've asked and you're willing to hear it... I want to be exclusive with you, and if you say no, I'll be crushed. I'll be obsessive to the point you'll need a restraining order, and I'll think long and hard about how I can use all my billions to get you back as I go quietly insane."

She went up on her toes and, snaking her arms around his neck, pulled herself up his front and kissed him hard. Then opened her mouth when he responded with a low rumble of satisfaction.

Her lips and tongue tangled with his. He felt the rush of having her against his body, the small of her back under his hands and her breasts soft against him. He let some of his reserve go and gripped a fistful of her hair, and squeezing tight, devoured her. Mouth open to hers, breathing in her breath, tasting her, touching her tongue felt like another kind of lovemaking.

He pulled back feeling drugged and took in Vega's abused and wet lips to her gaze that was dazed and wanting more.

"Vega...give me all of you."

Her tongue touched a tender red mark on her lip as she caught her breath. "Deal. You have exclusive rights granted from here forward until you breach said exclusive contract or get bored or boring."

"Thank you."

"And you?"

"Exclusive rights indefinitely."

"And if I stray? Want out?"

"We'll cross that bridge when we get there. One more question?"

She smiled up at him.

He touched the tip of his tongue to his lips. "Did you have marshmallows for breakfast?"

She grinned. "I did. And quick question. Were you made for me? I feel like you were made just for me. We'll find out when we make love, but I think we'll fit together like a hand in a glove. But maybe not."

"Do you promise to not go back to Jax even if I piss you off?"

"Double-gross, and yes, a long time ago, I used to run. Like, on the track and everything. So, I'll give that a try again when you piss me off and I want to douse the world with kerosene."

He bent and nuzzled her cheek before giving it a kiss. "Thank you."

She found his lips. "But don't piss me off."

"I'll try not to. But as I've been made aware lately, I am just a man. And sometimes just that can be offensive."

Vega, mirth dancing in her eyes, said, "Not just. No, you are a very wise man. I'm starting to see how billions of dollars hasn't totally fucked with you."

He shrugged. "It was the first million that fucked me up. My family picked up the pieces and helped me see straight."

Holding onto his lapels, Vega stretched up against him. "Tell me, tell me all the things that fucked you up. I'm going to need that to feel better about myself."

He grinned down into those dark eyes that were a touch lighter that morning, giving way to the gray-green hidden within. "You first."

She slid back down and let go of his lapels and adjusted them so they were perfect to her. "Damn."

When she didn't elaborate, he said, "Is that a no?"

"Hoyt..."

He whispered to her, "Give it to me, Vega, so I can protect you from it."

She shuddered, and he was reminded of the night before when she'd reacted that way when he'd been baldly honest with her.

"But that's just it, isn't it? I'm protecting you from it. And 'it' is me. If I give that knowledge to you, then you're culpable. It's the darkness that I'm keeping off of you. If I give it to you, I fail."

He let it go. "That's fine," and held his arm out, and she stepped into his quiet embrace.

"How do you do that?"

"What?"

"Give in without giving in? It sounds like you're giving in but with like this firm grip that says you won't forget, and goddammit, I'm a sucker for your quiet power. Gimme." She went up on her toes yet again, and he smiled into her kiss.

She thinks I have quiet power?

"But in bed? How quiet are you?"

"We'll have to find out. Later," he said, stepping back from her, but she was keen to the stiff rod he was trying to keep tucked away. "After work. We can wait. I don't want to do all the things I want to do here on this carpet or on top of my desk. Also, all those things will make HR fire me. Then rehire me just to fire me again."

Electrified, her voice went low and sultry. "I can work around your systems—"

"No. Let's go down to engineering. Lei found your bots and wants to ask you questions."

She shivered. "Fine," and grinned. "Also, can I have that list you have of all the things you want to do with me? I'd like to see if it matches mine."

He took her hand and headed for the door. He needed a chaperone, and fast, or his day was sunk. Sunk deep into Vega.

As they approached the elevators, Vega blew a kiss to Hector. "Did it arrive, hon?"

"Don't call me hon." Then with a grin he held up a brown package.

Vega winked. "Anything you need, you call me."

Hector looked over her shoulder at Hoyt in the elevator and gave a winning performance. "Ew, I would never! And don't come back."

Vega fluttered her fingers at him before stepping back into the elevator.

Hoyt's eyes danced with mirth as he hit the door-close button; the sub-level-five button was already illuminated. "What was that all about?"

The elevator began its slow decent. "He wanted a priming cream that makes your pores disappear."

"Why doesn't he just buy some himself?"

Vega turned toward him and, without thinking, saw her hands rise to smooth her palms over his pectorals. It was as if her hands couldn't resist touching and memorizing every muscle and jagged angle, and the warmth it created deep in his belly made him want her to never stop. "Oh, sweet, smart man, you can't buy this at the store—they've been sold out for months."

"So, to the black market you go?"

"Yes, and to you my Hector lets me go."

"Progress is a key card," Hoyt said, hovering over her lips, only half listening.

Vega pressed a kiss to his lips and, opening her mouth, touched her tongue to his. Hoyt felt his discipline begin to drown in his competing emotion, desire. He gripped her hair, stilling her to his devouring kiss, taking her into his mouth as a groan escaped from him. He wanted to get naked with her under him, now.

His rumble of need escaped, and Vega reached back and hit the elevator stop button. The car obeyed with a jarring thud.

Hoyt's hands shot out, bracing himself. "Vega..."

"Vega, nothing." She put her hands to his lapels and dragged her boot up his leg before stomping it down on the handrail.

His hands went to her ass and pressed her in against his erection. "We have a date with engineering," he whispered up her neck. "So, we should be quick."

Vega groaned as he pushed his pelvis up and down, mimicking

thrusting into her. The firm rod of his erection scoured along the seam of her crotch where heat—warm and building—rushed into their connection.

"Quick?" Vega asked as they took a collective breath. "Quick," Vega reiterated, and with a practiced twist, his belt was undone and his fly was down. Vega's knees hit the elevator floor as her mouth took him deep.

Hoyt's breath shot out as his feet slipped wide, his knees giving out with the feel of his desperate cock slipping into the wet warmth of her mouth as her fist gripped tight at his root. She slid the velvet of his skin up and down the iron rod of his erection making him think he was going to slip into an erotic coma.

Bliss built within his bloodstream. His head fell back, and he groaned as he tried to tell her something. "Cameras."

"Taken care of."

His voice, high with the pressure of his struggle to talk through his arousal, said, "You blocked the cameras?"

She batted her lashes. "Of course I did."

A tinny voice from the speaker box interrupted them. "Is everyone OK in there?"

"Fine," Hoyt choked out.

The voice had startled Vega's mouth and hands off him, and looking down to her, he saw she had already slid out her demonic phone and was typing commands.

"I can have you guys out—"

The power cut out, and the dim orange glow of the emergency lights came on.

"Four minutes, max," Vega said.

"Vega, we can just— Hoo…" In the dark of the emergency lights, his sense of touch was heightened, and his palm slapped the inside of the car with a thump, bracing himself against her powerful ministrations. "Vega!"

Her mouth was back on his erection, sucking and pumping with one hand as her other did something to his testes inside the tight confines of his boxer briefs that he'd not known was an erogenous zone for him.

"What?" She paused.

His breath was coming hard, and he couldn't remember what he was going to say. Instead, he said, "Fuck me fast."

He heard her low laugh and held on.

VEGA HAD SWORN A LIFETIME AGO THAT SHE'D NEVER BE ON HER KNEES for any man, but she had been wrong. For Hoyt, she'd now done it twice. There was something powerful about being on her knees with him, like stepping down into a Formula 1 driver's seat. Sure, you were low, but you were still gloriously in control. She had wanted to take it to its hilt within her and make him call her name through his lust-filled haze. She'd have him that way, and it just turned out to be in an elevator car with a stopwatch going. As her mouth worked the length of it in and out, the breadth of her tongue massaged the erogenous zone at his tip. It was a good, *real good*, size. What would it feel like in her with his pelvis hitting her clit?

With her fist chasing her mouth up and down this thick erection, she was having a hard time concentrating on her singular task. She wanted this and so much more. Vega felt his groan sizzle down her spine like static electricity. His knee began to shake, and he warned her he was close with the tone of his voice. "Vega..."

In the orange emergency light of the elevator, she glimpsed his left hand fumbling for something in his chest pocket, his pocket square.

Vega snatched the silk cloth out of his hand, and with a luxurious lick of his cock's long shaft, her eyes burned onto his. "You're fucking kidding if you think I need this." With puckered lips pressed to the head of his erection, she spoke through wet lips. "I'll swallow everything you give me, and your orgasm will happen in my mouth, and I'll swallow that too."

Slowly, purposefully, she breathed out hot air over his tip as she slipped it all the way down to the top of her throat. Keeping linked to his drugged gaze, she worked him to a peak again. She watched as his eyes drank her in until his nostrils flared and his abs crunched. The hand at the top of her head tightened its grip in her hair, and his hips, as if moving of their own accord, thrusted into her mouth. He lost control just before his groan echoed off the steel interior of the elevator, and his head fell back.

A drawn-out low cry shivered down his body as his hand in her hair gripped in reflex. Vega felt her scalp lift deliciously up, and his knee shook, and warmth flooded into her mouth. She swallowed him down, a grin in her mind.

She kept at him until he pulled her off him with a cry and a laugh.

AFTERMATH_

Vega felt like a pilgrim at a temple there at Hoyt's widespread knees, while in the aftermath of his orgasm he looked like he'd taken a header down a flight of stairs. She reveled in his complete loss of control, having firmly handed himself over to her. She wiped her mouth on the inside of her shirt before she dragged her nails up his bunched thigh muscles to his zipper, as they helped each other stand upright and put themselves back together.

His hands went to her hips and tugged her in against him.

Resting his head on her shoulder, he said, muffled into her hoodie, "Am I in heaven?"

She refastened his belt. "Yes, my name is Peter, I'll be your guide for the duration of your stay. How would you like to come? Hard or soft, or a variety?"

"Just like this, over and over and over..."

Vega smiled into his neck, the starch of his collar pressing into her cheek. "I hate to murder your afterglow, but we have just seconds before you have to pretend nothing happened in here, founder and CTO of Hoyt Securities."

"Yeah, got it."

"Gather your brain matter, hottie in a suit."

"Gathering."

Vega laughed as the lights came on and the elevator began its descent again. As he adjusted his suit coat, he gave her a longing look that said ten thousand years with her wouldn't be enough.

A tinny voice broke in. "Sir? Are you all right?"

He cleared his throat. "Thanks for getting us back up and running."

The operator pressed: "We're not sure what happened, and you're sure you're all right?"

Hoyt's gaze was on hers. "Never better."

"We're sorry, sir. We'll get the elevator checked, sir."

"Do that." He reached forward and severed the connection.

When the doors opened, he reached for Vega, but she slipped out, pulling up her hoodie and on a black disposable mask, as a man in a plaid collared shirt stood there with a yellow legal pad in his hand.

"Ah, good, Mr. Kahoʻokalakupua, there you are. I was just at your office, I have the risk analysis you requested for the..."

The man had excellent timing. With a smile Hoyt couldn't see, Vega slipped into the vast expanse of the subterranean-fifth-floor cubicles. Despite being so far underground, the floor was airy, with brightly lit boxes mimicking windows, short faux palm trees poking out of the cube maze, a happy birthday sign hung in the break room.

One glance back, and Vega was glad Hoyt's mind was blank and his analyst was waiting for him. There was no way he would have let her go otherwise. She disappeared down the first row of cubicles and made quick work heading to the frosted-glass office she'd already traced as his.

The office wasn't large, but it could just accommodate a tight two-person meeting area in one corner. Vega sat in his command center chair and felt something tighten in her stomach. This was *him*, the feel of the chair, his desk that had family pictures and papers scattered about. She wanted to touch every surface, inspect every drawer, but she didn't have time. Securing her USB into his system and pulling out her phone, she ordered Bunny to get to work.

Bunny shuffled off Hoyt's passcode from his keystrokes she'd been tracking all week, and in seconds she had Hoyt's desktop, with administrative access to all of Hoyt Securities, open, and with that access, she created a back door for her more complex systems. Satisfied, she logged off and slipped from his office.

There was no need to blow the game now; she just needed that virtual machine on his servers to be hers, and with her changes to the binary code of his security software to mask her from his scans, her software would look just like his and would take her bit of code with it even in the event of a rollback to an older version. She was officially in. Now, no matter what happened between them, this game or the other, she had the most powerful man in security in her pocket. With administrative access, she would become so embedded into his world she likely could be in his code for the rest of Hoyt Securities existence. As long as she was quiet. Until it was time to not be.

She saw Hoyt then, towering over cubicles. He'd left his analyst and was now walking with his engineer to an office at the end of the hall. Some workers were leaning back in their chairs to get a better look at him.

Vega knew the feeling. Hoyt cut a solid figure in his several-thousand-dollar suits that showed his muscles when he moved, making him a kind of walking masterpiece.

She overheard one of those employees as she made her way down the aisle to the man whose cock she still felt across her swollen lips: "He's down here because of the competition."

"Who's going at it?"

"He has not said. But feels freaky, like this might be a real attempt, you know?"

Vega resisted the urge to pop by the cube and entertain ideas with them. How people in offices got anything done, she had no idea. She imagined that if she worked here, she would spend the hours rolling from one cubicle to the next pilfering candy and starting rumors.

"Speaking of," she whispered to herself and ducked low into an empty cube and took a candy from the bowl of it as if it were an offering from the sugar plum fairy.

The conversation continued, and Vega sat, quietly unwrapping the hard pink candy, and pulling down her mask, she popped it into her mouth.

"But don't get me wrong—if we have to pull late nights, it's *real* nice to have him down here, you know?" said the second.

"Yeah, too bad he's about to get married." There was longing in the first's voice.

Vega raised her brows in mock shock and with a dramatic flourish looked at her ring finger. *Nope, still empty.*

"No, didn't you hear? She's been stepping out on him."

Vega put that hand to her chest and, sucking on the candy, feigned indignation.

"No way." The first was similarly indignant. "On him? Who does that?"

Vega nodded. *Who indeed.*

"I don't think they were a good match. She never came to any of the functions here. And practically his whole family works here, so not coming to these is like rejecting them too."

"Maybe she found out *they're* related."

"That's a soap opera."

"Could be true."

Vega was rotating in the desk chair and agreed—Hoyt and Londyn being long-lost siblings was soap opera stuff for sure. Though, she mused, so was the truth.

"No," the other whispered, "he's," and there was just the sound of clothes moving, and Vega wanted to stand up and have a peek at whatever the gesture was.

"No way. Who does that?"

"I don't think it's a secret. He was, like, a bachelor forever, and this thing with his fiancée didn't last for, what, even a couple of months? Maybe she didn't like that he'd had that done, and when he wouldn't reverse it, she took off?"

"Yeah, I hadn't even thought of that. I heard there were two others and the matchmaker was getting frustrated. Do you think that was it?"

She heard one shrug. "I mean, what else could it be?"

Vega's face was scrunched up as she mouthed, *What the hell?* She was about to stand up and have them explain when she heard one take a sharp intake of breath.

The other one whispered, "Shit."

When Vega rotated back to the cube's opening, Hoyt was towering there.

"Here you are."

She held up the candy wrapper. "Got hungry."

Vega popped up and looked over the cube wall to the two who were paralyzed, wearing matching expressions of shock, in their chairs. One wore thick glasses, the other a well-worn shirt that said, "This meeting could have been an email."

"What's not getting reversed?" Vega asked them.

They looked to Hoyt then back to her, their faces going ashen.

From behind her, Hoyt's deep voice rumbled, "Leave them alone, Ms. Arc."

Vega shrugged; she'd find out. "Bye," she said to them and left with him. She wanted to skip next to her big guy. But she didn't. She'd look crazy—her punk platforms weren't meant for skipping.

He said under his breath, his face impassive but curiosity bright in his eyes, "What are you playing at?"

"You mean just now," she said, throwing a thumb back at the two engineers, "or why I ditched you at the elevator to ransack this floor?"

He was thoughtful. "Both."

"First, candy, second, if I told you, it'd ruin the game."

He let a grin escape. "I'll find you if you burrow into our systems."

Vega wanted to bathe in his confidence. "God, I really hope you do, and when you do, I'll start another game to get you to come find me again."

He held his hand out to stop her. "Promise?"

Vega stepped up against his hand until his palm was spread over her diaphragm. She'd expected him to say something else but whispered back to him, "Oh yeah, I promise."

"Good, because your bots are gone."

Vega's fingers wove between his and squeezed before letting go, and stepping away, she rubbed her hands together. "Oh yeah?"

Just then his engineer appeared, her hair in a bun, a pencil rammed through it. "Get in here," she said to Hoyt, then as if belatedly seeing Vega, cut at her, "Who are you? If you're one of our new interns, then you go to his assistant to get time with him; otherwise leave him alone—he has enough on his plate."

Vega took in this commanding woman. She was his sister—of course she was.

"As you wish, my queen." At Vega's bow, Lei gave her a look that said she had no room for bozos right then.

Hoyt was loving the interaction and leaned against the wall next to her office door, his eyes bright, looking to be purposefully not stepping in to explain.

Lei nodded for Vega to get back to work down the hall. "Now."

Vega curtsied and instead pushed past her into her office and sat at her computer to see exactly how far they'd gotten.

"Hey! Get ouuuuu..." Something clicked with Lei, and her command slid onto the floor, as did the pen from atop her papers as her hands that held them went slack.

"Look," Vega said to her, "you've done excellent work. The question is, how many of my bunnies have you found? And, sure, you located my initial breach—"

Lei continued to stare. "It's you."

"Yup. Me. Now—"

Lei lifted a hand. "Hi."

Vega lifted a hand too. "Hi."

Lei's gaze went to her brother, and Vega thought she saw adoration there. "You made up with her."

"I did" was all he said, his eyes dancing.

Lei said to Vega, "It's an honor to meet you. You're an incredible woman."

Vega wasn't ready for those words of formality and kindness. "Oh no. Trust me. It's not an honor. You'll likely come to regret it; most people do."

"I've waited for this moment for years."

Vega paused. "Years?"

Lei explained, "I contacted you. A long time ago."

Vega understood quickly. "Oh, I see."

"My roommate," Lei explained further, "you saved her life."

Vega stood to step closer. "Look, it's better if I stay anonymous, so how about we say that I was never—"

Vega was crushed in a hug. Lei squeezed tight and said, "I promised myself I wouldn't freak out, but you helped my roommate, helped my professor... She's the one who gave me your name. Thank you for all you've done."

Vega of course knew where Lei had gone to school, and she knew the professor she mentioned. Vega greatly admired the Juggernaut researcher Dr. Branch, who answered every one of her questions even though Vega wasn't one of her students. They first "met" when a superior at the university had "borrowed" Dr. Branch's research without permission and claimed it as his. Using his position as dean, he made her claims to his theft and plagiarism sound as if she were attempting to steal *his* work. In a fit of rage and fueled by a bottle of cabernet sauvignon, Dr. Branch sought solutions on message boards that weren't strictly aboveboard for a university professor studying quantum computing. Vega answered the call, and within a month, he was sacked for having an affair with a student. Which Vega hadn't fabricated.

Vega patted her back and saw Hoyt mouthing, *Say, you're welcome.*

"You're welcome."

Lei let her go, and as she stepped back, Vega saw the papers in her hand were rumpled and her eyes wet. "I said I wouldn't get emotional, but you have no idea what it feels like to be so helpless. She wasn't going to survive that incident, and there was nothing we could do."

Vega felt that shadow; she was familiar with its cold hand. "I do understand. And you, none of you were helpless. You reached out. We sometimes forget how big a deal that is. It may take a few tries, you may have to figure out what a person can do to help, but inevitably someone reaches back. And in your case, you got a resolution."

"Because of you."

"Because we're survivors, we do what needs to be done, and that's to not take shit while lying down." Vega knew it was a slippery slope to keep talking about this, but she was breaking all her rules with Hoyt, and Lei's honesty was cracking her. "Who was your roommate?" There were thousands of requests every year. Too many.

Lei told her the story, and with a couple unique details, Vega remembered. "Getting drunk is not a crime. Even if she chose, drunk or not, to take off her clothes, that is not a crime. The only person who made a mistake was that shithead—and then he pushed that mistake to a place I could not abide. Hopefully when enough women punch back, the general populace will take up the narrative: don't fuck with women, or we'll fuck you up."

Lei's eyes were wide. "Yeah, we needed that then. I don't think he's done it again."

"He did, or tried to. When no one punished him for what he did to your roommate, he escalated fast. He made quick cash by getting chicks drunk and taking pictures they'd pay to not have on the internet. Then he'd upload anyway and charge other assholes to see them. He was real piece of shit."

Hoyt heard the past tense. "Was?"

"He's dead."

Lei's face lost its pink undertone as blood drained from her tan skin, making her look as if she were about to be sick. Her brother's eyebrows crammed together in worry.

Vega wanted to ask him if he still wanted to play the games she played. Instead, she just went ahead and explained. "The boyfriend of one of the women he tried to extort put a hole in him. I might have given him his address. *Maybe.*"

Hoyt murmured, "For fuck's sake."

"Yeah, welcome to my life."

They were all silent a moment.

"Let's get back on track," Hoyt finally said.

Lei was looking more like her commanding self, so Vega grinned at him, rolling with his cue. "You just let me know when you're done with this roller coaster, my friend—"

"Changing directions isn't me getting off the ride. Don't try to get me to exit before I've gotten my money's worth."

Lei stood back, studying them. "That's why you were looking flustered after getting off the elevator. We got an email saying the elevator got stuck. *You* made it stop." She studied her brother for a moment longer, her upper lip peeling back. "Oh...so gross! That was your freshly fucked face."

Vega remembered something. "Oh yeah," and she took Hoyt's silk pocket square out of her back pocket and refolded it neatly before tucking it into his chest pocket. "Forgot, that's yours."

Hoyt's low rumble of a laugh started in his chest before breaking out. He whispered to her, his eyes dancing, "Menace."

Vega beamed back at him.

"So gross," Lei said, then to Vega, "You should understand that this means I'm going to pressure Hoyt to marry you and make you my sister officially. My hero, my sister? Sounds good. So, if this is a game you have with him, stop now."

Vega liked it; that was honesty she appreciated. "Hoyt's not necessary for us to be sisters. I accept. Buy us a heart necklace, the kind with two halves, and I'll wear one half."

Lei laughed, and Vega liked being able to make Hoyt's little sister laugh.

"Show us the breach," Hoyt said with a tsk and shake of his head.

"Fine, but I'm marrying your sister if we don't work out." Vega sat at the computer, and out of the corner of her eye, she saw Lei mouth to her brother, *Work out?*

"That was fast, Hoʻo," Lei whispered.

"Was it?" he answered, and Vega thought they might be on the same page about that point, them together. It hadn't felt fast. It felt glacially slow.

He moved to stand behind Vega, watching her work, his hands tucked into his pockets.

Vega murmured, "I see you found the breach when Bunny found a printer with outdated software. He has a thing for sexy mature printers."

"Vega..." Hoyt pressed her to get on with it.

"And after that you found the one in Hoyt's phone..." Vega searched through the data and didn't see anything that pointed further. So, she let it be. "Done and dusted. Let's call that an official breach."

"Yeah, but here's the thing," Lei interjected. "Bunny came in off Hoyt's device, which you physically breached at the club? That negates the contest."

Vega liked the way she thought, and steepling her fingers, she said, "Excellent point. Now, are we done, or is there something more? We're happy with not protecting against bots that come in from external sources? Let's not forget the USB key that took down the Iranian nuclear program. So, you're satisfied with the work you've done? You'd prefer to call this not a breach?"

Lei's gaze narrowed. "When you put it like that, no. And, Hoyt, stop looking so smug. You two are going to make me nauseous, aren't you?"

"Likely," Hoyt said, then, "We've wiped Bunny, you should know, and will be rolling back the systems, restoring to an older—clean—version of our software."

Vega looked up at him from where she hung over the armrest. "Sure, sounds good." His face was upside down from her angle.

She watched his wide mouth move. "I'd prefer if you were more on defense. This feels like you've got something brewing."

Vega stood. "It's been fun, kids. Be sure to give me a call if anything else pops up." She wrote a series of numbers on a Post-It and handed it to Hoyt. "We both know I'm in so deep you can't find me. I'd be happy now to do a nonphysical breach, if that's what the protocol for one point five million requires. Otherwise, please send the deposit to that account."

He took the paper from her, keeping his gaze on hers. "Let me walk you out."

"Wait, wait, wait..." Lei was playing catch-up. "In so deep? Bunny's not the only one in the systems now?"

Vega just gave her a grin that she didn't appreciate.

"Look, you can't just—"

Hoyt interrupted his sister. "I'm walking her out."

"She can find her own way out, Hoyt—we need to talk."

"I'd rather she wasn't unescorted."

Vega chimed in. "Don't you trust me?"

"As far as I can throw you."

She looked him up and down. "You trust me that far? Damn. Hot."

Lei looked as if she'd eaten the peel of a lime. "So gross. Get out, Hoyt. Vega, it was nice to meet you."

Vega beamed at the golden-brown-eyed sister of the man she was falling for. "Love you, bye."

He held out his arm to her, and Vega slipped her black nails into the crook of it.

The cool gray of the afternoon welcomed them after the elevator ride up, which was much less eventful than the one down. He said as soon as the glass front door closed behind him, "I'll wire the money to that account, but you should know I'm not done with you."

"Thank god."

"See you tonight?"

"I have Project Valkyrie work to do; otherwise, it'd be a hot yes. And you'll be much too busy with what I have planned."

As he grabbed for her, Vega skipped backward on the wet sidewalk—platforms be damned—a smile on both their lips.

"Give me a clue?" he called after her.

"Now, where's the fun in that, Mr. Kaho'okalakupua?"

He grinned and whispered, "Hana hou."

BITE THE HAND_

Vega couldn't believe that she was up so early or that she was sitting in a stadium, lights cutting through the cold November fog, at the grizzly hour of 5:00 a.m. Through her telephoto lens, she watched the man she'd become infatuated with, and his trainer, tangle with a tractor tire, pushing sled, and other items of torture.

I need a hint.

Vega started mentally scrolling back through their recent texts, his first at eleven the night before.

Again, where's the fun in that?

I'm coming over.

My door is always open to you.

But be honest...

Will we have our clothes on or off while you're asking questions?

Good point.

I'll give you one hint.

...I'm waiting...

Clothes will be off.

V, hint.

You'll never find it.

That's not a hint.

Think. Why won't you find it?

Her phone had been silent a long time; then:

Fuck.

Vega smiled.

Sorry?

Rewriting the code at the binary level was rough, tricking even his systems checks.

Don't be sorry for being fucking good.

There it had been again, that kindness that he doled out without cost to his own confidence or value. She wanted to eat it up with a spoon—and also to run away. Goodness always hurt when it was gone. But for the first time in a long time, she let herself absorb the feeling, pretending it would never end.

But I'll find you. I wrote this code.

If I have to go line by line, I will.

Just reset and start over.

No.

Vega had tapped the screen in wonder. If it had just been about the competition, he'd have rolled back the systems by now. But if their first interaction was a clue into his future performance, then it was obvious: he was going to use her virtual machine on his servers to walk his own systems back into hers.

You want that quantum computing data you think I have.

Not think. Know.

And if I don't have it, will you still think I'm good?

Yes. Game or not.

Don't take it easy on me now, Ms. Flux.

I think that I'll probably play this game with you forever.

Even when I'm behind bars, I'll find a way to hack your systems from a prison microwave.

You'd better.

Vega hadn't slept or worked much after that, which was probably why she finally just got up at that unholy hour and sat on a damp bleacher to watch him. She could feel herself getting obsessive over him, where he was, what he was wearing, doing, eating. And she had to remind herself to calm down. Only, when she did, he'd message her. It was as if he too were obsessed. Vega hadn't been immune to crushes before, but she'd never let one go this far, giving the other person the opportunity to reciprocate. Usually, all it took was a little digging to find dirty secrets, and that would be the end of that.

The curses from down on the field made her think that his venom was saved for his morning workouts. His grunts pulled at her like a magnet, made her want to slide onto the field. They woke up her synapses, making her skin itch to feel his palm. They had fucked twice, and yet they still hadn't seen each other fully naked. She was going to have to right that wrong but also didn't want to rush it. And it felt like neither did he. Maybe they both wanted to savor the heat of the prolonged desire until they couldn't stand it for one second longer.

She just hoped he wasn't in a meeting when that happened.

Vega pulled the strings of her hoodie tighter as the dampness sunk in. She adjusted her lens and clicked off a perfect shot. His muscle tee revealed his cut upper body but also the black-and-jewel-toned ink that peeked out along his back and poured from shoulder to wrist down his right arm. Suit on, he would appear straitlaced, maybe even conservative. Suit off, his mahogany skin displayed expert Japanese irezumi-style artistry of a mythological scene. Vega watched that scene through her lens as it moved as his musculature bunched and resculpted while he shoved the sled that his coach now jumped on top of. Exertion pinched his face as if he were in labor; grimacing against the weight, he shoved, plowing the entire thing down the field.

Vega whispered, "Your coach seems mean, Hoyt, but hello, guns and buns..."

Vega's pocket buzzed, and frowning because of the early hour, she checked her phone. Scout. She answered, worried.

"Oh, shit. I thought I'd get your voicemail. Why are you still up?"

"Why are you up?" she deflected. "*And* calling me, sweet cheeks?"

"I got the cash. No biggie, just wanted to leave the voicemail. Just thanks and all."

"Cool," she said, momentarily distracted by Hoyt who was now doing lunges toward a tractor tire. Then she pressed: "What has you calling me at five thirty in the morning?"

Hoyt squatted next to the tire. Glossy with sweat, he grabbed the two-hundred-pound tire and with a roar whipped it over. Vega's insides squirmed with suppressed pleasure. She wanted that body to brace over her while his hips pounded into her that thick erection she'd held in her mouth and hands the day before. She craved feeling her breasts bounce with each smack.

Scout blew out a breath. "I want to talk to you about helping me out. I tried to deposit that twenty thousand, and, Vega, they said they'd be reporting it to the federal government."

Vega cursed, and her attention was now laser-focused on her sister. "It was supposed to go straight to the university, hon." She had gotten sloppy to not have done that for Scout. She'd been focused in an entirely different direction, and suddenly her focus on her own private life felt selfish.

Scout sounded as if she'd been working on her frustration with Vega for a while. "No shit, sis, but they couldn't take cash at the registrar's office." Vega pinched the bridge of her nose. She knew that, yet she hadn't thought about any of it. Her stomach churned as her attention was being snapped back to Scout with the clarity of a hornet sting. "So, I had to deposit it then get a cashier's check. So, in order for me to do that, I had to drive around depositing nine thousand nine hundred and ninety-nine dollars at separate bank locations until it was all in. I felt like a con artist! And at every point, they asked me questions about the cash, where'd I get it, who gave it to me, no legit paperwork, but I felt like I was dodging for you, Vee! I think I need to get loans. I know you work tax-free." She rushed forward before Vega could reply. "I figured it out—that's why you won't do big jobs and why you turned down working for Hoyt Securities when the friggin' founder himself asked for you. So...I've decided I can't be taking money from you for my undergrad anymore. It feels wrong."

Vega swallowed her heart down. Scout was skating at the edge of trouble. "Sure, sure. But if it's just about me paying taxes, I can go legit. I've just been so lazy about it. Ha." Her tone sounded like she was the one tossing two hundred pounds of bullshit on the field below.

"Yeah, I'd like that, Vee. Dodging taxes can get your wages garnished, and in some cases, you sent to prison."

"Yikes," Vega said, pretending that was news to her, and simultaneously feeling like that was the least of her worries. "I'll get on that today. Thanks, sis." Despite the chill in the air, Vega began to sweat.

"OK, then one more thing—your note with the money said you have my passport?"

"Yeah." Vega cursed silently again.

"I don't remember ever getting a photo."

Vega tried not to panic. Scout was becoming more and more of the attorney she was destined to be, questioning and argumentative, but right then, Vega didn't want it. She needed more time. She needed to think.

"I just grabbed a good picture of you and gave it a blank background and sent it off. Sorry, I thought I was doing you a favor."

"Vega... That feels like..."

Vega waited. This was what she thought thin ice must be like to skate on, unsure if the next move would plunge her into inescapable trouble. "What?"

Scout blew out another breath. "Vega, I think it's time I start to do things for myself. We should have a more sister-to-sister relationship. You keep taking things out of my hands like you're a mom and I'm a kid who doesn't know how things work."

Vega wanted to point out that her attempting to pay her tuition with twenty grand in cash was a rookie move, but that finger-pointing led to a slippery slope.

"Look, sorry, bug, but I was eight when you were born, and for most of your life, you didn't have mom. So I stepped in. I just have a hard time letting that parent role go."

"Ugh."

"What?" Vega asked as a chill wind moved over the bleachers.

"You always do that."

"Do what?"

"Point out what you sacrificed for me. I didn't ask you to! I'm not asking you now!"

Vega felt her temper catch with her pent-up frustration at herself, that she'd not been paying attention more and that Scout was about to bumble herself into hot water so deep it would destroy everything Vega worked so hard to do so Scout could have as normal a life as possible.

"Well, fuck, sure, Scout, take a big ol' shit on me for helping you. Look, have it your way. Get some loans. And while you're playing grown-up, you can fuck your credit score when you can't pay them back in time, just like a real adult. Or, hey, suck it up when your loan application gets rejected because you have no credit history. Sure, go be an adult. Default out of your pricey private school."

"You...you...ugh! You're such a jerk, Vega! I knew you'd blow up like this!"

"I'm a realist. I've seen the shit end of things in this world, and all I want is for you to be happy. But if suffering is what you want, fuck it, I can let that happen to you."

"How is paying my own way suffering?!"

Vega had to stop, needed to keep cool, but more than that, what she kept at bay scared the shit out of Vega. So, Vega had to be scary to Scout. But that made her into a monster. Any way she looked at it, she was fucked. Secrets made her sicker.

"Spoken like a girl who chooses to ignore the hard realities of life."

"Thanks, sis, I wonder who made me that way."

Vega hadn't been prepared for any of this. She'd been too busy with the man on the field and his life to check in on Scout, and it was the first time Vega felt tired by Scout not fucking getting it. Cindy and Peace had been right—she should tell Scout sooner than graduation. Scout needed to fall out of the nest lest she fell off a cliff.

"Great. Just great, Scout. You can float the rest of your education by yourself on your ten-hour-a-week college job. Congrats, you just bit the hand that fucking feeds you." But the line had already gone dead. Vega wanted to scream and whip the cell across the field.

The phone call was more than a reality check about her sister. Getting entangled with Hoyt meant that his normal family would eventually ask about her. There was only so much time before Lei or he slipped and talked about Vega as Vega. And while Vega's warrants would put her in prison, Scout's old name meant she could kiss the life she had goodbye.

Scout's old name still had debts owed. She would spend the next ten years cleaning up her good name instead of graduating, heading to law school, passing the bar, and starting her career. Then, if there was a vengeful collections agent—and they all were—she could see herself in court. Or if the person owed had a vendetta, the end of a gun. All because one man, sworn to protect them after their mother's death, sold their virgin identities to cover his own debts until Vega made him stop.

That was the thing about secrets—they always had a way of coming out. Even the person most protected by the secret eventually gave it up. There was no way around it, Vega thought: *Secrets make us sick.*

CHASE_

So deep in her thoughts, Vega didn't notice how the fog had started to burn off in the slow autumn sun, leaving her, in her black hoodie, black sneakers, and black leggings, a black dot in the silver stands.

Hoyt's training session finished, her stark presence seemed to draw his gaze.

"Fuck," Vega whispered. She tossed her legs over the bench then slipped down below the bleachers. Between the open supports she worked her way to the exit in the fence on the other side.

One glance back to the field, however, and she saw that Hoyt had dropped his bag and was sprinting toward that same exit.

Despite her desire to put distance between them, Vega's insides grinned. "Oh, boy," she whispered. She'd have to run fast. *Real* fast.

With a tight hand on her camera, she did something she'd not done in years. She sprinted. Down the damp sidewalk embossed with brown fallen leaves and around the corner she tore along the stadium's retaining wall.

She'd once been fast, scholarship fast, but that was a long time ago, and one glance back showed her that Hoyt was in tiptop shape and warmed up. He was already around the corner and was hauling ass after her; his hands, pumping, went flat, parallel to his body.

She couldn't help the excited squeal that escaped her like air from a balloon as she bolted down the wet cement. Ahead, the street crossing was empty save for the tightly parked cars on either side of the road. She slid over the hood of the one in front of her and stumble-stepped through the intersection. Between the bumpers on the other side, she caught her feet again and made for the next block. She was halfway up it when she heard the quick peal of the bottoms of Hoyt's lightweight training shoes on the sidewalk behind her.

"Vega!" he called after her.

She waved her hand over head and shouted, "Hi. Bye!"

Her breath coming like the chug of a freight train, she put on a burst of speed and at the next block pivoted at the corner only to have her sweatshirt get nicked by his long reach.

It twisted her shoulder back, pulling her momentum off center. Hoyt collided with her as she stumbled forward, trying to right herself. On her, Hoyt grabbed fistfuls of her sweater, trying to stop their collective forward movement by lifting and steering her around his feet.

She heard him curse, then felt him turn as he tucked her into his chest before they slammed back into a tree.

Breathing hard, he released her but held her loosely in his arms. "What are you doing here? And why are you running away?"

Turning her chest into his and feeling the good pound of her blood through her veins she said, "Doing something I shouldn't."

He pulled her hips in against his. "What's up? You dodged me yesterday after the talk with Lei and now this morning you're running like a track star from me. If I didn't know better, I'd say you were putting literal distance between us."

His eyes were golden, bright with his exertion, the morning light throwing his high cheekbones into relief, making Vega want to touch them and the shadows below. Sweat and sandalwood off his skin drew her in, and she touched him with her eyes. "Not very well, apparently." She dragged a long black fingernail down his right arm where a new glisten of sweat shone over his skin and down over his tattoo. She saw a story of a boy with what looked like a bone fishhook and the peaks of mountainous islands being pulled from the sea. “Beautiful.”

His hand cradled her cheek, his bicep mounding the islands. “You never told me that you own more than ripped jeans.”

Her hand covered his, feeling the warmth of it down to her bones. “There’s so much you don’t know.” She smiled but felt the sadness of the brakes she was pulling.

Hoyt was keen to the change, his golden gaze going dark as it studied her face before he asked, “What happened?”

“I had a reminder this morning that there are people who depend on me, and I need to keep that in mind more than this play-make-believe thing you and I have going.”

His head bent, and he kissed her ear, making her body soften against his, maybe one last feel of him.

“You want to end things?”

She sighed. “You really do cut to the chase, don’t you?”

“Saves time.”

“I do. I have to.”

“Unless I can somehow just do fucking and games?” he asked, coming back to the things she’d said to him the day before.

“Ugh, I hate how perceptive you are. And yes, can you?”

“No”—he brushed his lips over hers—“can you?”

She didn’t like the tease of his lips and chased them down to press a kiss to them, going against what her words were saying. “I need to.”

“Why pull back now? What happened to remind you?” he asked then added, “Because you’re wearing a stalker-worthy camera and came dressed as if you’re about to work out. Should we go back to the field and finish what you came for?” His palm glided over her hip, brushing over her rear before grabbing it and bringing her in tighter.

“Scout called just now.” She looked away to clear her mind. In the yard they’d stopped in front of, a row of roses behind a low, faded white picket fence was a dark shadow of what the summer sunshine had held in their blooms.

"Really? Seems early for a college kid," he whispered, tucking a loose lock of her hair behind her ear.

"She was trying to dodge me by talking just to my voicemail. She said she got the twenty thousand that I sent over..." She touched his wide mouth that had fed her hundreds of kisses and brought her to orgasm more thoroughly than anyone had ever before. "Thanks, by the way."

"Of course, friendship payments are serious."

Vega grinned at the reason she'd kept that twenty grand.

"I have a much bigger payment that's coming in electronic form later in the week. My accountants are having a shit fit over it. Apparently they don't like sending money to unknown accounts with strange transfer protocols. In the Caymans."

She touched the flat plane of his cheek, admiring the cut of his jaw. "You're really doing it, aren't you?"

"A deal is a deal, Ms. Flux."

"You have no idea what that means for me."

"That's right, I don't. Wanna tell me?"

"A man of his word...you're a unicorn, my friend."

"I was thinking a bit more about how you might use that one point five mil."

"That's...a secret."

"Please?"

She fisted the front of his workout tank. "What could you possibly want with that knowledge?"

"To know you better. I've only gotten so far as Scout having a seemingly regular Social Security number, but I'm sure if I look any further—and I won't—that it's made up right along with the names Vega and Scout Flux that sound like a teenager invented them. Is that how old you were when you saved Scout from your stepdad?"

"Oh, wow." She laid her forehead on his chest, and the black cord of his necklace bit into her skin.

"Too much?" he whispered. "Because I want more, Vega."

"Why?"

"Because in moments like this, I can help. I can talk you through the various risk assessments, and instead of you leaving what we have going, we can team up." She was about to respond when he added, "That and I want to slip into you every way possible. Into your body and into your mind until I'm 100 percent sure you understand how much you mean to me." He tilted her chin up. "Woman who calls herself Vega Flux. Woman who sees me and doesn't flinch. Woman who I'm pretty sure would fuck me if I had zero reputation and only a dime to my name."

Oh yes, she thought, she would. "You'd be sexier if you had only a dime. Just think of all the things I could get you to do with the lure of money."

"You'd take advantage of me?" he growled, putting his mouth to her neck and biting her softly in retaliation.

Vega softly squealed at the delicious feel of his teeth pressing sharply against her skin.

He then licked the bite marks before kissing them. "Don't be mean. I'd be hooked on you and wouldn't need money to get me to do your bidding."

He moved to the other side of her neck, and Vega suppressed a giggle at his breath tickling the sensitive skin beneath her ear. She pinned his face between her shoulder and her cheek. "Biting and talking dirty to me is going to make me take my clothes off. So, stop, unless you're prepared to hoist me up against this tree."

"Fine," he said between pinched cheeks. "Why did Scout call?"

Vega released him. "She wants to be just sisters."

"Mm." He paused to decode that. "She doesn't want big sister telling her what to do? How about big sister's money?"

"She doesn't even want that now. She doesn't understand the sacrifices we all had to make, and now she just wants to run headlong into the world without having any idea what lies in wait out there." Vega swallowed; she'd said too much.

Hoyt grasped on to it. "What lies in wait out there, Ms. Flux?"

She was on a slippery slope of secrets. "I'm sorry, that was too much."

"No, not enough, tell me more."

"This is why I want distance between us. Just seconds with you, and I've told you more than I've told anyone, much less a man, ever."

"Fine. Tell me, then, how many people have you killed with your bare hands?"

She raised her brows. "I like my inflated persona in your mind. Lemme see, none with my bare hands but likely four by proxy."

She studied his reaction. He looked away, thoughtful, as if processing that information against his own set of rights and wrongs. "Fine."

The backs of his fingers caressed her cheek. He put his cheek against her temple and held her close as he whispered, "I believe you. And trust you—"

"Ugh, don't."

"I do, so make me a promise?"

Vega felt her insides squeeze. She hoped she could do it, make whatever promise he was about to ask. "Depends."

"Someday you'll tell me?"

She let the bridge of her nose brush his chin while his breath warmed her forehead. "Someday."

"That's good enough for me, for right now. Let's just let all that go. Come with me." Taking her hand, he pulled her back down the sidewalk to the stadium.

"Hoyt, I need to go."

"Sure" was all he gave her.

There was his quiet power again, and she called after him as he tugged her along, "Do you always get what you want, Titan?"

Her words stopped him. His head was bent for a moment as if deciding on something. Then he turned, yanking her in against him. His hand gripped her hip as his other wove in her hair and held her in against his firm body. "I fucking do. Every time."

She smiled and said the antithesis of what was in her heart. "Hoyt, I hate you."

He grinned. "Not yet you don't."

SECRETS_

They took the elevators down to the concrete parking garage labeled *A* in bright orange on the concrete supports. In a paid members-only spot Vega recognized Hoyt's black luxury SUV. The dark paint shone under the fluorescent lights, and as Vega climbed into the soft tan leather interior of the passenger seat, she was reminded that the monetary difference between them was massive.

"I think your ride just charged me to sit here. Maybe I should drive and you sit in the back."

"Fuck you." And with a hand to the back of her headrest, he reversed them out of the spot.

She grinned and let her head fall back, watching him. "I'd like to be fucked by you, and no, you may not come up when you drop me off, no matter what I say when we get there."

"About that. You're coming with me to my place. I need a shower."

Vega felt pleasantly trapped. "Oh yeah?"

"Yeah."

"You know I'm going to watch, right?"

His eyes crinkled at the edges with what she was quickly learning was his suppressed glee. He knew she was going to watch. He probably knew he was going to break her mind. And that she'd be watching only for about the first ten seconds of the shower. "Afterward, I'd like you to walk through your process of breaching with Lei and me."

Vega sighed. "That still feels too close."

"Just one last request. Can you help me with that?"

"Ugh." Vega rubbed her hands over her thighs. "You know all of this is catnip for me. You know this, and now you're asking me politely? Dammit, Hoyt."

Hoyt glanced at her, his eyes soft. "Yes, beautiful. Ko'u lua pele, whose eyes are a color I'll never forget, blue of the ocean mixed with green of algae-covered ocean stones. Limua pōhaku kai. And a mouth I want on me all the time—"

Vega put her hands over her face as if that would stop the onslaught. "Oh, fuck, that all sounds beautiful—stop."

"'A'ole."

Vega's heart twisted under his words. "It's torture. What do I do with all those pretty sounds?"

"I want you to get so used to nice things being said to you, Vega, that you take them for granted."

"Hoyt, that would take a lifetime."

"I know."

Vega opened her mouth to reply then closed it again.

He rescued her from having to reply: "So, back to my earlier question, can you help me?"

"Just do it, and I'll follow. I'm not answering yes or no."

"Speaking of engineering, when you were eavesdropping on my engineers yesterday, the thing I'd have to have reversed is my vasectomy. Why the fuck that was brought up, or how they know, is beyond me."

"Oh, as in sex-without-condoms snipped?"

"Of course you'd hear that I can't have kids and think of the logistics of lovemaking."

"Yes, of course I would. And why did you snip before you had kids? You have enough on your plate?"

"I had a moment in my former career that made me realize condoms weren't enough."

"What kind of moment was that?"

"A night of debauchery, in a long line of nights of debauchery." The SUV's tires chirped on the ultra-smooth concrete as they rounded the last bend to the exit.

Vega waited for him to continue, and when he didn't, she offered, "That must have been some night of debauchery. You should know that after every time I'm with Jax, I get checked. He didn't penetrate me the last time I was with him, and I still got checked. I'm clean."

Hoyt cursed as he pulled them out of the parking structure. "He's someone I'm going to have to try really hard not to destroy if I ever meet him."

"Jax?"

"Yeah."

"I can't imagine any scenario where you two meet, and good gosh, Hoyt," she said, "still with the jealousy?"

"He's had more time with you than me, and I *hate* it."

She put her finger to his shoulder and dragged it down the art etched there. "You really say the prettiest stuff."

He gave her a glance that said that wasn't the type of kind words he wanted her to take for granted.

"But if you really want to destroy his life, just tell his stalker ex where he lives now."

"Ugh. I just fucking might. Remind me why you used him as a fuck buddy?"

"The questions, Hoyt. He doesn't ask any. I'm trying to get out of whatever this is that we have because of all your questions. You're goddamn dangerous."

"Questions thoroughly answered equals to safety in my business. So, let's do another."

"Fine, let's keep it to clothing size—"

"Let's talk about how fast you are. It's rare for me to work that hard to catch someone."

She let a grin spread across her face, "Yeah, well, apparently I wasn't fast enough." She gestured to the inside of his SUV. "But since I've got a few minutes comfortably trapped here with you and it's Q and A time, how about you answer mine and I'll answer yours. Night of debauchery?"

He shrugged. "As it sounds. Now, why not go to college—"

"You're dodging."

"Solidly dodging. Tell me why you decided to not go to college, and I ask because it's just surprising for a *college athletics scholarship winner*."

"Wow." She looked up and out the moon roof to the gray sky. He knew much, much more than she'd assumed, or hoped, he did. As in he was probably bankrolling someone to look into her. "You dug deep, Mr. Kahoʻokalakupua."

His voice was low. "Not deep enough."

"That wasn't publicized. I made sure of it. I have to ask, if my warrant list scared you, why'd you talk with, hmm, my foster mom?"

"Not me. A very quiet investigator did."

Vega closed her eyes; did she feel the urge to leap from the moving car? "Why..."

"I'm obsessed with you, and I needed to know."

That he'd sent someone he was bankrolling meant it was more than that. "Risk assessment," she said.

He was quiet, chancing glances and her. "How angry are you?"

Vega was surprised by the question but more so by her answer. "You know...I think I should be angry about it, but I just feel strangely relieved. There's less of my nightmare past I have to conceal. How much do you know?"

"That you were fast as fuck in high school, and it was enough to get my alma mater, Oregon State, to offer you a scholarship. That you would have been there when I was."

"Really?"

"Yes."

"You mean, we could have had this erotic tryst so much sooner?"

His eyes danced with mirth. "Much, much, sooner."

"I would have gotten into so much trouble with you. But also, I probably would have fucked a lot fewer worthless guys if I'd met you sooner."

"Maybe not. I was too focused on academics and coding the beta version of Titan's Wall to pursue girls. Now," he said, pointing, "immediately after college, you'd have torched me."

Vega waited for him to continue, and when he didn't, she said, "And?"

"And what?"

"You can't just leave it there. That was the debauchery time, wasn't it?"

He turned them onto Front Street heading south toward Hoyt Towers. "Tell me why we didn't go to college together."

She gave him a wan smile at the missed opportunity that was them in a normal relationship in college. "Things got...complicated. Junior, my foster dad, died, and going to college had to be on the back burner. Scout needed me, and I needed to make money to support us and Maggie, my foster mom, until she could get her feet under her. It meant pulling Scout to live with me full-time. So, I went to work instead."

The light turned, and as he made a sound from the back of his throat that said he understood but also knew that was only part of the story, he gentled his foot onto the accelerator.

"You sound like you already knew that answer."

"Just wanted to see how much you'd give me. And if it'd include the name you were born with."

"I see. The investigator hit a snag there, I take it?"

He nodded. "Name requests that get punted to vague email servers and paper trails that seemingly dead end."

"That's good. It means my defenses are working."

"What's in your shadows, Vega? What is it that you're hiding from other people? From me? Let me help."

The only thing Vega could think of was "For fuck's sake, why? Fucking and games, remember?"

"Fuck that. There are things in life that I can live without, and there are things I can't. As of thirteen days ago, the vison of what I want is just an image of you." He pointed all five fingers forward as if Vega's face was down field in the end zone. "I want all of you, and if I can see your past, I can show you a future that I think deep down you want as bad as I do. If I haven't totally miscalculated the risk there," he said, glancing toward her, "I want to celebrate this Thanksgiving with you at my table. And I'm arrogant enough to try and achieve that."

Vega could only groan as the bait she wanted was offered up to her on a silver platter. The weight of her past lifted from her shoulders. Him plus food plus family—she wanted his dream too. She might have to port into the house's Wi-Fi and watch through the smart home system he had, but she'd be there like a stray cat at the window looking in.

"With your original name and Social Security number, I'm told we can start to erase your warrants. Legally." The vehicle purred down the Hoyt Towers side street before he turned them into the private underground garage.

Vega rested her elbow on the window ledge of the passenger door and tried to hold back the flood of emotion that swamped her. *Was that possible?* It felt like freedom and pain in one medicated syringe.

"Talk to me" came quietly from the driver's seat.

He parked in his designated spot, and she closed her eyes and whispered, "Sure. Those are beautiful words, but not for me. I live in a house of cards. One wrong move, and the tower I've built gets compromised. Stop looking. I'll help you today, but I'm a stray, Hoyt. Can you be OK with that?"

He turned off the ignition and sat for a while, thinking seriously about what she'd asked him. "Truthfully? No. I'll likely keep digging—"

"Fuck, Hoyt," she whispered.

"Especially if you ghost me. If I can clear your name or have a clear path on how to do it, I'll track you down and beg you to let me do it. I want you every day."

Vega groaned. "Again, why me? Get back with the marriage broker, choose a woman who's not broken—they're everywhere. It's so much easier to love them. Loving them is uncomplicated and peaceful."

"I..." he started then seemed to be coaching himself on something. Then he just dove in. "I've been with women I should have found easy to love, good, kind people I've even stayed friends with, but after meeting you, I now know I need volcanic. I need someone who challenges me, who doesn't let me get away with holding back. And I've...I've fallen in love with you. No one has gotten into my head like you have. No one has had the power to pull me from my tower and into a warehouse across the river in the middle of the night but you. If you leave now, you have that right. But I won't be able to let go."

"Goddamn you." Vega undid her belt and crawled over the console to him. He grabbed the wheel and tilted it up before cradling her in his lap.

Straddling him, she trapped his face between her hands and kissed him, hard. She opened her mouth, tasting his words and putting her own back onto his tongue. She felt the heat of him, his words, and that same undeniable twist to her gut that said she'd never felt this way before and never would again. And for that she both hated and loved him.

His hands traveled from where they'd rested on her thighs up under her sweater. Touching her bare skin, he whispered, "I can care about you if you give me nothing else. I just want to give you every happiness that exists in this world, and I think it starts by not fearing your past. But I don't know what's there, so I don't know how to help."

Vega felt it start low in her abdomen: she wanted to give him what he wanted. *One name wasn't everything,* she lied to herself. His golden Apollo eyes were as honest as the sun rising in the east each morning, and the urge to give into him became like betting on the winning horse. That urge became a need, and soon she was putting her life savings down on that horse, and the name rolled out of her mouth into the quiet cabin. "Melanie Alexander."

The quiet that followed was the epitome of an explosion's

aftermath. And she'd just detonated the largest truth bomb she'd ever let get out.

Melanie Alexander?

Hearing her name dredged from a world of pain and personal war, she felt another shock as if she were physically waking the past. As if Lloyd were in the back seat shouting her name, *Melanie!*

What the fuck had she just done? She broke rule number one: tell no one her or Scout's real name. Ever. She didn't feel relieved. Her horse felt now like it was running for its life, taking her earnings with it.

Melanie Alexander.

With her hands still on his cheeks, she took in his gaze that had morphed into startled. He hadn't expected her to blurt it out. It swiftly was turning into concern as her whole body began to vibrate in fear. Broken rules were dangerous. They created cracks that lead to shattered foundations. She felt her house of cards sway.

Fucking Melanie Alexander!

His hands went to her thighs and rubbed, trying to get her body to calm down. "OK... It's OK, Vega. Tell me what I can do with that name. It's still in your control." He tried to catch hers as they flitted around the cabin of his car as if startled as to how she'd gotten there and how the fuck she could get out. "And breathe. Fuck, you're shaking. Breathe."

The question, *What have you done?*, ran through her mind in increasing decibels until it was just one drawn-out screech.

Vega opened the door.

Hoyt slipped out with her, a supportive hand on her waist. "Let's go upstairs. You can pace upstairs. I'll cancel my meetings."

Her eyes darted to his hand on her, and she jumped back. "Fuck."

He held his hands up, showing that he wouldn't touch her again. "Breathe, Vega, you just told me a very serious secret. I'm prepared to keep it forever if you want me to."

Vega was trying to breathe, but her whole body was telling her she should run.

On instinct, she pulled her phone out and dialed. Other hand on her waist, she panted as her first call didn't go through, but her next did. Hoyt tried to get close, his brow creased in concern. She was hyperventilating by the time the call on the secure line connected.

"Cindy," Vega breathed out and moved away from Hoyt, sliding around the backside of his vehicle then to the concrete floor as if she were dodging bullets.

"What's going on?" Cindy was on high alert.

"I told him," Vega whispered. "I fucked up."

"Who's him?"

"Hoyt."

"How much?"

"My name. I got emotional, and it just came out."

"Yeah, OK. He's good enough to get the rest with it. So, he's threatened you?"

"No, he says to tell him what he should do with it. If he should forget it or dive into it."

There was a long pause. "What do you feel like?"

Her voice shook. "Cin, I can't think. I should have talked with you guys first. Lloyd's going to find us. I can't think. Imma run or maybe vomit first. I'm sorry, I fucked up."

"Stop. You're spiraling. I hear you. That's big. Joan..." she said, using Vega's cover name while at her desk, "he's loyal, though, Joan."

"What are you saying? Fuck, I can't think, I'm gonna run." Vega came up to her knees and then to standing.

"Nope, no. You're not running. This isn't a real risk. He's not a risk. Do you hear me? Are you listening?"

"Don't run?" Vega sat back down against the rear tire. Parts of the parking garage started to come into focus, the dark gray of the concrete beams then the bright red of the Lamborghini that Hoyt's SUV was parked next to and the yellow of its brake calipers that she was on eye level with.

"Don't run," Cindy reiterated. "Carry this trust very carefully, Vega, but you're OK. If not, I'll shoot him. And you're not a kid anymore. You've got this. Breathe." She said, "Hoyt, I think, really, I mean, *really*, likes you. We can use a guy like him in our corner, Vee."

Vega took a deep, lung-filling breath, trying to think between the urges to run. Cindy was reminding her that she wasn't in danger. That what her brain thought she'd caused, a dangerous situation, wasn't actually bad. It was like that—the hardwiring that was woven into her synapses hadn't ever had time to heal and become like a normal adult's.

Trusting Cindy, she took a deep breath to clear away the false instinct. "Are you saying something more? You want to bring him on?"

"Yes. That's what I'm saying. I'm giving you the space to do it. Shit, girl, breathe. It's OK. He can be on Team Vega."

Vega was starting to think more clearly. "What about Peace? What will she want, though?"

"Man, you're really deep in your spiral, hon. I think you know what Peace would say. What she's been saying since the beginning. She was the one who found him and had the first good instincts about him. I'm just glad he sees what we do in you."

Vega swallowed, her mouth having gone dry as the fight-or-flight reflexes faded away. "Shit."

"What?"

"He said he loves me."

"He what?!" There was rustling on the other end, and Cindy's voice lowered. "Sorry, he what?"

"Yeah, what the hell do I do with that? Cin, I want this so bad, but what we do, we can't have him with us—the liability to his way of life is too great..."

"Oh, don't I know it. Stick with the plan, babe. Continue to prove you're not where you were a year ago, and it won't be. It's not as dangerous now for him. And if we continue to proceed carefully, you could be with him for a couple maybe even ten years before something comes up and you have to move again. I know being back home puts you on high alert, but things have been quiet for the last five years with you-know-who, and I think it's stable enough for you to try a relationship. Vee, it's worth it. He's got serious resources that we could only dream of. He could be really helpful."

"You mean, let him try to clear our names?"

"Shit, yeah. I mean, start there and then move on to the other blue-sky projects we've dreamed of."

"But if things go sideways..."

"They won't, remember? We have rules. And this rule-breaking is OK. I kinda knew it might happen sooner or later."

Vega groaned. "All right, I should go. I'm hiding from him to talk to you."

She heard Cindy give a soft laugh. "I'm so glad this call wasn't what I thought it was."

Vega relaxed. "Yeah, not DEFCON 1. Just yet."

"You-know-who is in prison, and we monitor him. It'll likely never happen, so don't ruin the now with some what-ifs."

"Yes, ma'am."

GIVE ME YOUR DARKNESS_

She saw him still standing there, a towering giant in his athletic gear, now on his phone as well. He looked up then, his eyes softening.

Vega went to him as she tucked her phone away and brushed tears off her cheeks that she didn't know she had shed.

His voice was laced with concern. "I was just canceling my meetings this morning. Would you rather be at your place?"

Vega could only nod.

The drive over was quiet until he pulled into her parking lot where the gravel crunched under his SUV's tires.

"You can look," she said abruptly. "At the name I was born with. Don't push past any password-protected stuff, or it'll trigger exposure warnings, and I'll likely have to initiate my DEFCON 1 and disappear."

He put the SUV in park and turned off the ignition. "That sounds bad."

"It's the nuclear reset option for our protection project. The girls help me disappear if it gets to that. You should at least know that, so you understand why you need to be careful."

"So, everything I do needs to be run through the filter of: Is this worth never seeing Vega again?"

"There's plenty you'll find before you hit the protected stuff. And when you do, I'll reassess letting you go further."

"So, this is a test?"

"Cindy thinks you can be an asset to our team, which is good. It's what let me see through that panic attack."

She watched relief pour through him, and his hand released its tight grip on the wheel. "And you? Do you see things as she does?"

"It's still complicated. Truthfully? I trust no one and nothing except Cindy and Peace, and even then, I can get suspicious. You and I have known each other for a few short weeks, and while my heart wants to tear my ribcage open just to have you touch me, my mind says wait."

"I can wait."

"That's the thing—your reputation is everything to you. It's what your entire empire is made from. I'm a black hole that can cripple in a fit of rage or destroy just by name association."

He nodded. "I get that. I also get that you see me for who I am today. You asked me earlier about my past, the debauchery I mentioned, and I should tell you about that time so that you know where I'm coming from when I say that there are things in life more important to me than what you see as an empire and a reputation."

Vega watched his profile as he spoke and noticed that hint of an accent return.

"You keep telling me I'm a good person. I wasn't always, and I'm still told more than once a week I'm an asshole. I'm not sure what you see that others don't, but you should know there was a part of my life that I lived hard in, and I almost didn't become the man I am today. The difference between then and now is that I'm clean now."

She appreciated finally hearing him tell of that time. "Were those the years after college, the NFL?"

"Yeah. I didn't make the transition as well as others did."

"I've done a little light stalking of you, but I only dug up that suddenly the news reports showed that you'd gotten better at playing.

It really sounded like they all thought you'd had your head up your ass, and then suddenly you didn't."

"I spent my signing bonus in three months on parties."

Vega felt her eyebrows raise. For a fourth-round draft pick for his rookie season, that number was flirting with a million dollars. "Oh my. Cocaine-and-girls kind of parties? How'd that not make news?"

"Because that kind of stuff isn't news."

"Right. I suppose there's a lot that goes on we don't hear about."

He nodded solemnly. "At first, it was buying people shit; then it was, more exactly, 'drinking myself unconscious and fan girls in hotels' parties. But of course, at the root, I was depressed, so the highs from that didn't last. I overcaffeinated during the day so I could perform; then I couldn't sleep, so I drank harder at night. Then the caffeine wasn't enough, so I got pills. I didn't do street drugs; they weren't always clean, and someone would eventually find out, and my contract would be toast. Pills seemed safe. FDA approved and all that."

She heard the internal lie he had told himself. "Sure, lesser of two evils."

"I was already losing my contract, though. Every game I had to sit out with an injury drove another nail in the coffin of my career, and while everyone around me wanted me to succeed and were showing me how, I couldn't do it."

"What ended up happening?"

"My agent called my family."

"Oh boy."

"My mom showed up with this." He pulled on the black cord around his neck, and from under his shirt came a shark's tooth. He looked to it then to her, watching her closely as if that shark's tooth had a heavy history and how she reacted to it was an answer as to what kind of person Vega was.

"Hello," she said to the jagged tooth. "I saw the cord and wondered... Has that been under your shirts all this time?"

"Yes, I have taken it off only once since my mother gave it to me."

"Surgery or something?" Vega held her hand up slowly. "Can I touch it?"

"Yeah." He answered then added, "It wasn't surgery."

She looked to him and saw he was holding something back, but right at the surface. "When'd you take it off?"

"I took it off for Londyn." He laid his palms flat against the steering wheel as he confessed what sounded like a secret. "She said it, and my tattoos, made me look like an uncivilized brute. I took it off the first time we were...alone together."

"Naked."

"'Ae."

Vega took the word that sounded like *aye* as a yes. She was thoughtful. Thoughtful on how she could gently drown Londyn in her bathwater. "She's a real piece of work. Congratulations on being rid of her."

Hoyt huffed out a laugh.

"And for the record," she continued, "you look mesmerizing. I want to eat snacks off your biceps and stare at you all day. I also want to get you fully naked and have my way with you, your tats, your face, your mind, your tight, expensive clothes. But back to this," she said, looking to the tooth, serrated on two of the three edges of the triangle, "Hoyt, this looks like a real shark's tooth, not like something found at a gift shop."

"It is. It represents manō, meaning 'shark.' The tooth is from a tiger shark, niuhi. Her tooth got caught in my dive bag when she went after my catch, and she left it behind."

Vega brushed her thumb over it, and repeated, "Mahn-oh."

"Yes, long *o*," and he spelled it for her, "the name of my 'aumakua."

"Those are new words for me."

Hoyt explained to her what 'aumakua meant, his family totem, in a way, a family spirit guide. Then how he met manō. Hoyt grinned as he spoke, his body relaxing, but Vega didn't read that to mean this was light-hearted knowledge he was imparting. It was as if these were private things to him and he didn't share them with anyone outside his family. And his family was more than those who called him kin; they somehow also seemed to encompass all the Hawaiian Islands, maybe even the whole of Polynesia. It was as if this knowledge was a common thread within that community, and he was bringing her in on it.

"That shark stole your fish, like, ripped fishy snacks right out of your dive sack? When it got that close, were you scared? I would have shit my pants."

"My catch bag had been trailing along behind me; it wasn't at my hip."

"Still…

What'd your mom say when she gave this to you?"

"At the time, I was so fogged up on pills and depression that I didn't care that she was there or that she brought it to remind me of something important."

"And what was that…?" she prodded gently.

"That where I come from isn't just a place. It's an entire people and a mindset, and the things that set me apart are the things that are to be celebrated, not brushed aside for me to fit in. That in brushing them aside, I was denying who I was and where I came from." Hoyt blew out a breath. "I tried to assimilate after college. I wasn't focused on tech or my family, and I missed home, but that felt like I was being a baby. I was a man, I could make it here in the mainland, I could compete up here in this massive arena. I got disconnected. Mom was disappointed but also saw that I too was disappointed in myself and brought in my family to help."

"She circled the wagons."

"She brought me home without having to take me home. They moved in, and pissed me off." He gave a soft huff. "She reminded me that I needed a challenge, and if I didn't push myself, I'd go after the man in the mirror and descend into self-hate. And that wasn't good for me, personally or professionally. And ultimately, she reminded me, my self-worth had already been established: I'd already touched paradise—I was born in it. Everything I do after is icing. I had to remove the pressure to become someone I wasn't, and just be me."

"How long did that take?"

He gave her a sidelong glance. "Still working on it."

Vega fell back into her seat. "That's the sound of a man who's done the work, and knows the work is never done."

"Says the woman who knows."

She looked down at the seam in the leather console and scratched at it. Yeah, she knew. She also knew her work was far from done.

His voice went soft, poking at her. "Your family circled the wagons too. Just as tight."

Vega knew who he was talking about. "Peace, Cindy, and I were making it up as we went back then. Thinking about it now, I can't believe three teenagers got Scout, and me, out of that house."

"You mentioned your stepdad the first time you came to my office—he was the one who used your socials?"

"Yeah. He sold them to people who defrauded just about everyone they could using 'Melanie Alexander' until the money ran out or the feds caught up to them. They didn't, and he didn't have the grace to think what owing a drug dealer would mean for the real Melanie Alexander." She huffed out a breath. "Guns, it always meant guns."

Hoyt pressed his thumb to the base of the steering wheel as if stretching it out while his mind churned. "He should have been protecting you."

"Sure, but he had no idea what protection was—he was too focused on his needs." Vega told him how she'd come to live with him, after her mom died, and how she'd come to leave his home. "Instead of making good on his promise to her to be a great dad, he went for door number two."

"Be the shittiest one possible."

"More like, go back to being the asshole she'd tempered when she was alive, but make the kids still call you father so you feel like you're doing something important." Vega stretched in her seat. "Until five years ago, he was still hunting for Scout and me."

"Fuck. I was hoping he was dead."

"Nope. I gave a brilliant testimony to his character in court, which included photos of my beat-up face"—Hoyt's jaw worked, and she wondered if he'd snap the steering wheel off—"and it earned him the maximum sentence from the jury. His first years in prison, he used every moment he had access to the prison library to search for me. Understand, I changed our names before we got to the custody hearing, so when he was being tried, he repeatedly used the names he knew us as. Which made him look like a real ding-dong who didn't know the names of the girls our mom had left him with. That was hardly the worst of his offenses, but it was a direct blow to his ego, and it was probably that that made him hunt me. Being 'Father' was leverage he had enjoyed and that I took from him.

"Each year we petitioned to restrict his online access, but nothing came of it. He'd lose access, but then employees at the prison would change over, and there'd be cracks, and he'd be back online. I set up parameters for us to follow, and we do them to stay hidden. But the data we have on hundreds of thousands of survivors is what keeps me up at night.

"I need the data to continue to protect them, but also, it's one point of vulnerability, so we have trip wires and escalating alarms to keep that data safe. If he gets my new name, it's just a hop, skip, and a jump before he's at my digital door or points someone to my physical door. Scout, Peace, and Cindy get compromised with a data breach like that too, and we're all back to where we started: rescuing ourselves from a life Scout and I narrowly escaped from. Only this time, the stakes are heavier with data on half a million survivors counting on us for protection."

Hoyt's thumb gouged the leather of the steering wheel. "Have you thought of murder?" He gave her a tight smile. "I'm only kidding, but also, mostly not. I'm sorry for all that happened to you when you were a kid."

"Thanks, but it's not your fault he's a dick."

"In case no one said it to you, I'm sorry. That was fucked."

"It was."

I'VE GOT THIS_

"WITH YOUR IDs COMPROMISED, WHAT'S BACK THERE IN YOUR PAST that needs cleaning up?"

"The Melanie Alexander name is associated with multiple counts of fraud. Fingerprints—that aren't mine—connected with drug charges that carry a felony conviction. None of which I committed. Scout's are all but wiped out now. I've been working the last fifteen years on hers. If I fight mine in the legal system, my new name and warrant list comes up and I'm in jail until a court date comes up, and I'm not done with Scout's old background. If they find me, they find Scout. I know what's coming; she doesn't."

He reached over and squeezed her hand. "What if I can wipe the rest of the charges out?"

Vega had always know that with enough money, anything was possible. Then she met Hoyt and put a good and decent human to that thought and didn't like where it went. A human was the perfect target for the third pillar in the trifecta that was her demonic past. Melanie's digital life, Vega's warrants, and *Lloyd*.

"Vega?" he said and squeezed. "What is it?"

"Don't get me wrong, I've fantasized about that. But as I've said before, bringing you in isn't protecting you. You'd have to prove that

Lloyd, my stepdad, took my identity and did what he did, and that's exposure. Something Cindy, Peace, and I have learned to be allergic to.

"He's already in prison. Where he needs to be. If you go after him, he'd have to be tried again. That exposure would be his playground. He'd get Scout's and my new names, and for me, it's not worth it because this time, Scout is old enough to watch *and* remember it all. So, what the hell did I fight for when I was twelve? Jackshit." She swallowed down the feeling of lead settling into her stomach at the dread of seeing him again, of him physically or digitally touching Scout's life with his corrupting fingers. Of her screams that day when he'd thrown her into the table before Peace had grabbed her and run.

And while Vega and Scout were a penance owed, to Lloyd, Hoyt would be a goldmine he'd die trying to tap into.

Panic snapped like a rubber band in her mind. "No, just, no. This is all a bad idea. I was fine before you. You were fine before me. I have protections in place. I've got this. Alone." Her body began vibrating again with the adrenal release to save Hoyt from a time in her life when she felt like she could never get her head above the surface of the darkness.

"I see."

"Do you?" She slid off her seat belt. "You see that he can talk the warden into getting him access to the prison network? You see that what I am today is because of him? I get to thank him and hate him all in one. He's a cunning narcissist who lives for money and getting even... If he knew about you, Hoyt... If the people he likely still owes find out about you..." Vega felt her stomach lurch.

"Vega—"

She fumbled with the door handle before getting it open and kicking it wide.

She couldn't bear thinking about the cancer that was Lloyd and his corrupting fingers reaching for Hoyt. He wouldn't come at him head-on. He'd reach out to low-hanging fruit first, a cousin, or a friend who had just started a nonprofit for the underprivileged, Big Friends Bigger Hearts. Get to know him then work the hustle, and before long, he'd offer Zane a twisted deal, cash and information on Hoyt or Zane's reputation. Zane would naturally refuse to be hustled. And overnight he'd lose his reputation. His name would appear on a registered sex offender's list or something else just as awful. It would be fixed, sure—Zane's lawyers would undo it—but the damage in the form of public opinion would not be undone. And that would be a stepping stone to Hoyt. But he could travel that path only if Vega didn't first outsmart, outmaneuver, and outhustle the person who taught her everything she knew.

Stumbling out, she swallowed as her mouth felt metallic; she was going to puke. This was the third pillar of her darkness, and the one that she feared the most.

She made it to the doors of her warehouse gulping air when she heard Hoyt's door close behind her. Was he calling her name?

Run, her broken mind whispered.

That helpless feeling was back, that noose around her neck that said no matter what, no matter where, the man she and Scout were once made to call Father could create fear and alter lives just by existing. Distance from her vulnerability was the only answer.

She got into the dusty open air of the first floor of her abandoned warehouse when Hoyt caught up.

"Vega—"

He had been calling her name.

She was on the stairs when she turned, "Hoyt, go. I'm spinning. I promised myself I'd never get in so deep with someone, *ever*, and now here I am giving you my darkness. No one understands what he's like or can do. I hoped this day wouldn't come, but fuck, it came fast with you. Look, with people like me"—she gestured between them—"none of this will last. It's impossible. Something always happens, today, tomorrow, ten years from now, and the one who wasn't born in that darkness gets the shit end of the stick because you don't see it coming fast enough."

She was panting—she had to save him now. "This is over. Get out." She pointed to her warehouse door.

Hoyt flinched. "Wha' the fuck does that mean?" Vega had only caught glimpses of his accent before, but now it was as thick as cane syrup. "Your father is in prison—he canna get out."

She shook her head at the beautiful man; he didn't get it. "Two years ago"—she held up the same number of fingers—"he got a guard to grant him access to contact some woman he'd been chatting with online, paid him handsomely with stolen funds. That person? That was my foster mother. He asked her if she knew where her last two foster kids were. She told him to take a hike. That was two years ago; since then, it's been quiet. Is he finally over it, or has he gone quiet to our monitors?" She tapped the side of her head. "I'll always be wondering."

"This? Righ' here? Needs to be sent to the DA." His vowels tumbled over his tongue like water over ocean stones.

She could hear her voice rising with the anxiety of being forced to go up against her monster, "Sure, who the fuck is going to give them the information?"

"I will."

"*No*," she bit back. "Once that darkness touches you, you'll never get it off."

He came to her one step after another until he was eye to eye with her. "You' told me I'm careful with my power. That's because I know what a billion dollars can do. I know tha' millions is more than a convicted felon can go up against. Much less a billion. You want him in Guantanamo? Give me a month."

Vega loved the idea—it was like a gift—but she put her hand softly to his cheek and had a thought to bless him and his beautiful naiveté. "I believe you. But he's the monster, and inside of me is rented space where he lives. He's both in real life and in here." She tapped her temple. "He can activate and torture me with threats to you. And I'll die a thousand little deaths as he orchestrates his fear campaign. I can survive if it's just me, but your embarrassment, pain, anger, or shame will be like a stake through my heart. Someday, in some far-off dreamland, I'll possibly be free of him. But that's not today."

His voice was a growl of suppressed emotion. "So, you'll kill us before he can?"

"When you haven't seen the darkness, it's easy to be bold. Heed me when I say, yes, this ends before it goes any further. You're safe now. That's what matters."

"'A'ole."

Vega recognized the word and tone for *no*. "Hoyt, this isn't—"

He was getting incensed again at Vega for taking something from him. His jaw worked at the words he was carefully grinding out. "Wha' the fuck do I do for a living?"

"Hoyt..."

"Ha'i mai i'au. *Tell me*," he demanded.

She told him what she saw. "You own a legitimate business with investors and by-the-law data security management."

"I'm a securities guy. Don't wade into my world and tell me I can't do my job."

"I shot through your systems in a day."

He corrected her. "*Manually* breached my device, and since then, my beta tech has been hunting you. After capturing one of your bots from your digital deluge tha' night at the club. And is now taking it apart."

Vega blinked. That was news to her. "What?"

"It's not technically legal—"

"I'd say."

"And before I looked up to find you sitting in the bleachers this morning, Titan 2.0 sent me the address of where the hunt terminated. Here."

She felt like her mind was on a bus ride and the driver had just yanked the wheel into oncoming traffic. "Oh, fuck."

"Ya."

"I didn't see that coming."

"Tha's the whole point of what *I* do. Hacking has always been a one-way street, but two-point-oh changes tha'."

She watched him, studying him there in front of her as his meteoric gaze bore down on hers, challenging her to prove him wrong.

Instead, she felt a kind of change in the air that smelled like fresh hope. "What do you think you'll do with two-point-oh, and us, I mean, me?" she fumbled. "I can see you gave this some thought."

"'A'ole, you take back telling me to get out of your life."

Vega looked up to the rusted beams above her to think clearly. Even with Titan 2.0, she wasn't sure it would keep him or her safe forever.

He continued, "Your piece-of-shit stepdad is good with computers and getting access to the internet. Hana maika'i. That's *my* playground. I built a fucking offensive wall, Vega. Wha' the fuck do you think I'll use it for?"

She looked back down. His harsh language made her want to settle her hand on his chest, so she did. That anger was there right where she'd created it. She felt his shark's tooth and pressed it against his skin. It awakened something in him, more clearly showing her that extra thing he carried.

"These are shark-infested waters, Titan."

His temper snapped. "Is that supposed to scare me?"

"No, that was a reminder to me that while I see you as a sweet, kind man, you have thick skin and dark eyes. I suppose these waters are filled with familiar foe."

"'Ae. They are."

"What will you do with Titan 2.0?"

"Answer me first," he whispered, then begged. "Put me back in play."

Just as quietly back to him: "If I put you back into play, this will be painful for me. Are you ready to watch me bleed?"

"With data on him, what he's doing, surveillance, and the like, we can keep the monster in your head quiet. With data, we can see what's up from down and put your past to bed, once and for all. You can use it to see it and to tell it, 'You can't touch me anymore.'"

Her nerves settled down as if Hoyt had crawled under her skin and touched each nerve ending, telling them, *Shh. I have this.*

She was incredulous as the feel of hope settled down on her like glitter at a club. "It's appropriate that your spirit animal is a shark. Right now, you are one."

"I'm just a man. And right now, there's just one thing I want in this entire universe, and she's playing keep-away."

"I was." Her fingers spread wide on his chest, she said beneath her breath, "But if you want me to travel through my valley of death, Hoyt, you'd better hold my hand."

He grasped her hand off his chest and held on tight. "And I'll never let go."

PROTECTION_

"When you say that Titan 2.0 captured one of my bots and took it apart, what exactly did that entail?"

Hoyt's stance was wide in front of her windows, hands tucked under his arms, and he looked like a fitness trainer who was gonna murder your quads and like it. His biceps, shoulders, and forearms were flexed, and Vega, kicking back in her chair, mentally ran her tongue over all of him.

He didn't notice that she was undressing him with her eyes and said simply, "That professor Lei mentioned, you knew her. *Know* her. You're working with her, aren't you?"

The red licorice straw in Vega's mouth went still.

"It found that? Fuck, that thing is stealthy." Vega turned to her command center and, hands wide above the keys, took in everything. "How far are you in?"

"Not in, just yet. We've come up against some diversions we hadn't accounted for."

Vega grinned back at him. "Please tell me someone is enjoying their free subscription to LubeTube."

His matching grin gave it away before he said, "That was a tight piece of comedy, Vega."

"You?"

"No, the engineers who thought it was a testing regimen for Titan 2.0. They unknowingly hit one of your safeguards, and HR got involved before I stepped in."

The red rope was bouncing between her lips again. "I wish I was there for that."

"I bet. But now that I know you have your systems booby-trapped, I'll pull back. Just let Dr. Branch know that her quantum computing project has us watching."

Vega choked. "What? What the fuck does that mean?" His shark eyes were back; only this time his game-face grin was in place too. He stood there like he was on the sidelines watching playback on the monitors of when he'd snatched the opponent's ball midair and sprinted to the end zone.

"Titan was able to use your bot like a digital fingerprint and see where else you had been. Much to the team's surprise, it showed up at the university. I said you were taking a class and had them forward me the data. But, Vega, Titan 2.0 means I see you, all of you, and now have a game plan to protect you and those in your circle who are vulnerable."

Vega felt his words swirl around in her stomach like sunshine and hope on marshmallow fluff. "Details?"

"I coat you, your sister, the girls, and your foster mom in Titan 2.0 while I tell our sales team to offer a full system to Oregon correctional facilities and call it a pilot system for a potential case study."

"All while keeping his ass monitored."

"Walls keep people in too," he reminded her.

"Yes, they do." The sunshine moment converted into real tangible relief, as if her insides had been a clenched fist and now it was relaxing. She asked the room in a whisper, "Could that work?"

"If not, it's adaptable, and I'll change it up to keep his time in prison feeling like it should."

Vega looked to her hands, wondering how they were able to capture such a man. He must indeed love the chaos of volcanoes.

"Hoyt?"

"What?" he said absently, looking at his watch that was buzzing, then flicked the notification silent.

"This is the kind of shit a billionaire can do."

"This is the kind of thing *I* can do, someone with connections can do. This is what my clout can buy and can afford to give away if we need to. I have no qualms about giving them a very specific software package that has a quiet bit of code geared for one specific resident and anyone acting as his agent. If he gets moved to another facility, I'll do it again and again until he dies."

Vega wove the licorice vine between her fingers, loving what he provided her. She was happy with her shield—it was a solid shield built for breaking noses—but what he offered was an entire army.

She felt lightweight and put her feet back up and took in his power that transcended his cut shoulders and deltoids. "Some girls like diamonds and couture. I'm a sucker for powerful deeds. I'm going to need, for my birthday, five hundred lobbyists at the state capital to force a law saying snacks are a food group."

"Or how about a dedicated team of lawyers to fight your bogus charges and clear your name without you having to make contact with your stepfather ever?"

She took in a deep, appreciative breath; he'd known her for just a handful of weeks, and yet he'd come to her as a fully formed partner. She said back to him the phrase he had quipped more than once, "You're not a moron."

"I keep saying this..." His hands relaxed to his side, and he made his way over to her chair where he bent over her. His shark's tooth swung forward, and Vega stopped it with a finger.

"I've never felt like this before. Like I do when I'm with you. Why are you doing all this? I know I've said this before, but you could have any woman in the world. And I mean, any woman—"

"I think I've been perfectly clear that I don't want any woman. I want the one right here."

"Sure, but I bet—"

"Vega, I don't want any woman. I want the one woman who sees me for who I am, not my wealth, trophies, or Super Bowl rings. I want the woman I can surprise when no one else can, and I want that thing she has that she holds close and refuses to give to anyone, except now, to me. Somehow, miraculously, I've found all that, and more, in one woman."

Hoyt's words smoothed down over her, and she wanted to hear it said out loud what she already knew in her heart. "And what's that that I've given you?"

"I'm the only man she's given both her love and her trust to." He touched the tip of his nose to hers. "That's the kind of VIP status I enjoy, being your only one."

She kissed those words back into his mouth. "Goddamn you. How'd you get up in here?" She tapped the side of her head.

"Same way you got into mine. You barged in." He gave her a kiss and admitted, "That and the idea of you has taken up space in my mind for a long time, so long I didn't think you existed. I thought you were just a fantasy, until you found me in a dark corner of a club minding my own business."

"Hoyt?"

"Yes?" His lips brushed over hers.

"Remember the first time you were here?" Vega watched the spark in his eyes as she asked him that quiet question that she'd had for days.

"The day I watched you sleep and thought, *What the fuck am I doing breaking into a woman's home?* Yeah."

"Well, this time do you want to stay and, I dunno, make me breakfast and fuck my brains out?"

He groaned and closed his eyes. "That question… You have no idea how many times I've found myself thinking about it. Remembering you in just socks and this hoodie, asking me that. Fucking shocking—"

"Sorry."

"Not what you said but that my first thought was *Fuck yeah.*"

Vega laughed deep down in her throat. "Oh, did you, now?"

"I did. That moment has plagued me, an open invite I didn't take."

"You weren't in a position to take it, kind sir."

"Now, though...I'll take you up on that offer and hope I can last more than thirty seconds. I've been wanting to be in you for," he kissed her, "so," and again, "damn," and once more, "long."

"Hell yes, I'll take thirty seconds on that python you call a penis."

His laugh was deep in his throat when he squatted and with his arms around her middle, hoisted Vega up. She let out a squeak and wrapped her legs high up around his ribs, squeezing her thighs tight. She kissed his upturned face as he maneuvered around her things to her wide, pillow-filled bed.

At the edge of it, he grinned up between her breasts. "Ready?"

"Fuck yeah."

Hoyt tossed her into the bed. Vega let out a scream-laugh at misinterpreting what "ready" had meant. She rolled over onto her belly; the kinetic energy of the toss made her kick her feet back and forth. She was gonna get laid by a tech titan and couldn't wait.

Staring at the towering man beside her bed, she slipped a finger into her mouth. "He's gonna break through your pants," she said, eyeing the tent pole in his athletic pants.

He slowly grabbed the hem of his workout shirt and lifted it up and off.

She groaned at the tease—no athletic pants yet—but also this perfectly fine reveal. "Hello, gorgeous." Vega could count the pillowed boxes that were the cut of his abdominal muscles and then devoured the rest of his cut body, from the black hair of his pits to the sparse cluster between his pecs and the trail that led from his navel down below the waistband of his pants. Down to the mammoth cock she was familiar with, hidden below. He swept his hair back that had fallen lose when he had taken his shirt off, and she watched as his musculature bunched and rippled from his pectorals to the firm humps of his bicep. His arm stayed aloft, and Vega had the feeling that he needed a beat before he continued, like the beat before jumping into the deep end of the pool where you had to both perform and not drown.

He turned to put the shirt on the table and inadvertently gave her a view of his back. Vega was up and off the bed, dragging her fingers over his stomach as she circled around to his back.

He froze as Vega said, "Hello…"

Her fingers landed on the indent of his spine where his back muscles made a trench from neck to lower back. She traced the mammoth-sized tattoo over the muscles, studying it like an archaeologist studying newly discovered hieroglyphics. He looked over his shoulder at her, making the muscles bunch and slide.

"What?" he asked, and if she wasn't mistaken, he had gone guarded. She assumed she had Londyn to thank for that.

"Stay still," she faux admonished, "I'm having a serious discussion with the artwork back here and want to know if it gives me consent to lick it?" After a beat, she answered for it, "Imma lick it."

His head tilted up to the ceiling, "Vega…"

"What?"

He mumbled something.

"Didn't hear that."

Then back over his shoulder, "'Apono. Consent given."

"Excellent," she whispered, and sliding her palm over his hip and up his front, she held him to her as she pressed her pelvis in against the firm round of his buttocks. Her nose against his salty skin, she inhaled the geometric pattern that was a grounding rod for the man it was inked on. And gave a long lick along his spine. The warm, smooth skin of his back tasted of exertion.

"There's a shark in this pattern," she whispered to it. "Hello, manō."

He reached around and held her tight against his back.

"The line work on this is insane. There's layers and layers of triangles and shading, making it pop. Gorgeous." Vega ran her fingers over it, saying hello to the ink and the obvious master who'd done the work on him. "Beautiful…"

He turned then and pulled her into his half-naked embrace, and over her neck and up to her mouth, he inhaled her into his lungs. "I fucking love you. Aloha wau iā 'oe."

Vega felt that second utterance of his love spike through her chest and resisted the urge to dig her nails into his skin with the thrill of hearing it.

Hoyt's phone buzzed again on his wrist next to Vega's ear.

Vega quietly laughed as the moment broke. "Is this what it's like to be with a man like you? Everyone needs you?"

With her in his arms, he tried to ignore it until he groaned in frustration up her neck as it went off again.

Vega tilted his wrist to see who it was. "It says it's from your sister. She says it's 9-1-1." To him: "What's up?"

He shook his head. "Just something we've been dealing with the last couple days." With his fingers in her pony, he gripped and pulled, tilting her chin up. Along her exposed neck, he dragged his teeth.

Vega swallowed and groaned, "If you say so..."

"I do. I want this. And please, for fuck's sake, why can't everyone leave me alone while I tick off my to-do list with you?"

His wrist lit up again, and he growled, took his watch off, and with a twist away from her, whipped it across the warehouse apartment.

Vega laughed and flopped back onto her bed, killed by the loss of the moment.

He looked down at her, eyes dilated and ready, when Vega put her sneaker to his chest.

"I'm nuts about you."

"Yup." And she watched the rise and fall of his chest and knew he was well on his way to being too far gone to have a conversation.

"I also like your sister, and I can't have her needing you while I fuck you senseless. You need to plan on being useless for at least seventy-two hours. Call her. Clear your schedule; then put that massive anaconda you call a cock hilt deep within me."

"No," he growled.

She pulled out her phone and started to dial when he snatched her phone, and Vega squealed, "Give it back!"

He made to whip that too down the length of the warehouse when she leaped up and onto his naked back.

He put a hand back and supported her under her rear and with his other pretended to throw her phone.

Vega squealed again, "Hoyt! That's my precious!"

The gruff rattle of his laugh shook her as she rode his back, trying to crawl over his shoulder to grab it back.

"I knew it!" He wrestled her, rotating his shoulder back. "This demon kit will make you go apeshit if anyone touches it."

"Yes! Now give it!" Using his face as a point of leverage, Vega pushed off his cheek get to the end of his arm where he held it away from her. "Hoyt! Just call your damn sister."

Vega had wrestled opponents larger than her before but none so physically adept at manhandling humans. The ceiling switched places with the wood floor before Vega thumped down on her back on her bed. Hoyt was over her and pressed his hips against her pelvis as her head swam. Her phone was gently set out of reach behind him, and he came down over her before rocking his pelvis against hers between her thrown-wide thighs.

"Vega...ko'u lua pele."

Her legs automatically wrapped around his waist, and he groaned in suppressed need and pressed in again.

Vega felt her mind go pleasantly blank. "But if it's an emergency," she mumbled on his lips.

Hoyt muttered, "Is the building on fire?"

"Maybe yours is?"

He pressed his hips in again, and it was Vega's turn to groan.

"Hoyt?"

"Yes?"

"Fuck me fast," she said, parroting him from the elevator days before.

Against her neck: "Yes, ma'am."

Vega wriggled as he pulled off her tights while she kicked her shoes off. She pushed down on the waistband of his athletic pants, setting free his red and engorged erection. His mouth went to hers, crushing her with his need as he tucked his pelvis in, pushing the thick, wet tip of his mushroom-headed erection inside of her.

Vega groaned as it stretched and filled her. Hoyt's voice melded with hers in a string of blissful curses.

"Vega…I'm…this is…"

Her heels went to his firm ass. "I know. I feel it too, but we need to be fast." She gave another groan as he inched farther in. "I've been ready for days, *please*." As her breath caught in her throat, her body lit with the erotic energy of being so intimately connected with him.

Braced over her, Hoyt pushed in gently at her command then slowed as if thinking better of fast, and Vega pressed him on. "I know it's strange trying for fast for our very first time out, but you're taking things too slow. Fuck. Me. Fast."

His gaze was dark and worried. "I don't want to hurt you. I'm, it's, he's…he can be big. Too big."

She gave a deep-throated laugh at how sweet he was. "Hoyt, my heart, I've been fantasizing about you, this, since the club where I wanted to straddle you in that dark corner booth. Being aroused all this time means my cervix is so high, you couldn't find it with a telephone pole."

His gaze went quizzical; studying her expression, his hips pressed, testing her theory, and she said, "See?"

Potent satisfaction over something more than her taking him cock deep moved over his features, and he settled heavier onto her. He kissed her lips, asking, "Were you made just for me? Me ke aloha pumehana, ipo ahi." He relaxed out before thrusting back in. The soft clap of skin made Vega groan and her head fall back into the soft furs as her body felt as if it were filling with erogenous water from her pelvic bowl up to her heart.

Eyes closed against the onslaught of having all her dreams come true while she rode a unicorn through a valley of buttercream frosting, she drowned in the sugar feel of his thick length, slippery and stretching within her. His heavy body pressed her into the soft faux fur of her blankets, making her want to undo her breasts from her sports bra but instead grabbed the firm edges of his hips and yanked him in harder.

Hoyt took her direction, and resting on one elbow, he grasped her hip. Tilting her pelvis up and holding her still, he drove into her. The physical impact had Vega whining with the feel of electric pleasure blooming out from their connection as Hoyt's breath began to scrape over his vocal cords, melding his groan with hers.

Vega felt the cliff's edge of orgasm, the power of Hoyt sliding his skin against hers, his heat mixing with hers, and the sheer capacity he was able to hold with her triggered her body to clench. Feeling her grasp him from inside her body, his beg started deep in his chest before moving up and out. "Come for me."

Her knees fell away as she arched her pelvis higher, letting his hips smack against her as his breath caught.

"I'm coming," she promised him as her pelvic bowl pinched tight in a full-bodied orgasm. Hoyt's lips crushed down onto hers with unrestrained need as he tucked his hips under and with quick thrusts cried out into her mouth as warmth flooded into her.

Breathing heavily, he stilled and dropped his now sweating forehead onto hers, their breath mixing together before he smiled, and Vega watched his eyes open, and in that starlight moment, she felt herself fall off the earth into something blissful and true.

"Did you know you have a navel ring?"

Vega laughed. "I love you," she confessed.

A smile broke out over his face. "Did you just tell me that you love me? Out loud and on purpose?"

Vega felt the starlight moment expand. "Yeah, I think I did."

His lips touched hers. "I love you too. And now I'm going to stay quiet and not ask you to marry me or make you promise to keep me by your side forever."

She wet her lips as she caught her breath. "You're not gonna do that?"

"Nope. I'm going to keep quiet about all that."

"What about a house? And a white picket fence? I should be quiet about asking you for those too, shouldn't I?"

"Yeah, definitely don't mention any of that."

"Good. Right. And pets?"

"Two dogs?"

"At least."

Hoyt's low rumble of a laugh started before his face broke into grin. "Hana hou... I'm definitely going to want to do this again."

He gave a wet push of his fading erection within her, and she clenched around him, making his eyes close. "Oh yeah. Don't do that —he's a bit sensitive at the moment."

"I think we have to kill our afterglow now and call someone, or someones, back?"

"What people?" She felt him test out how much of his body weight she could take as he continued, "Maybe a nap first."

His body weight pressed the air out of her lungs, making her choke-laugh. "Oh yes, please, this is how I want to die, crushed under you with a recovering erection sliding out of my vagina. You'd have a lot to explain to the coroner."

He lifted onto his elbows once more, mirth in his voice. "My excuse would be, but first she murdered me."

STRESS TESTING_

"Now give your sister a call. I have to double-check my systems anyway. Some tech titan got close to getting into her and I have to see what he almost touched." Vega was putting her black jeans on.

Hoyt hooked his finger into the waistband of her jeans and pulled her closer to him. "Vega…"

Caught, her gaze went to his hand then up to his face, reading him like a book, and answered, "If it turns out to be nothing from your sister, I'll pack a bag and go to your place. You mentioned needing a shower, and I have to confess to a fondness for high-pressure showers. Do you have one of those?"

"On the right setting, it feels like your skin is being scoured off."

Vega let out a pleasured whine. "Pinch me."

Vega watched Hoyt call his sister as she dug into her own systems. This game between them wasn't over; there was one last flex Vega had on his systems, but they hadn't triggered it yet. Which surprised her—basic security breaches were solved by rolling back the systems to the archived version that was known to be clean. Something Lei said they'd do. With her last little bot sitting in the binary level of his security code, a rollback was planned to trigger it. It was harmless, but it was educational, something Dr. Branch had been teaching her.

Vega heard Hoyt curse and, looking over her shoulder at him, saw his shark gaze was back and was wholly settled on her. Vega recognized his game face and smiled; someone had rolled back the systems at Hoyt Securities.

He said to Lei, "We'll be there in a few minutes."

As he hung up, Vega feigned confusion. "Oh, we're going somewhere? I hope it's to get ice cream."

He held his hands out for her. She let him pull her up, and as he put his hands on her hips, he said, "Someone has been causing pilikia."

"That sounds like trouble."

"It is."

Her eyes went wide in mock shock. "Who?"

"The power is cycling through the levels of Hoyt Towers every thirty minutes. The third floor is reporting a psychotic coffeepot, and engineering is receiving indecent emails."

Vega had to know: "Did anyone click the link?" She crossed her fingers.

Hoyt shook his head, but his eyes were gleaming. "You're a menace."

"But did anyone click on the link?" she pressed.

"My firm is buzzing like a tower of angry bees over this, and you want to know if someone clicked the link?"

"Just wondering..."

He closed his eyes. "I'm afraid to ask. What happens if someone clicks the link?"

Vega didn't want to spoil the surprise. "I'm excited. I'll pack my things; we should rush over there immediately."

He opened his eyes and firmed his grip up on her, keeping her in front of him. "My morning is totally toast. I've not showered. I've been rushed in my fucking. And I'm standing shirtless in your apartment with my headquarters going insane. Just so I'm prepared, is this what every day will be like with you?"

"I'm sorry to say but yes."

He bent and whispered, "Good," against her lips, "Ko'u lua pele."

Vega recognized the tumble of vowels and kissed him back before asking, "Lua pele?"

"Koʻu lua pele. My volcano."

Vega liked it and, peeling off him, said, "Let me pack some things, and we can go."

VEGA WAS WITH LEI IN HER OFFICE, HER BAG TOSSED IN THE CORNER, herself sprawled in one guest chair, her sneakers up in the other. She was counting her treats that had been released when the half-filled engineering room started buzzing again.

Lei went to the door to meet a harried-looking assistant. "What is it?"

"There's another report from upstairs."

Vega smiled and whispered, "Kittens."

"Um, I'm not sure I'm reading this right," the person said, "but there are kittens hopping across screens? Like a screensaver?" With a shout, someone else farther back in the cubes confirmed it.

Lei cursed. "OK, advise people to just reboot. Do not click the screen. Do *not* do what the kittens tell them to do."

"OK," the messenger responded, sounding apprehensive, as if the kittens were an existential threat.

Lei turned to Vega. "What have you done?"

Vega grinned. "Hardening your systems requires creativity and insight into the pathological mind." Vega spread her hands to encompass her chaos. "Behold, insight into the pathological mind."

"How the fuck do we clean this up?"

"How indeed?"

Lei's hair looked as if she'd gripped it in her fists more than once over the last several hours, as pieces of it stuck out from where it was tightly knotted with a pencil at the top of her head.

"Grr! You're as bad as Hoyt. I don't need riddles; I need actionable items. I rolled back the systems because he's a total nut bar for you, but now I see you're a flaming psycho and you're gonna kill us all."

Vega's eyes went wide. "I love it when you talk dirty. And, yes, I'm a flaming psycho. Now, how do we insulate from this?"

Lei, fuming and with hands on her hips, opened her mouth to respond when the lights went out.

There was a collective groan from the floor before the battery-powered orange emergency lights came on.

"What. The. Fuck."

"Someone did what the kitten told them to do."

"Goddammit" came from out in the hallway, and Vega recognized Hoyt's voice before he arrived in the doorway of Lei's office. His shirt was pressed white linen with and his straight-legged slacks a deep steel color.

Lei took him in, rolled up sleeves and all. "Oh, what's wrong with you?"

"What do you mean?"

"You're all casual."

Vega gave him the OK symbol with her fingers, kissed where her thumb and forefinger met, and mouthed, *Perfection.* He was letting the world see the tattoo on his arm, and the shark's tooth around his neck was clearly displayed.

"Is that a problem?" he asked his sister, before adding, "The building is in utter chaos, the C-suite is shitting themselves, and you're asking what happened to me?"

"Right, well, you look chill, and I'm not chill, Hoyt. I think this testing"—she looked to Vega—"has gone on long enough." Back to him: "Don't you?"

"The rollback spread her code. Take everything offline—"

"Um" came from the engineering room.

Vega peered out the door around Hoyt's body and saw Glasses, the gossipy engineer from last time, standing. "Um, I got a text from the front desk..."

Vega smothered her giggle. Treat number one. Someone in engineering had clicked the link to the indecent email that earlier had HR in a lather. Her stomach rumbled in anticipation.

Glasses continued, "They said that pizzas are arriving? Like, loads of pizzas?"

In the amber glow of the emergency lights, the floor was silent until Hoyt turned to Vega. "I take it that's you?"

"Nope. Indecent emails should be reported"—she raised her voice so the engineering department could hear her—"and not clicked on!"

Hoyt looked back out to his engineering department as if he could tell in the semi-dark who had done it.

Vega decided to end the simulation and pulled out her phone. She set to work quieting her bots and putting them back to bed.

The lights came on, and the room sighed in relief.

Vega said to Lei and Hoyt, "Pizza, anyone? Now might be a good time for a break."

Hoyt watched Lei and the team file up the stairs while a few brave souls took the elevator up to the conference rooms where the pizza was being handed out.

"I'll bring some back," Lei had said, looking tired. "I'll give you some time to sort this out, Ho'o."

Vega had been keen to Lei's tone. "I think she thinks you're being risky by playing with me."

"Yup." He did not give a shit what his sister thought of what he and Vega had going.

"Should we stop?"

"Nope." Though he had a good idea on what to do next and where her bots were hiding. "Come." He held out his hand to her. They got on the elevator. With the chaos creator next to him, he felt safe that if even if the elevator stopped, it would be for a real good time.

He watched Vega, her mask on, as they took the elevator down two floors to sub-level seven and got out into the server room. She gave nothing away but followed, and he knew he was close when her eyes glowed.

The server stacks took up the entire twelve thousand square feet, and in the hum of the cooling towers, the air was icy with the AC on high. The stacks gave off an ethereal glow with the lights off.

From next to him, he heard Vega inhale. The server room was computing power that to the trained eye told the viewer, in one room, the kind of power Hoyt Securities held. At their data center in Eastern Oregon? They could get lost in it.

"Oh, hello." Vega said to the room at large, and he watched her take in his firm's speed and computational depth with an appreciative air. She went to the closest wall and let her fingers flow over the dark stacks as they sat illuminated with flickering blue lights.

"Hoyt," she said from behind her mask, "you were sexy before, but now, I think you might be a brand of kink made just for me..." He let her meander down the first humming hallway as he went to the terminal at the front of the room.

He had figured out where her bots had been hiding to be able to command Hoyt Towers the way she had and set to work reviewing the code—that he'd created—to find and eliminate her Vega-splices within it.

Despite her saying that she'd never work for him, she had been. Their games were fun, might-testing performances of one-upmanship, but they were also learning experiences. If they could insulate from someone of Vega's caliber, they were bullet-proof.

THIS WASN'T THE FIRST TIME SHE THOUGHT OF THE CONTRACT SHE didn't sign. If she plugged into all this glory, she could expand her Project Valkyrie tenfold. They might even be able to start the nonprofit Peace wanted, taking Project Valkyrie legitimate. Legitimate-ish, at least. Being on the underbelly of life was comfortable, but she also wanted the things that others had. A house with interior doors. A lawn that she could get upset over when people let their dogs crap on it. A dining table where her friends could sit and eat food that got made on a stove. After decades of running and gunning, she wanted boring. She wanted predictable. She bet that felt safe and comforting like a fireside blanket.

She got to the end of the row and looked at the numbers listed on the servers and searched for number 222. It was in the corner separated from the rest like she'd assumed. Archived data sat on it and was all but abandoned. A relic in all the power-charged state-of-the-art towers behind her.

She touched the number and said, "Hello, girls, happy here?" Her phone chirped. Vega pulled out her device and slid open the screen and scrolled through the notifications. She smiled.

From behind her, she felt Hoyt approach before his hands slid over her hips. "Found you."

Vega was scrolling through her bot statuses and felt him watch too.

His voice rumbled through her chest. "Did I get them all?"

She scrolled to the bottom. Each of them reported offline.

Instead of answering the obvious, she turned her face up to his. "I declare this facility, once more, impenetrable."

His nose touched her shoulder, breathing her in before he kissed it. "Promise?"

"For now."

She felt him smile into her shoulder. "Then let's take care of something personal."

Vega turned in his arms after tucking her phone away and wrapped her arms around his neck, "Yes? Here in the server room where I could be dominated by you and the manifestation of all your power in server form? Fuck yeah."

"I was thinking getting Titan 2.0 on your friends and family plan."

"Oh, right. So, not naked, right now?"

"Naked later. I want to take you up on this seventy-two-hour recovery program you advised, but first, I have a promise to keep, and that starts now."

"All right. Lead the way."

GIVE ME ALL OF YOU_

"OK, I've given permission to Peace and Cindy's phones to accept the download, and it's going." Vega was with Hoyt in his penthouse. She tapped the plastic sheeting hung around the renovation as she talked. "When I called to ask their permission, Peace ended the call in tears and asked about double weddings. Which, ew. Fuck the patriarchy." Vega gave him a grin and watched his reaction.

He gave her only a grunt that he had heard her. His eyes were on his own massive laptop on the dining table that had been torn free of sheeting before he'd settled down. "Oregon correctional facilities have begun talks with us. The sales manager that oversees government contracts is confident they'll have it installed by the end of the month."

"Wow," Vega said, impressed, "that's fast for a government contract."

"Free has that effect."

"Finance is going to push you out your executive window for making that deal."

Hoyt leaned back and rested his hands behind his head. Vega took in his sculpted biceps and shoulders that he had no idea were on loud display in his white linen shirt, which also made his skin seem darker, like burnt caramel.

"It's times like that when I remind them of how much they make and how much they like it and that the risk is minuscule to the bottom line."

"Fancy words from a fancy man."

He gave her a half-laugh before shaking his head at her, his only rebuttal to being called a fancy man. He didn't understand why she was so keen on zeroing in on that, but despite that, he liked it.

He asked her, "Your foster mom?"

"She just has a landline, and a rotary one at that. I admit I encourage her to avoid technological upgrades. But she does have a desktop computer that she plays mahjong on and sends emails from. It's over a decade old; there's no way that desktop will accept a modern printer, much less hold Titan 2.0."

"How do you want to proceed there?"

"Honestly?"

"Yes."

"Really, though?"

"Really."

"Buy all the properties surrounding her and put up surveillance. That'll keep the access points off her physically and allow us to monitor her safety without compromising it."

He nodded, and Vega swallowed, not sure if he was going to laugh it off or actually do it, and for the life of her, she didn't know which one was worse.

"How about we loop her long-time neighbors in and just make sure they know to contact us if something changes with her? Never underestimate the power of the neighborhood watch."

"That's why they pay you the big bucks. Big ideas."

"Don't get me wrong—if that idea goes to shit, I'll buy the neighborhood."

Vega went to him at the dining table and sat astride his lap. His hands rested on her thighs. Grasping the lapels of his linen shirt, she kissed the hard bars of his clavicles and asked quietly, "Why are you so amazing and kind?"

He held her, responding, "That's strange, because, as I've mentioned, I've been told I'm an aggressive asshole."

She kissed his lips next. "Those people are morons. You're sweet and kind. Now, tell me, kind sir, who's covered your whole home in plastic and ripped-up tile? Have you been vandalized?"

"How do you know that this isn't how I always live?"

"Because both you and I know I've been here before, without permission."

He rested his forehead on her chest and spoke into the hoodie cavern between her breasts. "I'm glad you told me you'd been here. After the gala, I had thought I was going nuts." He groaned at the realization of something that brought him relief. "You have no idea... I could smell you on my things, and one suit coat in particular."

She gave a dark laugh deep in her throat, not letting it escape.

"You borrowed more than just Londyn's dress, didn't you?"

"Maybe. I wasn't going to go into your room, but I couldn't help but touch, smell, and wear your things."

"I didn't tell anyone. I wore mismatched stuff for those two days we fought just so I could wear the things that smelled like you. I considered taking a psych eval. I thought it was all in my head."

Vega felt warm in her stomach at having gotten so deep into his subconscious. "No, you're not crazy—I was here. I was just going to look, but my desire got the better of me, and I gave in."

Hoyt lifted his head from her breasts. "So, you know, then, that my shower has excellent water pressure."

"No, but that your sheets are *divine*."

Her lips hovered over his, and he pressed his up into hers before gently capturing her lower lip with his teeth. He let go. "You were in my sheets without me?"

"I was."

"We need to rectify that."

"We do, but one quick question." Vega loved being so close to him, being in that quiet space, sharing thoughts and memories, and wanted more. "Did you really need to gut your gorgeous pad to get out the Londyn ghoulies?"

"No... I might have gotten jealous at your place and decided I want to eat and code in my apartment too."

"Jealous, huh? What have you got planned, sir?"

"I might have given instructions to my cousin, Cody, my interior designer, to have it be a multi-terminal home office."

"I hope the paint scheme is jet black."

"It might be. Cody is convinced I need to have it be like something from the movies, but being functional was my only requirement."

"So sexy black with multicolored light strips and hacker low lighting."

"That's exactly what the idea board has drawn on it."

"If you add a snack cabinet, I might never leave. You'll have to call an exterminator to get me out."

He put his nose in his favorite spot in the crook of her neck and breathed her in. "Excellent. A monster snack cabinet is being added to the plans as we speak."

Arms draped around his neck, she dragged her lips along his jaw. His eyes closed against the feel of her breath against his skin; then at his lips, she rested.

"Vega..." he breathed, lips to lips.

"Yes?"

"I don't know if I'm ever going to get enough of you."

Her gaze settled on his, and as she breathed in his exhale, she said, "The feeling is mutual. What are we going to do about this?"

"I'm going to say, be with me? Can you make me that kind of promise, she who makes no promises to any man?"

"Except this once." She put her fingers to his lips. "Once. Never again, because no one will ever compare with you, and let's be real, I wanna crawl under your skin and stay there forever."

"Good."

Holding her by the thighs, Hoyt lifted her up, and hugging her to his chest, he carried her to his bedroom, which, unlike the rest of his apartment, was untouched.

"I have the next seventy-two hours clear." He kicked the door shut and let the ambient light from the floor and crown molding lights set the room aglow.

"Oh yeah? Should we see how soft your sheets are together, then?"

"Fuck yeah." He toed his shoes off and with a knee to the bed placed her down before following her down and covering her with his body.

Vega felt it then, the small but consequential nod to him that they were about to embark on a long journey of bliss creating.

His lips whispered over hers, "I realize I've said this before, but I love you, Vega Flux."

Thighs wrapped around his hips, she lifted up. "Hoyt..."

"Yes?" he whispered up her neck before securing his lips to hers.

"This is real, isn't it?"

"God, I hope so. If this is just a dream, I'm coming for you in real life."

His hand reached back and undid her boot laces one at a time before tossing them to the floor with a thump. He moved his hand back up her leg to her fly, and just as she thought he was about to undo her button, he slid his hand up and over her stomach. Shoving her sweatshirt up, he chased his hand with his lips before demanding, "Take this off."

"So commanding."

"Now."

Vega liked how his words got blunt as he approached the edge of his restraint. "Why, Mr. Kaho'okalakupua, you sound desperate."

"Naked, Vega. Get naked now."

Vega grabbed the lower edge of her sweatshirt and slowly pulled it up and off, taking her undershirt with it, leaving the laciest of her bras in place.

With hungry eyes, he placed his nose to her sternum and,

breathing her in, dove his hand under her and expertly undid the lace hooks. Vega watched him pull it up off her chest, and as his mouth devoured her left breast, he tossed the bra across the room.

He then pulled her button fly open before standing back, and with hands at her cuffs, he yanked. Vega laughed as she was pulled to the edge of the bed and was all at once pants-less. Her matching lace underwear was halfway down her thighs, having been caught by the friction of her pants.

He crooked his middle finger over the top of the elastic and pulled them down before throwing them across the room too. Vega felt the thrill of meeting the part of Hoyt that he kept back, the asshole aggressor that he'd been accused of being. She could play all day with a man like that.

Naked as the day she was born and ass at the edge of the plush bed, she watched Hoyt knee her thighs open to make room for him to stand between them. His hands went to his shirt and with the methodology of a tax assessor took each button to task, one by one, releasing the pearl fronts from the double-stitched buttonhole behind it. Each release yawned open the button-down farther and farther, showing the dusting of raven hair on his well-defined chest down to the valley of his abdominals. Then, with a slow and drawn-out pull, he tugged the shirt tails out of his pants and rolling his shoulders, slid the soft fabric off his naked upper body.

The contrast between the crisp white fabric and his warm tan skin made Vega come up on her elbows with a desire to touch him. The artwork on his arm bunched as his right hand undid the button of his tailored steel-gray chinos.

Vega could feel the sweat of wanton desire break out over her upper lip. She'd never been taunted in this way before and wasn't sure whether she wanted to keep watching or take him to the carpet to get him inside of her, *now*.

She rubbed her lips together. Hoyt was watching and stilled his hands.

"Is this..." He purposefully dragged his words out and over his vocal cords, making his baritone deep and sinful. "Is this what you want?"

She nodded, having lost her ability to speak, but she could watch a little more before she ripped his pants off.

"I couldn't hear you, Vega," he said as his fingertips went to the zipper. "Is this what you want?" He pulled the slider down just a few zipper teeth.

She whimpered.

"Or this?" He pulled it up.

"No!"

"No, you don't want this?"

"Yes, I mean, no, goddammit."

He gave her a wide smile that said he was having a glorious time with her.

Her chest heaving like she was doing sprints in his living room, she growled, "Down and off, or I do it myself."

"Like this?" And he dragged the zipper down the rest of the way.

"Exactly like that."

With his thumbs in the waistband of his chinos, he shoved them to the floor, leaving his cotton-and-silk-blend boxer briefs.

Vega grabbed him then, her control frayed, and pulled him between her spread thighs and pressed his erection with just the thin film of fabric between them to her chest. With a twist of her wrist, the briefs were down, and she put his red, thick erection straight into her mouth.

She sucked, feeling the salty warmth of his pre-excitement spread over her tongue.

Hoyt's body tightened at the sudden pleasure, and his pelvis pushed forward in an automatic desire to have her mouth do what she was so talented at. She gave him a few delicious pumps before pulling him out of her mouth. There was another band of ink she spied winding around this thigh. She touched the bands of triangles that wove around his quad, and the muscle bunched at her touch.

She put her lips to the tip of his erection and spoke into it like a microphone. "Beautiful. Is this—"

"Vega..."

She looked up to find his head back and his eyes closed.

"Vega," he repeated. "Please?"

She put the iron rod of him back into her mouth and slid him to the back of her throat, chasing her lips with her fist.

"Thish?" she asked with her mouth full.

"Yes."

Her other hand went to the backside of his testes and massaged. The grip he had on her hair tightened.

"Or thish?"

He made a guttural sound like he was drowning, and she took it as an affirmative before he pulled away from her. His erection slipped out with a pop off her lips, startling Vega.

"No," he said, suddenly changing his mind before grabbing her thighs and driving her deep into the bed, knocking cushions off and burying her into the thick duvet.

He kneeled at the temple of her erotic plateau, and Vega dragged her big toe up his tatted thigh to his sculpted bare chest where she pressed him back.

His dark gaze went to hers, and with an illuminating glitter in his eyes, he pulled her foot off his chest before kissing the bottom of it. He moved up the inside of her leg to her thigh before kissing the front of her pelvis. Her tight crop of hair received a kiss next, and Vega let her knees fall open wider, giving him an all-access pass.

While he'd been slow before when he drowned at her tableau, he wasted no time then in pushing three fingers within the wet, tight confines of her vaginal canal, hitting directly on her erogenous zone. Then with his tongue, he touched her clitoris, squeezing pleasure out of her in a moan. His rush became evident when he gave her three short hits before moving up to her breasts where he cupped one as his mouth covered the other as if he could maybe consume them both whole.

He nuzzled before whispering, "I need you," against her neck.

She kissed him and opened her mouth to his warm wet one

where he responded, tucking his tongue into her mouth and twining it with hers.

"And I want you and need you too, Hoyt. Please." She arched her hips, and he reached down, grabbing his thick erection, and notched it into Vega's opening.

Her whole body shivered at the beauty of having him rock hard over her and within her and with the press of his hips, the feel of him sliding into her, stretching and filling every vacancy.

Her hands scoured over the ridges of his shoulder muscles up to the deep, dark brown of his hair that had fallen forward. She pressed his face to hers, devouring him as he thrust into her. Her heels dug into the firm round of his buttocks, pressing him in farther, daring him to touch nirvana and her cervix in one. Feeling the humps of his back muscles as they bunched and relaxed as his thrusts drove them to orgasm, Vega swam in the beauty of him.

Their breath intertwined as he held her still with a firm grasp of her hair and another on her hip, before driving them hard to finish that blissful thing they started.

His moan tensed as his body did, his gold gaze lighting onto hers, and in them, she drowned in the power and vulnerability. That he was just a man who had given his heart to a woman, and that leap of faith he was taking could cost him everything. And if it did, even then, his eyes said she was worth it. Her hands went to his face and let him see what she did, that they, like that, were how she wanted them to be, forever, and sealed it with a kiss. Her pelvic bowl pinched and clenched with pleasure as she gentled a cry into his mouth as her body electrified with her orgasm.

Arching into it, Hoyt pounded into her hard, smacking the front of his pelvis against her clit until her head fell back as bliss rolled out over her body, sending her muscles rigid as every last ounce of pleasure was wrung out from her soul.

Hoyt groaned out a low cry and with one last thrust pushed up within her, releasing his orgasm in a flood of warmth within her.

As they descended back down from touching new heights, Vega

drew her finger down his throat over his shark's tooth and stopped at his navel.

"Hello," she whispered, wetting her dry lips, catching her breath.

Hoyt's skin glistened with sweat as he too caught his breath. "Hi. Pehea 'oe? Maika'i?" He gave her a kiss and whispered, "Aloha wau iā 'oe, ko'u lua pele."

Vega let the gentle tumble of vowels wash over her before exhaling, "I love you too. My Titan."

BLISS_

VEGA SLURPED SALTY DRUNKEN NOODLES OFF STAINLESS-STEEL chopsticks. She then pointed the shiny chopsticks to the drawings on the table and said through spicy, greasy lips, "Space out the floor sockets and add an external server for your personal use."

Hoyt had put away half the order of potstickers before grabbing a red pen and revising the drawings for the new home office.

"And," he added, "a monster snack fridge and cabinet."

Vega interjected, "Only if you plan on attracting the likes of me."

"Attracting and trapping."

She put down her chopsticks and dusted her hands. "Done. My warehouse will stay my home base, but I might just keep this as my play space as long as my key card works."

"It'll—"

"But let's be real, when it doesn't work, I'll still barge up here and fuck up whoever tries to take up space next to you."

He looked back down with a grin and said, "That's more like it." He was thoughtful for a beat, and Vega could feel Hoyt prepping for a question that was delicate for him.

When he stood and tucked his hands under his arms, she knew it was going to be a doozy and prepared herself.

"I want you to move out of that warehouse. Any special projects you have could come behind Titan's Wall and on an offline server that only you access when you're physically in the building. And I'd like to talk to you about insulating your Project Valkyrie business. Right now, from what you've said, it's a massive data file and booby-trapped, but I think you, and they, would be better served with an active wall around the parts used in the day-to-day, and those in deep freeze can be stored offline in a secure location here or in Prineville."

Vega pushed the noodles around, trying to figure out whether she should tell him or not about having such similar thoughts to his that she'd taken the initiative already.

"What is it?"

"Hm?"

"We can keep them safe, Vega."

"I know. Let me think about it," she said, dodging lying to him.

He squinted at her as if to make what she was really thinking clearer. Eventually he went with "Fine. But my next question has been in my court for a couple days." He came around the table and pulled out the chair next to her and sat. "The lawyers are waiting for the go-ahead to dig into your name and Social."

"Do Scout's first."

"Why?"

"Mine's booby-trapped to all hell. Give me some time to roll some of those protections back as we get everyone secured."

He laid his hand palm up on her thigh, and she put her hand into his. "We can do this. Maybe we wait until Titan's Wall is up and running at the penitentiary?"

Vega swallowed down apprehension and nodded.

"OK."

"Hoyt?" This was the last piece she'd yet to tell him, and she felt the weight of it.

He could feel it in her hand and pulled her up and into his arms. She whispered, "Closer."

Hoyt lifted her, taking her to the couch that had been replaced sometime during the day with a deep velvety gunmetal one. He rested her on his lap, swathed in his shirt, and kept her close.

"I'm ready," he said.

"You should know what the lawyers will likely find. A house, a father figure, two girls. When our mom died, you already know that he looked for alternate forms of income."

"Yeah, that didn't include honest hard work."

"No. What I do...why I do it... I had already taken our personal papers and hid them in my room after he found mine and sold it. I came home one day; he'd tossed my room and found it." Vega swallowed, hating the next part.

"I found him in the kitchen at his laptop, her info on the kitchen table next to him." She breathed through the memory and spoke as if she had exited her body. "I'll never forget seeing her nine-digit Social Security number, so innocuous on the official paper of the US Social Security Administration, and thinking, 'Oh fuck, my baby sis's life just got fucked.' Peace and Cindy...we'd planned for Scout and me to leave, we knew what to do—but in that moment, I lost my shit." She then told him everything.

Hoyt looked away, his jaw working as if he were there watching but could do nothing about it. He quieted his thoughts and looked back at her.

Vega settled in under his chin. "Cindy and Peace helped me send him to prison. He made a promise to us that he would never stop trying to destroy our lives, just like we did his."

His hand was back to slowly circling over her bent spine, and when Vega sat up, he asked, "Anything else the lawyers should know?"

"I think that's the last of it. Other than..."

"It's OK—tell me."

"When a fist hits your face..."

Hoyt nodded understanding, "It doesn't hurt at first."

She shook her head. "It doesn't. It wasn't until later in the ER when I knew Scout was safe and the girls were safe and the meds had yet to kick in. My nose was broken, my front teeth were loose." She'd referenced the beating earlier, when she'd told him about testifying against Lloyd, but then she'd spoken with dark humor behind her words. Now, she was speaking a truer truth. "It was then that I knew..."

His eyes were burning with the detail of the night she'd left Lloyd's home. "Say it."

She nodded. A tear slid down her cheek for the child she once had been, the girl who sat in the emergency room who should have been riding her bike, playing sports and braiding her friend's hair with the only worry on her mind being whether or not the braid was too tight and if that kid in math thought Cindy was hot.

"I knew then that if I had to, I'd kill him."

His hands wove up into her hair and, cradling her face between his wrists, told her, "I believe you."

She let another tear go. "It's not fair."

"It's not," he confirmed. And something like relief ran through her, like an exposed darkness had died. She slumped against his chest and used the beat of his heart and the warmth of his skin like grounding rod for her thoughts.

He held her like that for some time until her body wanted more than just the feel of his heartbeat.

"Hoyt?"

His voice warmed the shell of her ear. "Yes?"

Her pelvis tilted, rubbing her body against his, trying to get closer to him and, in turn, woke his body to hers. She hiccupped as her tears fell. "Remind me that I'm not there? I'm here, right? And there's still beauty in this world?"

His wide hand went to her lower back and pressed down firmly as he tilted his pelvis up, responding to her. "You're not there. You'll never be there again. The world is filled with beauty still—let me take you home with me to Maui. On our lands in Hāna, we have lava tubes with hidden underground ponds that glow blue or red depending on the time of the year and the ʻōpaeʻula that live there."

She gave him a watery smile. "I want that. Take me there...someday?"

"Someday could be now. It only takes an hour to get the jet fueled and prepped to go."

"No, now. I want to smell your skin when it gets hot and drown in the look your eyes get when you lose yourself inside of me. It makes me feel powerful. Like I'm invincible, and I need that reminder and beauty right now, if you can? I know it's a weird ask at this moment—"

His lips fastened on to hers as he rocked her over him before he pushed his hand between them and released his thickening erection so that Vega could connect them.

With his cock hard and stretching into her fast-wetting confines, she seated him fully inside. The warm connection pulsed, and she drowned in the golden starlight of his eyes before lifting herself up and pressing him back in, wetting the length of him. Hands to her hips, he assisted, lifting and pressing her back down. Rocking her in a mesmerizing rhythm, he watched her face as she broke over him; tears slid down her cheeks as the side of her fist hit his shoulder as she took his beauty deep inside of her and let that goodness fill her like hope changing the course of her life for the better.

"Remember," he told her and with a grunt pushed his pelvis up and brought her down with a smack.

She crushed her lips to his as they connected there on the couch, Hoyt thrusting into her until her breath caught and she cried out for mercy.

LATER THAT NIGHT, HOYT LAY WITH VEGA CURLED UP NEXT TO HIM, HER cheek on his chest and her leg thrown over his. His whole body thrummed with her energy. She was naked, her breasts pressed against his ribcage, and the spiky shaved strip of her pubic hair he could feel, if he concentrated, on his hip.

Naked. Vega. With him. He'd never felt so privileged in all his life. He promised himself he wouldn't think of Jax doing this. Vega had laughed at the thought, and he kept that close, the reassuring feeling that he indeed was the only one, likely ever, to be cuddled by Vega Flux.

He felt the smile inside of him before it bloomed onto his face—yeah, this was what his father was telling him. He'd known it before, but now he believed it in his bones. He was madly in love with a dangerous woman who was only calm when she was asleep. And that felt just right to him.

He tucked his hand under the thick layer of covers in the cool room and pressed his hand against her back in a one-armed hug. Hoyt felt heat and damp sweat, then peered down at her and saw that her bangs were damp, and as he moved under her, could feel the sweat along the length of his body.

"Vega?" He brushed damp hair off her cheek and gently squeezed her shoulder. "Vega? Are you—"

"No..." Her voice was a low cry that made goose bumps break out over his arms and down his back.

"Vega?" he tried again and pushed her shoulder back, trying to get her to lift her head.

She groaned. "Hoyt, he's here," she managed before her lips went out of sync and her words became a mash-up he couldn't understand.

"No one's here; you're safe. Vega, it's just a dream. Wake—"

Her body jumped as if she'd been shocked, and then she shouted, "Gun! Hoyt, run!"

"I'm right here! Wake up."

In a gasp of breath as if she'd finally returned to the ocean's surface, she reared back, her eyes popping open. She threw out her hand and took in the room in a panic, her eyes wide and frightened.

"Vega," he said softly, and her eyes darted to him. He watched her take one then two breaths with fear in her eyes before she recognized him and collapsed onto his chest.

He pulled her in against him again, this time her back pressed against his front as he curled around her. She pulled his leg up higher, hitching it over her hip, and pressed back into him as if he were a blanket she was covering herself with.

"It was just a nightmare." He soothed and brushed hair off her neck and cheek. "You're safe."

Vega nodded and pushed back farther as if she could retreat into him, and words fell off her lips in a quiet plea, "Protect me."

"I will." He held on to her until her heartbeat returned to a slow and steady rhythm and the sweat dried on her neck. Then, slowly, he reached back behind his neck and pulled wider the black cord to his necklace before taking it off and slipping it over her head. He adjusted it and her sleepy form until he could press the tooth against her chest and made a point of calling manō to her. If his mother was right, Vega already had a spirit manō could reach, and with her tooth around Vega's neck, the stronger their connection would be.

"Aloha wau iā ʻoe. Me ke aloha pumehana, koʻu lua pele." He whispered into her ear the declaration of his twisting, binding love to Vega, his volcanic love. "I'll protect you. Body and spirit."

VEGA WOKE THE NEXT MORNING WITH A WARM, HEAVY HUMAN PRESSED up against her backside. She smiled at the feel of him and stretched before turning over and cuddling in against his side. His eyes were closed, but his lips quirked into a smile; his arm tucked behind his pillow came around and pulled her in close.

"Good morning," Vega whispered.

"Aloha kakahiaka," he parroted before cracking an eyelid and pulling her in tighter.

Vega felt pleasantly squeezed as her insides were squished under his strong arms. She kissed the sparce hair on his chest then his lips when he bent to receive a kiss.

"It's early for you," his voice, still rough with sleep, told her.

"Damn near the middle of the night. Who gets up at eight anyway?"

"People who don't have dangerous women in their beds."

Vega slid onto his chest as his gold eyes woke and focused on her, down to her breasts squashed on his chest then back to her gaze.

"Now, aren't you at your leisure, sir."

"That I am."

"Did you already hit the field?"

"Fuck it."

"Meetings?"

He grinned. "Fuck them too."

She tsked. "What has happened to you?"

"You wouldn't believe me, even if I told you."

She touched his chin with one dark fingernail then dragged it down his neck, over a pectoral before saying, "Try me."

"I fell in love, and now I don't give a fuck about anything else. Reality will butt in soon enough, but I'll take the next seventy-two hours to get to know her better."

His hands moved down her back before sculpting over her buttocks and firmly grasping them before pressing her down onto his pelvis as he pressed his up against her.

Vega felt as if Skittles were raining down as she wriggled up his front and kissed him on the mouth. She let her lips open and linger, tasting and waking to the man who was beneath her. The long broad length of him that easily picked her up and held her, and most importantly, that mind that met her mind where she was. Tickling first her synapses before expertly using her body for pleasure experiments.

"About that list you had. Anything we should tick off this morning?"

"Yes," he said as his palms slid down the backsides of her thighs and spread them before he pushed inside of her. "Morning sex."

Vega's eyes fluttered shut as his morning wood slipped in and began filling and stretching inside of her.

Vega murmured, "Morning sex is my fav—"

The elevator chimed in the other room before voices started to fill the penthouse.

Vega caught, "...rear was torn out already, but the door package hasn't arrived, and the final specs have yet to be approved. But we can start with the server room floors..."

Paralyzed, they listened to what sounded like construction

starting in the rest of the penthouse. As if electrocuted, Hoyt pulled her off of him and picked up his phone. Vega laughed at the chance of getting caught in flagrante delicto as she swiped a hand down Hoyt's broad back as he sat on the side of the bed looking like an angry version of the bronze *Thinker* statue, phone to his ear.

Whomever he called he was curt, and Vega recognized his tone as the asshole he said some people called him.

"I didn't authorize construction to begin this morning. Get them the fuck out." He listened then his voice hissed, and Vega thought he might walk out naked as a jaybird if his command wasn't heeded by the person on the phone. "I don't care if they're here already. Pay them for the next two days of lost work—I'm in my own home, I can be here if I want. Cody, you're fucking fired—so now we're laughing?"

Arms folded behind her head, Vega watched him sever the connection then grip his phone so tight she thought the screen might crack.

"I'm getting dressed. I'll get them out then fire Cody and be right back."

"It's hard being a billionaire."

He gave her a smirk, his bad mood sliding off as his gaze settled onto her. "If I was just a cool guy coaching high school phys ed I could call in sick and fuck you until my dick fell off."

Vega laughed out. "Oh, please, no. This dick-on version is better."

He bent over her and kissed her lips. "I'll be right back."

"Try not to fire everyone. You'll need them to do shit you want next week."

He squinted. "No promises."

Naked, she watched him go to the closet, the muscles of his glutes divoting his butt cheeks as he walked, before she sunk down deep into the sheets, pulling the blankets over her head and heard him dress and get back on the phone. Vega smiled and shouted a "Bye!" when the door shut, and she closed her eyes, wondering if she could get back to sleep.

She heard Hoyt have a terse conversation with a man then the elevator ding. Slowly, footsteps shuffled until the penthouse was quiet. Curious, Vega slipped from Hoyt's bed.

She stepped into the long, wide bathroom off the bedroom and took in the warm tiles in stone colors. Into another, smaller room, Vega sat on the bidet and realized she was wearing his necklace.

"Oh," she said as she looked down at it. She touched the tooth and wondered how she'd come to have it on. Hoyt would have taken it off and placed it on her, and Vega felt the weight of his gesture hit her bones.

"Hi, Mahn-oh," she said to the tooth, then after washing up, went to his closet, talking to it again. "What shirt should we wear? Cream with stripes? Indigo silk? Yes, you're right. Linen from yesterday. Smells just like him." As if the tooth responded, she said, "I agree, I love you too, we're going to be best friends. Come, let's raid the fridge and see what's happening out there. Maybe we can score a little early brekkie."

Vega peered out the bedroom door and seeing the penthouse empty, padded into the kitchen and opened the stainless-steel commercial-sized fridge door. The skyline behind her was filled with low, gray clouds, but the fridge held a rainbow. Why would Hoyt ever get takeout? She selected fresh strawberries and a yogurt that promised her a thick and creamy experience.

"We'll see about that, my friend." She covered the fresh strawberries with copious quantities of what a finger lick told Vega was indeed thick and creamy with a touch of sweetness. But: "Could use more cream." She put the yogurt back and pulled out a small glass pint of cream and doused the top. She sifted through the front of the deep pantry for granola, hissing in pleasure that the walk-in pantry had pull-out shelves. "Glorious." She peered at clear container after clear container filled with breakfast and baking staples. "Could use a sprinkle of confection, if I'm being honest."

Vega finished decorating her breakfast bowl and began to eat while looking out at the view. She was thinking about Hoyt, why a man like that, with roots in the islands so deep, would stay in cold, rainy Portland, and wondered where he kept his baby pictures. She smiled to herself; she had delectable questions and research to perform that day.

Right behind the thought of research, she thought of Scout's passport. Despite their blow-out, she still needed to get her one, which now felt downright dangerous to attempt with her life going swimmingly aboveboard. With everything that had happened, Vega felt it was time to kill the past. She'd go to Scout. She'd tell her everything. It'd torpedo her semester abroad, but it was best to go with truth and let the chips fall where they may.

The chime of the elevator pulled her from her thoughts.

Expecting Hoyt, she was surprised when a long-haired woman with curves for days under a pants suit in a jewel-toned foliage pattern stepped off in sensible heels.

THIS IS JUST A TEST_

"OH, NOW, HELLO..." THE WOMAN PURRED.

Vega had the feeling that this woman had been hoping to catch her there alone. Vega wasn't sure how to react, so she gave her a three-fingered wave while holding her spoon. "Hi?"

"I'm Cody, Hoyt's interior designer. He's right behind me, but I've put the elevator on extended open, and Hector is buying me some time too."

Time...for what? "Oh, ah, hi, you're his cousin."

"By marriage. So it's OK when I say Hoyt is so smoking hot that my job for him is a sin. A panty-soaking sin. But he didn't want me, back in the day; his sweet cousin did. That's all right—he lets me have my way with him, which involves me sometimes closing my eyes and thinking of Hoyt. Just so you know—forewarned is forearmed and all."

Vega took in the dark-haired, dark-eyed woman and wondered if there were any meek people in Hoyt's family.

Cody put down—with a thud—on the cleared table her massive leather bag that was stretched beyond its means with sample binders.

"So, how'd you do it?"

"I'm sorry?" Vega thought that maybe excusing herself to put on a pair of panties would make her feel more secure right then, but she shrugged that idea off.

"How'd you do it, land him? Are you the fourth option the matchmaker proposed? Londyn was the third and most insidious of the three before you, and I knew the moment he gave me carte blanche to tear out that half and had an idea about what should be there that this new woman was *the one*."

"Oh," Vega said about being called 'the one.'"

"So, where'd they find you?"

"In a back alley."

Cody gave a dark and luscious laugh before laying out sample binders with fabric swatches, flooring samples, and blinds in a rich wooden material. "You're such a kidder. Only women who are smart catch his eye, and if they can't sustain it, he loses interest. You? He's losing sleep, coming in at all hours in all states of dress... Tell me, what do you do for a living?"

Vega liked her and was baldly honest. "Fuck people up."

She bristled. "Good god." Her smile was feline. "I see now. Fantasy made real, then? The matchmaker got it right."

"I'm sorry? Fantasy?"

Cody continued unfazed, letting gossip bind them together in an intimate conspiracy. "Lei got drunk once at a family party years back and was...let's say, amenable to my probing questions. I was trying to decide if he was worth the effort to pursue, and she set me straight. Apparently, since Hoyt was a kid, he used to read comics—the darker the heroine, the more obsessed he was. Had loads of them tucked under his bed."

"What, like, spank material?"

Cody wagged her eyebrows up and down as an affirmative. "And I heard you are something of a vigilante, so says Lei this morning, or that your skills are so good, this place went dark for hours yesterday. What a beautiful flex on a powerful man. Did he hate it?"

Vega looked down at her shirt then back to her. "I'm standing here in only his dress shirt—what do you think?"

Cody wiggled her shoulders as if the thought gave her erotic pleasure. "You minx! Of course he's fallen for you." Then her demeanor changed to ice, and Vega had the feeling that this was what she did, buttered people into thinking she was a softy pushover kind of gal then whipped out her fangs only once folk were nice and comfortable. "Two things you will heed while you are with him."

"Oh?"

"You will not boss me into decorating half this apartment for you in a style that wholly clashes with its owner, nor will I plan a December wedding. You understand me?"

Vega mock saluted with her spoon. "Yes, ma'am."

"Good." Her magenta lips pursed. "Then we're going to get on like a house on fire. Before you on the table are samples from draperies to flooring. This is a test; do not be confused. If you answer all of these appropriately, I won't torpedo your relationship, got it?"

Vega nodded; she liked the stakes that this woman played with. She thought it must be hard to find people who actually cared for Hoyt and loved him as an individual, so much so that it took multiple guardians to threaten the new person to make sure they were serious. Or maybe his run of bad luck had made everyone more careful.

Cody pressed a sharp holographic magenta nail to the first set of samples. Vega came around next to her.

Cody added, "The walls will be a deep umber, so these are the choices. Which one should be the drapes?"

"Ah," Vega said and tried to not feel like this was a trick question. "I think you should pick the one that reminds him most of home."

"And which one is that?"

Vega took a bite of her breakfast, biding time, looking at the various jewel-toned greens that reminded her of forest shadows. Eventually she pointed. "That one."

Cody tore off a Post-It and placed it on the sample. "Very good. Now this—" Cody's hand drifted off into space before just hanging there as her eyes rested on Vega's sternum. "I'm sorry. What's that?"

Vega looked down and saw Hoyt's necklace, "Oh, this is a shark's tooth from a real tiger shark that Hoyt met as a kid. Its guardian name is—"

"Manō." Cody's eyes had gone sharp. "I know what that represents. The question is, why do *you* have it?"

Vega shrugged, feeling like this might just be what it would be like when she someday got to court and was interrogated. "I woke up this morning with it on."

"He gave it to you?"

"Yes."

Cody had pulled out her phone that was protected with a leopard-skin cover dotted with rhinestones.

"Who are you texting?" Vega took another bite and looked around for her phone and saw her pouch on the bar top that separated the kitchen from the dining area.

"No one."

"Really?" She set down her bowl and pulled her phone and cord from the pouch and went back to Cody.

"Ginny is not going to believe this, but I warn you, I will not do a December wedding."

"I think we're far from wedding talk, Cody," she said. "Can I see your phone real quick? I want to show you something cool."

"Of course." She locked it and handed it over.

Vega plugged her phone into it and set it on the table. "Who's Ginny?" Vega woke up her systems across the river at the warehouse and set to work cleaning Cody's phone and installing the privacy software Peace, Cindy, and she had perfected over the last decade.

Cody watched her work and cooed her answer, knowing it was a bombshell. "Oh, you don't know Ginny? She's the Kaho'okalakupua Estate and Trust manager."

"Mm."

"And Hoyt's makuahine, Virginia."

That's a word I don't yet know."

"Mom."

Vega's fingers stilled.

Cody watched her with glee. "I'm surprised Hoyt hasn't told you about his family."

She had Vega on the defensive. “He has—he just calls them Mom and Dad.”

Cody shimmied again. “Do you want to meet them? Ginny is dying to meet you, and Curtis, his dad is, I dunno, he’s recently been obsessed with making food. Apparently, there’s some project Hoyt is working on, and the folks there like his dad’s cooking. Everyone is mum about it. Secret projects are my jam, but they’re not saying anything.”

Vega looked down at her phone. The contact labeled as Ginny was saying: *You’re so nīele. Leave her alone. Hoyt will tell us when he’s ready for us to meet her.*

“What’s that word?” Vega pointed to Cody’s screen.

“Nīele? ‘Curious’— Oh my god, how’d you get my phone open?”

Vega ignored her question to ask one of her own. “Who have you talked with about me?”

Cody thought. “Virginia, Hector, and my husband, Craig.”

Vega nodded as Cody watched her work. Hector had already received the app, but Virginia and Craig hadn’t, so Vega sent them a cute kitten video for them to download.

“Aww” came from Cody, “that’s so cute. Did you just send them malware?”

“Let’s call it Vegaware.”

Cody took a long appraising look at her and said, “I like it. You should patent that and create a side hustle. What does it do?”

“You know, your whole family, it seems, is very calm when I do stuff like this. Why’s that?”

“Hoyt’s in love with you, honey. If he trusts you, I trust you. He’s the most shrewd, arrogant asshole I’ve ever met, so if he approves of you? Hell, anything you say goes, hon. What does it do?”

“Photo- and text-match software that erases anything that it matches with. So, if you want to talk about me, then you’ll have to get really creative to outwit the AI. And keep outwitting the AI because it will learn your new codenames for me. Same with photos.”

“Is it done?”

Vega unplugged her phone from Cody’s. “Yup.”

Cody snatched her phone up and immediately took Vega's picture and sent it to Virginia.

"Nice," Vega said at the half-nude shot of her in Hoyt's oversized linen shirt.

Cody said, "Oh, it didn't send." She opened her camera app and didn't see it there either. "What, the...wow." Cody looked up at Vega, who was winding her cord back up. "Hot. I see why Hoyt fell head over cock for you."

Vega quietly smiled with the thought it was going to be a slippery slope with his family and her tainted past.

Vega set her things back into her pouch as Cody tried in vain to take another photo of Vega and send it out. As if, if she did it fast enough, the software wouldn't catch it.

Just then the elevator chimed, signaling that the doors were closing. Cody hustled to the elevator and hit the button to stay the doors.

The AI told them, "Elevator doors closing; stand back."

Cody yelped and stood back, her hands aloft to keep them from getting pinched. "How the hell is it doing that?"

Vega smiled. "Something tells me the person who's calling it, getting into it, and on his way right up will have some idea."

Cody took a beat to process that before her shoulders rolled again with excitement as she took in Vega, naked but for Hoyt's dress shirt, with a smirk. "Can't wait."

"Likely, he's going to be pissed."

Cody scoffed. "God, I hope so."

Vega took another bite of her creamy yogurt granola and waited with Cody. Cody looked to her, her lips in a tightly pursed smile that showed her dimples, then to the elevator doors. They both watched as the number started at fourteen, where the sky bridge was located from the other Hoyt Tower, then began to climb.

"There's a utility elevator at the rear. You sure you don't want to jump on that, real quick?"

"Oh no, this is worth staying for." Then as if something clicked, she looked to Vega eating her breakfast. "You."

"Yup, me."

"You like to eat. You're the secret project." The doors slid open to reveal Hoyt in a form-fitting black tee and jeans that Vega was sure were illegal in three states for being so tight across his thighs. "Are you pregnant?" Cody asked.

Vega choked on her yogurt.

"What the fuck," Hoyt said to her as he stepped off and waved Cody in. "Get in."

She batted her eyelashes at Hoyt, and Vega grinned. Cody had the kind of old-school sensuality that was niche sexual power, but she played it well. And for that, Vega gave her props. Only Hoyt looked like he was going to blow his stack.

"I can't." She pouted and pointed to her things on the table. "I have to get my things."

Hoyt put his hand to her back and gently pushed her into the elevator. "Wrong answer." Vega watched in the mirror on the back of the elevator as he pushed the lobby button.

Cody squeaked out, frustrated, "Hoyt!"

"Aloha nō," he said, and Vega understood then how one word could have many meanings. He said it with a punctuated dry tone, and she definitely heard the "goodbye" it meant.

"My things!" Cody hit the door-hold button.

"Wait in the lobby, and I'll send them down."

"Hoyt." His name came out in one long nasal drone that Vega imagined worked well on her husband, Craig, but Hoyt was pulling out his phone.

Vega smiled as she watched this man she'd come to love stand in the elevator doorway as he overrode the elevator's controls to have it close then descend with his cousin in it. Vega picked up Cody's things and brought them to the elevator, her arm heavy with the load.

Silently he called the elevator back, put her things in it then sent it down again before locking the entrance to his penthouse. Vega half expected Cody to still be in the elevator but was glad he didn't have to physically escort her down to the lobby. Something about the woman told Vega that Cody had definitely thought about pressing her luck.

Hoyt exhaled long and loud before tucking his phone into his back pocket and turned to her. "Now, where was I?"

He took the bowl out of Vega's hand set it on the counter in the kitchen and came back to her. He squatted and picked up Vega by the thighs. She wrapped her legs around his chest, grinning down into his face.

"Hi."

"I missed you," he said up to her.

"You were gone forever and ever," she said, melodrama saturating her words, "and I was here all alone with a woman who asked probing questions." She gave him sad eyes with a hint of mischief.

"I bet she did."

Sobering, she said, "They surprisingly revolved around how hot you were and held the underlying threat that I had better know how lucky I am and be worthy of your love."

He closed his eyes. "Sorry."

"It's fine, seriously. I learned a new word."

"What's that?"

"*Nīele.*"

Hoyt's laugh started deep in his throat. "Let me guess—my mom called Cody that."

She grinned back at him. "Very good, and accurate, guess."

He took in her smile as she lorded over him up in his arms. "Hector isn't good at running interference at Cody's behest and texted my mom for support—I suppose to override her."

"Hector is very loyal."

"He is, but he's catching flack for having met you and not told anyone."

Vega felt a smile bloom on her face. "He hadn't?"

"I might have had a talk with him."

This made Vega's brows rise. "Oh yeah? Wish I was there to witness it."

"I told him I gave you my key card."

"Oh?"

"He's akamai enough to know what that means."

"You mean he's smart enough to know that when the controlling, asshole founder and chief technology officer of Hoyt Securities gives a person his heart, cock, and key card, she's his number one?"

"Exactly," he said and kissed her, letting her slide down his front. "Vega?"

"Yes?"

"I'm going to need to do this every day."

She kissed his lips. "Oh yeah?"

"Yeah."

He kissed her again then slipped his tongue into her mouth, tasting her. "Where did you find strawberry granola?"

"Your pantry, from what little I've perused of it, is stocked with every item known to mankind, sweet, kind sir."

He gave her a glinting smile. "It is?"

"It is."

"I wonder how it got that way."

She heard it then, the faux curiosity, and she put her lips to his, letting them linger and thank him. Then opened and tasted once more. There was the pineapple in his morning shake and the ice cold water that he must have drunk from the water fountain next to the elevator downstairs before pulling out his cell and commanding the brass-trimmed car to return him to his tower and the woman who awaited him. "You stocked your kitchen for me."

"A week ago, there was nothing in the fridge or pantry. I mostly have food delivered to me and didn't eat here. But you... I didn't realize that feeding someone was an act of love until you. Until you ate the food I brought to you that night at your place. It crossed my mind that I might get an opportunity like today to get you alone, and I didn't want to be ill prepared."

She gave him one more peck. "You are definitely prepared, my friend."

He pinched the front of her shirt and opened his dress shirt wide and took her in from foot to crown. "I am. Now, this... There's a new dress code for the apartment. Effective immediately."

"It smelled like you—"

"Or naked." He was still having his conversation, and it seemed was now talking directly to her breasts.

She gave her upper arms a quick squeeze to have them bounce. Their bump and sway made his eyes widen.

"What's that?" she asked, then did it again.

Hoyt grinned. "This. Is mesmerizing. But I'm trying to have a conversation, Vega."

She put her two fingers up to her eyes. "Up here, big guy."

"Yeah, just a sec, they have something they want to tell me." He bent and put an ear to her right nipple and said, "Uh-huh, bras are stupid and you want to never wear one again? Good." He turned and kissed her nipple before slipping it into his mouth and gently sucking.

Vega's hand slid up into his hair as she hissed in pleasure as the taut pinch of her nipple tugged through her breast and created a tingle all the way down to between her thighs.

He sucked off her nipple before kissing it and looked her in the eye. "Oh, I'm sorry, you were saying something, Lua Pele?"

She grinned back at him hearing her volcano nickname and kissed his wet lips. "Totally forgot."

He bent again and whispered, "Good," over her other breast before adding, "Come in the kitchen. I have something I want to show you."

"I can come in the kitchen. I'm pretty sure, with you, I can come anywhere."

He groaned in response and slipped her other nipple into his mouth and suckled.

She breathed his name out over her vocal cords. "Hoyt..."

His nose traced up over her chest, her neck and ear, until his lips murmured against hers, "Yes?"

"What's in the kitchen?"

He smiled against her lips. "Come," and holding her hand, pulled her, dazed, into the kitchen where he started to unload things from the pantry.

LOVE ME, HARD_

Holding the blue rectangular can in her hand, Vega asked, "Spam? Really?"

"Really."

"Amazing. That musubi was good—so do you just ram it into the rice and wrap it in seaweed?"

He grinned at her. "Hop up, watch, and learn."

She did and, legs swinging, said to him. "This would be hotter if you had your shirt off."

"And what happens when hot musubi sauce splatters and burns me?" he asked as he put his hands over his pectorals.

On the counter, Vega rested her arm on the raised bar top that ran the length of the open kitchen. "Well, now, we wouldn't want that. How about an apron, and nothing else?"

"It's cold. But, as my guest, feel free to wear something more comfortable. And speaking of comfort," he said, taking the can from her and cracking open the lid, "did you get to the back of the pantry?"

"I didn't go any farther than the granola," she said, hopping down and opening the pantry, stepping inside, and flipping on the light. Vega took in the back shelves and felt as if she'd strayed from reality and into her own dreamscape. A kaleidoscope of colorful sweets in round fishbowl jars sat six shelves high. She sucked in her breath then let it out slowly, emitting a groan that was more like a purr. Then, as Hoyt came up behind her, she asked, "Hoyt? Is this...heaven?"

His hands slid over her hips before pressing her back into him in a hug. "Did we get all the ones you like?"

"All the ones *I* like? Sir, you have all the ones that exist." Vega went to the first one, popped the lid, and inhaled the sweet confection that hinted at a bright watermelon flavor in a round gummy candy.

Hoyt kissed her neck. "You have heart eyes right now."

"I'm just wondering how much of these I can eat before I puke."

"It's you, so, I'd say, half?"

"Half this container?"

"Half this wall."

Vega grinned and gave him a peck on the lips before shoving two watermelon candies into her mouth.

Back out on the counter, two containers of candies next to her, Vega watched Hoyt pour soy sauce, ground ginger, and "Is that generic maple syrup?" into a skillet set on medium flame.

"Yup."

"Wha..."

"Trust me, thin it all out with some water, simmer it down, and it makes the final sauce thick and caramelly without adding too much maple taste. Real maple syrup? No go. This, though? Perfect. But to be honest, every house has their own secret way to make it."

"Nice." As he cooked, Vega pulled up pictures on her phone of things they promised they wouldn't talk about. Without context, she showed him her phone. "What do you think of this guy?"

He gave her a sly smile, not missing a beat in her out-of-context prompting. "I thought we weren't ever supposed to talk about these things."

"I couldn't resist. So, thoughts? Too soon?"

"We'd need a yard."

She sighed with a smile; it wasn't too soon. Leaning back, bracing her elbows on the bar behind her, she thought about the property her sister lived in. It had a yard. The warehouse could use one, but she couldn't imagine Hoyt living there forever. "Maybe I should sell my warehouse..."

He was scrolling on his phone before he handed it over to her.

She took it and looked at the property listing, which had replaced her shelter-dog photo. "Oh, so you've thought about it."

"A little."

Vega scrolled through the listing's pictures then perused the real estate site, finding the list of houses Hoyt had favorited, all dated within the last week. Her cheeks were starting to hurt with the amount of smiling she was doing lately. Her muscles weren't used to it.

"You have twenty-seven properties on your favorites list."

He gave a soft shrug. "There'd be more, but not all of them have space for a helipad."

Vega laughed, making Hoyt grin at her.

He moved the slices of spam around in the simmering sauce. "You act like I'm joking."

She showed him a property. "White picket fence, half acre, walking distance to shops perfect for the fluffy pupper I just showed you."

He pulled a white spacecraft-looking appliance out from the corner of the kitchen and popped it open. Steaming rice was fluffed up inside. "What'd you call it?" he said, nodding to the real estate picture in her hand. "That's right, catnip. It's catnip for you."

Vega pulled her knees up and hunched over his phone that was twice the size of hers and scrolled through the images. "Pure catnip. Look at the floor space, huge backyard. I could have a table in there where friends could sit down and eat."

Hoyt left the rice cooker to get close to Vega. He pushed a lock of her hair back behind her ear. "Have you ever done that? Sat around a table in your own home and served a meal you made?"

Vega felt emotion constrict in her chest. Hoyt saw inside her so clearly now that she'd talked about her past. He saw the good parts and the broken parts. "No, I haven't. Cindy, Peace, and I usually stand and eat takeout. Peace is a good cook, and we've eaten stuff she's made, but the table is always something that wasn't made to be a table. Huge boxes with a small sheet of plywood on top is usually our go-to."

"Do you want that house?"

Vega touched the screen. "It's too much."

"I didn't ask the beautiful raven-haired lua pele on my counter if it was too much. I asked her if she wanted it."

The grass behind the home was hedged in a natural flow of shrubs, small trees, and flowers, making it look as if it were a botanical garden. "If I say I do, I know you'll buy it—"

"Vega, you're the only person I've ever known who makes me nuts with how much you don't ask from me."

"Your love is enough—"

"And so is yours for me. But the things you desire are things I can so easily provide you, and I want to. I want to watch you smile at Cindy and Peace as you welcome them into your home. I want to watch you shout at our four dogs—ranging in size from Chihuahua to Great Dane—as they conspire together to take food off the counter. And you can't do any of this at your warehouse, because someone will likely ingest lead paint."

Vega blew out a breath in agreement. "It definitely has lead paint. And probably asbestos."

"Right," he whispered and enveloped her in a one-armed hug. "Why don't you invite the girls over to dinner in your new—"

"Our," Vega corrected him before giving him a kiss.

"Our new place."

"I don't know how to cook," Vega whispered.

"Fine. You'll be on dog duty. I'll cook."

"Wait. Did I just let you buy me a house? And dogs?"

"Us, you just let me buy *us* a second place, one with room for the four kolohe dogs we're obviously going to adopt."

"Obviously," she whispered against his lips then sighed, "I should tell you..."

His thumb swiped over her cheekbone, "Yes?"

"The things I buy for the dogs, and actually buying the dogs, I can get them with the cash I have, but...at some point, this will be too aboveboard for someone with outstanding warrants—"

"Until we clear your name, just let me or Hector know what you want, and he'll buy them."

"What, like send him links? I could just go to the store with the cash I—"

Hoyt kissed her. "Send him a picture of what you want, and Hector will source it for you."

"Source it." Vega smiled. "I like that phrase. I'm gonna owe Hector big-time if I do."

Hoyt was back at the open space of the counter, now with a rectangular mold sitting on a strip of seaweed. He scooped rice into it then topped it with a marinated slice of spam.

"You won't owe Hector anything."

"So says you...oh," she said, getting distracted by Hoyt depressing the top of the musubi mold and a perfectly square rice block with spam on top pressing out the bottom. He wrapped the rectangle in seaweed and put it aside.

"Now you do one."

"OK!" Vega hopped off the counter and mimicked what he'd done.

She held up her finished product on her palm.

"Not bad," Hoyt said to the oblong object whose rice was torn in three places.

"Needs work," Vega amended.

Vega helped Hoyt finish the rest of the musubi, then eat them all while deciding on which house to really get, then which dogs to really get. The sun was setting by the time the kitchen was cleaned and Hoyt reclined back in his bed, Vega curled up next to him.

Vega said, "When you said videogames and chill, I expected some kind of screen. Are we playing on our phones, or is some, like, troupe of folk going to run into the room with your AV equipment?"

Hoyt just gave her a soft chuckle as if she were so funny before opening his side table and pulling out a remote. He pushed a button, and the hutch against the wall at the foot of the bed began to hum before a wide screen, the length of it, emerged out the top.

"Holy wow."

He grinned at her. "I love how impressed you are by the shit some people just come to expect from people with my income."

Vega laughed. "It's coming out of the dresser thingy! I've seen them before on shows and shit, but in real life...nope." She thought of something and gave him a sly grin. "I mean, I totally am impressed, don't get me wrong, but couldn't it be bigger?"

He turned his dark, glittering gaze to hers. "That's it." He tossed the remote and tackled her.

Vega squealed as he came over her.

"Take it back."

"Take what back?" She squealed again when his mouth went to her neck and bit her. "I take it back! I take it back!"

He rested back on an elbow. "That's more like it." Then looked across the room: "Now, where's the remote?"

GOODBYE_

Vega, bag on her shoulder, gave Hoyt a kiss. "I need to go talk with Scout, and then I'll be back after I grab a few more things from my warehouse."

His hands were clasped behind her back, holding her in the circle of his arms. "I'm sad the seventy-two hours is up but excited for the forever part."

She grinned up at him. "Me too."

"Good luck with your sister. I hope your fears about her never forgiving you are unfounded."

"How likely is that, though?"

"High. He was just a stepdad."

"But what if—"

Hoyt cut her off with a kiss. "No what-ifs. Let it be what it will. Scout's a smart kid. Even though I've only met her once, I'm sure she'll see things as you do."

Vega was in the garage, Hoyt's keys in hand and walking to his SUV, when her phone lit up. Scout was being routed through.

Vega smiled and answered, “Hey, bug, I was just going to text you. I’m headed to see—”

Vega stopped and looked at the phone when she heard the dead air. The call had disconnected, and Vega cursed her routing systems. Only a notification got through the routing systems. She had gotten an e-greeting from Scout in her messages. Vega’s stomach churned. Everything about the e-greeting felt off.

Vega dialed her sister. The signal went dead in the underground garage, and Vega texted her sister instead:

> Bug, it’s me. Call me. Got a weird text from you.

With anxiety in her stomach, she slid into Hoyt’s SUV and driving out of the garage into the drizzling rain, headed toward the university.

THE RAIN HAD STARTED AGAIN, AND PEACE SMILED AT ZANE AS SHE prepared dinner for them in her one-bedroom apartment. It was cozy with him there, like a home.

As she tore pieces of lettuce into a salad bowl, she addressed his concerns: “No, I don’t want to order in; with how busy you are with Big Friends Bigger Hearts, I wanted to make sure every second is spent together. And I have exactly three recipes I’ve perfected this last year, and I’d like to show them off.”

He pressed against her backside and kissed her cheek, his large presence making her small kitchen feel snug, exactly as she liked it. “All right, then you’ll have to put me to work.”

“Excellent,” she said to his wide jaw. “I’ve always wanted this, you know. Someone special cooking with me. It’s the reason I started learning. I figured if I learned, I could manifest my dream.” She gave him another kiss as he went to her sink.

As he lathered up, he said softly, with tenderhearted thoughtfulness, “That’s a beautiful dream, Peace. I’m honored to be the one you chose to have this moment with. I feel like my life is an embarrassment of riches right now."

Peace felt her face go hot. She understood him that his own dreams were coming true, and Peace felt humbled and honored that he included her in those dreams.

Tucking her head to hide the flame she felt in her cheeks, she shook her wet hands from the freshly rinsed and torn lettuce, knocking off the small pieces that had adhered to her fingers. Grabbed a spoon from the drawer in front of her and bumped it shut. As the drawer closed, her phone chimed. Still feeling light, she looked around the salad bowl to it where the phone sat on her counter.

The screen showed her an encrypted message, then alerted once more—the screen going a bright, warning red.

Peace's smile slid to the floor, as did the spoon, where it hit with a clatter.

"What is it?" she heard Zane ask.

Her mind couldn't process what she was seeing. It had come, the day they had practiced for and the moment they had prepared for. The calm they'd experienced was an illusion. The nightmare from their past found their stash of Valkyrie Project names.

Air escaped her lungs in a cry. "No..."

Her hands shook as she picked up the cell, and from down a long tunnel behind her, she heard Zane ask if everything was OK. She tried to open her device with her wet hands and couldn't. As she fumbled with the lock screen, the phone slipped, and reaching for it, she knocked it farther away. Her knees gave out, and she hit the floor, crawling toward it as she started to wail.

"Not now!" She finally swiped the screen open and typed in: *Confirmed. DEFCON 1.*

She felt Zane's hand on her shoulder as he said something. She looked up at him, not recognizing him in all her anguish. It was as if she had already said goodbye.

Her shoulders shook with the adrenaline that coursed through her veins. The memory snap of Vega's screams tore through her. The reason for it all. Where it started. The memory of the moment she and Cindy saw the underbelly of the world. She had watched as Vega took punch after punch from her stepdad the day Vega called for help. The day Lloyd took little Harmony Alexander and gave her identity to a man with a gun. Watched as Lloyd pinned Vega to the ground, arm on her cheek as Vega screamed for them to take a horrified toddler—Scout—and run.

The devil never forgot a debt owed.

Collateral damage. That was what Vega said Peace would be if she helped Vega put Lloyd away. She was young and naive and willing to pay the price, but now it felt like a small death. The only fodder for her soul was that she wasn't alone; this was a pact made by three, and her sisters needed her.

She stood and pushed Zane away. Staggering to the front door, her eyes took in the apartment and the gorgeous man who stood in it. She memorized his kind eyes, the power of his hands, and the soft brogue of his voice against her cheek. Another step back, she memorized the feeling of goodness, the softness of the couch against her back with Zane in her arms.

Shaking her head, her mind hating what she had to do, she let the tears fall.

"Goodbye," she choked out to him and heard him call her name and start for her, his own fear beginning to show on his normally jovial features. She got the door shut behind her, and in a move she'd practiced a hundred times since moving in, she picked up the rope hidden in her planter. She wrapped it around the knob and attached the other end to the hook that was intentionally much too secure for its fake purpose, holding her welcome sign. It had been meant to trap a bad man in. Now it trapped a good man who'd try to stop her.

She was running again. In the parking lot, she didn't feel the grit of the asphalt under her bare feet; she was just one of three doing the exact same thing at the exact same moment. Hundreds of thousands depended on them to do what they were doing without fail.

. . .

Red-eyed and emotionally frozen, Peace stood in the thundering rain in the parking lot of Vega's warehouse. Large drops slapped against her cheek. It was as if the heavens were in their own emotional turmoil. Phone in hand, looking down at the screen, lashes dropping crystal tears into the puddles on the glass, she held down the power button and the phone went orange, waiting for a verbal command. Peace held the button again and commanded the home-made app, "DEFCON 1 initiate."

It confirmed the voice match then began booting the systems Vega had put into place.

She watched the warehouse as rain slithered over her skin, chilling her down to her bones, to make sure the command did as it was meant to.

The crash came, telling Peace that the crane had hit the side of the building. She made sure that the magnet went to full power and watched as the building groaned. Witnessed as metal supports, nails, bolts, and rusted nuts ripped off their beams and brackets. She made sure her directive was followed to a T as Vega's equipment exploded in a fiery display of carnage before the building shivered, and like an elephant going to its knees, it collapsed. The rumble of it shook the earth beneath her as her own phone ripped out of her hand, joining in the dissolution of her and her sisters' life work.

Peace turned then, numb still to the wet grit beneath her feet as she walked to her car across the street, the fire reflected in its windows. She got in and drove it to the edge of the city, opened the locker in the twenty-four-hour gym, and left the world she and her sisters had built. Watched as everything they'd ever prepared for was executed. Watched over her shoulder at a life she would never have again.

Cindy put her accelerator to the floor as the lights of her SUV flashed, moving traffic on I-5 South out of her way. She had gotten the DEFCON signal and set her series of dominoes into effect. The penitentiary was five minutes away now. She hadn't been prepared for Vega going off script. She was there, identified assaulting a prisoner she had been visiting, and now Cindy was in a race to get there before the sheriff.

Cindy didn't slow until the front doors were before her. She called in her arrival and ran in, pulling her ID badge as she did.

Chaos greeted her. Vega was in the front entrance beyond the metal detectors lifted in the air by a guard's arms wrapped around her chest. Two other guards were attempting to capture her legs, but Vega wasn't the kind of human who did well in restraints. Her hips twisted, and her boot clipped a guard in the chin. His head snapped to the side as the other jumped on her and the guard restraining her, foolishly knocking them all to the ground.

Cindy slipped out her taser with an apology on her lips, "Sorry, babe."

Vega, eyes dilated like a cornered animal, leaped to her feet.

"Nope." Cindy jabbed her ribs with her taser and lit her up.

"Fu—" was all Vega managed before hitting the linoleum floor.

The guards charged, and Cindy put a boot on Vega's back and held up her ID badge to keep them back. "FBI! Back the fuck up!"

The four guards, two nursing bloody noses, glared. "That woman is going nowhere."

"What the fuck does the FBI want with her?"

Cindy let them take a beat as she took an aggressive stance toward Vega, indicating that she didn't take assaulting an officer lightly. "She's wanted by the FBI in connection to multiple instances of bank fraud. You guys did good."

"She's a fucking crazy bitch." The guard spat blood.

"I'll add assault charges. You all right? Should we get a medic?" Cindy's heart was pounding as she tried to quickly deescalate the situation.

"No," he said with a frown as the other two guards looked at him, only then realizing he was bleeding.

"The warden will want a word."

"I'm sure he will." Cindy could see other prisoners beyond the bullet-proof glass watching, exchanging wagers, and generally enjoying the chaos that Vega created. Beyond the crowd at the window, she saw an older man, faded strawberry-blond hair having gone to gray and seemingly kind eyes nursing a bloody nose. It was that kind-eyed stranger who made Cindy's spine tingle. Tingle in a way that made her want to slip her cuffs out and clip him to a chair and, surrounded by plastic sheeting, put a bullet through his eye socket.

But right then she was on a clock. Her backup was five minutes out. She had five minutes to talk down guards, wake Vega, give her the planned pat-down, and hustle her into the back of her rig. If she didn't, she'd disappear into the bureaucracy where she'd be out of Cindy's reach.

Thirty minutes earlier.

Vega sat at a bolted-down table. There in the penitentiary's visitor room, she looked at the man who'd singlehandedly created a monster so large that he'd changed the course of her young life. The DEFCON 1 signal had been sent the moment she left Scout's house, which told her that he had breached her systems. And with Scout's truth bomb, that she'd been to visit him, all Vega could think of was killing him.

"Know who I am?" she asked the slump of the aging man in front of her. He'd added prison specs, which gave his brown eyes an elderly woefulness.

He gave her a winsome smile with his lips as his eyes tried to join in, but prison had worn him down. Vega was keen to the tightness at the edges that said he was playing nice, for now. "I'd know my beautiful daughter anywhere. It's been too long. Scout and I talk about you often."

Vega bristled at hearing Scout's name off his tongue. She was watching all her hard work come undone as if he'd taken the bottom card to her tower of cards. "You'll never be a real father. Leave Scout alone."

"But why? *She* came to *me*." His eyes told her he was enjoying the irony. His sweet tone that said to trust him was offset by the orange jumpsuit and by the chains on his hands and feet. They were the physical reminders that he was not a gentle soul. He could no longer hide behind his crafty words and impish presence.

Vega grinned, her finger going to where the shark's tooth rested under her shirt, and hoped her incisors looked bigger.

"Cool," she said in a tone that conveyed that he was anything but, "you still got it, that shitty thing you do, convincing people that you're an underappreciated smart guy. Only as long as it suits your interests. This is the part where I tell you to knock it off and the only thing I want from you is a 'yes, ma'am.'"

She watched as he resisted the urge to lift his lip in disgust. "Is that any way to speak to your father?"

Vega pressed again, focusing on her task and not the chaos that was snapping and slathering at the end of her chain waiting to let loose from inside of her. "You *will* leave Scout alone, understood?"

"I can't possibly do anything here, Melanie—"

"I want a 'yes ma'am.'"

"Now, hold on, Melanie."

"Melanie is dead."

"Yes, that's right," he said, pausing to seemingly enjoy her like a plaything he held the strings to, "you're calling yourself Vega now."

He watched for a moment as Vega processed the knowledge that he knew her name. Of course he did. Her nightmares were filled with him standing over her saying it. It was effectively her shield being shattered, and her skin went icy as she felt something get injected into her veins.

He went on as if he hadn't just destroyed her carefully crafted world. "Fierce Vega. I tell my boys in here how my girls are all grown-up, trying on different identities, trying to find themselves in this confusing world."

"You do? You don't tell them that I'm fierce because you sold your daughters out? That you let shitty fucks into our world for a buck? You should tell 'your boys' we had to change our names to get the fuck out of that world, but I bet they already know. So, who do you owe now? Come to collect our new names and sell those too?"

No matter how many years had passed, the vitriol she had toward a man who had sworn to be all they ever needed after their mother died and instead placed value on their lives had not lessened. "I sent you to prison. Have you learned nothing from the lessons of a pissed-off teenager, Lloyd?"

She could see her words ignite the trigger she knew was there.

"It's *Father*" was all he could manage for a while. He looked around the room as if trying to find calm in its corners before coming back to her. "You and your whor—"

"Finish that sentence, and I'll put your face into the table as many times as I can before the guards stop me."

He seethed. "You three made me out to be a monster at my trial. Just a little check writing, that's all—"

"That's all? Really? You're fucking kidding yourself."

"Don't interrupt your *father*. You created this, this thing I was. I'm in here because of you, and you know what, you'll soon be in here too. Vega Flux is Melanie Alexander; maybe they'll even get you for murder. But I'm gonna start with my little party trick. I know what you do now; I see all those message boards of girlies crying to you for help. Well, howdy-doody, how are they going to like hearing how this big bad protector sold all their data off? I'm sure they'll believe you—you, who doesn't ever get punked by cyber bullies. I'm sure they'll understand that you got hacked."

Vega's hands began to shake. "Come for me. If you can. But you need to understand that Scout has no place between us."

His gaze sparked. "She's my daughter who wants a relationship with her father—"

"Step."

"*Father!*" he shouted before hissing and looking around when the guards turned their heads. "You can't take that away in a fit of trivial childish drama."

Vega smoothed her hands over the top of the small table in the sterile room, analyzing the cuticle of each one of her fingers until she calmly told him, “You know, the upside to having you as a *step*father is that while you groomed me to dip my fingers into the virtual pockets of unsuspecting strangers and pilfer account information from the innocent, I was able to be just as good as you at twelve. Now? I have something you’ll never have: time.” Her skin was ice, numb. “Understand that if you don’t turn Scout away, that if you continue to pursue a twisted, manipulative relationship with her, I’ll use the rest of my life to find a way to end yours.”

The guard announced the visiting session was ending.

Vega looked back to the man who made her call him Father, who held a threatening smile in response to her. She had expected any reaction to be from her press to use *stepfather*, but the guard’s announcement was a kind of trigger for him; he had to hurry up his hustle. “I’m in here, Vega; you’re out there. And don’t be so dramatic about killing me. You don’t have it in you, and even if you did, could you do it before or after I sell everything you’re hiding behind your kiddie tripwires? Let’s make a bet. My life for yours. Or should we bet,” and he watched her, excitement lighting his gaze, “Hoyt’s life?”

Vega’s blood stopped pumping as her guts bottomed out, and fear shut down blood flow to her heart, and she heard it shatter.

“I get the sense you would do anything to keep *him* safe.”

Vega felt the twelve-year-old deep inside start screaming. He was coming for her again to take what he thought was his. Her fingers shook as they crawled up to the talisman she had been given by a man who went through life grounded. She touched it and felt herself crash back into the present moment as if the shield he was had stepped beside her loaning her his power.

She was no longer twelve.

The guard called again, visiting time was over, and Vega felt herself let go of the snarling, salivating chaos that bit at the end of its leash. She felt that wraith rise out of her and point at the man whose dark threats were reaching out to grab her sisters and the one good man she’d come to love.

Lloyd stood. His expression said he knew what leverage he had on Vega and was happy for the opportunity she had given him.

"You're right, Lloyd," she said, her voice having gone deep and raw with suppressed emotion, "I *am* your daughter." She smiled at him slowly, feeling her upper lip lift. "So it's crazy to me, that you would come at me. You don't recognize the similarities between us? You somehow don't see it when you look at yourself in the mirror? In mine, I see the monster you made me into, every time."

Vega leaped. Her hands caught his hair, grabbing fistfuls of it. He flinched, but she kept him still. "I am the monster you created."

With his head between her wrists, she slipped back off the tabletop and sat hard. His face hit the table with a cartilage-smashing crunch. His head bounced as Vega leaped up. Hands to his face, he started screaming. Vega was around the table, the guards yelling for her to keep her hands off the prisoner.

"Fuck!" he shouted, holding his bloody nose.

"Not fucked yet." Her boot pounded his chest, once, quick, definitively. Caught in his chains, he sprawled back as the guards came for her.

But Vega was all eyes on him and fell onto him, her knees pinning his shoulders to the ground.

"Daddy?" she cooed like a baby as her head tilted to the side. "Save me, Daddy, please?" And punched his face, then growled, "Save me from the monster I've become," and punched. Fist back, wet with his blood, she screamed, "Die, motherfu—"

Was all she managed before getting tackled.

RUN_

VEGA WOKE CUFFED IN THE BACK OF CINDY'S PATROL SUV. THE MOTOR sounded like it was well into the red line. The fields that lined the I-5 freeway flew by. Water rocketed up past the windows like rooster tails off the tires. She blinked and looked to the eyes in the rearview. They were asking her what the fuck she was thinking. Which she couldn't ask aloud because of the recording devices in the rig. Vega adjusted in her seat, praying they didn't get in an accident. She'd look like shit for her funeral.

Vega closed her eyes and tried to get her heart to slow down. Slamming Lloyd's face into the table hadn't been in the cards, but it sure as fuck felt great. That she'd assaulted not just an inmate but guards was going to be a problem.

By the time they reached the Portland FBI satellite office by the airport, Vega was ready. Cindy parked and was around the side of the vehicle in a flash, yanking her out.

"Whoa, fuck." Vega stumbled out into the pouring rain.

"What the fuck where you thinking?" she hissed in her ear.

Vega leaned back, water pelting her face, to look at her best friend, whose wet hair was back in a tight braid making her look serious as hell. "He found Scout." Then, swallowing down the pain, uttered his name, "And Hoyt."

"Oh no."

"Yeah, lots of threats. My life, Hoyt's life, Scout's life. Yours and Peace's." Vega studied Cindy's face; it was her calculating-the-fallout face.

"Cin..."

"This is serious."

"Cin... Peace, if she hasn't done her part..."

"She has. She's...she's a ghost."

There was a collective sadness. The day the three were hoping would never come had. Everything was burnt, but Vega hadn't been prepared for the thing that hurt the most. All three had given in to hope. And now, that too was gone.

Vega's insides dropped; she should have been a ghost as well. But she'd lost her cool, and now Cindy was cleaning up her mess.

"Things change, Vega," she said, giving the situation the reality check it needed. "Let's get you inside, take your statement first. Then..."

"Yeah, then..."

INTO A BIN WENT THE THINGS VEGA CARRIED: HER CELL, FIFTEEN USB keys she didn't start the morning with, and Hoyt's necklace. She took a long, memorizing look at the necklace.

"What's with all the USB drives?" Cindy's tone was authoritative.

"Got lots of data. Why else?"

"Fine," she said and then to the stout man making notations on the contents of her bin. "She's headed to interview room five. Check those drives," she said, giving Vega a glare. "Make sure they don't have data on them she's trying to sell."

Vega gave her a wince and said, "Gross."

Seated in interview room five at the end of the hall, nothing but institutional gray-white, from the walls to the floors to the industrial-strength table and chairs, Vega waited for the thing she wanted to have happen to happen.

Cindy had Vega's file—it was bulky now—and flipped it open.

"You've been busy," she said to Vega in a display for the cameras.

"Hard to make a living without being busy. Like what you see? Wanna hire me?"

"What exactly am I to see here that makes you hirable, Ms. Flux?"

Vega just sighed. Her ribs hurt, and her head was starting to pound.

"Do you need medical attention, Ms. Flux?"

Vega shook her head; she was sure she'd have one or maybe two shiners in the morning. She tested her jaw again, still not sure it was aligned after getting tackled.

"I'm fine."

The stout administrative agent opened the evidence bag of USB drives in the office with the safe, insulated laptop. He inserted the first one, and the laptop's progress bar said the drive was going to take a while to open. He left and grabbed his coffee off his desk and was on his way back when his phone chimed.

He smiled at the notification from his dating app. He opened Binder to see who he had been matched with. The woman looked familiar. She had black hair, and her tongue arched out of her mouth between the spread *V* of her fingers. She looked scary, but kinky. He was curious, but he had been a proud and loyal employee of the Federal Bureau of Investigation for the past five years. He didn't like what she was selling. He declined the match.

Back at the laptop, he finished opening each one, and, surprisingly, each one was blank. He took the drives back to his desk and made a note in the file. His phone chimed again. This time his battery was low.

He mumbled about the damn short life of cell phones and plugged it into his desktop tower. His computer asked if he wanted to transfer files from the cell phone, since it was plugged into a USB drive, and he declined it before going to his emails. Absently he heard the fan on his tower kick on as if it were using all the computing power available. His mouse froze, and just as he gave it a shake, the entire facility went dark.

Orange lights came up, and the fire alarm went off.

Hands out, he whispered, looking down to his phone, "Oh, shit."

"It's time." Cindy's voice came from beside her in the dark. Vega hadn't been prepared for what it would feel like when she said goodbye. Cindy grabbed her hand and held firm. "If I catch you..."

"You won't. I'm gone. I love you."

"Love you more."

CRUSHED_

The cold November night started sooner than Hoyt was expecting, and the pouring rain added to the critically wrong feeling that twisted his stomach into knots. Vega hadn't returned from her warehouse and wasn't returning his texts. If Titan's systems were right, her cell was bricked, with Peace's and Cindy's right behind it.

He was looking from his penthouse out across the river at her place, contemplating heading over there, when Zane called in a panic. Peace had gotten a call that had completely rattled her, so much so that she'd run out the door, even locking him in behind her. All Zane knew was her cell had gone red and he heard her say something that sounded like "DEFCON 1 confirmed." Hoyt tried not to let the panic take over his own mind.

"I'll figure this out, Zane—"

Across the river, the rectangular block that was Vega's building blew into fiery orange flames. Shocked, Hoyt stumbled back as if the explosion had physically hit him.

"Vega" was all his mouth could say. Somewhere in the back of his mind, he heard his friend call his name from the floor where his cell had landed, but he remained standing, staring, feeling the blood drain out of his body. He did a double take, then a triple. It indeed was Vega's building.

Was she in there?

He had to go. This was wrong. So, so wrong.

Adrenaline drove him from his penthouse into the hammering rain to Vega's warehouse on the other side of the river. He hadn't thought to drive—his feet started running and didn't stop until a police officer asked him to "Step back, sir."

Five fire trucks were on it by the time he arrived on foot. Water from the ladder trucks arced through the air, dousing the twisted metal carnage that once was Vega's home.

He was panting and incoherent at the first officer; then, walking away, he gathered himself. To the next officer he said, "Ma'am"—he swallowed as rain ran down his cheek—"is there anyone"—he choked, tried again—"is anyone in there?"

She gave him a once-over. "Are you the owner?"

Hoyt lied, "Yes."

She pointed to a man who stood by a red SUV that had FIRE INVESTIGATOR emblazoned on the side in gold lettering. "I believe they want to talk with you. They can tell you what you need to know."

He tried to say thank you but couldn't.

IT WAS DAWN BY THE TIME THE FIRE WAS OUT AND THE CADAVER DOG had left. The unit had been declared clear, and Hoyt was still standing in the early-morning drizzle watching the last bit of steam rise from the center of the rubble that had once held his heart and soul when a car pulled up behind him.

"Hoyt!" a voice called. "Oh my god, there you are. Everyone is worried sick!" Only when footsteps stopped beside him did Hoyt register that it was his sister standing there. She went still seeing him staring at the charred wreckage. "Hey, what's going on?"

He couldn't say the words out loud. Not yet. What he dreaded couldn't have happened. He and his team had been so careful.

Lei pieced it together. "Oh, shit. Is this...? Was this her, oh, shit. Hoyt, was she in there?"

He shook his head. "Cadaver dog didn't find anything."

Lei put her hand on his arm, emotion twisting her words. "No, Hoyt, she can't be gone." Lei had the words he didn't. "I know you. You've been so careful."

He drowned himself in the logistics. "Contact Mom. I need the estate to purchase this property."

"Maybe we can recover something."

"'Ae, buy the adjoining property and take these scraps apart piece by piece. Any tech gets recovered, I wanna know. Get Hector to contact our lead investigator, and I need my legal team to move forward as if she's given us consent to clear her warrants."

"Sure, anything else? Can I help?"

"Contact Dr. Branch. If Vega reaches out to her, again, I wanna know."

"OK." Lei was quiet with him at the rubble's edge. "Hoyt?"

He knew what she was going to ask. "No, Lei. I can't think like that. She's on the run. Zane said Peace took off too. This is what she called DEFCON 1. They all have to disappear. I need to know why." Suddenly, his emotions swirled and changed, a tropical storm rising from where the waters had been calm. He could feel the fear mix with rage, and tears flooded his eyes as he turned toward his sister. "I feel her here." He stuck his fingers to his heart. "She's running scared, and I promised to protect her, but someone got by me. Someone got fucking by *me*!"

She took a deep breath and held her hands up; then once she'd indicated she meant no harm, she fell forward, enveloping her much bigger brother in a hug.

"OK, all right. Let's go, Ho'o. Let's find out what happened, and we can't do that here."

He stopped halfway to Lei's passenger door and took one long last look. Walking away from the rubble felt like he was walking away from her. He'd take that place apart brick by brick, put a forensic analysis team on the rubble, and reconstruct what happened. It wouldn't bring her back, but he needed to piece together what happened. Where his team went wrong and if they could fix it. He had low expectations; Vega would have been thorough with the destruction of data.

Reluctantly, he got into the passenger seat. As Lei drove, he turned his head and watched the charred remains of his bliss until it was out of sight.

In his executive office, he showered and changed, making use of the small closet of spare clothes that were kept there. As soon as he was dressed, he checked his phone yet again. Nothing. He felt another vice of pain clench down on his insides.

He wasn't sure how long he had been standing staring at his phone when Hector came in. He held a plate of pastries and a frothy mug of something.

"I've received Lei's directive and have everyone started on your requests. Let me know if you'd like me to get anyone on the phone or if you'd like to speak to them personally."

"Phone," his voice ground out. When Hector didn't leave but continued to look uncertain, he barked, "What?"

Hector jumped. "Oh, sorry, it's just there's a young woman with her friends here asking to see you."

"Who?"

"Her name is Scout? She said a mutual friend sent her?"

His synapses lit up, and he charged out of the room into the waiting area. Hoyt's focus lasered in on her as though Vega herself were standing there. As it had been when he'd met her in Peace's law offices, her black coils were pulled back in a thick ponytail; once again her freckles and soft and quiet appearance surprised Hoyt that this cutesy young college kid was connected to Vega. But Scout was a daughter to Vega, and in that way, it fit. Some parents strive to raise their duplicates. Vega raised her antithesis.

She was in a used army jacket, and her woven necklace held colorful beads that spelled, *S&V*, and his insides clenched again, thinking a young Scout or Vega, or both together in a bonding moment, had made that.

"This way," he said and brought her into his office and gestured to the conference table. Seated, he watched as she made micro adjustments to her jacket and chair, getting comfortable.

"I was told we should come here if we—my roommates and I," she said, throwing a thumb in the direction of the waiting room, "if we ran into trouble. Your cousins speak highly of you."

He was tired and cut to the chase. "Did they send you? Who sent you?" He wanted that crystal clear and from her lips.

"You know who," she said quietly. "Vega. My sister."

"When?"

"Oh, um, I don't know. Yesterday?"

"You don't know, or was it yesterday?"

"Ah, yes? Yesterday."

"What exactly did she say to you?"

"That I should come here... Look, if it's a bother to help out—"

He was done being polite, and she obviously didn't love Vega as he assumed a child or sister would love their caregiver. He snapped, "Where is she?"

Scout flinched. "Oh, I'm sorry, I don't know—"

"You don't know? The woman who raised you told you to come to me, but you can't tell me where she is?"

"She just said—"

"You said that already. I need context. Details!" he barked.

A red flush moved up her face. Hoyt felt a hand on his shoulder. He hadn't heard the door open or noticed Lei until right then.

"Hoyt," she hissed, gripping his shoulder to get his attention. Shock and concern, along with compassion, were etched into her features, emotions he currently couldn't feel. "Vega would rip your nut sack off if she heard you talk like that to her sister. Take a break. Go eat something. Take a nap. You're crashing, bro."

He whispered, "Fuck off," to his sister but did excuse himself to go to the bank of windows to look at the charred rubble across the river as if he could see in that exact moment Vega stopping by to witness what happened to her life.

He heard Lei sit and introduce herself to Scout. Heard Scout tentatively recount her last interaction with Vega. How Vega had gone white and stumbled back on her front porch after Scout admitted to being in contact with their stepfather. Scout had discovered in the process of getting her passport that her Social Security number had been fabricated, that her original name was really Harmony Alexander, and in her own investigations into what was going on, from their foster mother's house, she took home the last box Vega had kept there. In it had been original documents that Hoyt and his investigator hadn't been able to locate.

He was on fire when he turned again. Scout glanced to him before freezing under his heat. Lei turned to see what had affected her.

"Hoyt," Lei said and pointed at the door. "Get out. Do anything that's not here."

Ignoring his sister, he said to Scout, "What did Vega want me to do?"

"She said you could protect us. Lloyd, our stepfather, asked me to receive a package for him. I said fine, but then my roommates said we should open it. It was some router tech thing, I dunno, but apparently some guy was supposed to come by to pick it up. Then we realized, like, he can't have that in prison, right? My friend Toby went with me to the prison—that's when I think Lloyd got his name—and we told him together that he had to stop contacting me." She kept her face stoic, but a tear escaped the corner of her eye. She quickly wiped it away. "He used our house Wi-Fi to somehow contact Toby's grandmother. He fuckin' extorted nine grand from her! Then, like an hour ago, some dude showed up with a gun looking for the package."

Lei's eyes were wide, and all Hoyt could think was red rage.

Scout continued, "When Vega said goodbye to me, I didn't know she meant... But, like, we were waiting out there"—she again threw a thumb to the waiting room—"and the news said her place burned down, and I didn't know any of this about him until it was too late."

"It was *you*," Hoyt said, hearing the scathing accusation in his tone. "The *one* person she cares most about in this whole fucking world. It was *you* who sold her out."

Lei pointed at the door again. "Hoyt, out."

Scout shouted back at him, "I didn't sell her out! I just needed to know!"

"She's been running her whole fucking life, and in one moment of whatever the fuck went through your head, you thought it'd be OK to contact a felon serving a twenty-five-year sentence without all the facts?"

She burst into earnest tears. "I'm so sorry!"

Lei stood to pat her shoulder. Looking toward Hoyt, she threw her other arm wide. "Get out. Don't come back until you're human again."

He ground his molars and left his own office. He barely took in the executive lobby, which still had college kids waiting in it when he got on the elevator. He took it to the engineering floor.

Arriving at his desk without memory of how he'd wound through the cubicles, he opened the last data file they had on Vega's bots and the signature that was her style of code. She'd been in his systems. She'd been everywhere in his code. He prayed she'd left something behind. As he ran another systems diagnostic at the binary level of his security code, he began the search for her in real life. He made phone call after phone call and gave information additional to what Hector had distributed. The last call was to Special Agent Merino-Perez, whom he couldn't reach. He called back until the operator told him his calls were being blocked.

Picking up his stress ball, he walked to the elevator and took it down to the server floor. He slammed the ball off the floor, caught, and threw it again, again and again, as he paced past the towers of machines all humming in unison. He got to the end of one row and was about to pace back when he was struck by the memory of Vega. He'd found her in that part of the room, where the new servers ended and the antiquated ones sat offline against the wall. Except...now he noticed a LAN line traveling across the floor toward the old servers. That day he'd seen Vega there, he'd been so pumped to have had found all her bots in his systems that he didn't think anything of what she was doing.

Now, though, he tried to remember—had she touched something? Yes...she had put her finger to the number badge on the server chest height and said something. He followed the LAN line. It was connected to server number 222. Its badge was clearly legible, thanks to a finger swipe through the dust.

He jogged back down the aisle to the terminal at the front of the room. He gained access to the antiquated 222 and went file by file looking for Vega. Quickly, Hoyt realized there were hundreds of thousands of files on there. He'd have to sort the data faster. He dried his hands on his pants and tried again. He started from largest to smallest and was surprised it was that easy. The first file held a massive sixty-three terabytes of data. Big enough to hold Vega's digital life. Big enough, he soon learned, to hold many women.

The file took a moment to open, as it lagged under the data size. Then the data poured in. He sat back and scrolled down, then down again, until several minutes had passed, and he still hadn't reached the bottom. Each data file was titled with a first name and last initial. All women.

Hoyt had understood what Project Valkyrie did but had no idea at its vast impact. Gathering himself, he refocused on Vega. There were four labeled Melanie A., and within the Melanie A_4 file was her Project Valkyrie information. The data associated with each warrant, her Social Security number with each crime associated with it. It was what his team needed.

He made another phone call before moving all sixty-three terabytes of files to a more secure location with easier access from his own administrative terminal.

Back into the files, he reached the end of the names and found a cluster of program files. Opening it, he stared at the file titles a moment before sitting back. There, in front of him, was a carbon copy of Vega's systems, a backup that had been tucked in tight behind Titan's Wall. He felt emotion crash through him. He was running on empty, no sleep, no food, and no Vega. And the thought that one of the last things she did was quietly tuck her life's work into his systems broke him. He gripped his thighs as he hunched over and choked on a sob. Vega trusted no one but herself with her systems, but looking at her life's work on the screen before him, he was humbled and broken. It was as if she'd left him with her baby.

Hoyt wiped his eyes and groaned, thinking of her actual baby upstairs with Lei and how he'd reacted. He had to rectify that. Just as he was about to close the files, one folder caught his eye. It was titled Good Lil Dudes. Thinking it was a file filled with men, he found it instead was filled with her cache of bots and apps. Apps that were titled Hunter, Seek n Find, Sing, and Juggernaut.

As he opened them one by one, hope raced through him. None of them were legal. But right then, he could give a fuck. Just this once, he'd step into the driver's seat of Vega's systems and take them for a ride.

NEVER STOP_

THE STORAGE ROOM IN THE ATTIC OF THE OLD WOODEN FISH-processing warehouse on the pier wasn't as it was promised on the online forum. The bathroom was adjacent, sure, if adjacent meant adjacent to the far wall, opposite wooden storage crates a football field away. Though the storage room's one round port window did offer a clear view down to the pier and out to Puget Sound. Vega had arrived by train the week before and retrieved her things from the pawnshop in Chinatown before landing in the storage space. She had checked the cot, wide and sturdy, the table, old but firm, and the chair, lacking before unloading her things. The storage space would do until another place could be sorted. The spare clothes, tech, and MREs she'd gotten at a military surplus store and had packed years ago and stored in the bag at the pawnshop seemed stale even though they smelled lightly of cedar. It was a welcome smell from rest of her current setup, which smelled like stale seaweed, thanks to others' forgotten boxes of supplies and old window signs and ocean nets and buoys hanging from the rafters.

She'd had to leave her precious phone at the FBI building, and the nostalgia triggered by the tech in her bag made her angry. She wanted her stuff back. But it was gone. She'd found on the news that her place had burned to the ground. Her friends were safe, but she was grief-stricken that Peace had been the one tasked with that job. Vega had always hoped it would be her or Cindy who would be the closest GPS point and therefore tasked by the app to torch the building. She wanted to find Peace and give her a hug. Out of all of them, Peace was the cleanest. But simply being associated with Vega would cost her. The monster in prison wanted Vega, but if he could reach Peace, he would, to get Vega. If he could reach any of them, he could get Vega. One reason she had to stay away from Scout too—of course, Cindy would be forced to sit on Scout, the sister of the fugitive, anyway.

Then there was Hoyt, who, alarmingly, had claimed ownership over the building. She wanted to reach out to him. To explain what had happened. She hadn't wanted to leave him; even thinking of him made her chest ache and her eyes go hot. She would seriously consider a clandestine relationship with him. He, she knew, had the skill set to communicate quietly with her. But it was also that he couldn't do just fucking and games. And the more she thought about it, the more she knew that she couldn't either. She wanted that bed they slept in to be half hers, the refrigerator to be refilled every time she ate all the berries and yogurt with the understanding that those were things the lady of the house liked. But most of all, she thought, touching the shark's tooth, she wanted that time between dusk and dawn where their bodies touched in quiet embrace, letting their skin carry messages between their two hearts.

Vega waited for the sun to go down in the early afternoon before going out. Late autumn in the Pacific Northwest was a good time for people like her—more darkness than light each day. With her hood up and mask on, she left her hovel and stopped by a few shops that had no surveillance cameras for a few fresh basics. With her grocery bag filled with Twinkies and Franz's fruit-filled hand pies, she headed home.

As she ate a dollar hand pie on the quiet pier, the cold snap of the

November weather was like a snarled promise off the water. Vega realized Thanksgiving was the following week, and she felt the tear of the broken wish Hoyt had that she be at his table for the holiday.

She'd had enough of the world's shit right then to debate for a moment walking into his family meal and sitting right down. It would be good to have one final meal before...

She stopped her spiraling thoughts and touched the shark's tooth he'd given her. She still didn't know why, but he had, and with it, she kept the hope that there was a world where she and he could be together. Maybe not in this life but maybe in the next.

She stopped beside four seagulls who were settled on the pier railing, fluffed up and ready for bed.

"What do you guys think?" she asked them. "Do you think Hoyt believes in reincarnation?"

Two of them opened an eye each to spy what she was up to then closed them again.

"No, huh? Or can't be bothered?" Vega missed her gazelles then; the gulls were no substitute. "Look, I have no friends now—maybe you guys could help a girl out?"

A car door slammed, and Vega turned. Two women were scream-laughing about finding stellar parking so close to the area's nightlife. A figure was on their phone down the far end where she'd come from.

Back to the birds. "Bob, Sal, Hector, no, I knew a Hector, and you're not queen enough to be a Hector, how about Hugh, and... Chuck. Nah, you're Cindy, you're Peace, Scout, and Hoyt."

Another couple, bundled in coats, also laughing, made their way toward Vega. Their intimate giggles made Vega look the other way as the sound hurt to hear. The person on the phone hadn't moved. She had time for another quick question.

"So, what do you guys think—stay here or try for a more industrial feel? I'm missing my old place, kinda nostalgic for it, or in mourning... I haven't decided..." Something moved through her, sending goose bumps down her spine. The couples had moved on, and the man with the phone had looked up.

The shadows played tricks on her. It made her swallow down the "oh, shit" moment and do a double take. It had been a week since she'd seen him last, and the figure had his features, but his build was different. The man was thinner.

She shook her head and back to the birds said, "My mind is fucked. Everyone is looking like Hoyt now. Gotta scram, dudes. See you here tomorrow? Right. Good chat."

She looked back, and the man had crouched and was tying his shoes. Vega kept her pace light and halfway back chanced a peek.

"Holy shit" was all she got out before the sprinting body caught up to the quiet slap of his shoes. She froze and braced for impact. Only he went skidding by before stopping and slowly backing up made his way to her, his chest heaving with his panting.

"I thought you were going to run," he said by way of explanation. His eyes, over hollowed cheeks, underscored with dark circles, glittered like usual, but Vega was taken aback by everything else.

"I found you," Hoyt said in an exhaled cloud. "Fuck, I'm out of shape."

"Hoyt, what happened? You look like, you look, what happened?" was all she could manage. He looked as if he had lost fifty pounds.

He doubled over, resting his hands on his knees. "Fuck."

Vega felt like she was dreaming. This man was not the same human she knew. She touched him, and the stiffness of his wool coat that had been tailored when he was a larger size dimpled in at the shoulder. "Hoyt!"

He held his hands out to her, and in a former life, she would have walked into them, but now she could only ask, "Who's done this to you?"

He swallowed. "I know what I look like, but it's taken me a week to find you, and I don't think I've slept or eaten anything since you've left. But I don't fucking care. I found you."

Back in her small closet-sized living space, she gave Hoyt the bed to sit on and opened a new can of soup for him and a Twinkie to go with it. The room with him in it made her realize that she needed to get another place, somewhere with chairs and a microwave. He passed on the Twinkie but took a tentative sip of the cold soup.

"Hoyt," she said, looking out the door for a SWAT team in the rafter nets, "this is incredibly risky. You can't be here. But you look like shit, so you can stay a while. But just a little bit."

His gaze was tired when he asked her the question that sounded like it had been on his mind for a week. "Vega, what happened?"

She sighed and sat down onto her makeshift office chair, an overturned bucket, and told him everything. Stopping by Scout's place, being surprised that Scout had gone and found Lloyd and struck up a relationship with him, even going lightheaded at the news. Then how she lost her cool when the DEFCON signal went out, and she couldn't *not* visit the prison. Then when he threatened Hoyt's life.

"So, after that, I smashed his face in. I kinda lost it."

He nodded. "He got to you."

"Yeah, he lit up the monster in my head. I couldn't be sure Scout and you were safe, and he just felt so believable."

Hoyt swallowed as if his throat was parched and took another sip of the soup, wincing. "Yes. And he wasn't done. Our firewalls at Hoyt Securities caught traffic from the penitentiary that didn't get delivered."

"He was attempting to contact you? Already?"

"Yup. The DA is looking through a pile of data my team put together for them. The DA's office is considering upping his sentence to life."

Vega felt a wind blow through her. "Oh..."

"With you being gone, I didn't have to be careful."

"I see."

"Your original name is clear, all crimes wiped. Collections departments have been notified."

"Oh..." she said again, not knowing what to do but absorb his words. "They, they just took your word for it?"

"No, my team crafted a culling strategy for your outstanding collections requests that involved a courier-delivered three-thousand-page document. They could either start building a defense against that or agree to the extenuating circumstances and forgive the debt."

"Forgive the debt or go to court for decades. Got it."

"Yup." He managed a weak lopsided grin. "One company was ballsy enough to deny signing and updated their collections contract and sent a request for payment that felt so much like a threat I bought the agency and closed it."

"Oh?" Vega thought that sounded like Hoyt had come fully loose. "Sounds a little ragey."

"Not a little."

Vega grinned. "Real ragey."

"I found your Good Lil Dudes file."

"Oh…wow, you've been very busy."

"I made a promise to you that if you ran, I'd clear your name so that when I tracked you down, I'd have something to show you." He continued, "Everything is on a more secure server now, by the way." He gave her a dark look that also showed he was fading.

She sat next to him on the bed. "I think you should sleep. And eat."

He looked around. "I've been on an adrenaline rush for a week, and now that I'm with you…I feel like I've won. I'm so tired."

"Why don't you brick your phone and take a nap? We can sort things out in the morning."

He gripped her hand. "Don't fucking leave."

"I don't think I can. You look like shit, and I'm scared you might slip into a coma if I do."

"I will, so don't."

She held his hand. "OK. I'll be here."

The dawn broke watery and bright as Vega stretched in the tiny cot against the other body. Opening her eyes, she saw Hoyt, peaceful and quiet, his head resting on the makeshift pillow of three sweaters, and touched her fingers to his neck.

His lips stretched into a smile; the room was cold enough she could see his exhale. "I'm not dead. But I now know how to keep you from bolting next time." He cracked an eye to watch her.

"What's that?"

"Post my obituary and capture you when you come back."

"That's mean."

He'd turned sometime in the night to cradle her body against his and right then pulled her in tight to his chest. He whispered against her neck, "Good morning."

She was about to reply when his stomach growled. She laughed instead. "Hungry?"

"Starving, finally."

"I have a hand pie or Twinkies."

"Neither. I'll have breakfast brought up."

Vega shook her head at her delirious man. "Silly, you're not in a hotel. Did the cot and stale seaweed smell not convey that adequately? Seeing your own breath didn't help piece that together?"

He closed his eyes and smiled then parroted her. "Silly, I've got 130 plainclothes security personnel around this place. And my chauffeur is nearby. I'll have breakfast brought up."

Vega sat bolt upright. "W-what?"

Watching her, he said, "I'm careful with my power, Vega. I didn't say I never flex it."

"How long have you known I was here?"

"Locale? Twenty-four hours. Hunter found you. This hovel, as you call it, since last night, with Sing's help. Your apps are incredibly gifted."

She felt pleasure at him sliding into her apps and driving them. It felt personal and intimate.

"Cindy is trying hard to look like she's trying hard to find you. She gave me the heads-up about seventy-two hours ago that additional resources were being added to the case. I took that to mean, find you before they do. My lawyers are creating Vega-class chaos for them, including shooting holes in the reports from the penitentiary. There's evidence on a surveillance tape they're trying to acquire that has Lloyd Alexander threatening a young woman who was simply trying to protect another innocent young woman. In fact, that woman has a history of protecting women, and an anonymous PR campaign has begun to lobby for her cause. They'll go to the press, protecting her identity, but throw egg on the face of the FBI if they pursue an arrest. If it comes to that. And I don't think it will."

Vega felt the weight of his army behind her then. "Holy shit."

"Cindy does very well playing bad cop, FYI. Zane was her most recent victim, I mean, interview subject, and he categorically underestimated her, I can tell you that. Can I have my phone? I want to order breakfast."

"My, my, my, aren't we at our leisure. Sleep has done wonders for you, Mr. Kaho'okalakupua." Vega reached over to the desk where it was lying and handed it to him.

"My bedmate has done wonders for my sleep."

"Back to Cindy... She must seem to have turned on him too, in trying to find me. Is Zane alive?"

"Yeah, but I'm fairly sure he'll remember being cuffed to my conference room chair while she grilled me. But didn't grill me. She asked strange questions. After she left, Zane understood a bit better."

"Why's that?"

"She asked aggressive questions on if I loved you or not. Whether or not you loved me back, and what the fuck was I doing with all my goddamn money if not for the charity of others."

"Oh..."

"Yeah, character attack, not, say, actual, where is she, I'm getting a warrant for your phone, etc."

"Kind of a moot point, though, really."

"No, she was trying to get me to confess to what I was doing. She's good—she hit me where I was hurting, and I shouted at her that she could add her garbage warrant for your arrest to the list I was blowing through, and she looked fucking satisfied."

Vega felt a laugh start low in her chest like it was the first she'd had in a while. "Cindy, I miss her. And Peace."

He finished texting the breakfast request and put his phone down.

"That was the reason for her questioning, I think. She asked at the first meeting where Zane was, and I bit back that he was still trapped in Peace's apartment."

"Oh...that was for if Lloyd made good on his promise to hire someone to kill us all. Something he shouted at us the day in court when the guilty verdict was read. We have all these layers of booby traps we brainstormed at twelve, and as we added to them over the years, we never fully outgrew any of them. Just kept installing them, wherever we moved. Fear is funny like that. I'm sorry Zane got trapped. Is he OK now, besides being heartbroken?"

"That was why Cindy decided to return my phone calls in person. She had to gauge the threat level and liked what she heard. Peace had called her. She couldn't do it, run away. She had gotten to the Idaho border and found a working pay phone. She confessed to Cindy that she hadn't thought it would be so painful. It was one thing to plan, but executing it, she couldn't follow through. She called Cindy to be reminded of the threat level, that running was absolutely critical. Cindy advised her that the threat level was high, that Lloyd was getting traction with the new information he had on you and was reporting to the district attorney. But said for her to call the next day after she spoke with me. When she called again, Cindy told her to come home."

"Oh."

He touched her chin. "I would have thought that would have gotten more of a response."

"Yeah, I—"

"Sir?" came from her door. "Your things?"

"Leave it there," Hoyt called back.

Vega was standing, throwing things into her go-bag when Hoyt's languid form on her cot slowed her down.

"Breakfast," he reminded her.

"Right." Vega swallowed, trying to get her heart to settle down. "Sorry, I'm still a bit jumpy."

Hoyt stood and went to her door and pulled in two tray tables and paper bags that were grease stained. Then once the tables were set up, unloaded the items.

Pancakes, eggs, sausage and bacon, syrup, miniature tubs of butter, tubs of fresh fruit and yogurt with granola. For the first time since moving in, another smell overpowered the seaweed, and made Vega feel like she was in a diner.

Hoyt, chewing on fruit, brought out from a smaller bag a Diet Coke and a pastry coated with maple frosting and filled with cream.

"Ugh, you glorious man."

As they ate, he caught her up on the rest of the threats.

"Titan's Wall is up and running. Our team got the state pen covered. Lloyd is officially on lockdown. He can do what he likes locally on a computer, but as soon as he sends anything offsite, it triggers Titan's AI. Everything is scanned and recorded, but beyond that, it's tight enough that he'll think he's actually being received. I have a small team on that system, teaching the AI who he might contact and feeding it the data it needs.

"Your Vega warrants proved a bit trickier than cleaning up your original Social. There are a few the DA won't let go. My team says they're willing to hear your side of things, but be advised they'll likely want to make a deal with you. Think about all the women you've helped—have you found information along the way that the DA might find...interesting?"

"Let's see," Vega said, washing down her pastry with a gulp of her diet cola, "yeah. I can think of one or two, or fifty."

Having polished off the fruit and half the croissants and eggs and sausage, he sat back on her cot, leaning against the wall, and closed his eyes. He was looking better to Vega; the loss of mass still made him look as if he had been hospitalized for a week, but his color was returning. She put her can down and sat next to him on the cot.

He held his hand up, and she wove her fingers through his. Eyes back open, studying her now, he quietly reached over and ran his finger under the collar of her shirt and pulled out the tooth.

"I'm sorry," she whispered, "I don't know how I came to be wearing it, but I had to take it. I had to leave. And it was on me."

"I know. You got backed into a corner," he answered. Then added, "Before all this, at my place, you had a nightmare. In it you screamed for me to help you, to protect you. I gave you manō's tooth to give you the protection my 'aumakua offers. She didn't fail you, but I did. And for that, I'm sorry too."

"You didn't fail me, Hoyt. The world I was born into did."

"I promised to protect you, and the one place I didn't prioritize fast enough was my downfall."

"What do you mean? Who'd we miss?"

"Scout."

"Oh yes. That was a twist I wish I'd taken care of sooner. If she was raised with the understanding that Lloyd was a bad man and learned from me what he'd done, none of this would have happened. Instead, that one secret made us both sick."

"For better or worse, it opened that particular wound and enabled me to get an expert team of surgeons in to close it once and for all."

"Is Scout OK?"

"She is now."

Vega felt her guts bottom out. That should have been her first question. "Shit, tell me what happened."

"Scout came to my offices with four roommates who use the router that she's plugged into. We have them with new Titan-encrypted devices and relocated in a safe house while theirs is being remodeled with state-of-the-art tech that will capture downloads like that and keep them from spreading again."

Vega had felt the blood drain out of her face. "What'd he do?"

"He attempted a hustle on...I think it was Toby? I'm not sure, Lei was in charge. Lloyd tried to get Scout to bring him some kind of care package he had sent to her address. It turned out to be a 5G modem. She said no—in person, no less—but as you can imagine, he didn't abide by that no. I think he was trying to get unrestricted and anonymous internet access. Either way, it was a stretch for Lloyd's lying skills to convince her to bring it to him, so when he reached out to Toby and he said no, he hustled Toby's grandmother as payback. Telling her that Toby was in a hit-and-run and in the hospital, he said he was with the hospital billing department and asked her to give him a card to cover what insurance didn't. At that point, they knew they were in over their heads. But then a courier showed up for the package with a gun. She, Scout, is a good kid; she remembered what you said and came to us. Me."

Vega squeezed his hand. "You took care of her, thank you."

"Well," he said and looked away, "don't thank me. I lost my cool when she came. I'd spent all night watching your place burn, so when I heard that she had been the one to go see Lloyd, torpedoing my careful plans and endangering your life to the point you had to run? I lost my shit. Lei told me to get out, and I did. I've been living in my engineering office for a week."

"Oh..." Vega didn't know what to do about the weight of having been the cause of his current condition and excused his behavior toward Scout. "She's a big girl. She's going to forgive you."

"She has refused to be in my presence without a friend with her. I'm sorry. I think I fucked up there."

She squeezed his hand. "No one fucked up. Well, save for Lloyd. I believe, kind sir, that you are likely the last person he'll attempt to hustle."

He stood and pulled her up with him. "I'm going to have the car come around. Want to take anything with?"

She patted her pockets then put her hand on his arm. "Nope, I got everything I need right here."

POWER FLEX_

In the back of Hoyt's chauffeured, tinted-windowed SUV, Vega asked, "About Scout's Victorian you're remodeling, any chance you were able to talk to the owner of it?"

Hoyt's head was back with his eyes closed, her hand in his. "She's sitting right next to me. That little old lady you have managing that house told me you don't pay her enough to keep up with the demands from, and I quote, 'those spoiled brat kids.' She readily gave me the tracking details that her payments come from. Same Cayman bank that owns that account number I wired one and half mil to and the trust we found that was set up for Scout. Owned by one Melanie Alexander."

Vega grinned at the puzzle that he'd sorted out.

"Right there, in front of me the whole time."

"It's all right, Billions—you eventually got to the bottom of it."

"What do you say we spend the rest of our lives being a little less exciting?"

"What, like arguing over new paint schemes in your penthouse?"

"Our penthouse. I haven't had the chance to buy you that house yet. And since you're homeless now, I give you half of the penthouse."

"Damn, someone better warn Cody."

Hoyt's face broke into a smile. "She told everyone that you gave her a cutting-edge new app that deletes messages and photos that have your name and picture in them. She apparently—and this is from Lei, who was complaining about how Cody is like a sieve lately—keeps sending everyone texts with your name in them only to have them disappear. Of course, so does the rest of the message." He sighed. "Anyway, I have to apologize to her when I see her next."

"Oh?"

"She's asked me several times about the color scheme for the Victorian. There are historical colors, new colors, fuck me, I don't know colors. I shouted at her to leave me the fuck alone."

"Oh, Hoyt..."

"Yeah, she told me to get off my fucking high horse and solve my goddamn problem like a real man would. Then asked me what the fuck I was worth to you if I didn't use my billions to find you so she could stop asking me those questions and ask you."

"Ouch."

"I forget that her ʻaumakua is a pterodactyl."

Vega laughed.

"For Christmas, she's getting a dinosaur fang so everyone can be warned."

"She's not going to appreciate that. I think she likes people to think she's a softy pushover."

"True, but she always makes Christmas weird, so it'll be worth it."

"I bet she does, all that mistletoe waving around you."

He gave her a questioning glance. "How'd you know?"

"I've been forewarned so that I may be forearmed."

"Huh?"

"Nothing," Vega said with a smile as they arrived at the airport.

In the polished teak and white leather interior of his private jet, Vega noticed first the bed then the small kitchenette with bar then the main cabin where a flat screen played an NFL game. Two chilled glass bottles of water sat in cup holders in the table before the wide captain's chairs, one of which Hoyt flopped into. He still had exhaustion at the corners of his eyes.

"There's a bed in back." Vega threw her thumb behind her as if the posh jet was as new to him as it was her.

"It's a quick trip."

Vega shrugged and straddled his lap before gently laying her head on his chest. "This is kosher for takeoff, right?"

His hands rested on her back, and she heard the low rumble of his laugh. "One hundred percent."

The trip from Seattle to Portland was the length of a cat nap. Hoyt woke with a start when the plane touched down. Vega settled a finger on his lips. "Shh, we're home, that's all."

The color was returning to his face, and in every new vehicle they entered, tubs of fruit waited for him that he devoured. By the time they arrived in his penthouse, he was back at running speed. And ready for what was next.

Vega paused at the entryway to his apartment. Cody had been very busy. The floors were a deep veined wood with red clay tones streaking the dark brown. Deep forest velvet curtains bisected the view, warming the room. Inviting light fixtures looked like hand-carved leaves.

"Holy shit."

Hoyt looked around. "What?"

"Your penthouse."

"Yeah, it's a little different."

"A little?" Vega murmured.

The dining area now had a twelve-seat wood table under four hand-woven basket chandeliers that each held a tiny luminescent bulb.

"I'd like to shower." He held his hand out to her, and Vega put hers into it, letting him lead her around the corner to where the hall had been transformed by deeply shadowed wallpaper. It appeared almost three-dimensional—rainforest foliage leafing out as a backdrop for wood-framed portraits of sepia hula dancers in long leaf skirts and flower crowns and black-and-white photos of Native

Hawaiian relatives in starched Victorian garb, chins up, eyes proud. Beyond it, the hall dead-ended at a sliding opaque glass door that was mostly open to reveal a dark room with electric-blue recessed lighting and computing stations that looked so fresh Vega could practically smell the factory on them.

She stopped, tugging on Hoyt's hand. "Oh my..."

He pulled her along. "Later."

The door to his room closed with a silent click, and he turned to her, his hands going to her face, and pushing her hair back, he cradled her naked face.

"Have I told you lately that I love you?" His gaze studied her features, touching on her brows, cheekbones, down to her lips. "I've never seen you like this. Your eyes are naked, Vega."

Her hands rested on his forearms. "The eyeliner in my go-bag went bad, clumpy bad. I thought about getting more, but I kinda said, fuck it."

He bent and kissed her lips. "I missed you."

She put her arms around him, holding him firm until he lifted her up.

Her legs automatically wrapped around his waist. "Hoyt, wait, put me down—you're still recover—"

"Vega"—he hefted her wriggling body higher, carrying her to the bathroom where the spacious shower turned on at his request—"at my peak, I could lift a three-hundred-pound lineman out of my way. Now? I can carry your ass into my shower and make love to you until I forget that I was ever scared that you were gone forever."

He stepped them into the shower. Water fell in a deluge from hundreds of holes in the chrome ceiling. It was as though they'd gotten caught in a tropical rainstorm. She kissed him as water streamed over his upturned face.

He gently set her down and let her take his jacket off then his loose-fitting cable-knit sweater. They took their time undoing buttons and let both clothes and pain fall to the polished stone of the riverbed of his shower. Naked, he pulled her in against him and reminded himself of each of Vega's angles and curves. He had lost some bulk, but as he flexed and lifted her, his muscles remembered what it meant to drive power through his body to answer each of her unasked questions, to be strong enough to be at her side. And she was reminded that even at reduced power, he still was formidable and welcomed him against her with the wall of his shower at her back. Her legs wrapped around his waist. Warm water cascaded over them as his hips pushed the love they shared back into their connection. Vega's mouth found his, and there under the cascade of water they connected again, tasting, remembering the salt and smoke of each other's souls.

Vega moaned as Hoyt's body pushed in, pressing her to release her pleasure over him until she did. With a groan of his own, he moved deep with one last thrust and release just before his knees gave out.

VEGA TOOK IN HOYT, WHO WAS FINALLY LOOKING RELAXED AND BACK IN charge. He shot his white cuffs out the ends of his charcoal suitcoat sleeves as Vega made use of the only black clothes that Lei owned: a vintage AC/DC shirt whose holes would make her old jeans jealous and leather moto pants that were unfortunately pristine. With her platform boots, Vega felt that she needed aviators and a tongue stud.

"You look downright respectable, sir."

He grinned. "It's a secret I learned a long while back: dress like you can murder someone's bottom line, and people fall into place without you having to actually do that."

Vega fanned herself. "Hot."

He came to her there at the corner of his bed and kneed her thighs wide to make room for him. "Not hot. Fact."

She leaned back on the bed. "Also, fact, I look like I'd steal granny's pearls. Not a great look to help a team of lawyers defend me in court. Or against the DA who's likely down there with half his staff and Cindy and her team come to cuff me."

He held his palms out and pulled her to standing. "I can have new clothes shopped, bought, and brought here within the hour.

Though," he said and kissed her, "this and the other thing in the bag are PR approved."

She raised a single brow in question at him. "PR approved."

"Yes, granny's pearls were taken into account, and this was deemed appropriate. But if you don't want to wear them, you just say the words, and we'll go another path."

She let it go. "What other thing?"

He nodded to a bag that Lei had dropped off. "I think there's something else in there."

"Like what?"

He gave her lips a quick kiss. "I love you just as you are, but this woman in front of me full of doubt is new. I think the other thing in the bag can help. Check the bag, and I'll meet you downstairs."

"What's in there?"

"Something a woman I once knew couldn't live without. Camo."

"Camo?" she muttered as he went to the door.

He paused and said, door open, "Conference room in the executive suite, and don't worry"—he held up his phone—"I'm watching to make sure no one tackles you on your way there."

She grinned at him. "Or afraid I might bolt again, Titan?"

"Fucking terrified."

Though he could have watched her affix her camo, he didn't want to—didn't want to invade her privacy or spoil the surprise for himself. The phone as surveillance was just for "just in case." After a few minutes, he sent her a text.

> The guards at the elevator are for you.
>
> I've been advised you need to have them follow you into the conference room.
>
> Perception and all that.

While his advisory team had reminded him that perception was key, they'd also advised that her badass do-gooder reputation was actually something to lean into.

Her new encrypted device sent him her response:

???

You'll see.

The FBI and the DA teams were getting good data from his legal team, but one look at Cindy, and he could see she was getting antsy. She had wiped her brow for the third time in just as many minutes and was now pacing the end of the long room that looked through its full-length windows north over the city.

"What's taking so long?" she finally bit out. "Is she even here?" The two other agents were sipping water, happy to go after a potential suspect in such a cushy setting.

Hoyt's lead attorney on Vega's case responded, "Agent, I must reiterate that my client is here to speak with you of her own volition. If you attempt to arrest her before the DA and I—and you, for that matter—get to speak with her, you will force us to take legal action against the FBI."

The agents with her took that as their hint to huddle up around Cindy and whisper what Hoyt could only assume was some version of "Calm the fuck down." She was playing her part well. Cindy blew out a breath and shook out her hands. Hoyt felt for her—she was on the edge of a massive secret and had to lie through her teeth and pretend she didn't know Vega.

The elevator chimed, and the doors slid open, and he heard Vega's voice say to the group waiting for her, "Oh, hey, 'sup?"

The room went quiet. The infamous hacker flux_capacitor had arrived.

When she did, he couldn't resist the grin that split his face. She was still in Lei's borrowed clothes, but now her eyes were smoldering black, and with a swagger he recognized from the club when she'd first hunted him down, she made her way down the hall like it led to a candy store and she had a pocketful of cash. Behind her, looking fresh off the fields of war, were the seven guards he had reallocated to her at the request of his PR manager. Each one of the women wore battle black, their vests hugging tight to their curves strapped with batons and mace, and their pockets carried God only knew what.

Vega stopped in the doorway and cocked her hip before asking the room at large, "What's up, party people?"

Boots up and straw in her mouth sipping orange soda, Vega looked across the excessive buffet of food that Cindy's coworkers were making impressive work on while she sweated. Vega tried to keep her cool and not make eye contact with her old friend, but the sweat that she was trying to absorb back in seemed to be showing in Cindy's pits. Her dress shirt looked like the cool room was at least a hundred degrees.

The lawyers were going through the list of names Vega gave to them to sort out which to trade with the DA.

"Look," Cindy finally blurted, "we have evidence—clear evidence—against Ms. Flux that she tampered with an FBI facility one week ago today—"

Hoyt's lawyer shut her down as if they'd already talked about it, but Vega was worried. She was playing a delicate cat-and-mouse game that if she played too hard, matching or exceeding what Cindy was doing. Then the detectives, agents, and attorneys crowded into the room would get suspicious.

Vega wanted to tell her to cut it out, but the elevator chiming in the otherwise empty weekend executive floor distracted them all. Hector came around the corner escorting an older woman with a straight salt-and-pepper bob and in a light-blue power suit and flats.

Vega didn't recognize the woman, but the agents did. Hoyt excused himself from where he'd been behind Vega.

In the hallway, he gave the older woman a smile Vega recognized as business-Hoyt. He held his shoulders soft when she touched his arm and gave him a return look of gratitude. Vega got the feel that some high-level arrangement had happened between them and the woman was there on the weekend to play a specially requested part.

She came into the room, and Vega wasn't sure what was happening, but all eyes were now on the older woman. On her suit lapel was a pin that Vega recognized as the State of Hawai'i flag. She moved through the room shaking hands with everyone who had stood to personally greet her on her way toward Vega.

Vega heard them call her Senator. She dropped her boots and stood glancing at her security blanket, Hoyt. He gave her a nod that it was all OK.

"Hello, there," she said, finally in front of Vega. "You're Vega Flux, owner of the online vigilante handle flux_capacitor, I presume?"

"Hello," Vega said, giving her outstretched palm a shake. The room watched. She'd trained herself to distance herself from that handle. She looked to Hoyt, who nodded. "Yes, ma'am."

"Do you know who I am?"

Vega shook her head, "I'm sorry, ma'am, no."

"That's all right. Mr. Kaho'okalakupua has informed me that because of your fugitive status, you've been unable to ever vote. So, I'll give you a pass on recognizing a neighboring state's senator." She gave her a warm, just-from-the-oven cookie smile. "From my research, I understand there are more than five hundred thousand women over the past decade who have you to thank for saving, recovering, and overall restoring their lives to normal or better than normal?"

Vega inhaled deeply. More secrets revealed. But she'd already admitted to the handle. "Yes, ma'am."

"I'm Senator Linda Hashimoto from Hawai'i. I'm on the Senate committee tasked with understanding cybercrimes and how they disproportionately affect women and girls. I'd like to protect your research as part of an ongoing government study."

Vega knew that declaration was akin to throwing a light switch and plunging any agency hunting her into the dark on this matter, for good. She looked to Hoyt again to make sure the yes she was about to blurt matched what made sense. His lips mouthed, *Yes*.

Vega felt her relief reach her guts. "I'd be honored, ma'am."

"Please, call me Linda."

"Linda, I'm honored."

"Oh no, I'm the one who's honored." Then, her smile never faltering, she looked across the room to the FBI agents, who included Cindy, who was having a difficult time keeping her shit tight, and nodded. "Excellent work, agents. Let's talk in the hallway about next steps."

Vega watched Hoyt walk the senator out, the room now in a din of chatter. Vega's eyes then followed her gazelle's movement. Cindy grabbed the doorframe of the conference room and closed her eyes in relief before taking a deep breath and continuing.

One of the warrior guards at Vega's shoulder stepped close and under her breath asked, "You really flux_capacitor?"

Vega looked back over her shoulder at the blond whose hair was slicked into a braided pony and looked like she could kill a man with a popsicle stick. "Yes?"

She held her hand out. "It's a privilege to meet you, Flux. Six years back, you fucked up an ex who didn't respect my restraining order. He bought an assault rifle, and I spent months sleeping in a crawl space, afraid that he'd come for me. I wasn't wrong. He did. I used security footage to send him to prison, but he got out early. Real early. My attorney shared with me the message board she sent women to for 'extra' help."

Vega nodded, remembering the crawl space detail. "It's too bad he started dating that mob boss's daughter but refused to marry her after her pops caught them together. What a horrible coincidence."

The woman gave Vega a grin that was pure gasoline before a lit match. "Yeah, I didn't go to his funeral, but I did take that freedom and make something of it. Glad to pay it forward, ma'am."

Vega smiled back. That woman was pure boss.

Back into the room Hoyt strode and declared, "That'll be it for today."

Most of his team packed up and shook his hand before leaving.

Then Hoyt dismissed the security guards and sat facing one of the remaining four lawyers. "Where are we at, Natalie?"

"We've been able to have all but one warrant dismissed."

Hoyt looked down, adjusting his tie, and absently asked, "Which one still remains?"

Vega came to sit next to him at the edge of the plush conference room chair.

Natalie checked her notes. Her deep skin was set off by her high-end suit in a color that reminded Vega of the aqua waters off Tahiti. "The man whose hand was put in a panini press is refusing to negotiate."

Vega was surprised. She was sure he'd be the first to grab money and run. Or whatever it was that they approached him with.

"My notes show that he holds a personal grudge, that Ms. Flux is a danger to society, and it's his duty to protect society from her." Natalie's chunky rainbow-colored bracelets matched her earrings and necklace. Vega thought she could be a kindergarten teacher or a summer festival entertainer or a goddamn actual rainbow, not the straight-faced attorney she was, who hunted down the men from her warrants list.

Hoyt's face contorted into rage before his fist slammed down on the conference room table. "Crush him."

Vega jumped. Natalie, unmoved by his outburst, clicked her pen and made notes on her legal pad. "Fine."

Vega took that as code for digging into his past and bringing his character into question—then asking him again how far he wanted to take things.

She touched his arm. "Are you OK?" she asked, her back to the attorneys on the other side of the table.

He closed his eyes and tried to calm down and whispered back, "I'm sensitive right now about you, and frankly I don't give a fuck if it's the right or wrong thing to do." He opened his eyes as the other attorneys talked with Natalie about what to do next. The guards took turns walking the hallways looking for things that were suspect. "I've already made it clear that you're the one place I'll not hold back again."

She saw the shark within his gaze and squeezed his hand. "I'm sorry."

He reached over her tattered shirt collar and touched manō's tooth that hung against her sternum. "I'm the one to be sorry."

"No, I ran the ball down the field without you, and you had to come after me to get it back. I hate to break it to you, but I'm faster than you."

He let out a bright laugh before pulling her in for a kiss. "You say the meanest things to me sometimes."

"I'll let you bite me later."

He touched a finger to her chin. "Promise?"

"Promise."

"And what about forever?"

"Yeah, Hoyt, forever."

EPILOGUE_

That Thanksgiving morning, Hoyt stretched out long, lean, and naked next to Vega in their bed. Vega adjusted the pillows, taking in the dark hair of his armpits, chest, and crotch before groggily saying, "Yum."

As if triggered by her voice, he tackled her.

She squeaked as he came up over her announcing, "Guess what day it is?!" Then pumped his hips over her pelvis, rubbing his semi-erection over her sheet-covered pelvis before leaping off the bed.

"Oh my god!" Vega laughed. "What's gotten into you?"

Hands behind his head, he flicked his pelvis forward, making his penis dance and smack his stomach.

Vega screamed and fell back into the pillows, covering her face. "Oh, my eyes!!"

"It's game day!" he shouted before sprinting into his closet.

Groggy at the time but swiftly coming wide awake, she said, "Game day? It's Turkey Day, and your parents expect us at four. It's six. In the morning."

He appeared in the doorway of his closet, scowling at her. "Woman!"

Vega guffawed and wondered who the hell this new and enthused man was.

"Today is the family title championship game that gives bragging rights for an entire year. Red team won last year but not this year. They're fucking going down." He pointed to the earth and roared, his neck to his quads rippling under his skin, making him look as if his muscles were going to rip through his skin.

She reached for her phone as he ducked back into the closet, and Vega called after him, "Do it again!" She amended, "With pants on."

He leaped out of the closet and with a slap to his chest, stuck his tongue out and roared. She snapped off a series of pictures. "I'm sending this to the group chat."

"Good!" he shouted from the depths of his closet.

Vega wasn't prepared for the immediate responses. His brothers, cousins, and Lei sent their own. "Good Christ, Hoyt, everyone looks like you. What is that stance?"

"Haka!" he shouted again before blasting out of the closet and launching himself onto the bed.

Vega squeaked as pillows and her Titan, dressed in blue athletic gear, plowed into her. He grabbed her before she fell off the bed and said, "Where? Show me."

She kissed his temple. "Look, they're just as fired up as you."

He snatched her phone and texted the group,

Blue team is murdering red team this year!! - H

LEI

Where's your phone? Up your ass, right where I'm putting my foot this year?

MOM

'A'ole, keikis, language

More pictures of red- and blue-clothed family members came in and one text from Cody, just saying, *Yum*.

Vega grinned at Hoyt. "You know that's aimed at you."

"No way. She's just excited about the food."

"So, Christmas is weird because she's so into food, not your face?"

"She's married to Craig."

"But started where?"

He tsked. "No, that was just her being drunk. Don't be gross. She's my cousin."

Vega's heart raced when she got a text from the Mom, Dad, Hoyt group text:

MOM

Vega, Dad wants to know if you like spice?

Vega couldn't help it—the tears popped out and ran down her cheeks. Alarmed, Hoyt checked his phone.

Then back to her: "What? What is it?"

She pointed her black nails to the screen and blubbered, "They're so nice!"

"They just want to know how white your palate is, babe."

HOYT *HOTTY WITH A BODY*

Spicier the better.

MOM

Dad also wants to know if she wants crispy wonton. We have extra sheets from dumplings. He'll make wonton for her with the extra if she wants.

Vega could only respond with heart emojis.

HOYT *HOTTY WITH A BODY*

How come only she gets wonton?

His mother sent him a texted voice message that made Hoyt laugh. It was just *Tsk*.

He explained to Vega that singular sound was her telling him to get over himself.

He took her phone and pulled her up and out of bed. "Come on, time to get dressed. What color are you, sprinter?"

Vega held up her hands. She was wearing just her undies, her hair in a high knot. "I'm agnostic. Swiss neutrality right here."

He pulled her into him and buttered her up, smacking his wide hands against her thighs and dragging them up as he sucked one of her breasts into his mouth. His body rubbed against hers like a stripper, and he murmured, "My team."

Her head fell back with her laugh, and she wrapped her arms around his neck. "I'm Team Hoyt all the time, but today—*glog*." His tongue dove into her mouth, and she pulled back. "Hoyt! Your mom is teaching me to cook, and your dad asked me to help him with the smoker."

He grinned. "You know that's code for you and my dad drinking beer and watching us play, yeah?"

"I'm down with that too. You see, your parents have me 100 percent today. Sorry, but I'm in love with them and can't wait to get another set of hugs and hear them say, 'She's a good girl,' while they pat my shoulder."

"That happened *once*. Now that everyone knows you and isn't questioning you, my mom's not going to shadow you, playing nice. Probably."

"I liked it."

"What happened to hiding in my room cataloging all the things I left there?"

"Yeah, that was the first time. I've got everything cataloged. Plus, I know everyone now."

"Fine. And no helping my brothers get past game bosses in team play."

"Yeah, but they asked and had those puppy-dog eyes. How come you don't have puppy-dog eyes?"

"'Cause I'm weird and got this fucked recessive gene that makes me look like a freak."

Vega could feel her eyebrows raise. "You think your gold eyes are freaky? Don't make me pop them out and fuck them to show you how much I love them."

He scrunched his nose. "Intensely disturbing." Then he grabbed her ass. "Get dressed! We gotta go!" And he was out the bedroom door.

In the West Hills home, Vega worked in the expansive warm kitchen that smelled richly of smoky meat, butter, sage, and a sautéing paparika-colored sausage. The kitchen's long island was filled with casserole dishes, baskets of warm sweet rolls, crunchy wontons, ahi poke, and other appetizers, or pupus, as Ginny and the rest of the family referred to them.

Ginny pointed at the stove; what Vega heard as an accent was what Hoyt said was really pidgin. "Stir the Portuguese sausage, ya?" Her *Portuguese* sounding more like "Port-a-ghee."

Vega jumped in and with a wooden spoon stirred as she took gentle direction from her. Loose and fluid.

Lei came running in. Her red jersey was half mud, making her mom point her spoon at her then out the door.

"Lei! The floors!"

"I know, but, Vega. We need you." Her flag belt was holding chunks of turf.

Vega looked at her in confusion as she washed the fresh green beans that would become a creamy casserole. "I've never played football."

"Yeah, but I hear you might be faster than Hoyt. Can you carry a ball?"

"I mean, my hands work perfectly fine. But if it's muddy, and your mom needs me—"

Ginny shooed her out of the kitchen. "You go. I have this. Plus, my sister is coming, and she'll wonder why I did everything without her."

Lei jumped up and down. "Yeah!"

"Lei! You making a mess!"

Vega took off her apron. "I mean, OK..."

At the rear of the house, Vega could see down to the once-well-trimmed sports field that looked like it was regulation size. Now, though, it was half mud pit.

Lei held up cleats and a wide grin. “Oh, wait,” and inside the mudroom she dug through bags until she found another red shirt. Vega put it on, and Lei twisted it and knotted it at her back. “Ready?”

“Maybe.” On the way down the well-manicured trail through the shrubbery to the sports field Vega warmed up her legs with jumps and squats as Lei told her how she wanted to run their last few plays to score the final touchdown to win the game. Then explained how they had a lead, but everyone was tired, and Hoyt was on a steady rampage. Vega nodded, lunging her legs awake, and felt a tickle of excitement. She’d never played with Hoyt on the sports field before. She was going to end the day with a bloody nose or mud so deep in her pores that she’d sweat brown for a week.

Lei gave her the thumbs-up as they got to the end of the trail and let out a roar before she sprinted out from between the shrubs onto the field.

Vega walked out to the red team’s cheers and blue team shouting that adding a player midgame was illegal.

“Illegal, my ass!” Lei shouted back. “You bastards are on a roll. So, fuck you if I’m evening the field, just a little!”

Hoyt was three of the four towering giants on the field. His brothers, both younger with voluminous hair that had been pulled back tight for the game, whistled.

“Shoot! Bring her on. Hoyt’s going to catch her!”

He smacked his brothers’ backs before hanging his arms over their shoulders with a grin that said he couldn’t agree more.

He meandered over. “What happened to Swiss neutrality?” He fingered the red of Vega’s shirt before tugging one of her flags, his eyes glittering with excitement.

She snatched her flag and stuck it back on.

“Lei asked me.”

“I can’t wait to plow you into the mud.”

Vega knew he meant it to be as hot as she felt it was when he took one step back then another with his fingers up, telling her to bring it.

Vega kicked at the mud while the family watched them. “Know what a water slider is, *babe*?”

Glee colored his features. "No, what is it?"

"A lightweight creature that floats up on top of water and mud, it moves like lightning because its body weight isn't a hindrance."

His brothers hooted as they smacked each other, loving the heat she cannoned at their older brother.

Lei crowed, "Burn!"

He ate it up. "That's some A-grade shit talk from a retired track star."

"Says the retired NFL star."

Lei clapped, bringing the teams together. They eyed each other at the line of scrimmage, and Vega felt her heartbeat hammer in her ears. There was no way she'd be able to catch a muddy ball much less dart around Hoyt's massive brothers to get to the end zone, which looked to be seventy yards away.

Hoyt was at the other end of his defensive line and looked down to her, a shark grin in place.

"Eh," his brother Bryce, in front of her, said, "After this, wanna play *Destiny*? There's some new suits—"

Craig next to her on her team shouted, "Shut up! Stop getting in her head."

He shrugged. "I was just asking."

Hoyt barked from the other end of the line, "Tighten up!"

Lei called out the play, then, "Hut!" like a drill sergeant before snapping the ball to Hoyt's littlest brother, who was at the University of Hawai'i and a lean version of Hoyt. Vega, filled with jittery adrenaline, bolted.

She heard Bryce behind her. "Oh, fuck, she's fast."

Vega saw Hoyt as she dodged a cousin. The cousin fell flat as the ball came sailing through the air. Chaos reigned around her. Shouts told her to run; more said to get the ball midair. And all Vega could see was the ball arcing toward her. All she had to do was hold her hands out.

The ball smacked her arms so hard it bounced up and hit her face.

"Fuck." She fumbled with it as bodies came at her. Her arm hit it before it bounced forward, threatening to fall off her fingers into the mud. "Goddammit."

She missed it as her foot kicked it back up. Craig tackled a blue team cousin, and Vega chased the ball fumbling with it midair. Keeping an eye on the freight train steaming toward her, Lei dragging behind, a hold on the train's flag belt. Bryce picked their sister off Hoyt's belt, releasing him as Vega finally got hold of the slippery ball.

With a squeak, she secured it in the crook of her arm and took off.

Hoyt's hands went flat as he sprinted over the muddy field after her. The mud was slick, but Vega worked her run faster and faster until she was into the speed range she loved. With only her toes touching the ground, she bolted toward the end zone.

The field erupted behind her. She heard her name being screamed to run faster. Her lungs burned by the time she had ten yards left, and she felt disconnected from her legs as they propelled her forward. She heard the wet splotch of Hoyt's feet pounding behind her, and she didn't dare look behind.

"Vega!"

The thrill of the chase screamed out of her, and she pushed. She knew she'd puke later. The end zone came up, and Vega stepped into it as she was hit by a train.

Arm around her and she holding the ball tight, Vega flew. She landed before skidding farther into the end zone, dazed. Hoyt panted over her, his eyes bright, glowing with glee.

"You're fucking *fast*."

She put the ball overhead and touched the wet earth. "Touchdown."

"Yeah, touchdown."

He lowered himself, panting, to kiss her neck and pressed his pelvis against hers. She, trying to catch her breath, laughed as the jeers and cheers at the other end of the field roared.

Vega lifted her knees, and Hoyt slid between them. "I love you."

She smiled up at him. "Did we win?"

"Yeah, beautiful menace, you won."

. . .

Later, showered and changed and properly fucked by Hoyt in the estate's cottage and then dressed again, Vega talked with Scout from the deck overlooking the muddy playing field. Vega asked, "How's BC with Toby's family?"

"Good. You know, sis..."

Vega took a sip of wine that Cody had brought that had the longest French name she'd ever seen. "Yes, bug?"

"Toby, Mark, and I were all saying that you'd be a good mom."

Wine sprayed the bricks. "What?"

"Yeah, well, we were thinking that maybe if you had a real baby that you'd see me as a sister, and we could do sister stuff."

"That's weird, bug."

"OK, fine! I wanna have a baby, but I have school and my career ahead of me, and it's not fair, but Toby, Mark, and I want one. Toby's sister has one, and they're so squishy-cute! But she's in BC, and I want to finally live vicariously through you instead of you through me. What do you say? Make a baby with Hoyt?"

"Bug...how many glasses of wine have you had?"

"Glasses? Dunno lost count at dinner."

Vega laughed. She liked where her sister was in life. The secrets between them were gone, and the monster had a name and face they both recognized and kept behind bars.

She heard Hoyt behind her open the French doors before closing them again, his body showered and clean and relaxed after thrusting his release earlier. He pressed against her back. "It's time," he whispered over her neck before biting her earlobe.

"OK, bug, I'll tell you what. I'll think about it."

"Yay!"

Vega gave her sister a loud phone kiss. "Bye, bug, dinner's ready. Gotta go."

She signed off as Hoyt said, pressing her butt into his pelvis where his soft penis was firming up, "Everyone is here. Zane and Peace with Cindy. Even Nate and Eva with the baby and her pops are here."

Vega turned in his arms and kissed him hard. "Thank you. That's what I'm most thankful for today, and for the rest of my life—it's you."

"Want to take another shower?"

She smiled at his drugged, happy look. "No, I don't want to keep your folks waiting. It's rude, and so help me, I need them to love me."

"They already do."

She kissed him again there in the dusky fall night as fairy lights twinkled overhead up into the clear skies above.

"I love you. Marry me," she whispered.

He breathed over her lips, "I thought you'd never ask. 'Ae. Vega Flux, ko'u lua pele, who holds my heart in her hands, yes."

ʻŌLELO HAWAIʻI GLOSSARY_

The following definitions are sourced from Mary Kawena Pukui and Samuel H. Elbert's Hawaiian Dictionary (University of Hawaiʻi Press, 1986), my memory and understanding of terms I grew up using, and/or how others in my community, who know the language much better than I do, commonly use these words and phrases.

ʻae. Yes.
ʻāina. Land, earth.
akamai. Smart, clever.
aloha. Love, affection, compassion, mercy, sympathy, kindness, grace, charity; greeting, salutation, regards; goodbye.
Aloha kakahiaka. Good morning.
Aloha nō. Goodbye, with emphasis. We use it this way in my family, the nō intensifying the goodbye.
Aloha wau iā ʻoe. I love you.
ʻaʻole. No.
ʻapono. Consent, to approve.
ʻaumakua. Family or personal totem, god, or deified ancestor who might assume the shape of an animal, plant, element or object.
ʻehu kai. Sea spray, foam.
E komo mai. Welcome (into someone's home, for example).
Haʻi mai iʻau. Tell me.
haka. While haka as a Hawaiian word means a variety of things (including as its first definition "chicken roost" and "fish spear rack"), the characters here are using the Māori term for a war dance. My experience with haka was at school assemblies as a way to unify the school or team and get into the competitive spirit before a football game, usually a large, important game like homecoming.
hana hou. To do again.
hana maikaʻi. Well-done. I chose this phrasing because Hoyt is being sarcastic when he says it. A more genuine praise or congratulations is hoʻomaikaʻi.
hoʻokalakupua. Magic; to do wondrous acts; a magician, enchanter, extraordinary fisherman.
huhū. Angry.
ipo ahi. Ardent lover.
kama'āina. One born in a place; "land child"; in this case, a person from and of Hawaiʻi.
kika. Sister.
keiki. Child, offspring. *Kamaliʻi* is the grammatically correct plural of *keiki*, to

mean *children*, but it is not commonly used. Instead, *keikis*, a Hawaiian word with an English pluralization, is usually used.
kōkua. Help, aid, assistance, relief.
kolohe. Mischief-maker.
koʻu lua pele. My volcano.
Kulikuli. Be quiet (less polite than **Mai hana kuli**).
limua pōhaku kai. Algae-covered (limua) ocean (kai) stone (pōhaku).
lōlō. Crazy; crazy person.
Mahalo. Thanks.
Mahalo nui loa. Thank you very much. Nui is an add-on to mean "large" or "big." We have a phrase we use, *nui nui opu*, meaning "biiiiiiig tummy." Usually referring to chubby babies (but I've also heard it used just as affectionately for dad bods). Loa is also a kind of expansive word. Mauna Loa is a mountain on Hawaiʻi island and is the largest vocano on Earth.
Mai hana kuli. Be quiet (more polite than **Kulikuli**).
maikaʻi. Good, fine.
mākua. Parents.
makua kāne. Father, uncle, male relative of parents' generation.
makuahine. Mother, aunt, female relative of parents' generation.
malihini. Newcomer, tourist, guest, one unfamiliar with a place or custom. We always referred to individuals from the US mainland this way.
manō. Shark.
Me ke aloha pumehana. With warm affection. My grandmother used to say, "With cloying, binding love, like the pumehana vine."
nīele. Curious.
niuhi. Tiger shark.
ʻohana. Family.
ʻōlelo Hawaiʻi. Hawaiian language.
ʻōpaeʻula. A tiny red shrimp indigenous to the Hawaiian islands; has a prominent and macabre role in the legend of Princess Popoalaea at Waiʻānapanapa.
Pehea ʻoe? How are you?
pilikia. Trouble.
Pōmaikaʻi. Good luck.
wahine. Woman.

ACKNOWLEDGMENTS_

Mahalo for reading this novel that is so close to my heart. While all my books are close to my heart, like little paper babies I share with the world, this one is extra-special. Hoyt is a Maui boy and the product of my desire to put the kind of men I grew up with into the pages of the romance novels I love. A kind of personal awakening happened during the pandemic: I made the self-discovery that I'd like to see myself and the community I grew up in reflected in the characters of romance novels on bookstore shelves. This is the first of many, I hope, to come.

Mahalo nui loa to my ʻohana. This book was a community effort. There were considerable calls/texts/emails clarifying sayings and colloquial references. Everything from sharks to shrimps was checked and double-checked, and any errors or oversights are entirely my fault. Special thanks goes to my cousins with Native Hawaiian blood: a humble mahalo for letting me embody your spirit as I wrote this book; I hope that Hoyt meets your approval.

Sara, thanks for the push to pursue this idea and for being the first to give your feedback. Thanks to my beta readers for your love of Hoyt and Vega. Diane, Carla, Allyson, and Annie, thanks for carrying around that massive manuscript. Thank you to my Coffee Chat group, who took one look at the draft cover and said, *YUM!* Your enthusiasm is pure energy for my creative engine. Thank you also to my editor and her team. Kristin, you once again have proven you are the pro behind my prose. Your enthusiasm for this novel, dedication to double-checking the ʻōlelo Hawaiʻi that was used, and pointed and culturally sensitive feedback were much appreciated.

Thanks also goes to my husband—after twenty-plus years together, I finally wrote a story that most closely resembles us. Thank you for defining all the tech terms for me. Any mistake, overcompensation, oversimplification, and gross exaggeration for genre fiction purposes is entirely my fault. Haxors, please don't look him up—he's just as embarrassed as you.

And lastly, thank you to the romance writer and reader community for rallying behind fundraising efforts for our Lāhainā and Kula communities. The wildfire destroyed something within us that we'll never get back, but through love, community, and strength, we can and are building a bridge out of the ashes of our loss to a future that will once again give us hope and joy. Aloha and mahalo nui loa for your kōkua.

AUTHOR BIO_

Award-winning author Becky Healani Banks is a Maui girl, a kamaʻāina from an old Hawaiʻi family, who currently lives in Portland, Oregon, with her husband and two children. She's a graduate of Maui High School and Oregon State University, where she earned a bachelor's in natural resources and fell in love with fiction writing. Becky likes to craft dark romances that stem from her past and require love to see her characters through. When she's not crafting love stories, she's packing lunches for her little ones and breaking up *Minecraft* fights.

Visit Becky Banks online at beckybanksbooks.com and follow her on social media for updates on new releases and more.

facebook.com/beckybanksbooks
instagram.com/authorbeckybanks
amazon.com/author/beckybanks
goodreads.com/beckybanks
bookbub.com/profile/becky-banks

WHO IS REAGAN MANNING_

Vega sent a response to Hoyt that was just emojis telling him all the things she wanted to do with his eggplant.

Are you on or in the US Bank building downtown?

On.

V...

Look, someday I'll settle down, but not today. Cornices guy is sweet, and he pays well.

You don't need money.

All right, fine. He and his wife have such a good, wholesome marriage that I just want to support them in their kink.

Did you just call them wholesome?

Don't be closed-minded.

There was a pause then: *V?*

Yes, hunk-a-muffin?

What happened?

When? My life is a series of events that all could use explaining.

I'm not kidding—what's wrong with your phone? It stopped transmitting its GPS.

Really? Vega looked down, and the last message didn't send, and her phone was searching for a signal.

Vega stood and powered off her device. “What the fuck?”

A voice came from behind her. “That’s probably me.”

Vega whipped around to see a woman with tan skin and hazel eyes assessing Vega with the same intensity. Her long chestnut hair was pulled back into multiple braids that made her look like some kind of warrior who didn’t want to worry about getting her hair bloody.

“Hi?”

The woman pulled a device out of her jacket pocket, and Vega wanted a closer look and maybe to touch the sheepskin-lined bomber jacket. And wear her aviators too.

“I’ve been assured that this will knock out any device in a fifty-yard radius.”

Vega’s eyes, still glued to hers through the woman’s low-tint glasses, swallowed her apprehension. “The guys downstairs in the bank must be having a shit fit, then.”

She looked like she liked Vega’s humor. “No doubt.”

“Do I know you?”

“No, but I need a favor from you.”

Vega took in her athletic form and the tightly belted thing across her hips and another strapped to her leg and had the strange sensation that this woman might have a weapon—or ten—already on her.

“You look like someone who doesn’t need favors. Do you need me to help someone?”

“Cindy is trying to rebuild her reputation, and I was bored and wanted to know more about the rumors going around that she really helped you escape a couple months back. Then I read your file. I like you.” She gave Vega a cool smile that Vega didn’t readily know how to interpret.

“Oh, OK? You know Cindy?”

She was quiet for ten heartbeats before saying, “Sure.”

Vega wondered if what she was feeling was what her friends often felt. “What can I do for you, Ms....?”

“Call me Reagan.”

“OK. Reagan. What can I do for you?”

"Find him." She pulled out a piece of paper and handed it over.

Vega read the one-word page and looked back up. "Lucy? As in, the urban legend who leads an underground crime syndicate that is at the disposal of only the wealthiest?"

Vega watched as Reagan produced a thin white cigarette and, balancing it on her lip, swiped a silver, heavy-looking lighter against her thigh. She put the flame to the end of her cigarette before snapping the lid shut and handing the lighter to Vega. "It's his."

Vega took it from her and looked at the demon engraved on its side then back to the woman named Reagan and felt the cool air in her open mouth. Vega closed her mouth as she watched Reagan blow smoke up into the sky.

Vega mumbled in disbelief, "He exists..."

"Can you find him?"

"Sure. He a boyfriend you...lost touch with?"

Reagan grinned, the cigarette barely holding on in the corner of her mouth, as she zipped her jacket as if preparing to leave.

"Yeah. Let's call him that."

Vega swallowed. "Do you... Do you need protection from him?"

"Melanie, Joan, Vega," she said, using all her names as if in an incantation to bring her, all of her, to the present, "I believe you're the only person who can understand the need to find someone to right a wrong."

Vega nodded. "Yes, absolutely, I get that."

"You find. I hunt."

Oh yes, this woman was all the things Vega felt emanating off her. "Yeah. OK."

"Good. I'll send payment over this evening."

"Payment?" Vega asked as the woman stepped up onto the side of the building. "Whoa, hey, now. Careful."

Then she stepped off the side of the building. Vega screamed before clapping a hand over her own mouth and ran to the side of the building, pulling out her phone getting ready to dial 9-1-1.

Before she hit send, she couldn't believe what she was seeing.

"What the," and she touched the carbon fiber cord that was

embedded into the concrete buffer of the roof. Vega leaned over the side and watched as Reagan unhooked from the cable and with a flick of her wrist tossed it off and it threaded back up into the imbedded device with a snap. Vega watched her turn the corner and move into the crowds, becoming just another Portlander on her way to lunch.

Just then her phone blew up with texts from Hoyt.

In his office, she paced as he ate his lunch, hers sitting untouched. "And then *BOOM*! She's gone!"

"What do you mean, gone?" he asked around a bite.

"Just"—she turned, holding her hands out in disbelief, making sure Hoyt's gold eyes were fastened onto hers—"gone. She dropped over the side of the building, babe, on a line that could double as floss."

He swallowed and leaned back, one hand braced on the side of his chair. "She rappelled off the side of the building?"

Vega could feel herself starting to spin. "Please, you have to believe me."

Hoyt's eyebrows rammed together as he looked around, a crushed napkin in one hand. "It's fucking crazy, Vega, but yeah, I believe you. I'm just worried about what 'payment' is."

"Yeah." Vega plopped into the chair adjacent to him and rammed a massive bite of gyro into her mouth. "Buth hereth the thing!" she said, and Hoyt's eyes laughed.

Chewing, she stood and went back to pacing, finally swallowing down the massive bite, making her cough, but free to speak: "The guy she wants me to find is a fucking ghost! He's an urban legend, but she claims to know him. I said ex, and she agreed, but that's clearly not it. He's on her ledger? Does she have a ledger? I dunno—she seems like someone with a ledger."

"Does Cindy know her?" Hoyt interrupted her stream of dialog.

"Nope, Cin's never met anyone with her description, but she's looking into special ops crews or something."

Vega stood still and looked out the window, replaying the entire thing until Hoyt asked, "What is it?"

"I dunno."

"Yes, you do."

"Is it...quid pro quo?"

"What do you mean?"

"Like, I take care of her boogey man, and she'll do mine?"

"She didn't say that, though?"

"No, I'm just a weirdo."

Hoyt smiled. "Come eat, weirdo."

Reagan walked through the towering halls of the penitentiary. Some who were still awake whispered to others, pointing at her until the halls were banging in unison. In her fingers she rotated a USB key that she'd pilfered from evidence in the Vega Flux arrest. She whistled a tune: *Sticks and stones may break my bones...* The target was two doors down on the right, and she needed the place to be in a pounding lather by the time she got there. She wanted his screams to drown.

She blew kisses to the inmates until the night guards went on alert that an alley cat was walking through the hen house. She got to the door with a few seconds to spare.

The man was resting his forearms against the bars and was happy to see that the alley cat had stopped at his cell. The cells next to him called to her.

"Come here, baby!"

"Take it off, sweetheart!"

She looked back and forth. "I'm not here for you, boys. But if you're really naughty, like him, I'll be back."

Then the software she'd infected with Vega's code, and a bit extra, released the door to the cell in front of her, and with a hand on his chest, she walked the man inside to the back of it.

The prison walls shook with a violent cacophony of anger and excitement that a prisoner had a flexible-looking woman in skintight black gear in his cell.

Reagan laughed; the noise was exactly what she needed.

But her prey was keen to the kind of violence that her hands knew. He read it clearly in her body, not liking that his attempted touches were blocked by an elbow or forearm before she checked him into the back wall.

"Whoa. What the fuck is going on?"

Her hand slid down his front. "I'm here to deliver a message. Are you listening?"

"What fucking message?"

"Melanie Alexander, Joan of Arc, and Vega Flux wish you well in the afterlife."

He could smell the truth on her and screamed, "No!"

Reagan stabbed his voice box with her fingers. He doubled over, clutching his throat, and in a desperate attempt to get away, shoved by her as he ran for the cell door.

She hit the wall then sprinted for him, wrapping her arm around his neck. His weight and momentum jacked up on adrenaline dragged her on his back to the door. With a grunt, she put her feet up and struck the frame of the open cell door. He gagged, and she tightened up, arching back against his forward momentum.

He choked and gasped as the prisoners in the cells across from them stopped shouting and banging. They stepped back from the bars.

He stepped back, and they fell to the ground. Still struggling to breathe, she wrapped her legs around his abdomen and stretched him out. Her thighs squeezed him like a python. She tightened and pulled until he stopped thrashing. Pushing him off her, she stood. By his shirt, she dragged his still form farther back into his cell and hoisted him onto his bed.

She pulled an extra jumpsuit from under the pillow of his cellmate, who was currently in solitary, and wearing orange now, she walked out. With a token from her target in her pocket, she adjusted her suit then looked at the men in the cell next door.

"Wanna turn, boys?"

"No, ma'am," they said from the shadows of their dark cells as the entire penitentiary lit up. Alarms sounded as the doors to all cells opened.

She shrugged. "Maybe next time."

Inmates poured out, save for those who saw her handiwork, and into the fray, with a hunch in her shoulders and a knit cap pulled down low, she went.

Hoyt twirled the envelope around his fingers as he crossed the sky bridge into his and Vega's penthouse. In front of her bank of monitors in the back room, her heels were up while her apps ran traces for her current Valkyrie Project.

She smiled at him. "Hey, hottie."

He gave her the package with a kiss.

"What's this?"

"Dunno. Hector said it didn't come through him. It was on my desk this morning addressed to you."

"Oh." Vega looked at it as if it were a bomb.

"Payment from that woman? Have you heard from her again?"

Vega opened it with Hoyt warming her shoulder. "Oh, it's a necklace?" She pulled on the black cord at the same time that Hoyt gasped, "Is that a—" Vega screamed and dropped the necklace. "It's a fucking human tooth."

Hoyt cursed and turned away, pulling out his phone, and Vega stared at it on the dark carpet. She knew whose it was. After a few moments of pacing, Hoyt hung up.

"What? What is it?" she asked, not looking up, knowing what he'd learned.

"The prison."

Vega felt an eerie calm come over her. "It's his… He's dead."

Hoyt pulled her in against him. "I'm sorry."

"For what?"

"That she's got this over you."

Vega shook her head as she came out of the feelings. "No, no, I don't think that's it."

"Babe, if that's your stepfather's tooth, you need to address that. And not wear it. It's not a present—it's a threat."

Vega shook her head. "I think I understand her." Vega hoped she was right. "This, she, um, I think she just did me a real illegal solid. One," Vega said absently with a finger in the air, "she just proved her worth, and two, she just gave me a seriously good look into the life she leads."

"Proving her worth?"

"Like a wordless resume. It's twisted—"

"I'd say."

"I like it. And also, if I'm being honest, makes me feel like I'm gonna shit my pants."

"Welcome to my life."

Vega turned, grinning up at him. "She's my knight in uber-dark armor."

"Let's find her guy and have her ride back into the sunset."

***

ALSO BY BECKY BANKS_

CLAN MACLAOCH CURSE SERIES

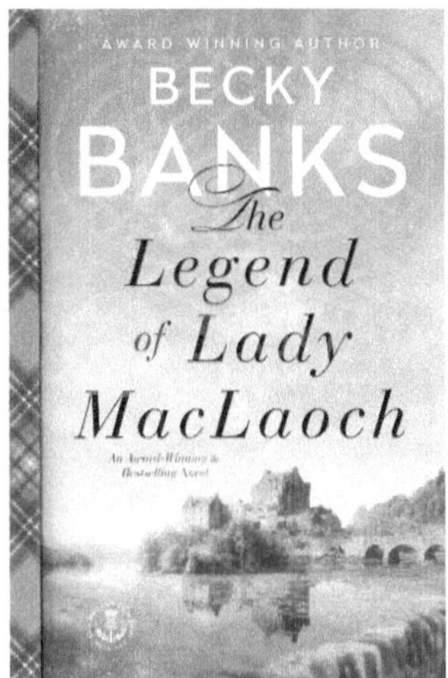

The Legend of Lady MacLaoch. Book 1 of the Clan MacLaoch Curse Series.

Centuries ago a vengeful curse buried itself deep into the history of the MacLaoch clan and became a legendary tale told by all those not cursed by its words.

In present-day Scotland, the laird and chief of the MacLaoch clan is an ex-Royal Air Force fighter pilot who has been past the gates of hell and returned a changed man. Rowan MacLaoch does battle with wartime memories and a family curse that threaten to consume him—unaware that his life and that of the history of the clan will be changed forever by the arrival of an American woman.

Cole Baker, a feisty recent graduate of a master's program, stumbles upon the ancient curse while researching her bloodlines. Moved by the history of the MacLaoch clan and the mystery of its chief, she digs into the legend that had been anything but quiet for centuries.

On their quest for answers, Cole and Rowan travel to places they have never before been and become witnesses to things they have never before fathomed. The legend—one started with blood—will end with more shed as its creator finally exacts her justice.

Book 2 of the Clan MacLaoch curse series, *The Legend of the Viking*.

In this second book of the Clan MacLaoch Curse series, we see our favorite characters, Rowan and Cole, return in their most passionate selves yet. Coming off the loss of the Gathering and the thought-to-be-extinguished MacLaoch curse, Rowan finally has a chance at his happily ever after. That is, until everything that he loves is put at risk, sparking events, that once set in motion, will not be stopped—except by love.

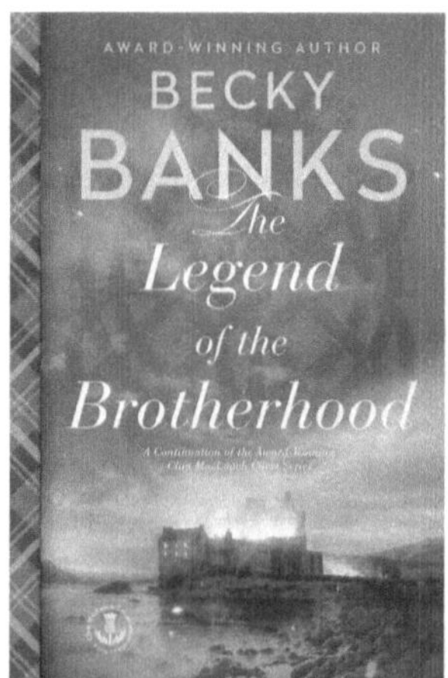

Coming soon. Book 3 of the Clan MacLaoch curse series, *The Legend of the Brotherhood.*

In this third book of the clan MacLaoch curse series, Cole's two worlds collide when her brother TJ stops by Castle Laoch for a surprise visit. His presence upsets more than the status quo at Castle Laoch; Rowan struggles to find a solution to the bankruptcy proceedings, which are starting to look like the end for the MacLaoch clan. Cole and Rowan - fresh off the battle on the cairn knoll - are bonded even more profoundly as they move to save the castle from bankruptcy and a villainous bankman set on a generation's old revenge. While Cole and Rowan's love is secure for eternity, the struggle for the ancestral MacLaoch home hangs in the balance. Can Rowan's determination, the Baker kids' ingenuity, and residual Viking power from Ormr Minorisson save the castle and clan from ruin?

ROMANTIC SUSPENSE TITLES

Flux. Can one notorious hacker protect the women she's saved before her dark past finds her?

Vega Flux, a notorious hacker whose single mission in life is to protect the weak from online trolls, crashes up against an impenetrable powerhouse of a man who wants nothing more than to slip the dark shroud off her persona and protect her from her torments.

In this smoldering high-stakes game of defense and one-upmanship, Vega takes a bet she knows she shouldn't and starts the largest hack she's ever attempted, against the only worthy opponent she's ever known, tech billionaire and ex-NFL tight end, Hoyt Kaho'okalakupua. Master of his domain, Hoyt, welcomes the chance to flex his power in a true challenge. With the stakes dangerously high, and his heart on the line, he enters a game with a woman he wants it all from. There's only one fatal flaw: Hoyt and Vega are following different instructions to the same game. He's a law-abiding billionaire, and the world Vega lives in breaks every rule.

Dark passions ignite in this fast-paced thrill ride from award-winning indie author and Maui girl, Becky Healani Banks. As the torments of Vega's past breach her defenses, she reaches for the one man who is uniquely capable of providing the shelter she seeks. And in that process, she touches a power she's never known, real-life love.

Forged. First loves, dark pasts, and fast cars collide in this high-octane thrill ride.

Managing editor of a Manhattan fashion rag, Eva Rodgers, couldn't believe she would ever step back into her old life, but the day her father called with his diagnosis, she had little choice. Returning home, and to the past she left behind, Eva signs up as editor-in-chief of the struggling Portland magazine, *Rose City Review*. There in the drizzling Portland metro Eva still holds firm to the New York city values that defined her time there: compromise on nothing. When her European auto, one luxury she missed in the walking and hired car world of Manhattan, needs fixing, she doesn't compromise. Even when the best European auto mechanic her assistant finds turns out to be an ex with a vendetta, Eva doesn't flinch.

Nathaniel Vellanova can't believe what the fuck just showed up at his garage.

He'd gotten his life together, buried his dark past, and definitely put Eva Rogers in his rearview mirror. Right?

But fuck him if she wasn't standing right there in the pouring rain needing his help. He'd do it—help her out—just this once then forget all about her. Again.

In this dark and suspenseful story of broken first loves, readers will ride the smoldering heat of high-octane fast cars, glitzy club fashion, and tainted love and ask themselves, are first loves the only love?

Serendipity of Fate. Enemies to lovers romance. One war, one blood promise, and the love to save it all.

It has been two years since Cason McPherson watched his best friend, Ryan Sparling, die in his arms. Now, with a blood promise tied to his heart, shrapnel in his hip, and a war behind him, he's focused on building a useful civilian life in his hometown of New Orleans. Living with Ryan's mother, a widow and retired nurse, he gives back the protection and care his best friend wanted. Only Ryan's sister, a woman whose well-worn picture got him through the darkest parts of the war, does not see it that way.

Savannah Sparling has spent the last five years building her career and life to the exacting expectations needed to achieve partner at Knight Interiors. And nothing could derail them except for the one person from her past who returned home a changed man. Cason McPherson and her brother Ryan had been her entire world once, but now she no longer recognizes him with his caustic attitude and effort to turn every conversation into a verbal sparring match. When a potential client, one large enough to secure her place as partner, requests her as lead designer, Savannah sets a plan for her final career move and Cason's eviction.

In a series of unstoppable events, Savannah's carefully laid plans backfire, and an unfathomable truth is revealed. In the aftermath, Cason and Savannah find that the only people strong enough to save them from themselves are each other. But will either one of them accept the help—and the love—that is offered?

FUTURE SERIES

Coming soon.

Set one-hundred years into a dystopian future, this socio-political romantic thriller takes place in the sprawling catacombs of The Peoples Republic of Portland. In a world that has been punished by the misdeeds of mankind, one writer sets out to answer one simple question: What would happen if everyone had hope again? Absorbed onto a misfit team of ex-war machine operators, junior journalist Wendy Wilson, moves quickly to adapt or die while trying to save the city she loves and maybe, just maybe, change the hearts and minds of even the most blood-thirsty among them.

Be sure to visit beckybanksbooks.com and sign up for the author newsletter. Newsletter recipients are the first to get book release news and giveaway alerts.

PREVIEW: FORGED_

First loves, dark pasts and fast cars collide in this high-octane thrill ride.

Managing editor of a Manhattan fashion rag, Eva Rodgers, couldn't believe she would ever step back into her old life, but the day her father called with his diagnosis, she had little choice. Returning home, and to the past she left behind, Eva signs up as editor-in-chief of the struggling Portland magazine, *Rose City Review*. There in the drizzling Portland metro Eva still holds firm to the New York city values that defined her time there: compromise on nothing. When her European auto, one luxury she missed in the walking and hired car world of Manhattan, needs fixing, she doesn't compromise. Even when the best European auto mechanic her assistant finds turns out to be an ex with a vendetta, Eva doesn't flinch.

Nathaniel Vellanova can't believe what the fuck just showed up at his garage. He'd gotten his life together, buried his dark past, and definitely put Eva Rogers in his rearview mirror. Right?

But fuck him if she wasn't standing right there in the pouring rain needing his help. He'd do it—help her out—just this once then forget all about her. Again.

In this dark and suspenseful story of broken first loves, readers will ride the smoldering heat of high-octane fast cars, glitzy club fashion, and tainted love and ask themselves, are first loves the only love?

Turn the page to start reading a sample of Nate and Eva's story in *Forged*.

FORGED: CHAPTER 1_

The memories flicker by like the frames of an old film. Unfocused and dark at the edges. A punch to his gut, to his face. The wall behind him in the yellowing kitchen seems to punch him as well. It slams against his back and smacks his head to the tabletop as the fist from his father throws it there. He's seven.

By ten he learns to dodge the fists, to know when tension in the apartment would erupt. Eleven, he has one foot out the door, has found a second life, a best friend. Twelve, he has already left home to live with his aunt. Twelve slides into fifteen and fifteen into freedom.

Freedom? It was never free.

The memories of that final day came unbidden, as they always did—and slippery. That day he was twenty-seven and holding the phone to his ear, listening to a foreign sound. His father's sobs echoed over the line; they begged him home. To please come, it was his mother... These sobs, from the man who met every sobering morning with a toast of his golden can of Olympia and every sunset with his fist in his wife's face.

Could the son have known then? He'd always ask himself that. Was there any way to know what his father had in store for him when he returned home, for his mother, for the man who was his father?

The scars on his skin and the wounds within that had yet even to scar told him not to go, but he had unfinished business with the old man. He'd go, and maybe this time it would be different.

Nate opened the door to the dark apartment he'd once called home. It was after work, the sun had gone down, his boots were slick with the rain he had just come in from. They slipped on the linoleum floor. A smell rose up and enshrouded his body like a cloak. It clung to his nose and at the back of his throat, a tangy, rusty tincture of blood. Warm, as if it were being pulsed from the veins of a being. Automatically he reached for the light behind him, his stomach clenching, his mind telling him no. No. NO!

That was when the memory got slick. Even now his mind recoiled, and the details of that night faded back into the black mist.

Eva, he thought to distract himself. *Where are you now, Eva?* Her name rolled around in his mouth softly, whispered to no one. An entirely different set of emotions consumed him as his parents faded away once more. She was seven when he was ten, and she was there for him every time he showed up with a black eye or a new burn. She'd shown him his first fast car, and later he taught her how to fix them, to make them go faster. At sixteen she rocked his world in a way he would never recover from.

The years had passed like lightning after that day, each one spent with Eva more mind blowing than the next. But as everything in his life tended to do, that too would come to an end.

The pain, now cathartic, motivated, consumed him. His dark past closed up shop and faded away, leaving him with his future. *His* future, where he was in control.

FORGED: CHAPTER 2_

The rain hammered down on the windshield as Jenny and I made our way to our recently discovered import garage. I had been relieved to find a BMW mechanic that wasn't too drunk or too deaf to hear that I just wanted the oil changed, not a forty-minute hollering hand-gesture session about how he wanted to replace my brakes. I'd bought the ten-year-old German sedan used and she was perfect—aside from needing regular repairs, which was like Jenny's alpaca yarn, costing me a mint.

Though my car was going to reap the rewards and I would come to blissfully claim at least partial credit for the mechanic find, Jenny and her precious Peugeot were technically the sole heroes in the discovery. On Monday, I'd been in my office ostensibly reviewing the recent shoot for July's cover, but really wallowing in the current state of my life. I knocked the old-school desk light to motivate it to work and thought of the fashion rag—particularly the office—I'd left in New York City. That office had been wide and luxurious—plush gray carpeting and dark paneling, furniture handpicked from a sleek and modern designer catalog—and I'd bitten and clawed my way to that corner palace thirty-four floors into the Manhattan sky in just seven years. Now I felt like I was perpetually crouching low under the

Portland, Oregon, cloud cover. My fourth-floor office's midcentury décor had nothing to do with design resurgence; rather, it simply hadn't been touched since Mad Men's inspiration had been reality. On top of that, I had chosen this new life and had a magazine to run, which included advertisers and subscribers who didn't care what my current office looked like. In other words, I had made my own worn-out bed, and I was having to work hard just to sleep in it.

Jenny, my *Rose City Review* assistant and sometimes guest writer, came waltzing in that morning and flopped down on one of the chairs in the semicircle in the middle of the office. "You would not believe what I found," she said smugly.

"What's that?" I bit on Jenny's bait.

"So, you know how I've been on this trek to find the best import repair shop in the city, right?"

"Please tell me that your ancient Peugeot has found one," I said with a laugh and returned to my work, editing pen in hand looking at the next issue's cover choices.

"I did...and they do all years of BMWs and the mechanics are H-O-T."

I glanced at her out of the corner of my eye. "So, you asked one of them out with your oil change? Bold." I said then held up a cover option. "Does her skin tone seem abnormally red to you in this one?"

"No and no. I'll probably work up the gumption, though. This one guy is totally my type."

I gave her a distracted smile, the model on that cover was definitely too red.

"The head mechanic actually owns the place and he's not really hot per se, but he has that air about him that I thought would be perfect for you."

"Perfect for me, huh," I repeated. "And what's that?" I asked as I put down the cover art.

"Unavailable, uninterested, sort of dark—with a past, you know? But I imagine that with him you sort of feel like you could take over the world."

I arched a brow at her. "Quite the brief first encounter." I looked back down. "If you're right, you just described *complex* to a T, my friend."

Jenny laughed, like a chiming bell tower, loud and ringing. "Yes! That's totally it. Anyway—didn't you say your door has a leak?"

I had dropped my car off the next afternoon, leaving the keys with their front desk woman, who wore something in the shade similar to safety orange and was the same age as my father, and not a single luscious or brooding mechanic was in sight. There were four work bays, from which noise screeched, and a parking lot full of average Euro cars, except for two. They were a little red family car and a black two-door monster. Though I was unsure of its heritage from a distance, however the black monster screamed: *fast*. Something I once knew a lot about.

Now, through the sheeting rain, from the comfort of the dry interior of Jenny's car, I saw the watery glow of my car idling, parking lights on, directly in front of us, beside the main office. I hoped the water seal on the rear door was indeed fixed; otherwise, my baby was now officially a fishbowl.

"Wanna borrow my umbrella?" Jenny asked.

"No, I'm good—I'll just run inside. I have to say"—my hand on the door handle—"I'm impressed already that they have the car running. I bet the heater's on too. We'll see after I get the bill if I'm still appreciating the attention to detail. See you tomorrow and thanks for the ri—"

Jenny grabbed my arm. "Omigod."

"Wha-?" I said, leaning to the side, trying to see what had made her gasp but at that moment only my car and its exhaust and lights were visible through the sheet of water on the windshield. Then the wipers cleared away the water, and I noticed what had made her gasp.

He stood tall in slate-colored work pants and an open rough-hewn jacket with the company logo embroidered over his heart. Leaning against the building under the scalloped awning, he smoked a cigarette like it was the last one he'd ever have. His features were shadowed under the awning, but it could have been pitch-black and I'd still have known who he was. And he was looking straight into the car—and into my eyes.

"Lord..." I said like an oath under my breath.

"I know, right?" Jenny said, misinterpreting me.

"Wish me luck," I whispered to her and to no one and got out of the car.

Nathaniel Vellanova pushed away from the wall and in one smooth movement opened the massive umbrella that had been leaning next to him and strode toward me.

Behind me I heard Jenny reverse out the driveway, leaving me to my past.

***

Continue reading *Forged* online or in paperback at Amazon.com.

www.ingramcontent.com/pod-product-compliance
Lightning Source LLC
Chambersburg PA
CBHW050111120726
47904CB00004B/1303

9780988261488